HUMANS

The Untold Story of Adam and Eve and their Descendants

VOLUME ONE: THE THESIS

(3ᴿᴰ REVISED EDITION)

EDITORIAL REVIEWS

Reviewed in the United States on November 4, 2019 by Misty s: "Great book good story line very interesting."

Erika Kraus wrote regarding Volume Two (Mjomba and the Evil Ghost): "Discussing this book was almost more important to me than reading it. Joseph M. Luguya is highly intelligent and respectable. I thoroughly enjoyed reading this book." (Goodreads, June 02, 2020)

Emily Nicole wrote regarding Volume Two (Mjomba and the Evil Ghost): "Mjomba and the Evil Ghost is a heavy read that requires your attention and thoughts. I really enjoyed this thought-provoking book." (Goodreads, July 29, 2020)

Melissa wrote regarding Volume Two (Mjomba and the Evil Ghost): "Interesting read. Well written." (Goodreads, May 23, 2020)

Mary wrote regarding Volume Two (Mjomba and the Evil Ghost): "Interesting read." (Goodreads, July 28, 2018)

Csimplot Simplot wrote regarding Volume Two (Mjomba and the Evil Ghost): "Excellent book!!!" (Goodreads, December 18, 2018)

Sasha wrote regarding Volume Two (Mjomba and the Evil Ghost): "This book for me was a very interesting read. I truly enjoyed reading this book. I couldn't put it down once I began reading it. I kept wanting to find out more. I would recommend this book to others. It is a very good read. I will be reading this again. This is an amazing author. If you haven't read any of his books you should." (Goodreads, July 30, 2020)

Connie wrote regarding Volume Two (Mjomba and the Evil Ghost): "I found this book uneven. Parts I could hardly read. Other parts I devoured. It is the story of a young man writing his thesis (think) and he somehow gets the devil to lecture him. It is never anti God. Always God is a real being in the story. It's the how and why the devil was banished and what his job has become." (Goodreads, December 20, 2018)

Mary wrote regarding Volume Two (Mjomba and the Evil Ghost): "Unique read." (Goodreads, July 1, 2020)

The Columbia Review of Books & Film:
-- Avraham Azrieli, **TheColumbiaReview.com**

Humans: The Untold Story of Adam and Eve and their Descendants is a substantial novel in three parts by Joseph M. Luguya, which explores good and evil through human, mythological and supernatural characters, much of it in the form of a grand debate, delivering an intricate theological saga.

Humans includes three volumes: "The Thesis" (Volume One), "Mjomba and the Evil Ghost" (Volume Two), and "The Demoniac" (Volume Three). The scene that launches Humans appropriately involves both mystery and magnificence: "The International Trade Center literally sat on the edge of downtown Dar es Salaam, the beautiful metropolis whose name fittingly signified "Heaven of Peace". Christian Mjomba's office was located on the twenty-seventh floor.

In an unusual move, using a key he took from his wallet, Mjomba unlocked a side door to his office and slid furtively inside." And from this opening of a mysterious door, Humans builds up to a complex yet compassionately humane story of Mjomba's fascinating journey.

In his earlier days, Mjomba had been a seminarian whose tangling with a monumental assignment on the "Original Virtue" led to an immensely challenging intellectual and spiritual quest—as well as a "Devil's bargain" of sorts. He fences with Satan and with its good counterparts while bringing into stark question many of the basic tenets of the church. In fact, "having in effect enlisted the help of Satan in the task of turning out a winning thesis on the subject of "Original Virtue," Mjomba finds himself "feeling quite uncomfortable filling the role of scribe to a creature that the sacred scriptures had pointedly referred to as "Accuser of our Brethren" (Revelation 12:10)."

And so, in a twist that makes Humans uniquely intriguing, Mjomba's sincere efforts to turn the most evil force into good and, thus, save souls, ends up placing our hero himself in a highly questionable—and dangerous—position.

Author Joseph M. Luguya brings to this novel enormous knowledge of religious concepts and historical records. Through the protagonist and the secondary characters, the reader becomes privy to a wealth of ideas and detailed arguments, many of them new and daring. While much of the book offers a multi-faceted, extensive dissertation that might appear dense to some readers, the author's creative use of Satan's own voice makes it hard to put down, not only when provocative arguments begin to attain logical flair, but also when the author brings in controversial historical figures whose legacy is open to debate—and to literary license—as Satan claims them to his side: "Take the so-called 'reformation' that I engineered. Believe it or not, but it was my idea. I used Martin Luther, a Catholic friar – yes, and a good one at that – and a reformer, to set it in motion."

Or this one: "… Joan of Arc who was labeled a witch and burned at the stake! You may or may not like to hear it, but I also succeeded in using that innocent girl to confound and drive other good souls in the Church to virtual despair."

Some of the arguments in fact ring true not only in the historical context, but in our current world, festering as it is with religious tensions and ethnic prejudices: "Later, during his oral defense of the thesis, Mjomba would comment that one of the legacies of original sin was the perennial tendency of humans to never see evil in themselves, and to see nothing good in other humans – especially those who were different from themselves in some respect." How true!

The author is especially deft at merging abstract ideas and structural visualizations into symbols that our hero's mind ponders in ways reminiscent of Dan Brown's symbologist Robert Langdon in The Da Vinci Code: "But the image of an inverted pyramid balancing on top of another pyramidal shape flooded Mjomba's mind with a force that made him feel like he might pass out. He attributed his ability to stay afloat and not drift off into a swoon to the fact that he was able to focus his mind on the peculiar design Primrose had produced using the blurb's material and its similarity to the letter "X"!

Humans is also distinguishable in telling a story within a story, cleverly utilizing several layers of imaginary characters. For example, here is our protagonist reflecting on his own created protagonist: "Mjomba shut his eyes and paused to think about Innocent Kintu, the central character of his 'masterpiece'. As images of the nurse's beguiling manner came flocking back, he came close to concluding that a non-fictional character like Kintu could in fact be considered fictional when contrasted with a character like Flora!"

In summary, Humans: The Untold Story of Adam and Eve by Joseph M. Luguya creates a dramatic confrontation between a virtuous young scholar and the most malevolent character of all, delivering an extensive, all-encompassing confrontation that becomes a metaphor for the very core of human existence. This thought-provoking, sprawling novel explores unresolved issues of faith and spirituality while the leading character valiantly defends all that he holds dear in the struggle between good and evil, life and death, and the opposing forces of divine creation. Readers will be enticed to contemplate the most fundamental questions of human existence and come away with a deeper understanding of both differences and commonalities that define us.

Significant and Memorable!
-- Avraham Azrieli, **TheColumbiaReview.com**

KIRKUS REVIEWS: Luguya (*Payment in Kind*, 1985) offers a three-part novel about one man's extensive views on Christianity.

When readers first meet Christian Mjomba, he's seated in his 27th-floor office in the city of Dar es Salaam, Tanzania. He has a pleasant view of the harbor and a degree from Stanford University on the wall, and seems to be doing fairly well. However, his dream of publishing a best-selling work remains unfulfilled. He does have a background in writing, though; as readers soon learn, he'd once been a member of a seminary brotherhood. During that time, he composed an extensive thesis on various aspects of the Christian faith, which strayed from official church teachings. Mjomba's intention was, in part, to "show unequivocally that the Prime Mover loved everyone irrespective of religious affiliation. "The book begins with an in-depth exploration of the protagonist's views; there's more action in later chapters, but the emphasis throughout is on ideas. They include Mjomba's annoyance with those who use the phrase "the bible says", and his meditation on the human body, which he says is "designed to be both a temple of God and a vessel of His grace." The book covers an extensive amount of theologically intriguing material; it's critical of many different parties, including the Apostle Peter, the devil, and people who revel in "mostly ill-gotten wealth..."

Readers looking for new interpretations of Christian thought will find them here, though those hoping for more thorough integration with plot may be disappointed. Its details of life in Tanzania, such as the notion that "Even though most spoke English very well, Tanzanians just loved to speak Swahili," are memorable. That said, the text as a whole is concerned with issues that go well beyond any single nation.

An insightful…array of spiritual material.

BOOKS WE'VE REVIEWED BY JOSEPH M. LUGUYA —**FOREWORD REVIEWS**

Joseph Luguya's book *Mjomba and the Evil Ghost* involves a sprawling discourse with Satan concerning the tenets and values of Christianity. Christian Mjomba is a Stanford-educated success story. The virtuous Tanzanian scholar is also an amateur theologian; in the book, he functions as a stand-in for Christian inquiry. Even his name is symbolic: "mjomba" means "fish" in Swahili. Through a twisting, dramatic series of debates and clashes with dark forces, he explores ideas about faith.

The opponent in Christian's debates is Satan, who is silver-tongued, slick, and convincing. Christian's arguments are human and sometimes clunky, so Satan often claims the upper hand. Referred to by many aliases and claiming to be "more catholic than the Catholics," Satan can debate any point. The two cover topics including the meaning of "victory of good over evil," the pre-lapsarian state of original virtue, murder, and the dangers of rationalization.

Both parties hold forth at length, with Satan picking holes in each of Christian's arguments with the expertise of a lawyer…The book's extensive, in-depth scholarship is excellent, educational, and exhaustive, but as a morality play, the book is too dense to be entertaining.

"Mjomba and the Evil Ghost" is a discursive novel concerned with the heresy that it views as inherent in scholarship; it works to justify the dogma of the Catholic Church.

Reviewed by Claire Foster
—Foreword Reviews

Joseph M. Luguya's *Humans: The Untold Story of Adam and Their Descendants* spins an ambitious three-volume fictional tale, in which he charts the history of the human condition…

In this novel, readers learn first-hand from Satan how humans have historically succumbed to temptation. Satan makes sure to present himself here not as villain but victim, and merely one who whispers suggestions to humans who then make unfortunate decisions…

According to the devil, he didn't instruct them to eat the proverbial fruit, but merely to think; they then concluded they didn't need the "Prime Mover" to make choices for them. The next instance was not far behind, when their son Cain listened to whispers and yielded to jealousy…

No pride-based offense is omitted, from that original fall through present-day power grabs by nations who justify their actions by claiming that they are for the greater good.

Readers must first digest the sum of Christian history, the Bible, all the major players (ex., St. Peter, Mother Teresa), and spiritual concepts (free will, sin, etc.) before being introduced to Satan and his apologetics…The author's own biblical study background is on full display, and he can accurately quote not only Scripture but also his scope of theology in general...**www.blueinkreview.com**

<u>www.Spiritrestoration.org</u>: In the same way that C. S. Lewis wrote **Screwtape Letters**, Joseph Luguya attempts to describe the spiritual realm from a human perspective. Luguya does very well at portraying the

character of the Devil...This book is one that every fan of C. S. Lewis should check out. Luguya has a very scholarly form just like Lewis...The Devil teaches almost more than the Christian. It is a very convicting book. Luguya is a great writer and well worth the investment in this huge book.

Fr. Gary Coulter: Joseph Luguya has written a very different novel, somewhat on the lines of C.S. Lewis' Screwtape Letters.

Stanford Business Magazine: In this novel, the fictitious author of a thesis on "Original Virtue" offers an African perspective of spirituality in general and Christianity in particular.

Midwest Book Review: Hellishly delicious, (Humans) is a novel about the devil's desire to claim his due, and one man's journey to hell and back...A worthy contemplation of good and evil, and highly recommended reading for its insights on humanity, its wordplay, and sheer devilish delight!

Hellishly Delicious... Sheer Devilish Delight!

Original Books
14404 Innsbruck Court
Silver Spring, MD, 20906, USA
Website: **www.originalbooks.org** (under construction)
Visit Amazon's Joseph M. Luguya Page

Library of Congress Control Number: 2015914304
ISBN-13: 978-1-7355649-2-0
ISBN-10: 1-7355649-2-3

3rd Revised Original Books Edition, August 23, 2020

Created and written by Joseph M. Luguya
Illustrations by Lorna M. Luguya
Printed and produced in the United States of America
First published August 2015.

About the Author

The author is a native of Uganda. He received his early education at St. Pius X Seminary Nagongera, St. Joseph's Seminary Nyenga, and St. Mary's Seminary Gaba. A graduate of the University of Nairobi, Mr. Luguya is also a former Sloan Fellow at the Stanford Graduate School of Business. He has lived and worked in Uganda, Kenya, Tanzania, Canada, and the United States. He is also the author of Payment in Kind, 2nd Revised edition (Original Books, 2017); The Forbidden Fruit (Original Books, 2011); and Inspired by the Devil Part 1: The Gospel According to Judas Iscariot (Original Books, 2007).

About the Book

Publisher: "The Thesis" is Volume One of Joseph Luguya's thrilling three-volume novel "Humans, The Untold Story of Adam and Eve and their Descendants". The other volumes are "Mjomba and the Evil Ghost" (Volume Two), and "The Demoniac" (Volume Three).

A virtuous but rather naïve member of St. Augustine's seminary brotherhood has a class assignment to turn in a thesis on "Original Virtue". But he has a runaway imagination, and easily gets snared into serving in a very strange role, namely the role of scribe to none other than Satan.

Misled by the practice in Rome that has one of

The cardinals (the Promoter of the Faith) play the role of the so-called *advocatus diaboli* (Latin for Devil's advocate) in order to argue against the canonization of the candidate for sainthood, he falls for the temptation to employ the devil as his mouthpiece for expounding on the doctrines of the church. He imagines that if he succeeds in doing that, he will effectively make Lucifer who is also known as Beelzebub work for the salvation of souls instead of their damnation.

And, incredibly, the seminarian appears to succeed in tricking the Evil One into working against his own interests and helping him craft a thesis that looks like a definite winner! Satan starts by bragging about how he derailed the father and mother of mankind, and it soon begins to dawn on the student that it is the Evil One who is using him instead of the other way round. Using the free platform provided by the unwitting seminarian, the devil indicates gleefully that he is in total control, and that his evil plan to consign everyone, Catholic and non-Catholic alike, the luckless student himself included, to hell is on track!

And that former "Angel of Light" and also "Father of Lies", in a master stroke of genius, succeeds in ensuring that humans are on the road to perdition by pulling off the most unlikely hat trick of all, namely shining as much light on truth as possible so that humans, who are already inclined to sin as a result of the fall of the first Man and the first Woman from grace, don't have any excuse at all when their time of reckoning comes - or so he leads the seminarian to believe!   The Prince of Darkness attempts in that manner to counter the Deliverer who, in the moments before His death on the gibbet, pleaded with His Father saying: "Father, forgive them, for they know not what they do."   Predictably the devil also brags that he is more knowledgeable in matters of theology than all the doctors of the church combined! And as he goes about shining light on the "Truth", the devil seems quite happy to use this opportunity to show the world that he does not just profess the Catholic faith, but he is actually more Catholic than the Catholics themselves!

Before long the student himself starts to see limitless possibilities of benefitting from the scheme, and dreams about riding on the cocktails of Diabolos and achieving fortune and fame by converting the "winning" thesis into a mega-selling blockbuster! While the devil is quite happy with that mutual arrangement and wants to see the student succeed, because disseminating "Truth" in whichever way now serves his purposes very well from one angle, from a different angle, because as the Father of Lies he is being coerced to act against his nature and sees it as punishment, all this now puts the student's eternal salvation in the greatest peril because of his central role in it.

This prodigious work dramatizes the battle between the forces of Good and the forces of Evil in a singularly effective manner, and would make for a really hilarious flick!

If **Humans, The Untold Story of Adam and Eve and their Descendants**, ever does get to hit the "Big Screen", the movie goers will actually accompany the seminarian in the final scene as he crosses the gulf that separates the living from the dead and, unrepentant, prepares to meet "His Mystic Majesty" face to face for his final reckoning only to find himself accosted by a totally enraged and menacing Satan who is at the head of a column of crazed demons. They are there to take him to his dungeon located at the bottom of hell; and it happens in the moments before the student's "resurrection"!

"**Humans**" is a treatise on the knowledge of good and evil; and it damns and convicts sinful and sinning humans one and all without any distinction.

This is the untold story of Adam and Eve and their descendants. Prepare to take off on a cruise into realms of spirituality quite beyond anything you had ever dreamed of; and be a witness to:

the Epic Battle Between the Forces of Good and the Forces of Evil

Watch the showdown as the devil and the Deliverer battle for human souls!

As you delve into "**Humans**", it will start to dawn on you slowly but surely that for a long time you had been wishing, albeit subconsciously, that someone would write a book exactly like this one. Your wish that someone would succeed in tricking Satan, that evilest of evil creatures, to spill all his dirty secrets, has come true at long last. Relax, sit back now, and enjoy Volume Two of "**Humans**"!

Disclaimer:

This book is a work of fiction. The characters, names, businesses, organizations, places, events, incidents, dialogue and plot are the product of the author's imagination or are fictitiously used. Any resemblance to actual persons living or dead, names, events, or locales is entirely coincidental.

Acknowledgements:

To my daughter Lorna for her imaginative illustration of the Prince of Darkness; and to my family, for being a great inspiration, and for their support; and to the many individuals who genuinely could not wait to see "Humans" in print.

Table of Contents

Volume One: The Thesis

HUMANS

THE UNTOLD STORY OF ADAM AND EVE AND THEIR DESCENDANTS

VOLUME ONE: THE THESIS

(3RD REVISED EDITION)

PART 1: THE DEMENTED SCHOLAR

The Port Authority occupied twenty-eight floors in the thirty-storey skyscraper. The towering structure, popularly known as the International Trade Center, enjoyed the distinction of being the tallest building in the country.

The site had been selected with great care. Consequently, as far as prime office locations went, with the exception of State House, the Port Authority did not have any rival. The International Trade Center literally sat on the edge of downtown Dar es Salaam, the beautiful metropolis located at the mouth of a natural sheltered harbor, and whose name fittingly signified "Heaven of Peace".

Christian Mjomba's office was located on the twenty-seventh floor. In an unusual move, using a key he took from his wallet, Mjomba unlocked a side door to his office and slid furtively inside. Mjomba himself did not recall ever using that side door. He seemed relieved that he had succeeded in gaining entrance to his office unnoticed by anyone, including his secretary.

Mjomba had never once employed the side door in that manner. Although he had occasionally thought of using it to evade unwelcome guests waiting in his secretary's *office en suite*, he had always resisted the urge to let himself out surreptitiously and disappear into the human traffic in the main corridor, as some of his unscrupulous colleagues did. He considered it demeaning to do that sort of thing.

Mjomba bolted the door shut behind him and eased his ample frame into a swivel chair by the fancy, glass-topped mahogany desk. He rested his elbows on the desk like someone in a daze, and sat slumped forward, so that his chin rested on the desktop. With his head thus bowed, Mjomba remained immobile for a long while.

As if to enhance his concentration, he kicked off his tight-fitting dress shoes, and rested his stockinged feet on the carpeted floor. The presence of Primrose, Mjomba's good and loyal secretary, was betrayed by the incessant pounding of typewriter keys as she worked away at her post.

The interconnecting door remained ajar from the time he walked through it with his leather brief case each morning - usually a little after nine o'clock in the morning - until he left to go home eight hours later. Primrose understood that this was her boss's wish, and was quite comfortable with the arrangement.

Primrose always exuded confidence that she could keep any unwanted visitors at bay despite her boss's office door being ajar. Which was just as well because, in the culture that existed at the Port Authority, the ability of a personal secretary to shield her boss from unwanted office guests was regarded as the hallmark of a good secretary.

As a matter of fact, it was partly as a tribute to Primrose's aptitude in that regard, and partly out of a desire to be different from everyone else that Mjomba preferred to leave the entrance to his office slightly ajar at all times. This applied even on those occasions when meetings were in progress inside, a sharp deviation from the general practice at the Port Authority.

Mjomba stared at the door and was glad that it was closed. He regretted that he was not in a position to actually bolt it from the inside. It still struck him as an unusual breach of custom for that door to be shut when he was right there in his office. It was odd enough that Primrose was unaware of his presence!

Mjomba's office had nothing special about it apart from the rich carpeting and the mahogany desk. A bookshelf to the right of the door was graced with the usual contents for someone of his station: Horngren's *Principles of Cost Accounting*, Samuelson's *Theory of Economics*, Drucker's *Management by Objectives*, a fat volume sporting the title *Ports of the World*, and Merriam-Webster's *Collegiate Dictionary*. *Group Think*, the title of a thin volume that was nestled in between the last two, was barely discernible from where he sat. Even though this was by far Mjomba's favorite publication in the collection, he would have been hard put to it to say who the author was. That had not been the case many years earlier when, as a grad student, he had to read it from cover to cover overnight as a part of his preparation for a seminar in Management.

Caspian Sea. Other traditions have him first preaching the Gospel in Judaea, and then in Aethiopia, a region of Colchis (in modern-day Georgia) that was also known as "the city of the cannibals".

Tradition maintains that the Apostle James who was the son of Alphaeus (and who is also known as James the Less) preached in Damascus in Syria and served as the first bishop of the Christians in Jerusalem. According to the historian Josephus, the "Just man" as James was also known was thrown from the pinnacle of the temple; and the scribes and Pharisees, seeing that he was not killed by the fall, began to stone him. But he turned, and kneeling down, prayed saying: "I beseech thee, Lord God our Father, forgive them; for they know not what they do." And while they were stoning him to death, one of the priests, a Rechabite or descendant of Rechab, screamed saying: "Cease, what do ye? The just man is praying for us!" Whereupon another one among them smashed the Apostle's head with a club.

The martyrdom of James the Lesser took place even as plans for the siege of Jerusalem were being finalized by Titus (the future Emperor Titus Flavius Caesar Vespasianus Augustus) and his deputy Tiberius Julius Alexander (the Egyptian Jew who was prefect of Judea). The siege and the destruction of Jerusalem and along with it the temple, described in graphic detail by the historian Josephus, followed the Jewish uprising that was spearheaded by the

"Zealots" (noted for their uncompromising opposition to pagan Rome and the polytheism it professed).

During that uprising, Romans, Greeks and their sympathizers were hounded and lynched. Josephus paints a picture of a truly desolate Jerusalem after the city fell and was sacked and razed to the ground. He wrote that the city was completely unrecognizable. Everywhere was slaughter and flight. Most of the victims were peaceful citizens, weak and unarmed, butchered wherever they were caught. He wrote that, around the Altar, the heaps of corpses grew higher and higher, while down the Sanctuary steps poured a river of blood and the bodies of those killed at the top slithered to the bottom.

Not even the trees that had lined Jerusalem's boulevards had been spared. According to one report, during the siege of Jerusalem, five hundred Jews were crucified every day in front of the city until there was no more wood to build crosses and no more space to stand the crosses. Describing the Siege, the historian Josephus wrote in his Antiquities: "So the soldiers, out of the wrath and hatred they bore the Jews, nailed those they caught, one after one way, and another after another, to the crosses, by way of jest, when their multitude was so great, that room was wanting for the crosses, and crosses wanting for the bodies…"

According to another report, Roman soldiers went to the extent of amusing themselves by nailing their victims in different postures! Thousands upon thousands died in the wake of the failed insurrection in Judea; and the Kidron valley which separated the Temple Mount from the Mount of Olives and the Valley of Hinnom or Ge-hinnom (or Gehenna) to the south side of Jerusalem (the valley that also served as the city's waste dump) were both filled corpses.

Josephus, who gives a blow by blow account of the siege and eventual fall of the Holy City and the destruction of the temple, estimated that a million people, including women and children, perished. Masada, the last "rebel" stronghold, fell to the Romans two years later.

According to one account, it had actually been Titus' intention to seize the temple and transform it into one that was dedicated to Roman gods. Titus, arguing that he had merely served as an instrument of divine wrath, and that the success of his campaign did not come about through his own efforts, would refuse to accept and don the crown of laurel (victory wreath) during the lavish victory celebrations in Rome.

The manner in which the apostles bore witness to the Gospel and their readiness to die for their faith without question constitute acts that are tough to follow. But then nothing less is expected of anyone heeding the call to be an *"Alter Christus"* ("Another Christ"). And it also explains why, when Peter proposed that the assembled disciples who numbered one hundred and twenty nominate two men to replace Judas Iscariot, after choosing Joseph Barsabbas (surnamed Justus) and Matthias, they prayed saying: "Thou, Lord, which knowest the hearts of all [men], shew whether of these two thou hast chosen, That he may take part of this ministry and apostleship, from which Judas by transgression fell, that he might go to his place"; and also why they went on to cast lots to choose the successor to the disciple from Kerioth.

But none of this should come as a surprise given what the Deliverer said: "The disciple is not above the master, nor the servant above his lord. It is enough for the disciple that he be as his master, and the servant as his lord. If they have called the good man of the house Beelzebub, how much more them of his household?" (Luke 6:40; Matthew 10:24; John 13:16; and John 15:20).

Made in the USA
Middletown, DE
16 April 2022

Mjomba looked bemused as he wondered if it was his manifestly inordinate admiration for whatever was between the covers of that "great" work that had effectively dampened any interest he might have had in its author in the interim. Whatever it was, it had effectively erased his/her name from Mjomba's memory for now!

A framed certificate on the wall immediately above the bookshelf attested to the fact that Mjomba had a Master's degree in Business Administration from Stanford. A portrait of his wife and their two children stared at him from its distinctive spot on the uppermost shelf.

Mjomba threw reluctant glances at a wooden tray to his left labeled "IN". The tray was stacked high with sheaves of documents, several of which had stickers proclaiming that they required his immediate attention. The tray labeled "OUT" was to his right and was empty.

To avoid being irked further by the sight of the pending work, Mjomba, acting somewhat impulsively, stuck out an arm and shoved the "IN" tray away from his sight so hard it very nearly tipped over. But he still found he had to spin his swivel chair around - nearly a hundred and eighty degrees - to keep the tray completely out of his line of vision.

He seemed well pleased with himself that the "IN" tray, with its load of pending work, now also occupied a part of the desk that was farthest away from the window. The desk was positioned so as to afford him a startling view of a busy section of the harbor, twenty-seven storeys below. It was a sunny and glorious morning as usual here on the East African seaboard. The view of the harbor was enlivened as usual by an interminable glow in the distance. The glow emanated from the oil refinery, a fixture on Dar es Salaam's ever-changing skyline since its construction a year and a half before.

The refinery itself was now barely visible on the horizon. Its tall chimney belched forth flames. Tongues of fire, they reached out into the clear blue skies as if in search of something to devour.

On a normal day, the usually flamboyant and carefree Mjomba would not have had any qualms about letting his gaze stray from work on his desk, or even individuals with whom he was in private conference, to take in the magnificent scene. It was, after all, constantly being remarked by his office guests that his office suite provided an angle of vision of the harbor that seemed quite unique.

On this particular morning, however, his chest caved in and shoulders slouched sideways, Mjomba had done something he rarely did if ever. He had buried his face in his arms, and appeared to be in a stupor of some sort. He had even allowed his elongated frame to assume a posture that made him resemble a hunchback! It was a far cry from Mjomba's usual appearance at the Port Authority, and he looked very odd in the otherwise serene surroundings of his office.

With the physical world effectively shut out and his sense faculties denied their usual indulgence,

Mjomba's faculties of the imagination and intellect went on a wild rampage.

Although physically present at the Port Authority, mentally and spiritually he was back at the rented bungalow on Msasani Peninsula, where he lived with his wife, Jamila, and their two children. In his imagination, he was reliving the events that had occurred there that morning as he prepared to leave for work. Judging by his appearance, Mjomba was resigned to the fact that those events had, for all practical purposes, already marred the rest of his day.

Even though crestfallen, there was something about Mjomba's mien that suggested beyond any doubt that he was determined to revive his spirits. Without moving, his lips seemed to be saying to him that dwelling on his early morning confrontation with Jamila was the surest way to bring that off! It was a ludicrous idea, to be sure; but one, nonetheless, whose appeal was irresistible. While he did not really believe it, he persuaded himself that to do otherwise, in the present circumstances was tantamount to running away from an intractable problem.

Mjomba, accordingly, decided to sit back and carefully weigh everything that had transpired that morning. He was unable to concentrate on anything else in any case. And so, oblivious to his immediate surroundings, he continued to mull over the sharp verbal exchange between Jamila and himself earlier that morning.

Mjomba was in this peculiar frame of mind when it occurred to him that it might be worth his while to put himself in his wife's shoes as it were, and to reconstruct what had transpired that morning from her perspective. And so, listless and clutching his head between both arms, he now began to imagine that he was Jamila!

In his mind's eye, Mjomba saw himself reclining on a love seat at the far end of their living room. That was where Jamila had proceeded after waiting on him. A quick mental inspection of himself - or rather herself - and he was satisfied that he looked and acted exactly like Jamila to wit!

So there "she" sat, one ear alert to any movement in the children's bedroom down the hallway, and the other listening to the clutter of silverware and china as the monster or ghoul (judging from Jamila's attitude that morning, she obviously thought of him as some monster or ghoul!) consumed its breakfast. Yes, ghoul and an unfeeling one at that! There it sat - the monster.

Mjomba retreated momentarily from the make-believe world of acting. Back in the security of his office at the Port Authority, he ruminated on the fact that he had not found it that difficult to imagine what went on inside his wife's mind while he helped himself on his breakfast. A natural actor, he had just let himself go and allowed his imagination free reign. It had been as simple as that! It was clear that nothing was going to prevent him from stepping back into Jamila's shoes and acting her part - if that was what it was going to take to establish what was really happening to set the record straight. Not even the fact that their physiques were dissimilar. He was convinced that he had done her no wrong, and was determined to establish his innocence.

By a simple process of metamorphosis, Mjomba was able, as he sat doubled up at his desk, to imagine that he was Jamila and was relaxing in the love seat in the living room of their seaside bungalow, savoring the aroma of the Arabica coffee. His large feet not only fit snugly in her tiny slippers, but he was also able to pretend that he was cuddling a nine-month-old baby inside his tummy!

Resuming his place on the love seat, Mjomba saw that, by all counts, the solitary figure at the dining table was enjoying yet another undeserved serving of pancakes, fried bacon, a sausage, and the almost obligatory scrambled egg on toast, all washed down with steaming black coffee. Most annoying of all was the fact that he always seemed to be in a rush at this particular time, and was consequently not in a position to enjoy the food she had devoted so much precious energy and time to prepare the way it was supposed to be enjoyed.

The clutter, lo and behold, came presently to an abrupt halt, signalling the end of Mjomba's morning meal. "Jamila" watched as, with a smack of his lips, "her" husband rose from his chair and stretched out his arms contentedly.

There was a break in Mjomba's train of thoughts at that particular point in time as he shifted in his chair and allowed himself the indulgence of a giggle. But the conviviality was short-lived. For, almost immediately, the guileless Mjomba relapsed into the sombre mood that had characterized his demeanour for much of that morning; and he allowed his flight of fancy to continue on its bizarre course.

And so, stepping back into his wife's shoes, he continued to playact in hopes that being so preoccupied was going to solve his problem. He - or rather "she"- immediately observed that "her" husband's movements, as he expressed his contentment with the meal "she" had prepared for him, revealed a tiny but noticeable bulge around his middle.

Even as Mjomba was thus engaged in his new role as the devoted and loving wife, he could not help indulging himself in escapades. In his mind's eye, Mjomba saw Jamila smile faintly at the fleeting thought that potbellies were a trademark of the affluent in this part of the globe. But the smile faded swiftly as the unpleasant things associated with excessive weight began to crowd in her mind: heart attacks, hypertension, an ungainly appearance - the list seemed endless! As Mjomba imagined it, his wife knew, or at least suspected, that all this while as she was thus engrossed, Mjomba took absolutely no notice of her presence in that house, let alone her condition and feelings.

At that point in time, the real Mjomba at the Port Authority was unable to put up with the make believe any longer. It was clear that apart from constituting an insult to his beloved Jamila, what he had just indulged in was quite reckless. How, indeed, could a person of his standing act as stupidly as he had just done! He decided forthwith that he could not let events be dictated entirely by a faculty of the imagination gone wild. Deciding that it was time for ordinary common sense to take charge again, Mjomba conceded that he had allowed his fertile imagination to run wild. He certainly did not believe that his imagination had enslaved him - at least not quite yet.

It did not seem conceivable that the problem that had led to his present predicament could have started the way he was imagining. It had to be more intricate than that, he avowed, as he finally stepped out of Jamila's shoes.

It had become apparent to Mjomba by now that the more he worried himself with regard to this whole thing, the more ridiculous it was all proving to be. But Mjomba was still irked by the fact that something about his wife's appearance, as he stepped away from his breakfast table and inclined forward to kiss her good day, had caused him to suddenly stop and exclaim: "What is the matter now, Jamila darling?"

Groping around now for something to use to reassure himself, Mjomba allowed that he was not normally given to voicing empty or harried expressions. He certainly knew that it was not characteristic of Jamila either to hurl words at him. But, in what seemed - to him at least - to be a fit of anger, she had shot back: "You are the one who looks like you have a problem!"

Mjomba recalled how, utterly mollified and reeling under the load of shame he suddenly felt for having started it all with his brash reaction, he had gingerly lifted his gaze to meet hers. He had always taken pride in the fact that he knew his spouse like the palm of his hand. He believed that she, too, knew him like the palm of her hand; and he even attributed the strength of their marital relations to this. He had, therefore, had no doubt that he was going to find Jamila's eyes, even at that late stage, a mirror of sympathy and understanding.

Mjomba was unable to stifle a giggle as he acknowledged that he had been really dumb to indulge in that false expectation. Indeed, his action had only had the opposite effect, eliciting words that seemed plainly calculated to have an even more devastating effect on him. The words, selected carefully, had come out of Jamila's mouth with a spontaneity which suggested that she had been lying in wait for him to make just the kind of mistake he was then making so she would let hell loose on him.

"What is biting you?" Jamila had continued with obvious relish.

It had been so unlike the Jamila he knew. Something now told him that she had been intent on hurting him from the start, and that she had added those last words for the specific purpose of rubbing it in!

Thinking back on the episode from the relative security of his office, the normally ebullient Mjomba admitted to himself that he was petrified all right as he faced his wife in their living room that morning.

"She is one of a sort!" he hissed, recalling how completely disarmed and helpless he had felt in her presence. He had also felt a stinging awkwardness as he stood there meekly, in a stance that could only be described as humble submission! Mjomba smiled as he tried to visualize what exactly went on inside her mind at that particular moment in time during their confrontation.

With everyone's emotions running so high, a lot more than what met the eye must have occurred in those extraordinary minutes. And, according to what Mjomba could now recall, he had tried to prepare himself for the very worst as Jamila, encircling her outsized tummy with ordinarily slender but now somewhat beefy arms, added nonchalantly: "For the whole of last week - for quite some time now in fact - you have been acting queer, as if the entire world's worries had all of a sudden been eased on your shoulders!"

Mjomba had felt considerable relief seeing his wife settle back in her seat after she had mouthed those last words. Almost immediately afterward, however, Jamila had inclined her head to one side, casting at him what he was only now realizing had been an accusing glance!

Mjomba mourned softly, and was deeply vexed as he wondered how his adorable Jamila, who was almost constantly on his mind, could even as much as insinuate that he, Mjomba of all people, was neglecting her!

Elbows planted firmly on top of the desk, Mjomba hugged his head at the temples with his closed fists, and shut his eyes tightly. The features of his face were frozen in a grimace. Opening his eyes moments later, something strange happened. It was a mere coincidence that he was gazing in the direction of the bookshelf when he opened his eyes. He instinctively began inspecting the meagre contents of his personal library at the office. But then he saw or thought he was seeing, nestled between Samuelson's *Theory of Economics* and Drucker's *Management by Objectives*, a thin but very handsome volume titled THE PSYCHIC ROOTS OF INNOCENT KINTU! It was there one moment, and the next moment it wasn't.

Mjomba had no doubt that his senses were playing tricks on him. At the very least he had to be dreaming, he told himself. The thought of becoming a victim of chicanery at the time he was trying to extricate himself from what he saw as big trouble involving his darling Jamila did not quite go down well with Mjomba. But, on the other hand, the temptation to take some time and verify that he was really seeing a printed and bound copy of the "masterpiece" he had been writing there on the bookshelf alongside the classics in his book collection, and that it was not a mirage, was too great to resist.

Mjomba rubbed his eyes hard, and then closed them systematically. When he opened his now heavy eyelids to peer at the spot where he had seen his "masterpiece", to his surprise and anger, it was no longer there! It was gone!

Mjomba rolled his eyes, grinned and allowed a huge smile to envelope his face. It was a gracious - and knowing - smile. Presumably as a result of being under prolonged pressure, Mjomba was becoming prone to whims of his imagination. While he wished to be realistic and admit that he had not seen any thin volume titled THE PSYCHIC ROOTS OF INNOCENT KINTU there on the bookshelf alongside those other masterpieces, Mjomba did not wish to entirely disappoint himself by ruling that possibility out altogether. He told himself that he wasn't doing anybody any harm or injustice by going along with the illusion that he was already a published author!

He was in a kind of a fix, of course. He had to be realistic and admit that his work-in-progress hadn't yet been transformed into a slick volume which could rub shoulders with works by the likes of Samuelson and Horngren, on the one hand; but, if he were ever going to succeed as writer, he occasionally had to kid himself that, for all practical purposes, he *was* already a published and celebrated author in all but name! In other words, he had to go along with the illusion that he was already a famous author. And if doing that meant that he had to use a bit of his imagination and pretend that a printed and bound copy of his book was sharing space on his bookshelf with the works of other authors, so be it, he reassured himself.

To the extent that he himself had read what he had written and liked it, he had in fact already been published and was a celebrated author. The fact that the nitwits he was writing for hadn't gotten an opportunity to read his material was relevant only in so far as the massive flow of revenues from his book into his bank account was concerned. And, if push came to shove, Mjomba wouldn't really give a damn if no one purchased his book. He figured that the real losers, if his work was not bought and read would be the readership he was targeting - and that included everyone, both literate and illiterate.

He had not only created the manuscript in its entirety, but he had also read and reread it innumerable times, not to mention writing and rewriting it almost as many times. He felt that if there was anyone in a position to announce to the world that there was within that manuscript at the very minimum the essence of a very good book, it was himself.

Judging by the changed expression on Mjomba's face, it no longer appeared to matter at all that everything about his "masterpiece" sharing the spotlight with the works of the likes of Drucker and Samuelson was so dreamlike and unreal. And it was evident that Mjomba had already decided - for the moment or, more accurately, for the occasion - that, regardless of the reality, THE PSYCHIC ROOTS OF INNOCENT KINTU had been published long ago and belonged there on the bookshelf, and that its handsome blue cover, designed by Primrose, was in fact hugging the ugly and worn covers of the works of Samuelson and Drucker!

Mjomba accordingly rolled his eyes this way and that, and continued to gloat over the fact that he was a published author whose fame would in time rival, and perhaps even surpass, that of the Americans.

Mjomba's eyes were wide open now, but his catalepsy continued uninterrupted. It actually no longer mattered an iota that the thin volume titled THE PSYCHIC ROOTS OF INNOCENT KINTU, sitting there on the mantle, was a figment of his imagination. Almost everything he had seen since waking up that morning seemed cut out for a work of fiction any way, and it seemed unlikely that allowing himself to be deluded in that manner was going to alter things that much.

Even though it was something that Mjomba's fertile imagination had fabricated in its entirety, the "vision" was real enough while it lasted to make the messy pile in the In-Tray vanish completely from sight along with the in-tray itself.

The gloom that had plagued him not long before and the mysterious woe-be-gone expression in which his face had been engulfed became things of the past as a grinning Mjomba continued to gloat over his tome. He did not believe that anything could be more beautiful than the sight of THE PSYCHIC ROOTS OF INNOCENT KINTU as it shared a rare platform with the works of Samuelson and Drucker among others.

Confidently, Mjomba reclined back in his seat and stared in the direction of the oil refinery, which was framed by the wall of glass representing his window. The refinery's chimney was clearly visible in the distance; and the incinerating flames, surging up and disappearing into the ethereal blue, made a beautiful sight indeed. But there was something about them that was starting to remind him of Jamila, and he immediately looked away. That also caused him to spin the swivel chair around, so that he found himself once more glaring at the In-Tray which was still piled high with urgent memoranda, vouchers, audit schedules, accounting reports that were crammed with figures and stuff like that, much to his discomfort.

His hands were clammy, and beads of sweat started ringing his forehead. But his gaze remained transfixed on the In-Tray - as if keeping watch over it made any difference to the fact that someone, if not he himself, would have to review the tray's contents and take necessary action on the individual documents!

Mjomba remained still for a long while. He was clearly at the end of his tether, and his countenance said it all. The bout of depression he had been battling since jumping into his car to drive to work that morning had evidently gotten the better of him, and the expression on his face seemed to acknowledge that much. And, as was typical of people who found themselves in situations of that nature, he had been inclined to think that it was natural - and, in fact, quite

OK - to seek refuge in distractions of one sort or another.

The favored distraction in Mjomba's particular case apparently had been employing his imagination to picture himself in extreme situations of euphoria or of doom. Reliving his earlier experience at home and then persuading himself that he was already a celebrated writer were undoubtedly the two ways in which he had sought to distract himself and escape from reality.

Mjomba finally succeeded in stirring from his lethargy. But he did so only to realize that it was now the image of his manuscript as a can of worms that was firmly stuck in his mind. As if that was not bad enough, he also discovered that it was not going to go away easily. And his suspicions that his book project was the root cause of his problems now, predictably, aggravated his depression.

Mjomba first got an inkling of the fact that his "dark night of the soul" was over when his prized "masterpiece", THE PSYCHIC ROOTS OF INNOCENT KINTU, vanished from its place besides the works of Drucker and Samuelson.

Yes - dark night of the soul! From the time he was introduced, as a minor seminarian, to ascetical works featuring the likes of Francis of Assisi, Jerome, and others who, because they were beloved of God, were almost permanently under assault by demons and had to live through innumerable so-called "dark nights of the soul", Mjomba always imagined that "depressions", because they too supposedly caused their victims unspeakable spiritual torment, amounted to "dark nights of the soul"!

Mjomba was able to track the real whereabouts of his masterpiece to the topmost shelf. Transformed into a plain blue file folder and a stack of neatly typed sheets of paper, perhaps two hundred or so in number, the manuscript lay there, innocently, not far off from the framed portrait of his loving Jamila and their two children.

The folder and the neat stack of papers comprising the manuscript appeared to be staring down at him menacingly from where they were perched. The folder, which had been cut to size and spotted a plain white sticker on its topside, was leaning ever so slightly against the neat stack. The legend on the sticker proclaimed in large bold letters: THE PSYCHIC ROOTS OF INNOCENT KINTU.

Mjomba seemed both puzzled and troubled that his book manuscript with the colored folder Primrose had designed for it had not caught his eye earlier. They both made such a distinctive and striking sight

A visibly relaxed Mjomba now took time to survey the bookshelf's other contents. It was the second time he was doing so this morning; and this time around, he made a point of reading the titles aloud to himself. He did so not once but twice. And he would have extended his hand to touch and feel the books themselves if they had been within easy reach.

A touch of unreality surrounded Mjomba's every move. Although the library he maintained back at his beach side residence was much more extensive and impressive, he appeared to relish every moment he was spending examining the bookshelf's contents.

Mjomba rolled his eyes uneasily, and stared up into the ceiling for a moment or so in a meaningless gesture before returning his gaze to the bookshelf. The fact that nothing had changed seemed to signal that he had regained a measure of control over his life. It was at that juncture that he made a point of reminding himself that the folder, and certainly the manuscript the folder was designed to hold, were things he had to continue to keep concealed from his wife - for now at any rate.

Shifting in his seat, Mjomba changed his stance and, relaxing his fists, buried his head in his open palms. It was while in this new position that Mjomba started reminiscing over his decision to not let Jamila in on his book project until such time as he would deem appropriate. And doing so inevitably led him back to the topic that, to all appearances, he had been trying to avoid.

With no immediate obstacle in the way, Mjomba's faculties of the imagination and intellect now of their own accord became transfixed on the events of that morning at his beachside home. Mjomba would even have sworn that there was absolutely nothing in the whole wide world at that particular point in time that was capable of distracting him, even only momentarily, from doing what he had to do - namely concentrate on that early morning encounter.

A fleeting idea exactly to that effect in fact crossed his mind just as the palms of his hands relented their grip about his temples. Then, as if calculated to prove him wrong, his office door flew open and Primrose burst in. The single, pink sheet of paper she clasped between the index fingers of her right hand fluttered to the floor as she careened to an abrupt stop.

"It is you?" she gasped. "For a moment I thought I was having a vision!"

In response to the "Hi" that Mjomba muttered under his breath, Primrose, who had already sensed that her boss was not in his usual mood, quickly retrieved the sheet of paper from the floor, and was about to place it alongside the book manuscript on the shelf when Mjomba held out his hand.

"The blurb," she said in a virtual whisper. She handed him the sheet of paper and retreated, closing the door behind her. It was the final draft for the blurb for his forthcoming novel. With very little work on her hands, Primrose had gone out of her way and in effect used the blurb to produce a design of sorts for the book's back cover. She had produced an ingenious design by typing the blurb's text in the shape of an inverted pyramid balancing on top of another pyramid.

The strange pattern on the sheet of paper as it fell to the floor had caught Mjomba's eye, and its likeness to the letter X of the alphabet had caused the expression "X-Generation" to immediately spring to his mind. Mjomba could not help leaning forward for a closer examination of the peculiar pattern. He noted with a smile that it was, indeed, the proposed blurb for his book that his resourceful secretary had employed to create the bizarre pattern. He did not know whether to applaud her effort in that regard or to get angry with her. At that particular juncture, he found himself unable to resist reading the text aloud to himself:

'Exquisitely lush, incredibly picturesque and spell-
binding, Zundaland is situated on the
Equator in Africa's heartland. It
is probably also the
original Garden
of Eden.
Until the arrival of
missionaries from Europe,
the Wazunda, in accordance with
time-honored customs and traditions,
accorded Lhekha-Zinda, father of the Zunda
Nation, and the rest of their ancestors
the full respect that was due to
them. Not surprisingly,
in the ears of
the
tradition-bound
and, indeed, proud people
of Zundaland, the "New Testament" the
strangers were proclaiming, continued for quite
sometime to sound truly like a "*Novel Testament*"!
Unfortunately for Lhekha-Zinda and the
Venerable ancestors, it was

a situation that was not
to last for very long.

The previous day, as Mjomba was dictating the blurb's text to his secretary, he could have sworn that it was the very final version. He had actually spent an enormous amount of time and energy drafting the blurb for his "masterpiece", the one word that most often came to his mind whenever he reflected on his literary project. In Mjomba's mind, revisiting it not only was out of question; it would be to no avail because it was so perfect. He had effectively persuaded himself that there was no way his blurb could be improved further!

But now, scarcely twenty-four hours later, it occurred to Mjomba that the blurb as it stood outlined a story that was completely different from his original one. It also dawned on him that none of the names featured in the blurb appeared anywhere in the body of the manuscript!

Mjomba's spirits were, arguably, already at a low point; and the realization that he was in a new jam dampened them even further. But it also provided a new and undoubtedly welcome distraction.

And so, relegating his early morning brawl with the mother of his children to the back of his mind, Mjomba turned to confront the new situation that had just cropped up. He made a mental note that the only other option - rewriting the manuscript - was completely out of question. The manuscript, he told himself, was perfect as it was and any attempt to rework his book would damage it irrevocably.

Mjomba had no doubt about the fact that the material in his book would make delightful reading for anybody. He also thought the blurb was kind of long-winded, and certainly not suitable as an introduction to a work of great stature like THE PSYCHIC ROOTS OF INNOCENT KINTU. This was despite the fact that he still liked the blurb as it was currently fashioned very much.

On the spur of the moment, he decided that he was going to polish it just a little; and he would do it right there and then. He liked the original blurb, and wasn't intending to alter very much. But he was confident that no one would notice any conflict between the blurb and the book after he was done! Since he himself liked both the blurb and the manuscript, he did not think it was asking too much to expect his readers to do the same. They were a dumb lot any way, he mumbled to himself. As for the publishers, he did not have any time for them really. If they proved tardy in jumping on the bandwagon, he could easily take care of that situation by setting up his own publishing company, and making the masterpiece he had worked so hard to produce his first title!

With a flourish, Mjomba set the sheet down, took a silver-gilded pen from his shirt pocket, and began scribbling in the margins: "But the greatest respect and honor", Mjomba wrote "was reserved for *Were*, the all-knowing, life-giving Wind. When the

Wazunda went hunting in the forest, planted crops, celebrated a good harvest or the coming of age of their youth with feasting and dancing - or, indeed, when they did anything involving two or more adult members of the community - they always did these things to the greater honor and glory of *Were*."

Mjomba circled the material he had inserted in the margins, and drew an arrow to indicate where the new material belonged, namely just before the last sentence but one on the sheet. He skimmed through the revised blurb rapidly from beginning to end, struck out the last two sentences of the original version of the blurb, and scribbled the following in the space immediately below: "Not only did the 'New Testament' which was being proclaimed by the strangers sound truly like a 'Novel Testament', in the eyes of the general populace, the new doctrines constituted a brazen assault on their mores, and on the hallowed traditions of the land. But for Annamaria Mvyengwa and Victor Nkharanga, both of whom were misfits in their society, it was a Godsend!"

Brimming with obvious pleasure at this latest demonstration of the creative genius in him, Mjomba was in the process of returning the pen to his shirt pocket when he stopped in his tracks.

Something told him that he had not really done anything to the blurb to make it sell his "masterpiece" the way he wanted it to do. The entire blurb seemed to be about religious beliefs, said little or nothing about political domination and social change, and not one word about the author!

In a rare display of impatience, the young up-and-coming executive cum celebrated author brought the expensive-looking pen crashing down on the glass desktop; and, seizing the sheet of paper with the amended blurb, he crumpled it into a tiny ball using both hands. Then, without any hint as to what he was about to do, Mjomba aimed the jumbled remains of the blurb at the certificate on the wall, just narrowly missing his mark. He worked swiftly and furiously, as if the gesture was going to compensate in some fashion for the fact that he hadn't been doing what he was supposed, namely brooding about the events of that morning in the living room of his beach-side home.

Up until this time, Mjomba had gone about the business of amending the blurb hesitantly and may be even reluctantly. But a strange force now took over, inducing him to get into high gear and to go about that whole business really aggressively and purposefully. The change that came over Mjomba was as sudden as it was unpredictable.

The fact that he was now operating under the influence of some mysterious force somehow did not detract from the meticulousness that normally characterized Mjomba's approach to creative activity. Indeed, the fact that he was having a little help from the "mystic" powers actually appeared, if anything, to be facilitating the job of producing a revised blurb. For one, he did not now require a pen and paper to do so!

True to form, Mjomba began by taking note of a tiny, translucent screen-like object somewhere at the back of his skull. He felt an irresistible urge to read the messages that appeared thereon at the same time. The minuscule screen, which was visible only to the mind and not to the eye, presently blossomed into a giant screen, not at all unlike those employed for screening films in drive-in cinemas. The first thing that appeared on the screen, predictably, was the introductory section of the new and, he had decided, final version of the blurb for his forthcoming book.

Mjomba's face was a mask of equanimity as he turned to scan the text of the blurb as its lines came streaming into view on the mysterious screen from nowhere. He did so by grinding both fists against his temples, narrowing his pupils, and staring straight ahead of him into the mysterious void! He closed his eyes slowly and then opened them again - slowly and apprehensively. He was clearly weary lest he did anything that would either cause his mystic powers to vanish or that, alternatively, would jolt his senses back to reality and its boring routine. Without letting go of his temples, Mjomba leaned back gently and continued to savor his newly found freedom. He found himself propelled on by the mere thought that his imagination was enjoying a totally unfettered and indisputably free reign once again.

Even though a virtual prisoner in his *office en suite*, Mjomba felt as free as a bird. He was surprised to find that he did not actually have to exert himself in anyway to be creative, and he certainly did not have to think hard to get results. Once the first lines for his brand-new blurb materialized on the giant screen and started drifting one by one to the lower end of the screen, others just kept popping up at the upper end.

As he pressed on with this new burst of creative effort, Mjomba could not help noticing that whenever he opened and shut his eyes, that act of blinking in and of itself assured the appearance of additional material on the screen! This did not strike him as strange at all. If his experience was anything to go by, the strangest things happened in the creative realm, and especially when one gave one's imagination free reign to explore uncharted ground.

Mjomba generated the new blurb so effortlessly, it felt like he was simply lifting or, possibly even, plagiarizing the material from some other original source. At the end of that exercise, the individual lines of the new blurb were indelibly etched in his mind.

As the ideas for the new blurb translated themselves mysteriously into text on the invisible screen, a suggestion (which just seemed fascinating and did not appear strange in the least) also kept popping up in his mind. It was to the effect that this new blurb summed up the material covered by THE PSYCHIC ROOTS OF INNOCENT KINTU much more accurately and succinctly than anything else he could have produced. Mjomba found this comforting, even though he suspected that it was not quite the case.

As had happened earlier, he could not resist reading aloud to himself the text of the new blurb as it flashed on the screen.

"This is a fascinating account of a community" he began, "whose members find themselves almost overnight under new political masters. A proud people who treasure their cultural traditions, they not only find themselves now a subjugated people, but they are also confronted with very rapid social change which quickly culminates in a new social order!

"The new social order, furthermore, comes complete with a new theocracy which is centred around the 'New Testament' as it is called. In the eyes of the general populace, the New Testament, proclaimed by the strangers, sounds truly like a 'Novel Testament'!

"But it is also the story of a maniacal scholar with a runaway imagination (the forerunner of a new breed of scholars?); and his bizarre antidote for a ravaging, hitherto unknown disease with no known cure.

"Dubbed 'Brain Death' by the peasants, the disease appears to single out for its prey those individuals in the community who display the greatest loyalty to the new social order. It just so happens that members of the country's tiny elite belong to this group; and, consequently, the general consensus is that the disease has its origins in the West."

Mjomba found everything about the new blurb quite fascinating. Reflecting on the reference to "Brain Death", he was wondering if it might be all that hard to write a novel with that title when all sorts of ideas started flooding his mind. He knew that he didn't have the power to stop the flood even if he wanted. It did not matter that he still needed to apply himself or at least get his train of thoughts going before the floodgates opened. He had just made himself comfortable in his seat when his mind became deluged with ideas about a mysterious ailment which had suddenly becomes the focus of everybody's attention as it struck deep in the heart of Africa.

Mjomba did not need any further prodding to come up with a plot for such a novel. All he needed to do to get it registered permanently in his mind was to locate the tiny, translucent screen-like object at the back of his skull, and begin scanning the text as it materialized thereupon. He did just that, and watched as the tiny screen instantly blossomed into a giant screen, making his task really easy.

Everything went just as expected. In his mind, Mjomba saw the first lines of the plot for the story about a hypothetical pandemic in Africa's heartland begin to materialize on a giant screen, just as the latest version of his blurb had done. To make things even easier, a mystery voice, rapping in a peculiar but easily discernible fashion, echoed the individual sentences as they began forming at the top of the screen and then continued to stream downwards.

"An unknown disease with no known cure is detected in a fast developing, exceedingly lush, region of sub-Saharan Africa" the mystery rapper said in a whisper. "The disease, a debilitating brain condition which the largely peasant population refer to as 'Brain Death', strikes following a specific but as yet unpredictable cycle. To the consternation of everyone, the disease appears to single out members of the lettered minority, and especially those who are intellectually endowed. Curiously, the peasantry, whose members are largely illiterate and tradition-bound, display a relative immunity to the mysterious disease. Also, because the intellectual elite in these parts by and large are the product of missionary schools, the disease's victims are invariably fervent Christians!

"Enter Mjomba, a member of the seminary brotherhood, and a student of philosophy and theology. He thinks he is already toast and expects to be the next one to fall prey to the brain disorder for which there was no known cure. He does not want to die in that fashion and become a statistic, and he concludes early on that his only hope lies in he himself unravelling the mystery behind the dread disease.

"Undaunted, Mjomba sets out on his mission which appears doomed from inception. He is armed only with his aptitude for applying the Scholastic Method (which he has learned about in Philosophy class) to the most implausible situations, and a dubious knack for translating perceptions in the metaphysical realm into common words!

"Mjomba's interest in the disease has actually been triggered by what befell a close pal of his by the name of Innocent Kintu. A member of the seminary

32

brotherhood like Mjomba and a fellow tribesman as well, Kintu has, sadly, been reduced to a vegetable by the disease; and he has been consigned to the care of Professor Claus Gringo, a renowned psychiatrist..."

The mysterious voice trailed off just as the screen went blank, a sign that he had actually ran out of ideas. He had, in any case, begun to notice that some of the material with which his mind was being fed for incorporation in the plot for the hypothetical novel was coming straight from THE PSYCHIC ROOTS OF INNOCENT KINTU!

It was also at that point that, suddenly and without any warning whatsoever, Mjomba picked up the pen from the table and, with a sudden jerk of his arm, transformed it into a missile of sorts. He seemed decidedly relieved that he had sent his pen hurtling toward the far end of the room. Ignoring Primrose, who had heard the commotion and was peering at him through the half-opened door, Mjomba stood up and rammed the glass topped desk hard with his fist. He sank back into the chair as the door closed, and his secretary's face disappeared behind it as silently as it had appeared. Then, as if for lack of anything to do, he proceeded to bury his head between his arms, clutching at his temples with his fists just like he had done on several previous occasions.

It was evident, at the end of the long moment that passed, that Mjomba had finally woken up to the fact that he had betrayed his beloved Jamila.

Contrary to his earlier solemn resolution, he had, rather sadly, gone back on his word and allowed his attention to be distracted from the matter at hand!

He now looked more dishevelled than ever. But, contrary to appearances, his thoughts were actually more focused than at any time before. Focused once again on the events that had transpired at the bungalow earlier that morning.

The silence, which had reigned momentarily, was broken by sounds which came from the adjoining room as Primrose apparently continued to chuckle to herself. Listening to her chuckles caused him to instantly recall what he had done to the original blurb. Looking around, he easily located the crumpled piece of paper. It was perched precariously on top of the manuscript!

Mjomba forced a smile at the thought that it was the same spot where Primrose had originally intended to leave it in the first place. But the image of an inverted pyramid balancing on top of another pyramidal shape flooded Mjomba's mind with a force that made him feel like he might pass out. He attributed his ability to stay afloat and not drift off into a swoon to the fact that he was able to focus his mind on the peculiar design Primrose had produced using the blurb's material and its similarity to the letter "X"!

Even in the middle of his adversity, Mjomba could not help fantasizing about a boundless market out there for his book consisting largely of members of the so-called X-Generation. It was not quite the most auspicious time to fantasize about that sort of thing; but Mjomba found himself recalling that, on a couple of occasions in the past, he had come very close to tossing out his manuscript with his office garbage! He had persuaded himself on those occasions that he would be better off devoting the time he was taking to write and rewrite it on more useful things.

In retrospect, it now looked so ridiculous that he had even contemplated doing such a thing. He even wondered if there hadn't been anything the matter with him for an idea as absurd as that to have had any appeal. It was so totally unbelievable. Mjomba found himself struggling to contain himself. The loud explosion of Mjomba's laughter induced a shrill but short-lived rejoinder from Primrose in the adjoining room.

Mjomba checked himself quickly. This was even though he did not care less if his secretary sometimes caught him with the wrong foot down. Prim, as his secretary was popularly referred to in the corridors of the Trade Center, was a conscientious employee who firmly believed that a *personal* secretary was, by definition, also a *confidential* secretary. Mjomba's trust in her could be gauged from the fact that he had entrusted her with the task of typing up the final edited version of his book manuscript. She was the only other individual who knew about his literary project.

Primrose had seen her boss at work on the manuscript on countless occasions, and had arrived at the conclusion that being a good writer not only required enormous concentration, but staying the course represented the greatest drain imaginable on the energies of a human being. She had, therefore, no doubt that her boss regarded THE PSYCHIC ROOTS OF INNOCENT KINTU as very important work. As for her own accidental involvement, she preferred to think about it as a simple labor of love. And just knowing that he trusted her to keep the project a secret from Jamila until the book was ready to go to press made her feel really honored.

Mjomba knew that he could get into serious trouble if his use of office resources for his private project were discovered. He also knew, however, that his secretary, who alone was in a position to blow the whistle on him, wasn't the type to ever want to see him in any trouble, leave alone trouble of that kind. To make doubly sure that she would never be tempted to turn traitor, he had made a special point of giving her the very best employee evaluation ratings and also a raise every year.

In spite of that, Mjomba recognized the seriousness of the situation which was underscored by the fact that there was always the remote possibility that Primrose could decide for whatever reason to screech and, in his words, hand him over to the dogs. But Mjomba was easily able to rationalize away any feelings of guilt and to justify his actions in that particular regard simultaneously, thanks to his fertile imagination and abiding sense of humor.

While he understood that he was in the wrong and risked ruining his career by being in breach of such a fundamental workplace canon, he always told himself that if he was doing any wrong, it was could only be in an academic sense! Thus, while Mjomba knew that the violation of a rule of that nature, particularly by a senior member of staff who was also expected to set a good example, carried with it extremely grave consequences, he saw it very differently in practical terms.

The dangers inherent in the misuse of one's office were lost on Mjomba almost as quickly as they surfaced. In his view, the one thing that was paramount in all of this business was not the observance of a rubric. It was creativity. He even rationalized that being a published author was in fact going to benefit his career. Since this happened to Europeans and Americans who were published, Mjomba reckoned that there had to be an even greater likelihood of it happening to him here in this so-called Dark Continent where close to ninety percent of the populace still had to discover the three R's!

Talking of Europeans and Americans, Mjomba once in a while entertained the truly weird notion that his own peculiar literary style - a narrative mode dominated by monologue or, more precisely, a kind of rap that took its inspiration from the bible - would one day become the style of choice in the West as well. A fan of Western pop (the Beatles was his favorite group), he once confided to his personal secretary that something similar would occur sooner or later in the pop world, with some bizarre rapping clatter becoming mainstream and completely eclipsing Western pop music as they knew it!

An incredulous Primrose had even heard him suggest that, languages being what they were, the Queen's English, which had already been unbelievably corrupted by the injection of Americanisms, would be corrupted further by Rap to a point where "rapping" would not only become fashionable, but the only accepted style of articulation! She had responded that she could not wait to watch BBC news casters, ABC, NBC and the other American television anchors "rap away" on television in the new style at prime time!

Still weighed down by anxiety for the physical and mental state of mind of his darling Jamila, Mjomba could not resist spending some more time mulling over different aspects of his manuscript. He would, for one, have preferred not to be in that situation. He would have liked, at this particular time, to be preoccupied with Jamila's condition and nothing else. But, like the proverbial trespasser whose spirit was willing, but whose body was weak, he found himself altogether unable to steer clear of the temptation to dwell some more on his book.

And so, against his will, so to speak, Mjomba continued to mull over his "blockbuster" which he sometimes also referred to as "The Masterpiece". While he initially seemed to be moving in that direction reluctantly, it quickly became clear that some strange force was propelling him along, and not only induced him to get into high gear, but also to go about the whole business aggressively and purposefully. Exuding a sense of confidence that the energies he had expended on the "Masterpiece" were finally about to produce long awaited results in the form of riches and fame, Mjomba got up and paced to the window.

From where he stood, he could count ten cargo ships in Dar es Salaam's inner harbor; and he made out the silhouettes of about the same number that were moored in the outer harbor. He now imagined all twenty vessels loaded with copies of "The Masterpiece" as they raised anchor to sail away after their next call to this "Heaven of Peace"!

Mjomba always thought he was lucky to be an individual with a fertile imagination, and he credited that faculty with his impending success. It was also the faculty that came to his rescue time and again as the anxiety for Jamila's wellbeing threatened to overwhelm him. He was, of course, aware that applying the faculty of the imagination was akin in some people's view to giving in to one's lowest instincts. According to them, only a dimwit or imbecile could get himself or herself into the kinds of situations he had found himself in; and, according to those same people, certainly no normal person would try to find solutions to problems in that fashion.

Mjomba would have conceded that they were not entirely wrong. He would have been the first person to admit that he sometimes felt like a real nut when he allowed his imagination such unfettered reign. He would also have been the first person to admit that he often let his imagination go wild because he considered it therapeutic to indulge in that sort of thing! In Mjomba's view, the real difference between himself and these other people who did not see any good in applying one's imagination to the solution of problems - who only saw themselves as sages - was that this latter group suffered from what was in effect *irreversible*, and for that reason also incurable, madness. He clearly did not believe that diseases of the mind were so mysterious as to be entirely incomprehensible.

Talking about diseases of the mind and insanity, Mjomba was of the view that everybody, including himself, was insane! Which almost amounted to saying that insanity was the normal human state, and sanity the abnormal state. And he also associated insanity with the use of one's imagination.

Whenever Mjomba found his mind dwelling on arcane ideas, or even just wondering, he always used the occasion to remind himself that he was really insane for entertaining ideas as crazy as that. But by the same token he also comforted himself with the thought that to be a true visionary - by which he meant to be a creative individual - one had, after all, to be insane. And he was sometimes tickled by the idea that he was likely, one day, to commit the ultimate act of madness by stopping to get up every morning to go to work like other ordinary folks so-called, and devoting the rest of his life to creative writing! But having discovered that he was at least on the brink of insanity if not actually insane, Mjomba naturally had developed a yearning to know exactly how he got there.

Mjomba was confident that his literary project had enabled him to essentially kill three birds with a single stone. For one, everything pointed to the fact that he was using it successfully to establish how he had come to be on the brink of insanity, and also to explain away madness! That was in addition to assuring him riches and fame if people who had money saw THE PSYCHIC ROOTS OF A NUT for what it was and made a point of getting themselves and their friends copies to keep! It wouldn't really matter if those who bought his masterpiece just placed it on the mantle for display and didn't even read it, as far as Mjomba was concerned. Everyone was insane after all.

Mjomba had no sooner warmed up, for perhaps the umpteenth time, to the notion that he was on the verge of bursting out onto the world as a renowned author and a great thinker than he suddenly recoiled at the grief that his very first work-in-progress was already causing him. The thought that he could still be a prisoner of his imagination caused him to turn away from the window and hasten to his seat at the mahogany desk. There he sat, slumped listlessly into the swivel chair.

Mjomba marshalled every ounce of his will power, sat up straight, and put on his best face on a sudden impulse. He looked so much his usual self, it would have been impossible for a newcomer on the scene to even suspect that Mjomba was just in process of recovering from the worst bout of depression he had ever had in the twenty-six years of his life. As soon as he was sufficiently composed, Mjomba started to rock gently in his chair. He leaned over toward the telephone set presently and, his gaze transfixed on the manuscript as it lay there on top of the bookshelf, was about to buzz his secretary when he froze for no apparent reason.

But his mind was obviously still wandering. This was more than evident from his reaction when the In-Tray and its load of unanswered correspondence accidentally came into his line of vision. It took Mjomba a while to accept that the contents of the tray did in fact represent work that was pending.

Mjomba got up on a sudden impulse and, moving with his back to the In Tray, approached the bookshelf. Once there, he retrieved the manuscript and the blue file folder along with the crumpled blurb carefully, as if they were objects that might sustain damage if handled in the normal fashion, and returned with them to his seat. Unaware that his swivel chair had moved from its place, Mjomba realized a little late that it was not where he thought it was. He lost his balance and, to save himself from a nasty fall, had to let go of his precious load so he could free his arms and use them to hang onto the mahogany desk for dear life's sake.

In the immediate aftermath, Mjomba did not appear at all concerned about his wellbeing. He seemed to be more preoccupied with the fate of his manuscript. He could not believe that those papers strewn all over the place were in fact the pages of his manuscript. The single word that sprung to his mind as he sought for a way to describe the scene was "desecration". Mjomba was aware that different people tended to have different impressions of things or events. In this particular instance, as far as he was concerned, the sanctity of his work of many months, indeed of his lifetime, had been violated!

Picking himself up very cautiously this time, Mjomba sat himself down in his executive chair. He appeared dazed and seemed to be wondering how the fine mess had all come about! He dearly wished that there had been someone else there on whom he could pin the blame for what had happened. He certainly could not blame the chair which was, even now, helping him recover from his traumatic experience.

Wondering why things of that sort happened to people, Mjomba was on the verge of stopping and blaming Providence when it occurred to him that there might be something human beings, himself included, did - or omitted to do - that set the stage for misadventures like those. Fearing that he would find himself entirely to blame, Mjomba decided against pursuing the matter any further. But the fall, which left parts of his body aching wildly, also left him wondering if human beings, despite their vainglory and vanity, were not very frail creatures who were also entirely at the mercy of some Supreme Being.

It took the wail of the siren announcing the twelve o'clock shift at the Docks to bring him to completely. Notwithstanding his frayed nerves, Mjomba's first impulse was to roll up his sleeves as he was supposed to do, and justify his five-digit monthly pay by clearing his desk of the pending work. He even looked in the direction of the In-Tray on the far side of his desk and recalled that he had earlier deliberately moved it so the sight of the label "For Immediate Action" would not cause him any agony. He even seemed like he was about to extend an arm to pick up a sheaf of documents for scrutiny when he suddenly appeared to lose heart.

But he could not ignore the spectacle on the floor. He would have to be nuts not to realize that the reality of that situation, involving as it did no less than the blue print for his masterpiece, took precedence over everything else. The sight of the pages of his manuscript strewn every which way he cast his eyes and with the lovely sky-blue file folder which was supposed to hold them nowhere in sight, caused his heart to sink.

When he reported for work that morning, Mjomba had undoubtedly been a victim of a pretty serious depression. To call the gloom and despondency that now descended on the expectant father this time around severe was to seriously misconstrue the situation. If appearances were anything to go by, Mjomba saw, or at least thought he saw, a large rock come falling from the skies and threaten to drop smack on top of him - or something of the sort! At that moment, at any rate, he looked everything like someone in that predicament.

In a flash, the idol thoughts with which he had just then been preoccupied were forgotten and became a thing of the past. And the same went for the In-Tray's bulging contents; and also the throbbing pain in his knees, elbows and side. It was a different story, however, with regard to the manuscript.

Springing up from his seat, Mjomba seemed in haste as he gathered up the manuscript's pages and painstakingly arranged them in a neat pile on his chair. He even took time to arrange them in page order, before tucking them neatly inside the blue folder.

Mjomba paused to stare one more time at the manuscript which he had placed just inches away from the In Tray and its contents of work files, payment vouchers, and unanswered correspondence. For the first time he felt a sting of guilt, albeit momentary, for having employed his secretary as well as office equipment and stationery in its preparation.

Mjomba had never been really bothered by the fact that he himself sometimes worked on his book during official working hours; because, as a senior officer of the Port Authority, he was not entitled to any additional pay for the many special assignments he was often called upon to do outside of the so-called official working hours. But the fact that Primrose had apparently finished work on the glossy folder for his manuscript and on the blurb, and delivered them to him only that morning, heightened his feelings of guilt somewhat. Now, however, it was guilt for something else altogether that now really rocked him and deflated his spirits beyond all measure.

Then, at long last, with what seemed to be a jolt, Mjomba awakened to fact that he had been very unfair to his adorable Jamila. He found himself mulling over the fact that he had fallen into the habit of spending his luncheon hours at the office instead of driving home for his usual three-course lunch, as had previously been his custom, ostensibly to save on gas. But it still took him a long while to concede that over the past several months he had been conducting himself as if he had a responsibility to the world. And when he finally did, it was with such a sting of remorse, he actually lost several heartbeats.

Immediately after that, all hell seemed to break loose with Mjomba sensing that he was again losing control over the direction of his thoughts. And while some of them dealt with some of his favorite subjects such as his sojourn in America for instance, others dealt with certain aspects of his own background that he had never really wanted revealed at any price.

One of those "dark" secrets was the fact that he had been a member of the seminary brotherhood. There were several reasons for this. On leaving the seminary, Mjomba had learned almost immediately that being an *ex-seminarian* was, in the eyes of a goodly number of people, synonymous with being a sex maniac or even a sex predator. More importantly, however, Mjomba feared that if that part of his background was not hidden from the world, readers of his proposed "best seller" would be tempted to jump to the conclusion that his masterpiece was in fact just an autobiographical work.

Not that there was anything intrinsically wrong with writing an autobiography. When the time came for him to write one, and he hoped that time would come in due course, he would definitely give that also his best shot. He would do it "with body and soul" - to borrow the expression Mjomba enjoyed using when he was urging Primrose and other subordinate staff to get on with some urgent or important task.

For now, however, Mjomba's sights were firmly set on landing a position in the world as a best-selling novelist, and he wanted THE PSYCHIC ROOTS OF INNOCENT KINTU to stand as a creative piece of work, pure and simple.

Goaded on by a mysterious force, Mjomba again travelled back in his thoughts to his beachside bungalow. The children were still asleep, and his early morning confrontation with his wife was continuing. Staring Jamila in the eye, Mjomba was this time about to confess that it was all his fault. But he was also going to add that it was his preoccupation with the novel that was to blame! He had written the last word and thought it was the right time to disclose to her his long-held secret.

Mjomba stared at his wife, intent on doing just that. Even though he was only imagining that he was at home on Msasani Peninsula with Jamila, it all felt very real.

As he opened his mouth to make the confession, a most extraordinary thing happened. He was snatched up by the same mysterious force that had caused him to begin thinking about the confession, and immediately transported in spirit to St. Augustine's Seminary. Once there, he found himself hovering all over the place, just like he was a spook.

He floated around freely, gaining entrance into various buildings, including the chapel, effortlessly through chinks in the roofs. He was doing this when he was suddenly confronted with what was clearly the real reason for the mystical journey to his alma mater. For it was, indeed, whilst Mjomba was a student at St. Augustine's, many years before, that he had commenced work on his book.

What exactly had gone wrong from the moment he first got the idea of writing a book to the present time, when everything that had anything to do with the book appeared to spell trouble? It was a question that became uppermost in his mind as he cruised around St. Augustine's Seminary like a phantom, and also one that represented - for the moment at any rate - the most plausible explanation for his spiritual pilgrimage to his alma mater.

The former member of the seminary brotherhood found himself detesting the place without any apparent reason. And the more his dislike for the place, the more his mind sought out aspects of seminary life on which he could pin blame for his mounting personal problems and their cumulative effect on his book project.

And that was also when memories of something that had in fact marred his stay at St.

Augustine's returned to haunt him. Mjomba had never appreciated the fact that a label proposed by one particular fellow he had no particular liking for had stuck on him.

To be sure, Judas Iscariot was not exactly the sort of character that Christian Mjomba - or anyone else at St. Augustine's Seminary for that matter - would have wanted to be nicknamed after. But the fact was that Mjomba had never made a secret of his views on the world. Everyone in the seminary brotherhood knew his stand on apartheid and things like that; and his views in their regard were considered very liberal. In the conservative environment that prevailed at St. Augustine's Seminary, they were also tantamount to betrayal! That "man of Kerioth" was about the most unsavory character that anyone could have wished to be associated with. Be that as it may, that was the label he had got stuck with.

Everyone knew, besides, that it wasn't some uninformed gentile or misguided unbeliever who had betrayed the Deliverer and handed Him over to His killers. And Judas Iscariot wasn't just anybody either. Judas was one of the twelve who had been handpicked by the Deliverer to form the core of the convocation that would become the *Sancta Ecclesia*. In addition to being the Deliverer's purse bearer, Judas Iscariot also drank wine from the same cup as his Master! The man who would betray the Deliverer with a kiss was a member of the inner circle of the burgeoning Christ Fellowship; and, before long, his name had become so repulsive even among Romans, it had replaced that of Brutus, the friend of Cæsar who had conspired with others and stabbed the emperor in the back, not metaphorically but in the literal sense (Cæsar was stabbed by Brutus and his co-conspirators a total of twenty-three times), as a symbol of betrayal. A traitor par excellence!

It was, Mjomba reflected, quite extraordinary – the extent to which humans, created in the image of the Prime Mover and all of them descendants of Adam and Eve without any exception, could turn on each other just like that and become traitors and quislings instead of being each other's keeper! But then, it mirrored the betrayal by Lucifer and the legion of angels who joined him in his plot against their Maker, and also Adam and Eve's betrayal of the Deity that had caused them to bounce into existence out of nothing when they decided to eat of the forbidden fruit from the Tree of the Knowledge of Good and Evil, an act that got them booted out of the Paradise of Pleasure! Mjomba would write in his theology thesis that humans were free to do anything they fancied without regard to the consequences as long as they were kicking. But they effectively lost that freedom upon kicking the proverbial bucket. And that seemingly was also when they faced the consequences of their acts of omission and commission!

Whenever Mjomba thought about Judas' betrayal of the Messiah of the world with a kiss, it was not the act of betrayal itself that came to mind. It was not even the chilling words "Would'st thou betray thy Master with a kiss, Judas?" that were addressed to the betrayer by the Deliverer in the moment when Judas, no doubt representing all humanity, embraced the Nazarene and kissed him on the cheek so the temple's constabulary wouldn't grab and take into custody the wrong person! It was the Deliverer's address to Peter a little earlier on in the Upper House as the fisherman, who would himself swear that he did not know the Nazarene, not once but three times, in front of a shivering crowd not long afterward, balked at the notion that the miracle worker and Son of Man could stoop to wash his (the fisherman's) dirty feet, namely: "Not all are clean, Peter!" And that was, in all probability, after Judas's feet had already been washed by the Nazarene.

That, in any event, was the character after whom Christian Mjomba had been nicknamed by his buddies in what he initially regarded as something that was itself an act of betrayal. The traitors! As if they didn't know that this was the man that Dante had not hesitated to confine to the fourth ring of the ninth circle that was reserved for the worst sinners in his Divine Comedy! But even if they thought nothing about that because the setting was the figment of Dante's imagination, they surely knew how others had referred to that "renegade" apostle! Pope St. Leo the Great and a Doctor of the Church had branded Judas Iscariot "the wickedest man who ever lived"! St. Matthew, the Evangelist, had of course provided a somewhat different take when he wrote in his account of the goings-on in Jerusalem at the time the Deliverer met His death on the cross as follows: "Then Judas, who betrayed him, seeing that he (the Deliverer) was condemned, repenting himself, brought back the thirty pieces of silver to the chief priests and ancients, saying: I have sinned in betraying innocent blood". Still Pope Leo the Great wasn't alone. St. Augustine had stated in *The City of God* that when Judas killed himself, he killed a wicked man, and passed from this life chargeable not only with the death of Christ, but also with his own! And St. Catherine of Siena had referred to the sin of the betrayer in *The Dialogue* as one that was unforgivable!

Christian Mjomba could not understand how people could be so insensitive about the feelings of others! And even though he had never said it, he had never liked it a bit - until he started work on his theology thesis.

He, admittedly, didn't really have any choice but to accept the fact that individuals rarely chose their nicknames or, for that matter, any other labels that enemies and friends alike used to refer to them. These were things that were bestowed upon them by others. But before long, and certainly by the time the seminarian was searching for themes for the thesis on his chosen subject of Original Virtue, he appeared to have undergone a transformation of sorts. At some point during that transformation, instead of being something that was abominable, all of a sudden "Judas" had stopped striking him as a "disgusting" label. In his mind, it didn't have to be since it *was* a very appropriate label.

Only the Immaculate Virgin Mary and her Divine Son were sinless, and no other human, members of the seminary brotherhood included, could claim that label. Christian Mjomba found that it was in fact liberating to accept those facts for what they were. If there was anything to be ashamed of, it was clearly the reluctance of people to see that they all were betrayers! In retrospect, Christian Mjomba was thankful that he had been singled out as deserving the nickname of Judas. For it was that association with the Deliverer's purse bearer and betrayer that would spark his interest in the much-maligned apostle from Jericho, leading him to devote an entire section of the thesis on his namesake.

Mjomba was completely lost in reverie by now. But his reasoning was faultless. How appropriate, he said to himself, that the senior seminary was named after St. Augustine of Hippo, who was easily the most illustrious and scholarly amongst the so-called Fathers of the early Church. St. Augustine's Major Seminary, as it was officially known, was the only institution of its kind in the region and was ranked on a par with senior seminaries in other parts of the world.

Young men aspiring to the holy priesthood came here from different countries in Eastern Africa to receive advanced training in the doctrines of the Roman Catholic Church. Those who did so had at least one thing in common: they had survived seven years of rigorous discipline in junior seminaries in their own lands!

Seminaries undoubtedly inspired a certain amount of awe in the minds of East Africans. But Christian Mjomba imagined that the situation of the Israelites who had heard about the twelve men who had heeded the Messiah's call two thousand years earlier to leave all and follow him was no different; and he saw nothing unusual in the mystique that surrounded the seminarians and their preparation for holy orders. Mjomba thought about the batch of seventy-two other disciples whom the Deliverer appointed and sent out ahead of him into the villages and cities that he planned to visit "as lambs among wolves", and with instructions that they take along "neither purse, nor scrip, nor shoes" and that they "salute no man by the way"! That second batch of "laborers", probably clad in white robes or cassocks just as the first wave of "seminarians" who were hitting the road in Eastern Africa (Christian Mjomba among them) were in the habit of doing, must have initially felt a little out of place as well.

Christian Mjomba would never forget how, during his first ever retreat years earlier as a Minor Seminarian, he had tried putting himself in the shoes of Peter at the time the fisherman received his call; and he had concluded that Peter and the other candidates for apostleship would have been abnormal if they had not felt a little funny themselves as they struggled to keep pace with the Nazarene, a member of the Godhead, and to internalize the dogmas and everything else He taught them over the space of a mere three years! The retreat took place during the third term; and before it was over, Mjomba, who still had to complete Prep as the freshman class was referred to, had no doubt that the chaps in Low Figures, High Figures, Grammar, Syntax, Poetry, and even in Rhetoric Class shared his view in that regard.

That was not to say that seminaries were accepted by East Africans with no questions asked. Actually, many people, particularly those who had exceptional attachment to traditions of the land, initially regarded the seminary institution as something of an anachronism in this part of the world, and practically doomed to failure. This was principally because the seminarians were expected, amongst other things, to lead celibate lives.

In the eyes of many inhabitants of sub-Saharan Africa, where polygamous marriages were not just an accepted custom but a tradition that was deep rooted and highly revered, the idea of celibacy struck a code that was not exactly enchanting. Not surprisingly, the first missionaries to arrive in sub-Saharan Africa had the tendency to regard African customs, including the polygamous marriages, as evil and totally unacceptable, forgetting that whilst according to Genesis 2:24 "a man shall leave his father and his mother and hold fast to his wife, and they shall become one flesh", some really notable figures in the Old Testament at any rate openly practiced polygamy. Abraham, Judah, Gideon, Samson, David, Moses and King David were all apparently into this practice with Solomon, the third king of Israel who reigned from around 968 B.C.E. to 928 B.C.E., said to have had a harem that included seven hundred wives and three hundred concubines! (1 Kings 11:3)

Be that as it may, the first impression the requirement that aspirants to the priesthood lead celibate lives evoked in the minds of the "natives" was that this practice (celibacy) was something unnatural. At the very least, it had to be suggestive of serious deficiencies in the sexual makeup of members of the societies in which ideas of that sort took root and became accepted as a norm.

Sexual instincts were such a fundamental part of the nature of not just humankind but of all living forms of life, both animal and vegetative, the preference for a life style of that sort in their view had to be a symptom of something gone really wrong! While conditions in their own society precluded abuses of any significance in the realm of sexual matters, the people of sub-Saharan Africa supposed that Western society had been tolerating abuses probably for generations. When that happened, the abuses became pervasive and they were also apt to obscure the very purpose of this vital aspect of human life.

When things got out of hand like that, the role of sex where it really mattered, namely in procreation, stopped being seen as vital and unique; and the abuses became a real threat to the family institution. And, consequently, society ceased to regard the family, that bastion of strength for any nation in both victory and defeat, as vital and unique.

They rationalized that, for society to invoke sanctions of that gravity against any of its members, the abuses such sanctions were designed to discourage had to be really gross and mind-boggling! It was quite conceivable that there were societies in which individuals, and eventually a majority of members of that society, for one reason or another, chose to regard the sexual instinct as something that wasn't originally designed for conception or procreation, but simply for amusement and recreation! People in this part of the world suspected that, at a certain point in time, Western society as a whole had actually fallen for that bait.

In any case, the argument the inhabitants of these parts would have advanced as their strongest one against the so-called chastity belt would, of course, have been that living species, whether animal or vegetative, were made the way they were for an obvious reason. It was the same argument that anyone who engaged in the excesses they condemned probably would use to justify their actions; but that was obviously something they could do very little about. It was in any event quite funny that such extremes in behavior and philosophical thinking could become espoused by an entire people or society! This was a situation that seemed quite inconceivable.

Their forefathers, who were revered in the same way righteous Christian men and women were revered upon their departure from this world to the next one, had always urged young men to seek out and find themselves not just one but, if possible, many wives so they could beget many children. And, naturally, the more children a man begot, the more respect he earned himself in the community. The reasoning of Africans was similar in many respects to that of Viola when she urged Olivia not to "lead these graces to the grave and leave the world no copy"! Children were regarded as the key to the survival of the human race.

A married young man who was unable to beget a child was despised. But a healthy young man who could not get himself a wife, irrespective of the reason, was despised more. And, while marital infidelity was outlawed, voluntary celibacy *per se* had never been deemed a viable option. It was generally agreed that anyone who pretended that he or she could live up to that state was up to something else. The consensus was that it was not just good for society but critically important for the survival of the human race if the number of births were at least equal to, but preferably more than, the number of people who were dying either of old age, illness or in battle. The only problem, of course, was that things were changing, and disagreements over those traditional values were setting in. Mjomba imagined a scenario in which more humans were dying than were being born, and the opposite was happening to their livestock. In that scenario, one only needed an abacus (or counting frame as that antediluvian calculating tool is known) and not a computer to establish the exact date and time when there would be no more humans on earth, and cattle, sheep, goats, swine, chickens, etc. would be the ones roaming around in the houses, palaces and temples that humans had built and left behind, and even the hospitals with their operating rooms and high-end scanners, anaesthetic machines, and flashing operating room lights where the last humans to die had sought treatment, and desecrating everything in their path!

Still, while an avowal to lifelong celibacy traditionally bordered on the presumptuous and continued to be so in the eyes of many, for the growing number of people who saw Christianity as the key to literacy and immediate financial prosperity, the idea amazingly was winsome and, in some cases, even patently enthralling. In fact, in the end, for any disdain that celibacy as a notion earned the Church, there was lots more respect gained.

The explanation appeared to lie in the claim that success in keeping a vow of celibacy could only be attributable to the workings of something entirely novel in concept called divine grace! But mystery was no stranger to Africans and, anyway, logic itself appeared to support that stance. Indeed, one could not achieve a feat that was so clearly beyond the power of nature without the intervention of something supernatural, namely divine grace!

And when the time finally came for those few diehards, who actually succeeded in surviving the full fourteen years of seminary life, to make a solemn renewal of their perpetual vow of chastity at the time of their ordination to the priesthood, it seemed only natural that they did it with great pomp and circumstance. And the community of Christians supported them all the way because the catechism stated that seminary life was synonymous with years of rigorous and exacting discipline.

PART 2: THE THESIS

As usually happened, whenever sexuality was at issue, Mjomba invariably found himself recalling the fall of Adam and Eve from grace, and the original sin into which all members of the human race were subsequently plunged at conception according to Catholic dogma. More often than not, that in turn brought to mind what Mjomba himself now accepted was an idiosyncratic thesis that he had advanced in a controversial paper he wrote while at Augustine's.

Students chose the subject for their theological thesis. Mjomba's thesis was titled "Original Virtue". In it, Mjomba sought to develop a profile for members of the "invisible Church" using what was essentially a combination of fact and legend; and he argued that Man's inclination to sin in the aftermath of the rebellion of Adam and Eve was the result of the struggle between the forces of good, represented by Original Virtue and the forces of evil represented by Original Sin. Mjomba theorized that humans who did not belong to the visible Church but still belonged to the invisible one did so by virtue of Original Virtue!

In selecting the subject for the thesis, Mjomba was influenced by his views on the nature and origin of man. Unlike so many other people for whom "Adam" and "Eve" were mythical characters that had nothing in common with the reality of the evolution of man, Mjomba believed that the first Man and Woman happened into the world almost at the same time, and that Adam came complete with male characteristics while his companion, Eve, had female characteristics.

Creatures who were willed into being and given an existence by an all-knowing and almighty "Prime Mover", and whose blue print or nature had been in the Prime Mover's mind from eternity, Mjomba believed that Adam and Eve were spirits. As would happen with the rest of their posterity, the "spirits" became automatically incarnated and acquired a physical body at the time they came into being.

But even though they were spiritual beings, the bodily matter in their nature, while it allowed them to develop and thrive in their temporal earthly habitat, hindered physical contact and normal interaction, not only with the "Non-Creature and Master Craftsman", but also with other creatures that were pure spirits. Consequently, "Adam" and "Eve", the first "humans" ever to walk the earth, were constantly faced with the temptation to think that they were all on their own and owed no one anything, and that they might even be the real masters of the universe instead of just creatures enjoying a temporary lease of life there. But they remained well aware that their days in earth are numbered, and that they were expected to use their time and talents to prepare for eternal bliss with the Non-Creature and Master Craftsman, the only kind of happiness that could fully satisfy them and round out their self-actualization.

The humans, according to Mjomba, had not been around for a long time when they did something very bad - they broke their covenant with the Non-

Creature and Master Craftsman who had gratuitously willed them into existence. They actually didn't want to feel that they owed Him - or anyone else for that matter - anything, a rotten idea they got from a rebel creature that, unlike themselves, was completely invisible because of the fact that he was a pure spirit.

After that dastardly act, the humans had been so ashamed of themselves, they had cried out to the heavens and begged the skies to fall on them, pulverize them and reduce them to the nothingness from which they had originally come because of their sin. Seeing the compunction of Adam and Eve, the Non-Creature and Master Craftsman, and also Lord of the Universe, had felt sorry for them, and immediately promised them help in the shape of a Redeemer whose act of atonement on their behalf would be acceptable to Him.

Mjomba wrote in his Thesis on Original Virtue that it took some persuasion on the part of the Prime Mover to get Adam and Eve to accept that the idea of their Prime Mover sending his only begotten Son into the world to redeem humankind was workable. Quoting from the Rwenzori Prehistoric Diaries, he wrote that Adam and Eve were initially adamant that humans were irredeemable. They both believed that they would vaporize if they set their eyes on the Prime Mover. Mjomba quoted Adam as interrupting the booming voice of the Prime Mover to make his point.

"No! No! No! Almighty One", Mjomba quoted Adam as shouting, his voice hoarse from crying and mourning the loss of state of innocence; "It is too late…this will not work! We traded in our birthright for what we now acknowledge is mere fantasy; we just deserve to die. Leave us alone!

"And as for our offspring – the poor things are doomed as well! There is no conceivable way that they can come into this world without the stain of our sin. Poor things – they will even never understand what happened! They will never know how Eve and I, who came into this world as innocent creatures who were ministered to by our guardian angels and who had none other than you yourself as our, could have been so dumb! How we could have allowed ourselves to be hoodwinked by Lucifer of all creatures? We blew it!

"This human nature of ours, fashioned though it still is in your image, is now infected with a dreadful, uncleanable virus - thanks to the lies and chicanery of Old Scratch. And now, not only are we both inclined to sin; but our children, their children, and their children's children will be inclined to sin from birth! That can only mean that the generations to come will find themselves in a world that will be awash with selfishness, greed, and the array of unimaginable evils that stem from there from!"

It was at that point that Eve interjected saying: "Oh, Prime Mover, the sun has not even set yet since we both trespassed against thee. But this Adam who is supposed to be my companion – he is already giving me murderous looks! I admit that I am the one who led him by hand to the spot where the Tree of the Knowledge of Good and Evil is located. But I am now afraid – this Man is going to kill me, Oh God!"

"Yes, you have to be careful, girl!" the Prime Mover started. His voice booming as usual, He had continued: "You and your companion Adam indeed now belong with the Evil Ghost and the angels that joined it in its rebellion. And it is also the reason I now insist on sending my beloved Son into the world. I, the Almighty and Holy One, knew from the beginning of time that you humans would fall for the lies of Old Scratch. But I also knew that, unlike that damned Lucifer and the host of demons who opted to follow in his footsteps, you were going to feel sorry for your transgression. Already at that time, I committed to sending you a Deliverer. Eve, you and Adam can escape from being consigned to the Cavern of Darkness or 'hell' only by virtue of the graces that will be merited for you by the Son of Man at the time of His visitation."

Even after they had heard the Prime Mover reiterate that the Deliverer was on the way, Adam and Eve both still wished that the heavens would fall on them so that they would be no more. The reason became evident as Adam, his voice vibrating hoarsely, said in response.

"No, no, no! Ooh Holy One!" Mjomba quoted Adam as shouting. "We are irredeemable - leave us alone! And tell the Son of Man not to venture here into this accursed world of ours, lest he be overtaken by harm."

"Exactly" countered the Prime Mover, His voice booming as usual. "Lo, the Son of Man - and know that it is through Him that all creation, including Michael the arch-angel and the host of angels who minister to me here in heaven, Lucifer and the demons in hell, and you humans, has come to be - cometh. I love the world so, and behold! I send Him so that those humans who believe in Him might be delivered from the clutches of sin, and from death.

"As for the Son of Man Himself" the Prime Mover said in conclusion, "no one can take His life away from Him, but He can lay it down on His own initiative. He has authority to lay it down, and He has authority to take it up again. In obedience to my command, even though the Son of Man is Lord of all, He can be obedient even unto death – and he will!"

The *devil*, as Adam and Eve called the evil spirit which had been instrumental in leading them astray, was sworn to the dirtiest campaign imaginable against all who intended to stay loyal to the Non-Creature and Master Craftsman. Variously known as Diabolos, Beelzebub, Satan and Prince of Darkness, the evil spirit had the notoriety of being the most dangerous creature that ever came into being, and was proud of its horrendous record which included misleading a host of pure spirits like itself into following its example and revolting against their *divine* Creator, and now also successfully tempting the first Man and Woman, and causing them to disobey their *God*. It was because Adam and Eve had shown they were determined to be good and faithful creatures during their probationary period on earth that they had become targets in the first place.

With the promise of a Redeemer, the invisible tempter, who never had such a second chance after he himself strayed from righteousness - he would never have been interested in a second chance out of pride any way - swore that he would give the humans a run for their money as long as he existed. The disenchanted spirit vowed to devote all its energies and talents, particularly its sharp wit, to being a real spoiler, particularly in view of the promise of a Redeemer.

Mjomba, of course, believed that the promised Redeemer - the Son of Man as He called Himself - eventually did come to earth, had paid the price for Man's redemption, and had ascended back into heaven. And if it had turned out that the Son of Man was actually the only begotten Son of the Non-Creature and Master Craftsman, who was united to His Father in a bond of Love that was itself so strong it constituted a distinct Person equal to God the Father and God the Son, it only seemed logical in his mind.

Later, while speaking in defense of his thesis, Mjomba would say something that was quite remarkable but true, namely that Beelzebub, while he was not a member of the Church Triumphant because he had flunked the Church Triumphant Entrance Test, had at one time been a member of the invisible Church!

Mjomba had espoused these views from his early days as a child in a deeply Christian family where leafing through pictorial books of the Old and

New Testament had been regarded as completely normal. And, as it would happen, the events that would vindicate those who, like him, subscribed to views of the origin of Man that were dismissed as primitive and simplistic with no real scientific merit by the "scientific community", would actually unfold in his own lifetime!

The Rwenzori Prehistoric Diaries...

It was only lately that entirely new but quite credible information about Adam and Eve and the kind of lives the first humans led had been unearthed in Uganda. And, that was while the world of archaeology was still reeling from two other absolutely mind-boggling archaeological finds that had occurred almost simultaneously just months earlier. Those archaeological discoveries had rocked Christendom and caused turmoil among the hitherto disparate Christian churches.

The first archaeological find on the scene had been dubbed the "Canadian Scrolls"; and they contained a mine of information on New Testament figures like Judas Iscariot and St. Stephen in Palestine, and other information that exploded the twin myths regarding "redemption by faith alone" and "*sola scriptura*" as the only Source of Revealed truth!

Besides, the treasure trove included information that not only corroborated the four gospels and the Acts of the Apostles in many respects, but also included a biography of Judas Iscariot! The betrayer's biography was written in Hebrew by someone who signed himself simply as Nicodemus, but included many anecdotes that suggested that its author was none other than the Nicodemus whose exchange with the Deliverer regarding spiritual regeneration through the sacrament of Baptism is recorded in John 3:1-21, and who also features elsewhere in St. John's Gospel (John 7:50-51 and John 19:39-42).

A group of Canadian tourists, trudging through a valley near the Dead Sea, had stumbled on these scrolls, and hence their name. The scrolls apparently dated back to the time of the apostles, and even contained new information on the apostles Peter and John, and on Mary Magdalene, amongst others. They also identified the character alluded to in Luke 9:49-50. This was the "independent" New Testament exorcist whose activities had attracted the attention of the Deliverer's disciples enough that they sought to know what the Deliverer's stand regarding him was.

But the scrolls proved to be of very great significance in one particular respect: a close study of the parchments by world's top archaeologists left no doubt that it was the Church of Rome, headed by Peter's successors, that indeed was the Church the Deliverer established!

To the disappointment of the many disaffected "Christians" who had chosen to break ranks with the Church of Rome for one reason or another, and did not recognize the authority of the pope, the scrolls corroborated the writings of the so-called early

Church fathers, amongst them Clement of Rome (died around 110 AD), Polycarp of Smyrna (died in 155 AD), Irenaeus of Lyons (died around 202 AD), Tertullian of Carthage (died around 240 AD) and others, pertaining to the foundation of the Church and the primacy of the bishop of Rome. The parchments specifically cited the passage from the writing of Matthew that stated: *Tu es Petrus, et super hanc petram Aedificabo Ecclesiam meam, Et portae inferi non praevalebunt adversus eam: Et tibi dabo claves Regni coelorum. Quodcumque ligaveris super terram, Erit ligatum et in coelis; Et quodcumque solveris super terram Erit solutum et in coelis.* (You are Peter, and on this rock I will build my church, and the gates of hell will not prevail against it: and I will give you the keys to the kingdom of heaven. Whatever you bind on earth will be bound also in heaven; and whatever you release on earth will be released also in heaven.)

It was also quite plain from studying the new archaeological finds that the accounts of the evangelists, whether they were accounts that subsequently received the stamp of approval of the apostles as being among the most reliable accounts available - what came to be known as the *"imprimatur"* - or accounts that merely contained useful supplemental material like those of the historian Flavius Josephus (36-100 CE) corroborating what the surviving apostles taught, took second place to what the apostles presented as being the authoritative teaching of the Church.

Already at that time it was, for instance, regarded as being of little significance that the accounts compiled by the evangelists remained fragmentary and incomplete from the perspective of the infant Church; and the parchments included discussions concerning the fact that the evangelists Mark and John did not include details of the place where the Deliverer was born. And even the accounts that did (the ones Luke and Matthew had just finished compiling) did not agree on whether Joseph and Mary travelled to Bethlehem for the birth of the Deliverer or had lived there for a while in the months before the Deliverer was born.

The Canadian Scrolls included incontrovertible evidence that the leadership of the nascent Church, led by Peter, urged converts to focus, not on the ostensibly unending debate regarding which account of the gospel was more accurate, but on the fact that the divine Messiah and also Deliverer of humans had come and, in the wake of His ignominious death on the cross and His subsequent resurrection from the dead, had formally inaugurated His Church, and commissioned them to head out into the world to spread what they called the "Message of the Crucified and Risen Savior of the World". The Church's clergy harped on the importance of following in the Deliverer's footsteps by "preparing the way of the Lord, making his paths straight, and keeping the commandments".

According to the evidence, all the eleven surviving apostles, while they lived, had urged the converts to the faith to always remember what the "Deliverer" taught concerning the life and destiny of humans, namely that their happiness, or lack thereof, after they crossed the gulf that separated the living from the dead, would depend entirely on the extent to which they led self-less lives whilst back on earth, their participation in the life of the "Mystical Body of the Deliverer", and above all their love for their neighbors.

The Canadian Scrolls completely undermined the argument of latter-day self-styled "reformers" to the effect that it was the written Word of God alone or "*Sola Scriptura*" as they labeled it, and not the teaching authority or *Magisterium* of the Church, on which followers of the Deliverer needed to focus. This was in addition to emphasizing that "keeping the paths straightened", whether by Jewish or non-Jewish converts, did not at all entail keeping the (old) Law of Moses or abiding by the Jewish customs and rituals, things that the Deliverer Himself had done for the purpose of fulfilling prophecies of the "Old Testament".

And so, by making it clearer than ever before that the "Word of God", represented by the collection of writings forming what was known as the New Testament, were authoritative only to the extent to which they had a stamp of approval of the fledgling Church with the fisherman at its helm, the scrolls completely undermined the position of the break-away churches, because these "churches" claimed that authority for what was believed and taught in those churches derived from the Word of God *per se,* and did not depend in any way on the "*magisterium*" of the Church or anything like that. That also effectively meant that being "in communion" with the Roman Catholic Church was absolutely critical for membership in the *Sancta Ecclesia* founded by the Deliverer!

Furthermore, the scrolls included entirely new material pertaining to the relationship between the Old Testament and the New Testament. The material consisted of statements attributed to the apostles that had apparently helped in resolving the controversy in the early Church surrounding the initial reluctance of some at the time to proclaim what Peter termed the good news of peace (Acts 10:36) to Jews and gentiles alike without discrimination or favour.

There was ample evidence that the material had been compiled with the intention of including it in what we now know as the "Gospel According to Luke'. The discovery of the Canadian Scrolls would immediately give rise to speculation as to the reasons that led to the exclusion of statements of such import from the canonical gospels.

After scrutinizing the "Canadian Scrolls", some biblical scholars voiced the opinion that what the tourists had alighted upon were "notes" that either Luke himself (or a scribe whom he had commissioned) had compiled, after interviewing the apostles, relatives of the Deliverer, including the Deliverer's mother Mary, the holy women of the New Testament, Simon of Arimathea, and others who represented his "sources". That conclusion was based on the similarities between the Canadian Scrolls and the known writings of Luke (*The Gospel according to Luke* and his other self-published work titled *The Acts of the Apostles*). But the reason those "notes" did not make it into the canonical gospels would remain a mystery, albeit not for long.

For, barely three weeks after news agencies from around the globe started buzzing with the news surrounding the Canadian Scrolls, a treasure trove that included the handwritten epistle the "Apostle of the Gentiles" wrote to Timothy turned up in Alexandria, Egypt. Construction workers, preparing the foundation for a high-rise in Alexandria, realized almost too late that they were burrowing into a stash of ancient manuscripts. Dubbed the "Alexandria Gusher" because of the vast amount of information the stash contained, the find in Alexandria corroborated the Canadian Scrolls to the hilt, adding to the turmoil in Christendom.

As if the archaeological finds in the Dead Sea valley and in Alexandria weren't extraordinary enough, while the world was still reeling from the news surrounding them, and exactly one month after the construction workers in Egypt struck their "gold mine", copper miners in the Rwenzori Mountains in Western Uganda dug up parchments that turned out to be diaries that the first Man and Woman who had ever walked the earth had apparently kept! Known as the Rwenzori Prehistoric Diaries, the parchments, undoubtedly Archaeology's rarest find, were embedded in molten rock inside a cave.

Other evidence found suggested that the cave had provided shelter to Adam and Eve for a prolonged period, perhaps as long as ten years. Archaeologists from Uganda's Makerere University, the University of Addis Ababa, Stanford, Harvard, Oxford, and other eminent institutions of learning from around the globe speculated that the volcanic eruption had occurred several generations after Adam and Eve had passed on, and that the fossilized human remains found nearby likely belonged to Adam and Eve's great grandchildren.

The scientists also stunned the world with their announcement that the evidence had buried in one fell swoop the long-held notion that humans had evolved from primates! And, using new and experimental "genetic" dating methods, they revised the dates for the appearance on earth of *'homo sapiens'* to sometime between three hundred thousand and four hundred thousand years ago.

But the big question that would remain and continue to engage biblical scholars and theologians - and now also archaeologists - for a very long time was whether that cave had been the home of the first Man and the first Woman, whom they renamed *"Msaijja"* and *"Mkailli"* in conformity with the way Adam and Eve had signed their names in the Rwenzori Prehistoric Diaries, prior to their fall from grace, a finding that would effectively place the cave within the boundaries of the "Garden of Eden".

There was no disagreement in the scientific community regarding the authenticity of the diaries.

The faded parchments were universally attributed to the first Man and Woman. The letter symbols or codes employed in compiling the diaries bore amazing resemblance to the Ge'ez alphabet that forms the basis of dialects spoken in modern-day Ethiopia! The scientists ruled out the possibility that the parchments might be twentieth century forgeries!

In the months following their discovery, teams of archaeologists flocked to Mount Rwenzori from around the world with the primary objective of conducting excavation that might yield the bones of the First Man and the First Woman. This and the influx of tourists into Uganda to see the "Garden of Eden" - or at least its environs - caused a huge metropolis to spring up in no time in what had previously been virgin tropical forest inhabited by gorillas and other types of wildlife.

In her own diary, Eve (or Mkailli) had fondly referred to Adam as "Msaijja" on occasion. But the biggest surprise of all was the fact that there was ample evidence in both diaries that Adam (or Msaijja) did in fact live to the ripe old age of nine hundred and thirty years (930) years - exactly as the Book of Genesis said. It was also clear from the diaries that Eve died when she was just shy of her one thousandth birthday! This came as a shock to everyone including the Roman Pontiff, even as he found himself compelled to promulgate a special dogma affirming the authenticity of the Rwenzori Prehistoric Diaries. The Holy Father simultaneously issued a special Church cannon mandating the study of the Rwenzori Prehistoric Diaries by all Catholic students of Biblical Exegesis, including catechists and candidates for the priesthood.

As for the newly unearthed Egyptian scrolls, it was soon established authoritatively that these had been part of precious archives that had been maintained in a fireproof subterranean vault underneath the famous library in Alexandria that the Romans, led by Octavian, torched along with the Egyptian fleet as they pursued Cleopatra. The fact that the invaluable collection, that included some really ancient scrolls, had remained undisturbed suggested that the Romans, after torching the Egyptian fleet, had systematically wiped out the city's entire population; and that everyone who had known about the library's underground vault and its treasures had been put to the sword. And then, incredibly, some of the archived material corroborated the contents of the new Dead Sea or "Canadian Scrolls" and vice versa.

Christian Mjomba, who had just started work on his "Thesis on Original Virtue" when these events unfolded, could not be more delighted. This was an unbelievable coincidence in every respect. In his thesis, Mjomba did not fail to point out that, roughly one hundred and fifty miles as the crow flies from Mt. Rwenzori, the most celebrated of the legendary Mountains of the Moon, to the southeast over Lake Victoria lay the Ngorongoro Crater, the eighth Natural Wonder of the World. That was the crater that had also been dubbed "Africa's Eden" from the time the adventurous Dr. Louis Leakey had wandered upon the skull of *Zinjanthropus* or the "Nutcracker Man". Mjomba reported that, with the discovery of the Rwenzori Prehistoric Diaries penned by "Msaijja" and "Mkailli" (those were the names that Adam and Eve use to refer to each other in their historic blogs), archaeologists were unanimous in their conclusion that the belt stretching from the crater where the Nutcracker Man had his home to the fold mountains northeast, where Msaijja and Mkailli first met and then set up their own home, did indeed comprise the "Cradle of Mankind".

It was, according to Mjomba's thesis, well documented that it was from the foothills of the Mountains of the Moon where the "little men from the land of trees and spirits", also known as Pygmies or the "Twa", who worshipped a God known as Bes, had started their four-thousand-mile trek along what is now known as the River Nile to the northern tip of the Red Sea, where they set up home and established what later became the Egyptian civilization.

PART 3: PROPOSITIONS ADVANCED BY MJOMBA

Mjomba (and any serious student of theology of his time for that matter) had no doubt that, using the newly found data, he could reconstruct events that took place in the lifetime of Adam and Eve, and also dispel many of the myths surrounding the Church's early work and teachings. He was not alone. Mjomba's position had very much become the standard among students of theology and/or biblical studies of his time - those worthy of the name, at any rate. And as he pointed out in the preamble to his thesis, he also hoped to show, without compromising orthodoxy, that the Church was in fact more inclusive and less inhibiting to join than it had been made out to be by both its supporters and detractors.

That was Mjomba's official stance. Actually, Mjomba's real objectives, which he kept strictly to himself, were two-fold: to show unequivocally that the Prime Mover loved everyone irrespective of religious affiliation; and to demonstrate that the Second Person of the Blessed Trinity had *all* humans, without exception, in His sights when, refusing to be deterred by either the betrayal of Adam and Eve or by the fact that humans would continue to misuse their freedom until doomsday, He agreed to be their intercessor and accordingly proceeded to take on His human nature.

In the final analysis, the difference in Mjomba's official and private positions was only in emphasis because, in addition to believing that salvation was only attainable through the Deliverer who had said *"ego sum via et veritas et vita nemo venit ad Patrem nisi per me"* (I am the way, and the truth, and the life; no man cometh to the Father but by me), Mjomba also firmly held that the Deliverer had staked out authoritatively His positions on everything ranging from the nature of true sanctity to the nature of the Deliverer's personal relationship with His Father and the Divine Spirit. It was also obvious to Mjomba that it was the Church the Deliverer took pains to establish that alone could claim to be the guardian of those sacred truths!

But while it was usual for Catholic apologists to stop there, it was not to be for Mjomba. He went on to infer that, if it was indisputable that all humans were not just fashioned in the image of the Prime Mover, but came into being through the Word, regardless of their individual circumstances, as invitees to the divine banquet, they all without exception belonged to the Church Militant - until they refused to receive the apostles and to hear the apostles' words when the latter got to their house or city, that is.

The first "humans"...

As outlined by Mjomba in his thesis, which drew extensively on the Rwenzori Prehistoric Diaries, Adam, endowed with extraordinary shrewdness and alacrity, which flowed from his closeness to his

Creator, had been quick to note the immense similarity between Eve, whom the Creator had fashioned from his own rib, and himself! They looked very much alike, and yet were also dissimilar in some quite important respects. For starts, he was male and she was female!

And, as Adam confided to Eve on one occasion, their frontal features - he had seen reflections of his own face a countless number of times in the clear waters of the spring behind the cave they called home and so knew exactly how he himself looked - both bore a strange resemblance to the shape of a triangle. A keen artist, he liked to pass his time tracing the shape of that triangle over the pictures of the human faces he scrawled on boulders, tree trunks and in the sand.

But, even though Adam had been anticipating the creation of Eve, he was apparently caught off guard when he woke up from what appeared to be a deep slumber on the afternoon Eve was created and noticed, first her silhouette, and then the figure of a human being approach the coach on which he had been reclining in the moments before he passed out.

Perhaps it was the pain Adam felt in his side as a result of losing a rib. But his behavior, according to Mjomba's thesis, bordered on the atrocious with Adam initially believing he was seeing an apparition - the apparition of a creature that bore great resemblance to himself! The "humanoid" was beautiful. Yes, a devil of a beauty. The creature was also "butt-naked" or whatever you would call that; and it was flashing what looked decidedly like a devilish smile.

Trying hard to remain calm and keep all his senses about him even as he stood there regarding the humanoid with unease, Adam noted that there was something about "it" that was causing him to feel off balance - as if he was about to "lose control" of himself. There was something "electrifying" about it. Adam was clearly mesmerized by the deep dimples that appeared on either of the apparition's cheeks when "it" smiled.

Adam felt helpless as "wicked" images invaded his mind. It was the first time in his life that he had found himself in that position, and he had no doubt in his mind that the creature was the source of those images, and that it was responsible for making him feel that way. He closed his eyes instinctively. But even as he did so, he could not help wondering why the "humanoid" looked like that. Adam initially thought that although the creature resembled him, it could not possibly be human because it was missing some parts! Also, where the nipples should have been, there were two big swellings or "boobs" that were voluptuous and stuck out in a way that (strangely) made him look stupid. And it spotted long hair the color of cinnamon. His own hair was matted and black.

Still, the creature could only be a spirit in flesh, because it was different from the animals that inhabited the earth. The animals Adam found inhabiting the earth did not have souls, but this creature definitely had a soul - if it was a creature and not a mere apparition. It was something Adam thought he clearly discerned as he himself attempted, albeit unsuccessfully, to stare the creature down.

His eyes still shut, Adam noted that, when looking over the creature, he had been able to trace an invisible but discernible line that run from the center of its forehead, down between its eye-balls and along the ridge of its aquiline nose, and then over its ever so slightly parted lips, and down its chest, passing over the navel and stopping at a point where the creatures' hips were joined together. Reflecting on the fact that the apparition had all the markings of a humanoid - an invisible, straight "line" that was capable of informing and giving a solid shape to the bag of chemicals that represented the humanoid's "body', Adam now imagined that, even if the creature had been fully "clothed", he would have been able to tell that it was endowed with a soul by just staring directly into its round, sparkling eyes!

When he opened his eyes, Adam had the distinct feeling that the humanoid, as it took its turn to stare him down, was also tracing an invisible line that started somewhere on Adam's crown, and run down between his own eyes and the rest of his person. But he doubted if the creature had any feelings. And in the event that it had, Adam could not imagine that they would be the sort of feelings that could threaten to throw the creature off balance in the same way his own feelings had come close to making him lose his nerve.

Adam concluded from his observations that, even though it was not exactly realistic or even practical to ascribe shapes to spiritual entities, the best way he could picture to himself a soul was by ascribing to it the shape of a straight line! Which appeared to signify that a spirit that also existed in the flesh was at its best behavior when it was standing or kneeling in an upright position, or lying prostrate on the ground, rather than leaning slothfully against the trunk of a tree or lying curled up as if in agony.

Adam regarded it as something of special significance that the creature was flashing a smile, albeit one that looked as though it was wicked or devilish. Apart from himself, the apparition was the only other creature that Adam had seen smiling! Even though intrigued by the fact that certain if not all of the Prime Mover's creation had the habit of reacting to things around them - Adam had not failed to notice that morning glory, for instance, had the habit of opening up and "showing off" the glamour it commanded at the first signs of the sun's light - he did not believe that there as any other creature on earth that could smile.

From the very beginning, Adam had associated his ability to smile with his ability to exercise discretion in ways that lower beasts could not. It all boiled down to one thing: only a creature that was endowed with a conscience had that capability. And that capability clearly set him apart from all the other creatures with which he shared the earthly habitat, all of which were able to get by only with the help of their instincts. He, Adam, could choose between good and evil, something these creatures were definitely incapable of. It was the reason Adam just turned and walked away one day when a wild cow he had been trying to milk suddenly lunged forward and kicked him with its hind leg in the groin. He had done that even against his instinct which was clamouring for some sort of revenge. His reason, according to which a creature that had no conscience effectively could never do any wrong, prevailed!

And Adam had arrived at another obvious conclusion: unlike soul-less beasts that had been created for his benefit as a humanoid and were therefore expendable, he not only was extremely precious in the eyes of the Prime Mover, but he was also fully accountable for all his actions; and, similarly, each and every humanoid after him would be both very precious in the Prime Mover's eyes as well as accountable to Him for "its" actions. This would be so regardless of the humanoid's social standing in "society" and other circumstances.

Adam reasoned that, because of the nature of humanoids and the way the human conscience operated, only the Prime Mover was qualified to pass judgement over anyone of them. And, in the "hypothetical" situation in which the number of humanoids was such that it became imperative for some humanoids to exercise authority over others, it was obvious that authority exercised by a humanoid over another could only come from the Prime Mover; and that also automatically meant that its misuse would be a grave matter for which that humanoid would have to pay very dearly on the "Day of Judgement".

Adam was, of course, aware that, as a creature that was so elevated in the sight of the Prime Mover and that, moreover, shared the same last end as the holy angels (which, namely, was the exultation and worship of Him Who would in time reveal His divine nature to Moses with the words *"ehyeh ašer ehyeh"* (I am Who am), the failure on his part (or on the part of any humanoid for that matter) to live as befitted a child of a divinity would be tantamount to betrayal of the highest order.

That would be the case if for instance he gave in to his lower animal instincts and decided to lead a life of "debauchery" which was the converse of eternal happiness for beings that were fashioned in the Prime Mover's image and had a soul. And Adam understood quite well that "passing" pleasures or joys, because they were transient and fleeting, when they did not immediately turn sour, essentially begun to evaporate at the moment they were supposed to start. That could happen if his appreciation of the works of creation turned into self-indulgence and/or self-love, and became his last end instead of redounding to the glory of the Prime Mover who was his true last end.

Adam knew that debauchery and the temporal pleasures that accompanied it were the converse of eternal happiness in heaven in the afterlife - happiness that had nothing in common with a life of make believe, came from being true to one's conscience, and was bolstered by participation in the sufferings of the Deliverer. And Adam certainly did not think that there was any formula that a humanoid could employ to capture and prolong material joys indefinitely, just as he did not believe that there was any formula that a humanoid could use to grow young instead of growing old - or to stop ageing altogether.

Adam recognized that it was actually a blessing that living creatures - with the obvious exception of angels who were consigned straight away into their afterlife at creation - grew old, and their days on earth became numbered with the passage of time. That was what guaranteed their passage into the afterlife where they could rest in peace. In his particular case, "resting in peace" of course meant being filled and fulfilled by the Holy Spirit who also united God the Father and God the Son together in an eternal, albeit mysterious, divine union. Sometimes Adam thought that he could not wait for the moment his soul would say "Bye, Bye" to his body so it would be on its way to a union with its divine Creator that was not inhibited by "matter".

Adam of course understood that it wasn't just a question of trading a life of hedonism on earth for one in his afterlife. He appreciated the fact that spiritual happiness, unlike a life of materialism on earth, entailed total giving and self-abnegation. Adam did not associate happiness in heaven with the satisfaction of his physical or even spiritual senses. In fact his idea of happiness in the afterlife, in the presence of the Prime Mover and in the company of angels, was predicated on total self-denial on both the physical as well as spiritual plane. Because only then could a creature be fit to be a vessel of grace that was freely given by an infinitely loving Prime Mover.

The pursuit of material happiness was driven by self-love or selfishness, both of which were the opposite of generosity. Happiness or joy in heaven, on the other hand, was incompatible with selfishness.

To understand the nature of happiness and ecstasy in the afterlife, Adam frequently meditated on the subject of divinity, and the nature of the Prime Mover. Adam, who spent long hours contemplating the creation of the world, had noted that the Prime Mover had taken sometime to "create" the world and the earth, and everything that was in it including himself. Adam did not fail to take note of the fact that in the beginning - ever before there was any created thing, including the angels - there was the "Word" (Adam's name for the "Framer of the universe in whom and from whom and through whom all things were true which anywhere were true, and in whom and from whom and through whom all things were wise which anywhere were wise, and in whom and from whom and through whom all things lived, which truly and supremely lived, and in whom and from whom and through whom all things were blessed, which anywhere were blessed".

He had also noted that a Spirit, which he envisioned as some sort of cloud, had come over all the works of the Word or "creation" presumably to bless and sanctify it. That had led Adam to conclude that the "Godhead" consisted not just of one, but of three separate and distinct entities or "persons". He referred to them as "God the Father", "God the Son", and "God the Holy Spirit".

Adam reasoned that because no one created the Prime Mover, the Prime Mover in turn did not need anything from anyone, and that was true for all three persons of the "Holy Trinity". In spite of that, it was apparent that "giving" was perhaps the most important attribute that the three divine persons of the Blessed Trinity had in common. The infinite generosity of God the Father was very much in evidence as He exercised His role as God the "Father" and "Creator" while at the same time giving full credit for His works of creation to the "Word". That was self-effacement and humility that Adam initially found hard to accept as an attribute of the Prime Mover. Still, it was there for anyone to see.

Then, Adam could not help but admire the fact that God the Father and God the Son (who was also the Word through whom every creature had come into being) did not just get along with each other like two individuals, but were really and truly united in a bond of love that was so strong "it' constituted a separate and also quite distinct divine "person". Adam saw that as another example of the obviously infinite goodness and love and self-effacement of God the Father *and* God the Son.

It spoke to the infinite "godliness" of the two divine persons that the way they regarded each other pointed to the existence of the Holy Spirit that united them both in such a way that instead of just an act of "infinite love" for each other, their divine love itself translated into a separate and distinct divine person who was nevertheless completely one with them. Consequently, Adam associated the attributes of "outpouring" and "infinity" with the work of the Holy Spirit during his meditations.

And when Adam contemplated the Second Person of the Blessed Trinity, he could not but marvel at the total obedience to the Father of the "Son of Man". It was a sonship that held back nothing, with the Word apparently prepared to defer to the will of God the Father notwithstanding the fact that He was Himself a full and equal member of the Holy Trinity. For Adam, it was these "activities" occurring in eternity and without let up that made the Father, the Son and the Holy Spirit a God who was infinite Goodness and infinite Perfection.

In Adam's view, the notoriety of Beelzebub, a creature and now an implacable enemy of the Prime Mover, was grounded in that creature's attempts to turn the tables around and have selfishness, possessiveness, pride, self-aggrandisement and similar "vices" replace charity, self-immolation, giving and humility as the basis or foundation of existence. That naturally did not alter the fact that to join the party in heaven, a soul had to be selfless. As a reward for being selfless, and because the soul had received its existence completely gratuitously, the Prime Mover and Author of all - who Himself was infinitely and unreservedly loving - would feel comfortable filling and fulfilling the soul in accordance with His divine plan.

As far as Adam (who always thought out of the box and liked to imagine a world that was populated with other humanoids besides himself) was concerned, souls that had love for their creator and for others, and were not focused on themselves, not only would have a capacity for more love upon leaving this world for the afterlife, but that capacity would be multiplied a thousand-fold. But selfish souls that focused only on themselves would have whatever little capacity they might still have left for appreciating the good things in others and in their Creator taken away!

Still, Adam feared that, in spite of those rationalizations, a time might come when he, Adam, would be tempted to underestimate his own worth as a creature that was fashioned in the image of the Prime Mover. Adam recoiled at the possibility that either he himself or some humanoids that would come after him might be tempted to think either of themselves or of each other as being not quite so deserving of their blessings.

For now, however, he had no doubt whatsoever in his mind that it would always be a grave error on the part of any humanoid to treat another humanoid as expendable - like cows or goats that he was free to slaughter at any time he felt like enjoying a meal of veal. Adam prayed, as he stared at the apparition, that no humanoid would ever be tempted to regard another humanoid in that way; that it would always be thoughts and feelings of love - sacred love - and never thoughts and feelings of hate that would define relations among humanoids.

Standing there gazing open-mouthed at the creature that had appeared out of nowhere, Adam could not help reflecting on the fact that the existence he himself had been enjoying as a humanoid was entirely gratuitous. That reinforced his view that he would be making a grave mistake for which he would pay dearly sooner or later if he were ever to treat another humanoid as expendable - and in a timely manner too, because he was starting to wonder if his standoff with the stranger might not have to be settled violently, with either himself or the stranger being forced to concede defeat.

If only the creature hadn't borne so much resemblance to him. In the event, he would probably have decided to charge it in the hope that "it" would bolt and flee into surrounding bushes. That was something he definitely would have enjoyed doing, if only for the kicks. But this particular creature bore too much resemblance to him; and, if he did that, may be it would be a "brother or sister humanoid" he would be hounding. Adam recoiled at the thought that, unbeknownst to him, a "brother" or "sister" could end up living in the forest, alone and surrounded by wildlife, when he could share the little he had with the newcomer and make him/her feel welcome.

Now, because of his suspicion that the creature he was seeing might be a humanoid, Adam was leery of jumping to conclusions about its disposition. And that may, conceivably, have given the impression that he was faltering in his resolve to face up to and challenge the 'stranger'. For it was then that Eve, trying her best to make Adam feel relaxed and at home, broke into the equivalent of *a Sultan's Dance*. That only caused the conscientious Adam to imagine that what he was seeing approach was the cunning "Satan" and archenemy in an ingenious disguise! The fact that the strange "creature" which had materialized from nowhere, and which he continued to have in his sights just in case it staged a sudden assault on him, did not display a tail, the face of a goat, a horn or even the proverbial "devil's claw" made it all the more suspect.

Adam had already confronted another "creature" which fit that description in a dream; and he had concocted the name Satan for it in jest - a name he, however, soon begun to use whenever he made any mental reference to the Enemy. For some time already now, Adam had been harboring the notion that the archenemy loved disguises and sported the things mentioned, and that he somehow needed to behave that way to be able to pass on his corrupting influence to others. But Adam, all by himself in the whole wide world, was determined to be careful and avoid any trouble.

Adam was on the verge of bolting and fleeing, and he was in fact prepared to abandon the Garden of Eden for the "adversary" rather than consort with "him". Fearing the worst, the First Man had jumped to the conclusion that the intruder could not possibly be someone of good will. Spoilt and pampered, he did not at first see that he was expected to rationalize and arrive at reasoned conclusions about strangers. What was more, he did not hear the reassuring voice of the Prime Mover, booming like thunder overhead, reiterate that it was not good for Man to be alone, and urge him to step forward and accost Eve, his future bride! Instead, as he stood there paralysed in the shadow of a large apple tree, he noticed that the stranger continued to approach.

It was, according to Mjomba, a learning process that was quite interesting for both Adam and Eve as they glared one at the other suspiciously, and sized each other up. It was Eve, supposedly, who took the initiative to break the ice. Using gestures similar to those used by horse breeders in the initial stages of taming and grooming wild horses, she had gradually caused Adam to drop his guard and come to terms with the fact that he was in the presence of a real creature, if one that was still very much a stranger, and that he wasn't seeing an apparition.

When Adam eventually allowed Eve to come close enough, she had reached out and offered him her right hand, allowing him to touch and massage it. Instead of taking flight, Adam began considering the possibility that this stranger might in fact be the companion he had been promised by the Prime Mover. Because, in addition to proving that she meant him no harm, Eve had also shown - or at least hinted at the fact - that she could actually fill the role of companion if he stopped treating her as though she were an alien from another planet.

Still in shock, as Adam gazed upon the creature he would eventually end up referring to as "My Eve", he had given vent to a completely involuntary exclamation - actually the very first words that Adam succeeded in giving expression to since he was molded out of clay by the Prime Mover.

As he would subsequently write in his diary, Adam had stuttered in a dialect he himself hardly comprehended: "How on the blessed earth could Thou, Oh gracious Prime Mover, bring into existence a creature that could perform a jig like the one I just saw! If Thou were not the One and the Only Prime Mover, I wouldn't have attributed the apparition of this dancing humanoid to you, Oh Holy One. I would probably have attributed it to the Evil One!"

Quoting from the Rwenzori Prehistoric Diaries, Mjomba wrote that Adam, confronted by the spectacle of the new arrival, whose very first actions were clearly intended to catch his attention, had immediately concluded that the Prime Mover had in any case to be a most accomplished Artist, and one who obviously enjoyed and also loved what He did, to bring into existence a humanoid such as the one he was seeing for the very first time - if his imagination wasn't playing tricks on him that is!

Citing further evidence in the Rwenzori Prehistoric Diaries, Mjomba wrote that it was not until a couple of days later that Adam started to appreciate the importance of having a companion. This was even though during the six months or so he himself had been around, he had had occasion to observe that the other creatures around him - gorillas, elephants, lions, whales and under-water creatures, reptiles, birds, and even insects - all belonged to "families". He had yet to find a living creature that lived all by itself just as he did. It had been quite plain that all the creatures with which he shared the earthly habitat, including moths and vegetative life belonged to distinct families, and he had been envious of them because of it.

There was even this particular flock of birds - he coined a name for them which thought was quite fitting - "mocking birds" - which seemed to know his predilection and apparently liked to mock him by swooping low and "buzzing" him for brief periods before flying away and out of range of the rocks he would hurl at them. They stopped doing so the moment Eve came on the scene - perhaps at the Prime Mover's command. But now that he himself had someone of his own kind for company, he actually would have loved to see them swoop low and fly around him and Eve. Instead of being irritated by their action, he would have seen in their action a reminder of the goodness of the Prime Mover in remembering that he, Adam, needed family just like them and creating Eve from a rib He took from his side. And as time went by, Adam even began wondering how it was he hadn't gone nuts in the days he had been all by himself on earth with no other human around!

But even after Adam had finally come to terms with the fact that the world's population had effectively doubled with the appearance on the scene of Eve, and even though he also understood that the newcomer and himself were meant for each other, Adam had apparently expected that the new addition to earth's human population would be an exact mirror image of himself. It did not help matters very much when it turned out that Eve also, after looking over herself, initially assumed that Adam, her companion, was going to turn out to be an exact replica of herself. Adam, who had been around longer and had seen examples of male and female creatures all around him in the world of animals, reptiles, birds, insects and even plants, should of course have known better.

It was only gradually, according to Mjomba's thesis, that Adam came to accept that Eve, even though human like himself, was radically different - and the same for Eve. And the discovery came as a great surprise and also a great relief to them both, because they now understood that they were expected to cohabit as husband and wife in due course, and eventually go on to procreate and fill the earth!

Members of the last "animal" species to arrive on Planet Earth, Adam and Eve, perhaps because they were still so innocent, were frequently agog at everything they saw. Finding themselves in a place as exotic as that and in such fabulous earthy company, they were often beside themselves and quite titillated by it all, unable to believe that they could have been so fortunate as to arrive in the Garden of Eden at the time and in the manner they did.

Unschooled in the ways of the world, Adam and Eve marvelled adoringly at the practiced manner and the ease displayed by beasts of the earth, birds of the air, mammals of the sea, etc. Baffled at first that some of the creatures they saw looked like they were inadequately endowed by nature to survive the challenges they faced and might already be endangered species, Adam and Eve invariably found that it was they themselves who had been fooled, as what appeared to be lackadaisical and defenseless creatures suddenly took off with incredible speed either to evade predators or to themselves capture an agile prey!

The first Man and Woman tried to grasp how it had come about that creatures with only short spans of life were the ones that multiplied fastest. At one point, Adam and Eve even conceded that, if they themselves had not been temples of God and in a state of grace, they might have very easily found themselves according these lower creatures the respect due to deities, just seeing what they were capable of doing. A good deal of it seemed to border on the miraculous, given that these creatures only acted on instinct and could not actually think. Many of these "lower" creatures were capable of accomplishing many things that Adam and Eve themselves couldn't; and they did it in style and often with a flourish that was quite boggling to the human mind.

But there was, of course, always the bigger question to which, because Adam and Eve had a ready and perfectly rational reply, fortunately could only be asked in a hypothetical way. The reply was grounded in their own experience. But even though they already had an answer to that question, they felt they needed to keep asking it because the response to it represented something extremely important, namely an anthem of Thanksgiving they felt they needed to sing whenever they had a free moment.

The hypothetical question hinged on the assumption that there was no such a thing as a Prime Mover, a being who was not just intelligent but Intelligence itself; and who combined those qualities with being almighty. Assuming, therefore, that a Prime Mover did not exist, the big question was: How come such handsomely crafted and endowed beings - beings of all stripes and variety including themselves - had all come to be? Absent a Prime Mover, Adam and Eve still would have had to come to grips somehow with that question, especially considering that, with all their intelligence, they did not feel that they were even up to the task of just envisioning unaided a scheme as grand as that of creation? The answer to that "big" question was so momentous, Adam and Eve felt that they needed to keep reflecting on it. And the best way to do that was by reiterating the same question differently. It was the beginnings of the *Pater Noster*, a different version of which would eventually become the *Credo*!

"*Omnia ad gloriam Dei*" - translated "*Everything you do, do it all to the greater glory of God*" - was the motto that guided the lives of the first Man and Woman from the very first moments of their existence, according to Mjomba's controversial thesis. He argued that the lower life forms followed the exact same adage spontaneously - by intuition. Adam and Eve, who could rationalize about these things because they were endowed with the faculty of the intellect in addition to the faculty of the will, saw the Creator's image and likeness in themselves and to a lesser extent also in animals, birds, reptiles, marine life, and even in inanimate objects.

According to Mjomba, the curiosity Adam and Eve had about themselves and their origin and also about the reality around them was rooted in their nature which, unlike that of the Prime Mover, was separate and distinct from their existence. Rational animals, they sought as a matter of course to achieve self-actualization, and to fulfill the will of the Prime Mover in the process. It was evident that lower life forms sought to fulfill the divine plan in a similar way albeit instinctively. But above all, Mjomba wrote, the likeness of Adam and Eve to the Prime Mover made their hunger - be it for food, knowledge, or self-actualization - a hunger that was ultimately for the perfect good. A hunger for "that greater than which cannot be conceived" and which, when finally acquired, was alone capable of imparting complete fulfillment.

Both Adam and Eve, according to Mjomba, were very keenly aware of the unique gifts with which they themselves were endowed, in particular the spiritual faculties of the intellect and will. That awareness also led them to recognize the fact that their role in the divine plan was a very unique one. It was up to them to harness not just the earth's resources, but everything in the universe, including the properties of the sun and the rest of the interplanetary system, for their self-actualization, and accord the Prime Mover His due honor and glory in the process of doing so.

From the beginning, Mjomba wrote, the First Man and the First Woman had been at liberty to take the necessary steps to exploit the universe to any extent they desired, their freedom in that respect being circumscribed only by the laws of physics and other laws that governed the universe. And so, rational animals - as opposed to the irrational beasts which depended on instincts instead of reason to get by - the representatives of the human race also pretty well understood that the manner in which they chose to exploit the earth's resources also had a bearing on the expected results. For sure, they did not yet have to sweat - at least not the way they would have to sweat just to survive later after the rebellion - to see results accrue from their enterprise. But it was imperative that they understood that different approaches employed in harnessing the earth's resources yielded different results.

Adam and Eve knew that choices made by them as they went about their business in the Garden of Eden had certain consequences, there was also no question they knew that a decision on their part to accord the Prime Mover the respect due to Him (or to desist from doing so) would have immediate and dire consequences. They had to decide to acknowledge or not to acknowledge the fact of the Prime Mover's existence, and also the fact that their own hopes and desires ultimately rested with Him on Whom everything else inside and outside the universe depended, and the way they decided was critical.

Knowledge *per se* had, of course, never been designed or even intended to stifle human liberty. And so, until the day they decided to embark on their ill-advised pursuit for independence from the Prime Mover, they both were very much aware of their obligations, remained faithful to their conscience and in communion with the Almighty. It was a relationship that translated into a genuine, deeply sincere and abiding love for the Prime Mover.

At this time, Mjomba wrote, Adam and Eve could not help being very curious about their surroundings. And because they shared their habitat with animals, birds, reptiles, plants, Mother Earth and the planets, they devoted a good deal of their waking hours learning about those things.

Describing the first outing of Adam and Eve together, Mjomba wrote that when they ventured out into the wilderness and discovered that they were not the only creatures roaming the earth, Adam and Eve did not at first know what to make of it. The very first beast that accosted them was a she-gorilla, which was scampering from one tree branch to another. A cub, perhaps only days old, was spread-eagled on her back. A he-gorilla, balancing his weight on his hind legs, watched the two execute the spectacular trapeze act from nearby.

Eve at first thought the three were fellow humans and extended her hand to the he-gorilla expecting that they would greet and embrace each other only to be rebuffed. It was an incident Adam would, for many years, love to use to wheedle his companion and cause her to laugh whenever he thought she needed to laugh and be jolly. But Eve also had something stemming from that first encounter to use to cajole her companion.

She would invariably remind him that he was the one who persisted for a long time after that in his belief that birds, animals, reptiles and other living creatures belonged to a higher order of beings and that they might even be "immortal" or even "divine"! That was until both of them were able to establish that, of all the created beings, it was only they who could laugh! Mjomba wrote that from then on Eve delighted in referring to Adam as the Smiling Brute while he on his part referred to her as the Laughing Animal.

Adam and Eve reasoned that if these creatures could not laugh or smile, there was less chance that they could rationalize and connect with anything that was beyond matter, and consequently an even lesser chance that their being and existence transcended their physical selves or that a part of them was pure spirit. Adam and Eve were subsequently in agreement that, all the theatrics of those other creatures not-with-standing, they were the only ones in the whole wide world equipped with the where-with-all for an afterlife, namely reason and free will, and thus in a position to lay claim to immortality.

According to the evidence, Adam and Eve spent hours and hours observing the antics of wildlife, and were surprised at the peculiar manner in which these creatures "celebrated" the greatness of their Prime Mover, which they did just by pursuing their individual self-actualization.

They found it very exhilarating just observing animals of the forest go about their usual business. Wondering across herds of African elephants, they were mesmerized by the way these strange looking creatures went about the business of fending for themselves in the wilderness. Eve in particular was greatly impressed by the way grown-up elephants surrounded the baby elephants while warning hostile intruders to keep their distance by hooting loudly. She was out in the forest by herself picking wild berries one day when she witnessed a confrontation between a family of elephants and a lioness that appeared to be eyeing a baby elephant in the herd. For a moment, Eve thought she was hearing the sound of an oncoming avalanche until she realized that it was one of the older elephants in the herd caterwauling to scare off the lioness, which was nowhere to be seen by the time she recovered her wits.

Mjomba supposed that it was Eve who was really overwhelmed by the fact that certain beasts of prey - including alligators, lions and hyenas - were almost always outclassed by the very animals that kept them from starving when it came to celebrating the joy of life. Adam and Eve felt a lot of sympathy, Mjomba wrote, for these czars of the wilderness which appeared contented to roam the steppes of the Garden of Eden in search of occasions to prove that "might is right!" while weaklings like deer and their cubs, sometimes completely oblivious to the dangers lurking in the bushes, were cavorting, prancing and romping about for hours on end, and in general getting far more out of life.

But it was Adam who conceded to Eve that he was completely spellbound at the loving manner in which baboons of either gender cradled their young and charged leopards, hyenas and even lions when any of them threatened to steal the kill reserved for the baby baboons. The hunting habits of hawks, orioles, parrots and other bird species mesmerized Adam and Eve, with Eve confessing to the man she had found already ensconced on Mother Earth that the way hawks stalked their prey from very high up in the air or from atop a high mast was so enthralling she could scarcely concentrate on anything from the moment their activity attracted her attention until the moment they sprang on their surprised victims. That had only goaded him on to make his own confession. He had turned to Eve and mumbled in the dialect they had perfected and were using to communicate with each other that the clever way certain birds that were potential targets of hawks and other predators laid low and did all sorts of clever things to avoid falling victims to the hunters, taking steps to mislead the hunters regarding the actual whereabouts of their nests and so on, said something about the Prime Mover, namely that He was another one.

Adam and Eve did not fail to notice that families of certain animal species went to great lengths to curve out territory for themselves, and then proceeded to ensure that trespassers, even if they were of the same species as themselves, were kept out. But again it was Eve, according to Mjomba, who drew Adam's attention to the fact that male members of the pride of lions went to the extent of fighting over lionesses during the mating season, with the brawls sometimes proving fatal for the vanquished lion.

That only provoked Adam to proffer a reply that Eve found a little surprising: "That will never happen among humans who should be able to control themselves and put the love of a neighbor first!"

Not wanting to risk losing the only woman on the planet by engaging in anything that might have had the appearance of sexual harassment or improper conduct until he was certain that the moment to propose to her was ripe, Adam had up until then successfully reined in his libido, and wanted to impress Eve with his reply that he was the perfect, if undeclared, suitor.

Adam and Eve, while charmed by the reality around them, were even more perplexed that there could be creatures like themselves roaming the earth. Mjomba suggested that it was only rational, as they sought to grasp what their existence in the Garden of Eden really meant, that they should begin their inquiry by initially focusing on the lower life forms, and then move on to ponder the fact of their own existence in greater detail later on after they had learned more about the world around them and were reasonably reassured of their safety in the environment into which the Prime Mover had thrust them.

It was this, more than anything else, which explained why Adam had been coy about rushing into a marriage proposal. As things stood, the first Man and the first Woman were still preoccupied at this time with satisfying their curiosity about many other things, not least of them, the fact that while both were human, they possessed dissimilarities that, in some respects, appeared quite radical. They were both certain that their eyes were not deceiving them. Still, it was strange that one of them was masculine in gender and the other one female. Shy about confiding in each other on the subject, they each of them wondered surreptitiously how they came to be so different from each in the first place!

A lot of what they were discovering, as they studiously observed the antics of creatures in the animal kingdom amongst others was thus proving helpful in clearing up many of their earlier misconceptions about themselves. But neither Adam nor Eve was prepared at this time to take a step even remotely resembling a date proposal, let alone a marriage proposal.

That is not to say that they were completely indifferent to each other. From the moment Eve arrived on the scene and assumed her role as the matriarch of mankind, Adam found himself fantasizing in all sorts of ways about her quite spontaneously; and the same went for Eve. Arguing that the faculty of the intellect of the first man and woman at that time was unimaginably sharp, Mjomba wrote that the corresponding faculty of the imagination too was very fertile. Consequently, the images and scenarios that invaded their minds were sometimes beguiling and suggestive in the extreme.

Mjomba supposed that, in their pristine innocence, they initially went all out to stifle these fantasies and to erase the unsolicited images from their memories. Such action probably resulted in these temptations coming faster and more furiously; and it was easy to see how those images could become titillating and provocative to the point Adam and Eve would think they might not be able to desist from indulging themselves in the manner and ways suggested. But the upshot of all that, according to Mjomba, was that Adam and Eve, being in a state of grace and in constant communion with the Prime Mover, used those involuntary flights of fancy to strengthen the bond existing between themselves and the Prime Mover.

Mjomba argued that the first Man and Woman treasured that bond immensely for one additional reason which, namely, was that they might have ended up hurting each other for nothing if it had not been for the fact that they both held their Lord and God in awe. Contrary to what some believe, even before their fall from grace, Adam and Eve had to struggle constantly to keep their tempers and things like that in check. Perhaps it was because it was just the two of them in the Garden of Eden.

Quoting from the Rwenzori Prehistoric Diaries, Mjomba wrote that there were times when something in Eve made her hate everything about her companion. Similarly, there were times when Adam felt like he should take flight and go live on some distant planet, because something in him made him hate everything about the creature his Maker had given him for a companion.

Whenever those spontaneous moods, which were involuntary and unwelcome, got the better of them, they always felt like killing each other. The thought that thrust itself into Eve's mind was that she should get rid of Adam by lacing his food with toxin taken from the glands of a cobra. For his part, Adam sometimes found himself wishing, completely involuntarily, that Eve would die in her sleep so he would not have to put up with her constant prattle about things being in the wrong place in their little hamlet and stuff like that. What saved the day was the fact that both Adam and Eve usually sought refuge in prayer to their loving Maker immediately, imploring Him to save them from themselves during the period they were on trial.

They were not yet thinking about marrying each other and rearing children; but, reeling from shock on discovering that the human mind could conjure up thoughts that were as vile and mean as those, they also frequently prayed that if they were ever blessed with offspring, in addition to giving them their daily bread, He condescend and insulate their children and their children's children from their own evil thoughts and the wiles of Satan.

Even at the height of those temptations of the flesh, Adam and Eve continued to see their Divine Master as the source and origin of all good things of this world. Mjomba supposed that Adam and Eve in the process discovered, probably to their amazement, that they were actually very frail and completely dependent on God when it came to staying upright and virtuous.

They came to understand that those provocative images were pure fantasies that would turn out to be as unreal as dreams if pursued; and that pursuing them would be a diversion from the reality of committing themselves unreservedly to the service of the Omnipotent Being who was also the Perfect Good. But they no doubt also understood in the end that, removed from the mystical presence of the Prime Mover and devoid of the strength that their closeness to Him imparted, they would in fact be as nothing in the face of those temptations of the flesh.

According to Mjomba's thesis, Adam took the opportunity presented by Eve's confession relating to the curious habits of lions and their combative nature to reveal to his companion that, even before she came onto the scene, he himself had found the contrasting habits of black and white rhinos extremely enchanting. So much so, in fact, he had been debating with himself about the propriety of capturing black and white rhinos - at least one male and one female rhino from each specie - and placing them in a zoo or some place like that for an experiment. He was curious about the consequences of crossbreeding black and white rhinos on their divergent habits! Eve's response, which seemed to make a lot of sense at least then, was to the effect that such action would be tantamount to interfering with nature, and would be bordering on sin if not actually sinful!

Encounter in the shadow of the Alps...

Mjomba made extensive reference in his thesis to Adam and Eve's tour of the world, and he also described their first face-to-face encounter with the Prince of Hades. According to the thesis, Adam and Eve had set off on their world tour and were negotiating their way through lush prairie-land in what is now known as the Sahara Desert when they came across herds of mules.

Their belongings which included collections of precious stones, a variety of animal hide which they used to construct tents, a variety of elegant bird feathers that Eve had taken to using as livery, and other collectibles, were already voluminous; and they needed help carrying them as they journeyed from place to place admiring what they rightly deemed as their real estate. They did not find it very hard to entice about a dozen mules from one herd by dangling yams and cassava roots in front of the animals and so cajole them into becoming members of their travelling party.

Mjomba wrote that it was as those first humans and their dedicated and quite dependable mules were heading in the direction of the North Pole and negotiating their way at a steady pace along the picturesque slopes of what we now know as the Alps when they made a hideous discovery. Eve was the first to notice that a flock of sheep that appeared to be grazing by the way side was acting funny. Adam looked once at the herd and stopped in his tracks. He had observed sheep while in all sorts of situations and understood their behavior and antics even better than he understood the behavior and antics of Eve. And so, he had shouted that there was something the matter with that particular herd of sheep. It was after he had undertaken a protracted and discerning examination of the animals from a safe distance that he came to the firm but grisly conclusion that the herd was operating under the influence of Beelzebub. In other words, the animals were possessed!

Adam and Eve had been warned by the Prime Mover about the existence of Satan who headed a rebel band of spirits. He had also specifically alerted them about the devil's trickery and cunning ways, and had warned against ever getting into any sort of dialogue with the Evil One. But, somewhat presumptuously, Adam and Eve had written the devil off as a spent force that would never succeed in planting a wedge between themselves and their Prime Mover. They certainly had never expected to encounter their foe in the flesh so to speak, much less in such picturesque surroundings.

It had never occurred to Adam and Eve that Satan could be so brazen as to mount a challenge just as they conducted their very first tour of the length and breadth of Mother Earth. In whispered exchanges, Adam signalled his agreement with Eve's point that the devil's objective was to frighten them, and hence his choice of time and place for the encounter. Eve, for her part, reassured Adam that even if they were distant from home and in unfamiliar terrain, the devil's tack, which was to try and isolate them from the Prime Mover, was doomed to failure, since their Divine Master was everywhere.

According to the thesis, Adam and Eve stood their ground; and Eve, using her right hand, traced the shape of a triangle in midair in a gesture that supposedly was designed to signify their total dedication to doing the will of the Triune divinity. Then, apparently taking the Evil One by complete surprise, she had commanded him to tell her who he was, and to leave the innocent animals quickly in any case before he got hurt.

The devil, mistaking the triangular shape she had traced in mid-air to be the sign of the cross, had been thrown into a panic. Declaring through the sheep in a dialect that Adam and Eve could barely decipher that he was Beelzebub, the archenemy had left the animals abruptly, leaving them traumatized and permanently scarred.

The fact that it was Eve and not Adam who had decided to take him on had been somewhat enervating for Satan. A pure spirit who did not exist in space and time, he had nonetheless succeeded in divining, by turning his faculty of the imagination down side up, that even though he would one day succeed in persuading Adam and Eve to eat of the "forbidden fruit" from the "Tree of the Knowledge of Good and Evil", it would all eventually come to naught. For another woman would come along who would have the sun itself for her raiment and whose "*Fiat*" would cause all Beelzebub's efforts to throw a wedge between the Prime Mover and his human creatures to come to naught!

Mjomba wrote that the devil had briefly hesitated, unsure if this woman who wanted him gone post haste was Adam's regular companion or that other woman with whom he did not want to meddle in any way whatsoever. As he scrambled to get out of the determined Eve's face, he even thought he was already able to divine the powers of that mysterious woman, even though it would be many centuries before she would appear on the scene. Power that, indeed, would begin taking effect as soon as the Prime Mover, in his infinite mercy, promised mankind deliverance in the wake of the rebellion of Adam and Eve.

Even though he had accosted the father and mother of the human race in the shadow of the Alps with no sun in sight, the devil was apparently terrified to the bone. But what really caused him to take to his heels immediately and not look back at least for now was Eve's physical likeness to that other woman - the woman who would be responsible for bringing his hitherto uninterrupted reign in the world as well as the

Underworld to a disastrous end. It did not seem to matter that the figure of Eve, who was not even wearing her makeup, was not bounded by the shimmering halo that would be Mary's trademark. Eve's determined stand had caused Satan to cower as if he were an earth-bound reptile, instead of a spiritual essence. He even briefly took on the shape of a creature which was half beast and half human, and which spotted a grey cloak complete with a cap similar to that of Robin Hood.

The devil then surprised Adam and Eve by whipping out from underneath his mantle a frightfully scarred paw resembling the limb of a goat that had been exposed to the naked flame of an acetylene touch until it had turned black. After brandishing it awhile with the obvious intention of terrifying Adam and Eve further, the Evil One suddenly changed his mind, and decided to use it to conceal his ugly head, which was half beast and half human, from view.

According to Mjomba, Diabolos regretted that he had summoned his powers of divination in his confrontation with the two humans, because he quickly found out that he could not withstand the image of Mary that Eve signified. Mjomba went on that it was Satan's fear that he might be inadvertently tampering with the woman who would consent to become the Deliverer's mother which made the devil sense that he could get hurt really bad (and he already knew what getting hurt meant) if he did not get the blazes out of there fast.

Adam and Eve were themselves surprised at the speed with which the Evil One abandoned his position, and retreated into the bowels of the earth. They could tell that it was where he was headed because, for the next couple of minutes, the enormous mountain range shuddered and rumbled, and belched what appeared to be fire and brimstone. Luckily the travelling party was far from the perimeter of the volcanic eruption set off by the Prince of Hades as he returned to the place where he belonged.

Later that evening, after chanting hymns of praise and gratitude to the Prime Mover as they usually did at the end of the day, Adam and Eve reflected back on the incident according to Mjomba's notes. They agreed that the devil posed a far greater danger than they had initially thought. They were especially concerned that he had been able to make his presence visibly felt even though he was a pure spirit; and they thanked the Prime Mover for keeping the tempter in check, and not giving him lee way to pose a greater danger to them than that which they had been able to withstand with the help of His grace. Mjomba added that they also thanked the Prime Mover for providing them with guardian angels.

They did not know it; but it was actually their guardian angels who had organized things in such a way that Eve rather than Adam stepped forward to do the exorcism. Consequently, Beelzebub, who had put all his bets on Adam and had accordingly devised a plan to engage him in dialogue, had been caught completely off guard. But if Adam and Eve believed that Diabolos was going to give up so easily, they

116

were wrong. For as Adam slept that evening, he was taunted once again by Satan who was wearing a disguise when he appeared to him in a dream. The Infernal One looked just like Eve and, until it was all over, Adam was convinced that it was Eve he was conversing with.

As Adam narrated it to the good woman the next morning, "Eve" had pointed to the stunning vista which included the Alp's highest peak and sighed: "Adam, my love, I know you have been too shy to lay your hand on me up until now. I now invite you to do so, but on one condition: you must pick up courage and join me in telling you-know-Whom-I-mean: 'Now, this is a beautiful piece of real estate - this Mother Earth! Bye, Bye...You made a mistake and brought us into being. That was your mistake. For our part, we now see the idea of independence - total independence - as a good one, and we are determined to go for it, the fact that we are created in Your image notwithstanding! Starting now, we are on our own. We no longer need You or Your bureaucratic regime of 'Thou shalt do this' and 'Thou shalt not do that'! Adam, my love, do I have a deal?"

The outrageous suggestion by "Eve" that he, Adam, disown his Maker was so infuriating, Adam was prepared to commit murder! But as he raised his fist to carry his threat through, the cowardly Satan, fearing he would get hurt, had turned on his heels and vanished into thin air. That caused Adam to awaken from his fitful slumber - which he did only to discover that his companion was sound asleep on her mat and could not, therefore, have had anything to do with the evil scheme the devil had been proposing. It was a great relief for Adam to see Eve resting serenely in her corner of the tree shade; and his only regret was that he had not struck out fast enough with his fist and beaten the hell out of Diabolos!

One of the things Adam learnt from that experience was to take things in life a bit easy and not jump to conclusions about others' intentions based solely on appearances. The dream had been so vivid, it made him abhor Satan as if their encounter had been in daylight while he was wide awake.

If anything, Adam now hated the Prince of Darkness more because it was not only evident that the devil observed no rules and was prepared to hit you below the belt if he saw the opportunity, but he was apparently dead serious and leaving no stone unturned as he went about his dirty business of sowing seeds of discord between Man and God as well as between Man and "Man". Adam shared his feelings with Eve after she awoke, calling the tempter an *evil* creature that deserved to be called *devil*, his abbreviated expression for the words *the embodiment of evil* in the lexicon they had developed for touching base with each other.

It scared the hell out of Adam and Eve to think that they were dealing with a liar who was as atrocious as that, and whose intentions were so evil. From their point of view, it was in fact impossible for evil and badness to exist. Their reason told them that "being" - sharing in God's *Esse* - was something that could only apply to virtues like goodness, kindness and love, with God being the ultimate Good. The devil clearly lacked all those good things, and had to be full of every conceivable vice - both himself and his hosts of rebel spirits! If "evil" could be defined as an absence of virtue, that effectively meant that the sphere in which the fallen Lucifer and the demons that joined him in his rebellion against the Prime Mover had to be somewhere between reality and unreality! While they still continued to "exist", they were actually "dead" spiritually at any rate! Adam and Eve wondered what that state of being in existence and alive while being dead at the same time might portend. These things were an enigma that actually elicited the pity of the first man and the first woman.

Knowing the joy which came from being good and faithful servants of God, Adam and Eve had every reason to believe that the existence 'enjoyed' by the devil and his band of crazed - yes, deranged - followers, being the obverse of happy, was something else altogether. It had to be an existence that was full of contradictions; and a veritable hell if for no other reason - an existence in which 'hope' itself had absolutely no meaning. And that explained one other thing... It explained why Diabolos was all over the place like a raging buffalo that was itching to destroy anything it spied moving for lack of anything else to do.

But that also made Adam and Eve fear for the safety of their scion and led them to actually to offer up prayers for their posterity even before they had formally discussed the subject of marriage to each other. In almost an instant, it had become apparent that their life on earth was itself fraught with real danger. They were not just caught up in the raging battle between good and evil; they were at the center of it!

In the glorious days (before the fall)...

Both Adam and Eve were greatly intrigued by the habits of the wild donkeys, goats and cows they came across as they approached their homestead near the Equator. They decided that these were creatures they could domesticate without unduly interfering with the laws of nature; and they accordingly captured a male and female member of each of those animal species for that purpose. The same fate befell sheep, swine and what eventually came to be known as poultry.

Mjomba wrote that if Adam and Eve found animal, marine, and bird life and the lives of reptiles beguiling and captivating to watch, their awe at the wonders of creation became simply boundless when it came to biological and physical matter. Smarter overall than their modern ancestors, the first Man and Woman had quickly figured out that matter was made up of atoms and molecules, and that bursts of energy lay at the core of physical substances.

As they roamed the steppes of Eden, plied the waters of rivers in a canoe, sailed the high seas in a dingy and mapped and recorded their discoveries, Adam and Eve also discovered to their amazement that they were artists who loved not just to design but to actually fabricate and manufacture all sorts of things. Taking their cue from birds and even land and marine-based creatures which displayed extraordinary adroitness at picking up speed as they traveled from one physical point to another, Adam and Eve in due course designed and constructed conveyances which enabled them to travel with speed between different points of the globe.

To their amazement, as they travelled north from the Equator, crossed the North Pole, and then again south, over the South Pole and back to their original place of abode at the source of what had to be the longest river on earth, Adam and Eve found that there was always something new to learn from birds, reptiles, insects, and both land and marine-based creatures. Of course, just learning that there were in existence contrasting creatures like crested cranes and kites, woodpeckers and hawks, sea gulls and snakes, dolphins, sea cats and walruses, polar bears, hippos, alligators, horses, cows, goats and sheep, and so on and so forth was of enormous significance in and of itself. And that is not mentioning the variety of plant and insect life, rock formations - and what have you. Suffice it to say that by the time Adam and Eve arrived back at their hamlet, they were feeling very small and humbled.

They could not help feeling awestruck and agog at those "wonders" of creation. Aware that they themselves were a bundle of mystery, they felt constrained to bow down and humbly court the audience of the Prime Mover as often as they could, singing canticles of praise and anthems of love.

And, reviewing the artifacts they themselves had created to enable them to return home quickly and safely, they were not a little grateful to the one and the only Mysterious and Incomprehensible Source of it all - the Mysterious and Incomprehensible Source in whose image they themselves had been fashioned - for having endowed them so richly.

After they fell from grace, Adam and Eve would recall, with great nostalgia, those good old times when their sharp intellects, unburdened as yet by the effects of original sin, allowed them to swiftly translate into practical reality almost any original or borrowed idea, provided that the idea met the test of the laws of chemistry and physics. They would regret that they had ever entertained the idea of revolting against their Prime Mover; and they would hate themselves for allowing themselves to fall for the archenemy's ruse, and to opt for evil. They would particularly regret that they had fallen for a ruse that caused them to go after something that was ephemeral and wanting in substance, as well as damaging to the future of the entire human race.

In the meantime, as they traversed the globe on their journeys of discovery, the first Man and Woman were cognizant of the fact that they owed their being to the same Divine Principle or Being that "knew all that now existed long before there ever was any of it", and then freely chose to cause it all to burst into glorious reality. Adam and Eve were not simply mesmerized. Their faith and trust in the one and the only Being, whose essence and existence, unlike their own, was unchanging and therefore had no need for causation, was immensely reinforced.

The first Man and Woman were mollified to a degree they had never expected as they came to grips with the fact that, even though they were undeniably lords of the universe, they were effectively eclipsed in many respects by creatures that were supposed to be less endowed. These were creatures whose nature they regarded as less perfect than their own. Knowing that they could never match the ability of a chameleon at camouflage, muster the strength of an elephant, sprint as fast as a gazelle, summon the courage to face an irate rhinoceros, fly unaided in midair as birds and certain types of insects did, match the skills of a beaver at constructing a dam, and so on and so forth, caused Adam and Eve to temper whatever satisfaction they derived from any personal accomplishment with a genuine sense of humility.

That knowledge also caused them to bear with the shortcoming of the various life forms around them, and also with each other's shortcomings; and it predisposed them to practice the virtue of patience as they went about exploiting the earth's resources and the properties of the sun and the interplanetary system. According to Mjomba, the magnanimity that Adam and Eve displayed toward each other and to the lesser-endowed creatures mirrored the unsurpassed goodness of the Prime Mover who had intended that things be that way.

The fact that Adam and Eve already advanced in their practice of virtue, coupled with the fact that they were always concerned about the future of their posterity, made their subsequent revolt against the Prime Mover all the more despicable, Mjomba stated in his thesis. But he was also quick to point out that these things also worked in their favor. They assured them a sympathetic ear when they immediately made an about-turn in the wake of their criminal action.

Precisely because they had been such keen practitioners of virtue, in particular the virtue of charity, the Prime Mover easily welcomed them back into the fold when they reined in their pride and accepted their wrong doing, making it possible once again for Man to inherit eternal happiness in the presence of Beauty, Love and Wisdom personified. Mjomba suggested in his thesis that it is this that gave rise to the adage, popularized by a medieval recluse, that Charity covers a multitude of sins!

Emphasizing that the humility of the first Man and Woman was deep, genuine and abiding, Mjomba cited as evidence the fact that Adam and Eve did not regard it as being below their dignity to studiously observe and examine the ways in which the birds of the air, the beasts of the earth, the reptiles, insects and other living forms, including certain species of plant life communicated with each other. They were then able, Mjomba wrote, to incorporate the things learnt into the lingo they developed for their own use. Learnt, he added, with the speed with which a newborn observes and grasps the intricacies of speech, and other things. And they were richly rewarded for their endeavors. The result of their research, a brilliant combination of sound, signs, gestures and scribbled techniques, contained the building blocks of human speech, literature, and philosophy!

Mjomba described the symbols Adam and Eve developed and used to communicate with each other - the first human language ever - as sounding a little like Gaelic, and looking like the ancient Ge'ez script found in Ethiopia when committed to writing.

According to Mjomba, Adam and Eve at this time lived in a kind of a Utopia in which only good reigned on earth; and also one in which an extraordinary, almost celestial, sense of well-being held sway. That sense of wellbeing was brought on by the fact that everything in creation moved in strict consonance with the divine will – everything, except the devil and his rebel band, that is. Mjomba likened the methodical way in which things "moved" to a perfect symphony, and suggested that the telltale beauty, grace and sophistication accompanying all movement in creation Adam and Eve observed in the course of their investigation derived ultimately from the Prime Mover.

Were it not for the fact that they were still "on trial", the Garden of Eden would have been a real heaven, Mjomba asserted! But even though they were on "probation", they nevertheless felt the enormous weight of responsibility, as the "pre-eminent" residents of Mother Earth, for ensuring that the harmony and unity of purpose on parade continued unhindered.

And so it was that, in these glorious days before the fall from grace, the sight of a flock of swan, geese, bats, crows and other bird species in flight evoked images of legions of angels in perpetual adoration. A flock of gazelle bolting with a luckless cheetah on their heels brought to mind images of a company of angels on a mission, while a school of dolphins massing in the calm and clear waters of a coral reef caused Adam and Eve to imagine Cherubs and Seraphs on patrol. A pair of giraffes grazing serenely in a clamp of trees reminded them of their guardian angels, and so on and so forth.

The state of calm and tranquillity that was predominant in the otherwise rough and stormy world was described by Mjomba as pervasive and edifying in a most sublime way. Among the so-called lower life forms, it was a sense of well-being that ironically did not diminish even as members of certain species sacrificed their lives to ensure that other species did not face extinction as called for in the divine plan!

Chaste and sinless, Adam and Eve were of course called to attain a higher level of sanctity than they had already realized at that juncture. It is precisely this that explained their current status in the Garden of Eden - the status of being on trial. The fact of the matter was that, even though Adam and

Eve were in a state of grace and close to the Prime Mover in a way in which their hapless descendants - conceived as they would be in original sin - would not be in a position to grasp easily, the scope for getting even closer to the Mysterious Source of all creation and for attaining greater holiness was very much there. Their efforts in that direction were in fact supposedly indistinguishable from the exertions that would result in their self-actualization!

It was very significant that, when they finally decided that they were going to defy the Omnipotent, Adam and Eve did so by expressing a longing to be like Him and not like animals or any of the other earthly creatures. The urge to be like the lower creatures, Mjomba wrote, was nonexistent or weak at best.

Even though the existence these creatures enjoyed on earth, while it lasted, was glorious, that was really all there was to it - apart from the impressions of it stored in the "minds" or instincts of the surviving brother and sister creatures. Knowing that there was no after-life for these other creatures, it would have been witless and rather crass on the part of Adam and Eve to think that a short-lived banal existence, however delightful, would be compensation enough for abandoning their lofty place in the universe.

That was precisely the reason for fretting about a diet they thought would prolong their lives indefinitely; and it was this that would eventually lead the first Man and Woman into sin. And, once they had disobeyed and fallen from grace, the single most powerful motivation for getting back into the fold promptly was, understandably, to avoid death and everlasting damnation - the direct consequences of sin Adam and Eve had apparently not bargained for.

But sin or no sin, Adam and Eve knew what was good for them and what was not. They recognized that a life of temporal bliss which would come to an abrupt end at the end of their days on earth (as was the case with lower creatures) was patently not good enough for a creature as richly endowed as Man. They knew that to embrace it would be as retrogressive a step as any imaginable! Mjomba wrote that it seemed completely out of character for Adam and Eve, given what they had demonstrated up until that point in time, to sink to that depth.

The transient vis-à-vis the eternal...

According to Mjomba, Adam and Eve were devotees of Tai Chi Tchi Kong, Acupuncture, Transcendental Meditation, and what we now know as Oriental Zen. Their preoccupation with these techniques, which they considered important for keeping spirit and body attuned to each other, was (Mjomba suggested) incompatible with a life of wanton self-indulgence or a craving to satisfy base animal desires. All the more reason, Mjomba wrote, for believing that the focus of our first parents, even as they were plotting the rebellion, did not by any means shift radically or significantly from the eternal to the transient as is widely held.

Mjomba was apparently able to somehow reconcile this position with his belief that what Adam and Eve had essentially been attempting to do was to stage a coup d'état and assume control over Planet Earth and the galaxies surrounding it - claiming all these, including the Garden of Eden and along with it all the creatures which made their abode therein, for themselves in a blatant act of betrayal - in preparation for the permanent imposition of their personal rule over the whole wide world!

Arguably, they did not really need to own all of those things to achieve self-actualization; and they, moreover, had never had any intention of compensating the Prime Mover in any way for His loss. Some would accordingly have characterized that, perhaps justifiably, as the lowest form of human degradation - greed that was worse than if they had merely connived to satisfy their animal desires clandestinely while putting up the appearance of being loyal subjects of the Prime Mover!

Mjomba, for his part, went to great lengths to make it clear that, regardless of the form or nature of their rebellion, the real test of a successful coup remained immortality. Guaranteed to them in the afterlife by the Prime Mover if they remained loyal subjects, immortality was also at the heart of the rebellion.

If they could revolt and, while at it, also succeed in attaining immortality, their apostasy however disgusting would be a success. But any success in throwing off the yoke of bondage to the Almighty One, if it lacked on that score, was not success but a farce at worst and a show at best. And the problem with an act of rebellion whose main focus was the satisfaction of carnal and other animal cravings was that fulfilment in all these instances was fleeting and transient by its very nature.

It would have been very much out of character, Mjomba concluded, for Adam and Eve to pursue gratification of the body's senses for its own sake without any regard to the eventual fate of the body itself. And so, while conceivable, it was very unlikely (Mjomba wrote) for this good man and good woman, who probably committed only that one mortal act of sin in the Garden of Eden in their entire lives to pursue gratification of the body's senses without giving a thought regarding that same body's origins or its eventual fate - or, indeed, the origins and eventual fate of their own person.

Mjomba supposed that even after they disobeyed and sinned, they continued to regard self-indulgence with disdain. Their basic reasoning was that self-indulgence was exactly the same as "knowingly involving oneself in a dangerous and pointless undertaking which hindered you from being productive and useful in society; and, once mired in it, adamantly refusing to acknowledge the danger lurking therein; and instead embracing blindly the idea that your reward will be measured by the extent you are prepared to go in your reckless abandon!"

According to Mjomba, Adam and Eve apparently had no difficulty accepting that the pining by human beings for material pleasures (which, while real, was strictly temporal and in any case far from being timeless or eternal and in that sense mere distractions) was just so much additional evidence of our deep-seated longing for the One who personified Perfection itself. Arguing that wanting to be satisfied (or loved) and wanting to satisfy (or love) were one and the same thing in the final analysis, Mjomba suggested that true love inevitably translated into a union, and that what Man really yearned for was the reunion with the Incomparable, Supreme Good who also happened to be his Maker.

And, granted that the Perfect One had created Man in His own image and likeness, the conclusion that He alone was capable of satisfying Man's hunger became inevitable. In Mjomba's view, the fact that no human being was immune or exempt from the innate desire to be fulfilled only went to reinforce the position taken by Adam and Eve.

The legacy of original sin...

As far as the first Man and Woman were concerned, self-indulgence, far from being something that a creature of their standing could regard as a fulfilling experience, was in fact self-deprecating. And, contrary to the belief of all but those few truly upright men and women whose lives were modelled according to those of children, and who consequently were childlike and not driven by self-love (Mjomba wrote), gratification of the senses had no place or relevance in the afterlife. The same applied to the gratification derived by individuals from performing so-called "good works".

According to Mjomba, it followed from the fact that the human body remained subject to the laws of Mother Nature even after it ceased to be a suitable abode for the spirit that informed it up until then - at the time its owner passed on to the afterlife - that the particular shape and condition in which it might have been maintained up until that point did not have any direct bearing on the eternal fortunes of that individual in his or her afterlife. He wrote that the importance accorded to temporal things, just like the importance that Adam's descendants attached to the body, also seemed largely misplaced in view of this.

And, naturally, if none of these things themselves curried favor with the Prime Mover, the dissembling lives of many public and not-so-public figures, the duplicity and cunning of individuals who spent their lives striving to undermine others in hopes of furthering their own material fortunes thereby, the double lives people lived, the make believe and lies that were paraded as truth for personal gain could not possibly translate into a fulfilling afterlife. And Mjomba had a list of other things in that same category, and it was long.

❖ The coldness and insensitivity on the part of those who inflicted immeasurable pain and suffering on others in the name National Security.

❖ And then, there were terrible acts of cruelty perpetrated by people in positions of public trust against the defenseless in the name of the Rule of Law.

❖ The willy-nilly, unbridled pursuit of profits by owners of businesses and their surrogates that amounted to exploitation of the unwary consumers and of members of society who were guileless and vulnerable, or the pursuit of profits that was completely blind to the bodily and/or spiritual well-being of those involved in generating those revenues, or to the harm done to the well-being of the body politic as a direct result of their activities.

❖ The selfishness of those who were wealthy, and their reluctance to share their wealth with those who were in need.

❖ The hypocrisy of managers of organizations that trumpeted their commitment to the principle of equal employment opportunity, but where discrimination in one form or another was the rule rather than the exception.

❖ The brazenness of those who were paid to manage publicly funded organizations, but did nothing to ensure that appropriate policies pertaining to personnel, purchasing, financial management, etc. safeguarding the public interest were in place; and who instead routinely gave the small fry who had the misfortune of working under them a hell on the slightest pretext.

❖ The insincerity of those who presided over religious orders where the virtues of charity and self-sacrifice were extolled day in and day out, but whose own treatment of subordinates amounted to humiliation and persistent abuse, even as they passed themselves off as models of holiness.

❖ The mendacity of those who run organizations whose declared mission was the advancement of the rights of workers, but whose own employees' rights were flouted regularly and systematically in ways that made a complete mockery of the principles those organizations supposedly stood for.

❖ The impertinence of the managers of corporations that habitually shelled out millions publicizing their dedication to customer satisfaction, but who were really committed to the production and marketing of substandard and even harmful products to the gullible public.

❖ The madness of those who managed organizations set up to promote the welfare of children, the elderly, those who were physically or mentally challenged, and others who were disadvantaged in one way or another, and who even used the scarce resources of these organizations to proclaim loudly for the whole world to hear how well they discharged their weighty responsibilities; but who routinely ignored the needs of those they were supposed to serve and even misused the funds entrusted to them for that purpose.

❖ The shamelessness of managers of corporations that bragged about being in the forefront in the war on diseases by reason of their pioneering discoveries and consequently innovative practices in the production of drugs and pharmaceuticals; but yet consistently priced their products beyond the reach of those who most needed them.

❖ The silence and/or collusion of those whose duty it was to fearlessly point out injustices irrespective of the nature or source.

❖ The hypocrisy of the vast majority of present-day moralists, many of whom would undoubtedly feel devastated if suddenly everyone became irrevocably saved and they went out work. Some of them, Mjomba wrote, acted as if the Prime Mover was their personal possession and had no ability whatsoever, save with their permission, to communicate, inspire or do any favor of any sort to other men and women!

❖ The greed and selfishness that drove law makers even in so-called advanced societies to craft statutes that violated natural justice, had no regard whatsoever for the sanctity of family life and things like that, or statutes that were designed to promote the domination of one section of society over others.

❖ The hypocrisy of members of legislatures and administrations around the world who pretended that all was well when those served by institutions they presided over were subjected on a daily basis to undeserved pain and suffering, were routinely and systematically terrorized and made to endure unspeakable crudities and humiliation at the hands of the functionaries running those institutions with all avenues for appeal against the injustices committed against them blocked; or when the inmates of those institutions were left to fight for survival in conditions that are dehumanizing.

❖ The altogether reckless and unjustified preoccupation by leaders of rich nations with the development of weapons of mass destruction, while pouring scorn on the inhabitants of underdeveloped and developing nations and ignoring their own role in keeping those poor nations poor.

❖ The unconscionable, wholly unpardonable actions of leaders in those selfsame countries that had resulted in the development of germs and viruses that had a way of collapsing gradually or instantaneously the immune systems of those who were exposed to them because, unlike natural germs and viruses which could be fought with medication, these man-made germs and viruses were themselves immune to treatment.

❖ The political, economic and military policies crafted by leaders in these same countries that were designed to advance their interests regardless of the short and long term harm the policies in question have on the well-being of millions of innocent people around the globe.

❖ The inaction of members of the Church hierarchy in wealthy, so-called "Christian" nations where the hype was "family values", but where the legislation, enacted under their noses and left to sit unchallenged on the books, sought to attract professionals and skilled workers from other nations to relieve existing internal shortages cheaply at the expense of the basic family unit; and where immigration laws, presuming to override God's laws, ignored the fact that the head of a family was indeed the head of a family, and denied dependents the right to accompany and live with the bread earner in his or her new country of residence; and where immigration laws, flouting all Christian norms, separated wives from husbands, and minors from their parents just because the families at risk were immigrant families.

❖ Pointing out that, in some of these countries, the legislation unashamedly made ironic, almost mocking, references to "family categories", Mjomba wrote that the laws deliberately prevented spouses and children of permanent residents from joining the "permanent resident" until years later - by which time the possibility of members of that family staying together as one family unit would be no more. He decried the fact that the Church's hierarchy paid what amounted to lip service to the needs of families that were separated as a result of the operation of those "weird" laws. He wrote that, in contrast, obscure organizations with meagre resources went out of their way to lend a much-needed helping hand to those adversely affected by the "anti-family" legislation. It was, in any case, inconceivable that such "anti-family" laws existed on the books of rich nations that claimed to be "Christian" when similar "anti-family" laws were unheard of in much poorer, non-Christian nations!

The general indifference of the Church hierarchy to the needs of the poor. Mjomba wrote that the tendency of the clergy to refer those in need to "Social Services" rather than deal with the immediate problems of the needy appeared to be pervasive. He made reference to a notice posted on the door of the rectory of one Catholic Church in an American metropolis which seemed to suggest that it was none of the Church's business to provide for the poor and homeless; and that the right place for them to find such shelter was across the street at an establishment operated by an obscure Protestant church organization that, unlike the church where the notice was posted, presumably could afford to put Charity before Orthodoxy. Mjomba said it reminded him of the story of a dashing American cardinal who reportedly was prepared to contribute to the cost of completing the demolition of a collapsing inner-city Baptist church which also catered for the poor and homeless, but not to the cost of erecting the new one!

During Mjomba's oral defense of his thesis, he would remark that, platitudes aside, being a good Samaritan and being a member of the Church's hierarchy, seemingly compatible in theory, did not appear to be so in practice for some reason; and he would go on to suggest that the parallel with the attitudes of the scribes and Pharisees which the gospels repeatedly referred to seemed plain enough.

Mjomba would also make reference to the fact that the Church in America openly and consistently supported conservatives, even though it was well-known that the conservatives there were not beholden to things like higher minimum wages, universal Medicare, universal suffrage, affirmative action for the disadvantaged minority even as affirmative action for the already empowered majority was still ongoing, and so on and so forth; and that they were staunch supporters of the death penalty and things like that, in addition to being the darling of exploitive conglomerates.

According to Mjomba, the Church did not appear to see that it was facing a dilemma of sorts given that the policies advocated by both liberals *and* conservatives in America had major flaws from the point of view of Catholic doctrine.

Citing one survey Mjomba wrote that, with roughly a quarter of the population identifying themselves as Catholics, America boasted the fourth largest concentration of Catholics in the world. However, according to that same survey, just one-third of those "Catholics" actually believed in the Real Presence - that the bread and wine actually become the body and blood of the Deliverer at consecration during Holy Mass (or Transubstantiation).

Assuming that the survey he was citing was reliable and two thirds of American Catholics did not believe in the Church's doctrine of Transubstantiation, then America likely also boasted one of the largest concentrations of so-called "cultural" Catholics in the world! Admittedly the phenomenon of "cultural Catholics" was not confined to America; and Mjomba supposed that the number of "cultural Catholics" as a percentage of Catholic populations around the world varied from country to country, and was presumably the result of many different factors, one such factor being the quality of catechetical instruction availed catechumens - or so

Mjomba imagined. The labors of folks like St. Alphonse Liguori, St. Catherine of Siena and St. Bernard of Clairvaux without any doubt had their impact not only on the numbers of converts to Catholicism, but also on the prevailing number of cultural Catholics of their time. But, then, there was only so much that even Alphonses, Bernards and Catherines could do; and they moreover couldn't be everywhere.

Still, the number of "cultural" Catholics in America, if the survey the seminarian was citing was reliable, represented a truly shocking statistic - or so he thought. In which case, Mjomba wrote, that the true number of Americans who professed "Catholicism" in the true sense of that word was just that, namely a third of those who found it convenient to identify themselves as Catholics, as it was a dogma of the Church that the bread and wine actually become the body and blood of the Deliverer at the time of consecration; and a Catholic who knowingly and willfully repudiated that dogma was excommunicated *latae sententiae*. Mjomba, after making a passing reference to the conditions prevailing in Europe at the time of the Protestant Reformation so-called - conditions that predisposed hordes in Germany and the Scandinavian countries to embrace Martin Luther's heresies - added that he supposed that the two thirds American "cultural" believed and acted the way they did because of a deficiency of some sort in the catechetical instructions they were availed. Mjomba wrote that, if ignored, the phenomena of "cultural Catholicism" could easily end up as a modern-day "neo-Protestant Reformation"!

But what else did the two thirds not believe, Mjomba went on? Was it just fine if the successors to the apostles merely succeeded in getting hordes to "identify" themselves as "Catholics" as and when they found it convenient to do so? What exactly did the word "evangelization mean? What is the exact import of the words [echoed in Pope Francis's *Evangelii Gaudium* ("The Joy of the Gospel")]: "And Jesus came and spake unto them, saying, All power is given unto me in heaven and in earth. Go ye therefore, and teach all nations, baptizing them in the name of the Father, and of the Son, and of the Holy Ghost: Teaching them to observe all things whatsoever I have commanded you: and, lo, I am with you always, even unto the end of the world. Amen. (Matthew 28:18-20)

The Deliverer, Mjomba wrote, had also told His disciples: "Truly I tell you, if you have faith as small as a mustard seed, you can say to this mountain, 'Move from here to there,' and it will move. Nothing will be impossible for you." (Matthew 17:20-21)

And the Apostle to the Gentiles, writing to the Corinthians, had stated: "And if I should have prophecy and should know all mysteries, and all knowledge, and if I should have all faith, so that I could remove mountains, and have not charity, I am nothing." (1 Corinthians 13:2)

Mjomba wrote that unfortunately many "preachers" interpreted that to mean that it was none of their business to call out anyone - Catholic and non-Catholic - who misrepresented the doctrines of the *Sancta Ecclesia*. And as if that was not bad enough, others were quite happy not just to selectively turn one single issue in Catholic social teaching into a "litmus test" for determining whether an individual was a faithful Catholic, but to proceed to weaponize it in the political sphere to the advantage or disadvantage of their favorite political party, while ignoring all other equally important issues, and effectively reducing the common good to just that one, single issue and minimizing the importance of the other issues.

Such actions, particularly when carried out by prelates (who were the successors to the apostles) or their surrogates had consequences. They could, for one, prejudice those members of the political party that was not the prelates' favorite and cause them to look with disdain on the *Sancta Ecclesia*, and what it stood for, and thus become an obstacle to their conversion. Moreover, Mjomba added, the Deliverer did not come to save those who were righteous; He came to save sinners! (Mark 2:13-17)

As he penned his thesis, Mjomba tried to figure out why the kinds of situations he had described came about. There was the Protestant Reformation that was precipitated by the ninety-five theses that Martin Luther, a member of the Order of the Hermits of St. Augustine, nailed to the door of the Schlosskirche (Castle Church) in Wittenberg in 1517. And before that there was the East–West Schism that came to a head in 1054 when Michael Cerularius was patriarch of Constantinople. But history was also replete with other instances of Catholic prelates, among them cardinals, among them cardinals, who were explicitly excommunicated by a pope or ecumenical council for spreading heresies.

And when you thought that things couldn't get any crazier, there was this one pope who had his predecessor exhumed, tried, de-fingered, briefly reburied, and then thrown into the Tiber! Then there was another one who gave land to a mistress, murdered several people, and was in turn killed by a man who caught him in bed with his wife. Then there was another one who "sold" the Papacy! There was another one who complained that he did not hear enough screaming when Cardinals who had conspired against him were tortured. Another one, a spendthrift member of the Medici family, succeeded in spending on a single ceremony one seventh the reserves that his predecessors had labored to amass. And there was another one, also a Medici, whose power-politicking with Spain, France and Germany got Rome sacked!

Mjomba thought that it was quite extraordinary that Judas Iscariot, who was among the Deliverer's twelve handpicked apostles, didn't just betray his Master, but did so with a kiss!

But then, out of the host of angels that the Prime Mover caused to bounce into existence out of nothing (creatures that were "angelic" by definition), a goodly number of them had ended up as demons who were so vile, the Prime Mover had no choice but to consign them to the "hell" of their own making!

And, finally, there was Adam and Eve, the first humans who were created in a state of grace, and were placed by the Prime Mover in the Paradise of Pleasure. Caught filching forbidden fruit from the Tree of the Knowledge of Good and Evil, they were banished from the Garden of Eden as a result.

Mjomba now worried that, for all he knew, he himself could quite easily end up a heretic for some of the things he was expressing in his thesis, as he saw nothing special about himself. Then, thinking about the hordes whose views on the world were at complete variance with the dogmas of the *Sancta Ecclesia*, and who sincerely believed that Catholics were the ones who were the crazies, having been brainwashed, he mused that there would be lots of drama at the end of time as the truth hit home for all those "poor people"!

As expected, Mjomba's views on the political situation in America would be hotly contested when the time came for him to defend his thesis. This would be even more so with regard to his charge that actions of members of the Church's hierarchy were wanting in many respects. It did not therefore surprise Mjomba at all when Father Damian, a nonagenarian whose nick-name was "Honorary Dean of the Dogmatic Corps" because, in addition to teaching Dogmatic Theology at the seminary, he was the one who cleared diocesan publications requiring the bishop's *imprimatur*, shot his fist into the air to signal his disenchantment with Mjomba's views on that score.

"*Godverdomme!*" the old man swore in his native Dutch tongue before launching his own counter attack.

Fr. Damian wore rimless eye glasses, and his small, glistening eyes burrowed into Mjomba as he continued, his quivering voice shattering the dead silence that had descended on the Convocation Hall in the wake of his unorthodox oath: "Do you agree, Reverend Mjomba, that there is such a thing as anti-Catholicism? And can you provide us any reason why we shouldn't take your position as anti-Catholic?"

"You are probably right on the money" Mjomba had replied. "Still, is it not true, Father, that anti-Catholics inside the Church and the prevalence of unbecoming behaviour by priests and bishops - and even popes - are phenomena that are quite consistent with the definition of the Church as the Mystical Body of Christ? They are after all also consistent with the description of humans as the poor forsaken children of Adam and Eve. We are not surprised that actions of priests and scribes under the Old Testament, and even actions of important figures like David and Solomon, occasionally left a lot to be desired. I would have thought, Father, that we Catholics - and especially members of the Church's hierarchy - would grasp at each and every such opportunity to examine ourselves to see if we might not be acting like the priests and the Pharisees who, two thousand years ago, not only fabricated the case against the Deliverer, but made certain that He met a grizzly end on Mt. Calvary - or am I wrong?"

As he gave his impromptu sermon, Mjomba did not once bat an eyelid, with the result that Father Damian's gaze and his were locked on each other while the exchange lasted. Mjomba did not regret that he had decided to stand his ground because, by the time it was all over, it was evident to him - and perhaps no one else in that Convocation Hall - that the old man was feigning, and knew from the start that Mjomba was on rock solid ground. But everyone else there appeared surprised when the exchange did not develop into an acrimonious debate especially as the priest had begun, somewhat uncharacteristically, by swearing.

The evil deeds that humans routinely did to one another with seeming impunity and, in particular, the scale of those misdeeds were just two measures of the depth to which integrity and morality among humans had sunk, Mjomba wrote in his thesis. They were also an indication of the self-deception they were capable of at the same time.

Another measure was the extent to which humans acted as though they were the original authors of life itself, and the presumption that they could substitute the original objectives and purposes of created objects with completely new purposes and objectives that were almost entirely self-serving.

Soon enough however, in a demonstration of total irresponsibility, humans took to doing whatever they did without any purpose to their actions - as though they were automatons or zombies! Mjomba quipped that a human who was lost - specifically a human who was lost and did not wish to be redeemed - apparently did things purposelessly and without any objective almost by definition.

In any case, having lost their innocence and then chosen to abnegate their responsibilities as creatures endowed with reason, they inevitably suffered from a kind of inferiority complex as a consequence of their transgressions; and it was that inferiority complex that ended up as the motive force behind their actions thence forward. Precisely because they were endowed with a free will and an intellect, the situation could not get any worse than that.

It could be said that anything humans did at that juncture was done to please - to look good. And it was not as if humans really needed to sink that low. For, reviewing the results of His work after He was done with creation, the Prime Mover Himself had declared that it was good.

The strange thing about all that, Mjomba wrote, was that a good deal of the untoward things humans did would cease being misdeeds and would actually qualify as meritorious activity, if only they were done with cleaner intentions. But the problem was that humans thought they could have it both ways - namely be both good and bad at the same time! This is what made them, in Mjomba's words, such a weird lot.

The satisfaction humans would otherwise derive from conducting themselves in an upright manner would also be real, and not hollow or faked. That satisfaction would be measured by the weight of responsibility shouldered in relation to the gifts that particular human was endowed with.

Mjomba confessed that whereas he had some idea as to what the expressions "satisfaction" and "gifts" meant, his understanding of the expression "responsibility" was vague to the point of being nonexistent.

According to him, the pleasure and satisfaction humans got when conducting themselves like automatons was not very different from the pleasure and satisfaction a lion or other beasts of prey which had already had its fill obtained from going off on a senseless hunting trip. And just as hunting in those circumstances only benefited other predators, actions humans did for the sake of doing so, or to maintain their place among the Joneses, merely profited the devil and his cohorts.

The funny thing was that even after humans found, after indulging themselves over and over again, that the pleasures of the body were short lived and quickly came to naught, they never seemed to learn. If anything, the experience seemingly rendered them less capable of determining from a set of obvious facts what really was or wasn't in their own best interests! Not even the fact that in the course of "enjoying" they had wasted valuable time during which they might have done things that were slightly more useful seemed to matter; or the fact that the blind pursuit of those pleasures frequently ended up harming them in important respects - physical and mental health, social standing and careers.

For some humans, the preoccupation with material things apparently was incomplete unless it went hand in hand with an all out effort to make the lives of those around them as miserable and difficult as possible - as if they were determined to ensure that there was as little charity as possible left in them to cover even some portion of the multitude of their sins.

Mjomba also made reference in his thesis to transgressions involving the misuse of power by individuals in positions of authority who had no interest in justice and fairness. He claimed that some of them exploited their subordinates and treated those who did not happen to be their close pals as if they were entirely expendable. He contended that the time would come when these "foxes" would be told, just like Pontius Pilate was told, that the authority they wielded and misused had been entrusted to them by the Prime Mover, and that they had to provide an accounting for the way they used that authority.

Mjomba claimed in his thesis that humans were sometimes so irrational, they gave the impression they were about to exchange places with one of the lower animal species that the Prime Mover in his infinite wisdom had not endowed with reason and a free will. A good example of their irrationality was their propensity to take life. Some humans even killed in the name of the Prime Mover.

There was a time in history, wrote Mjomba, when some humans killed in the name of the divine emperor, while others killed to placate other kinds of gods. Since then, the number of gods had increased rather than decreased; and one of them went by the uninspiring name of "Choice", Mjomba quipped. Worshipping at the altar of "Choice" reminded Mjomba of the action of Adam and Eve in deciding to put their own wishes ahead of their conscience and also ahead of the corresponding demands of their God-given nature.

Elaborating on that particular "god", Mjomba went on to state that humans who believed so passionately in Choice in the sense in which it was popularly used forgot that they would not be capable of choosing anything if they themselves did not exist. But they seemed to think that because someone "chose" to let *them* live, that in turn gave them the right to choose to allow a life to flower to full maturity if they happened to like that, or to cut it off prematurely if they found that more convenient.

Mjomba argued that any action that violated the rights of any individual to choose was bad enough. Indeed such action hit at the very nature of humans, who were differentiated from lower creatures by their ability to rationalize and to choose between what was good and what was lacking in goodness or evil. Fighting for the right to choose in the latter sense was, Mjomba wrote, quite commendable.

But, regardless of the personal circumstances of the expectant mother or the imagined circumstances of the unborn, action that prematurely ended the latter's existence for the sake of ending it, while demonstrating that humans did indeed have the right to choose, denied their victims not just the right to continue to exist like everybody else for better or for worse, but the action to terminate life automatically denied the victims the chance to get to that point in life where they too could exercise their choice between different alternatives.

When quizzed about his opinion regarding the right of women to choose with respect to anything, including matters that affected their bodies, Mjomba would respond that he had an opinion about both men and women exercising rights that went with being human beings. When women were singled out and asked to defend their inalienable rights, it was invariably with ulterior motives - the same motives that, according to him, were behind the historical discriminatory practices against members of the so-called "weaker" sex.

Mjomba argued that when some humans tried to abrogate the right of others to choose, it was called slavery, and that it certainly was never the idea of the Prime Mover to relegate women to the role of slaves. The evils of slavery, imperialism, colonialism and the traditional discriminatory practices against women that had been perpetuated in all but the few matrilineal social systems still in existence around the world stemmed from the same thing, namely the original sin. According to Mjomba, the relationships inside marriages which themselves started out as contracts between two free individuals, did not at all have to be at the expense of the exercise by women of their inalienable rights.

Mjomba acknowledged that the right to choose aside, choices had of necessity, to be seen in their proper context; and choices made by individuals - regardless of whether they were men or women - could be more or less heroic depending on the circumstances. An example of a heroic choice, according to Mjomba, was that of Mary in agreeing to be a virgin mother albeit of the "Son of the Most High". Being human, Mary must have been devastated by the suggestion of someone who was a complete stranger that she bear a child despite her vow of chastity and the fact that she was already "betrothed" to Joseph, the carpenter, for her protection from a society in which women's rights were severely curtailed.

There was a parallel of sorts, according to Mjomba, between Mary's consent to become the mother of the Deliverer and consent by women who were victims of sexual assault or rape to be involuntary mothers. In many respects, Mary's decision was the more difficult and heroic since it placed her not only at odds with herself and her desire to be chaste all the days of her life, but also at odds with Joseph (to whom she was wedded in the eyes of the world) but also with society since she essentially was agreeing to be a mother out of wedlock.

Mjomba suggested that many opponents of abortion had motives other than the preservation of the life of the unborn, adding that many anti-abortionists were not only the staunchest death penalty advocates even in circumstances in which the equitable and fair administration of justice had been called into question, but also tended to be the most vociferous supporters of things like "regime changes" in other lands, "pre-emptive strikes" against so-called rogue states, and other military adventures that took unnecessary lives. He claimed that if they genuinely respected life, they would respect all lives, everywhere and in all circumstances. But they would, above all, be at the forefront in working for the peaceful resolution of conflicts; and, instead of pushing for the death penalty and expansion of the prison systems, they would be working to address the root causes of anti-social behavior.

Thinking aloud, Mjomba said a new kind of world order in which humans were increasingly turning on each other, and swearing to physically eliminate each other had evolved. According to Mjomba, there was an unmistakeable similarity between the present tendency by groups to demonize each other and the time of the crusades when two opposing groups of humans decided that the other group was on the side of the devil, and that there was only one solution to the "problem", namely to drive the other group into the sea! The crusades of the ages gone by did not yield any victors, and neither would the present "crusades" against so-called "terrorists", Mjomba surmised. In this nuclear age, *both* sides - indeed the whole of humanity - stood to lose out. The world, according to Mjomba, was fast sliding to the brink, propelled on by those who were worshippers of the god called "Choice".

Judging by the activity surrounding that "god", decidedly more men than women idolised "it". These were men who strutted about with buttons on their lapels that proclaimed "Neolib" or "Neocon"! They believed that even though only a handful, they had the wherewithal to re-draw the world map to their liking and also to "convert" the rest of the world to their own distinctly "super power" or "American" view of the world. Included among those who worshipped at the altar of the god called "Choice", according to Mjomba, would be a new breed of clergy - typically "American" priests and bishops - who would "leave the Church" without even suspecting it, and take zillions out of the Church with them by failing to speak out in support of Pope John Paul's condemnation of the American invasion of a Middle Eastern country as morally unjustifiable.

Mjomba wondered if members of the Church's hierarchy, who should have been in the forefront of defending the rights of all, and the rights of the "weak" in particular, had again not been complicit in what had become the institutionalized denial of women's right to choose. He also wondered if their own "masculine" gender did not have anything to do with it, just like the race and religious affiliation of many churchmen blinded them to the murder and mayhem committed by the "crusaders", and the evils of slavery and imperialism.

Mjomba was adamant that the doctrine of infallibility which applied to St. Peter's successors when they were enunciating dogmas of the Church appeared to have served as a cloak for members of the Church's hierarchy to get away with failings of human nature to which they were subject in the same way everybody else was. And because churchmen had the tendency to hide behind the Church, it was the reputation of the Church - the Mystical Body of the Deliverer - which suffered.

Mjomba argued that it was accordingly to the Church's advantage if members of the hierarchy owned up to the fact that, even though called to share in a divine priesthood and anointed in a very special way, it was sometime before they would themselves graduate and become members of the Church Triumphant. Until they owned up to that fact, it was unlikely that they would be understanding of the failings of others; and it would be especially true of the failings of those who, for reasons best known to themselves, did not believe in what Mjomba referred to as the official "road-map" to heaven represented by membership in the visible Church.

The numerous references by Saints Peter and Paul in their epistles to their own unworthiness as they toiled in the service of the Church sprang from their deep humility. It took a lot of humility for John Paul to apologize for the actions done in the name of the Church by many individuals in the near and distant past, Mjomba said. He added that it would definitely take a lot of humility for Princes of the Church all over the world to occasionally include an admission that they and the devoted priests whose work was so critical to the Church's mission of spreading the faith, far from being perfect, needed to forgiveness seven times seven times a day!

Mjomba wrote that he did not think that there was anything anyone could do to another that was worse than denying him/her the right to continue to exist. Doing so on the pretext that they were exercising their own right to choose was what elevated the practice to worship, according to Mjomba. Since humans were commanded to love one another and to even sacrifice their lives for others if that became necessary, Mjomba did not believe that there could be any justification for deliberately terminating a life whether of an unborn child or of a member of the security forces of some other country that was going about harnessing its resources for the good of its people in the same way other countries were harnessing their resources for the good of their citizenry.

During the ensuing discussion on justified and unjustified wars, Mjomba made the controversial point that, from the moral standpoint, nations that launched unjustified wars became liable for restitution in the exact same way robbers who decided to help themselves on other people's property had to own up and agree to return the loot before they could become reconciled with their divine Maker. In Mjomba's view, declarations by the Holy Father to the effect that wars in given situations were unjustified were binding in every sense of that word, and could not be taken lightly.

The decision by one mortal human to be rid of another member of the human family came with such a high cost that, even in purely economic terms, it had to be labeled a bad one – and particularly so when the requirement for restitution was figured in. In philosophical terms it was an illogical decision because it not only ignored the basic right of other humans to exist, but effectively took away permanently from the victims in the process the option to themselves choose, even as the individuals making the illogical choice were using it to make a statement about their own right to choose. In theological terms, that kind of choice, between freedom and responsibility without regard to the interests of others, was completely unjustifiable. And because it could never be argued that the end - be it the continued physical or mental health of the decision maker or mere convenience - justified the means, even in purely practical terms, the decision to terminate a life or lives - particularly the innocent ones - was not one that could be defended, according to Mjomba.

The decision to do away with the life of another person was also a stupid one that did not take cognizance of the fact that even the killer had a firm appointment with death - the very thing the killer was visiting on others. Mjomba elaborated that all humans, including those who went around in bulletproof vests and surrounded by bodyguards all the time, eventually kicked the bucket just the same. And the moment they did so, the tables were turned as even they themselves might have figured out in advance. Those they falsely accused back on earth became their accusers in the afterlife, and they did not do so by their own choosing out of vengeance, but as a duty on the orders of someone who had undergone a very similar fate here on earth - the Deliverer and Judge Himself.

Mjomba quipped that the cheek and swagger of killers also ended right there, and that it was in all likelihood a painful transition because, according to his thesis, killers did what they did because they thought they were "more equal than others" and therefore had a right to stay on here longer than others. And unfortunately for the killers, it was at the time they kicked their own buckets that they would also discover - somewhat late - that, instead of seeking to make war with fellow humans (which also automatically meant declaring war on the Creator) or being preoccupied with acts of vengeance, they should have devoted every moment of their lives working to foster peace in the world and at all costs.

Talking about worshipping gods or more correctly *false* gods, Mjomba wrote that the worship in olden days of waxen calves and idols made of stone, so long as it did not involve human sacrifice, was decidedly more preferable to the worship in modern days of "Choice". But he lamented that because the latter seemed to be so obviously wrong, it also automatically provided the modern Pharisees and scribes the opportunity - and one that was apparently much sought after - of taking up stones to cast at those adjudged to be sinners.

Just as in the case of the New Testament prostitute who found herself on the verge of being stoned to death (and who, according to legend, was none other than Saint Mary Magdalene), perhaps all those who appear so itchy to cast the first stones are themselves not so innocent after all, Mjomba wrote.

Well, all the characters involved were, of course, human, Mjomba wrote. That being the case, standing in line to cast the first stone was, arguably, the occupational hazard of those who were "apostles". This was because they often forgot the reason the Deliverer, who called them to be apostles, came down from Heaven; which, namely, was to bring back those who had strayed from the right path to the fold. Without humans complicating it further, life, Mjomba wrote, was already complicated enough as it was, and of course also full of many paradoxes.

But, more than anything else, the "human factor" as he called it made life a lot harder and more paradoxical than it otherwise needed to be. And even then, the medicine invented by humans to cure ills that sprung from the human factor itself invariably proved to be worse than the diseases it aimed to cure!

Correcting himself, Mjomba went on that calling it a problem of the human factor was a gross understatement, if not entirely false. Because, as he pointed out, while those who were so eager to cast the first stones in the matter of the "Choice Worshippers" might not have been physically involved in, or contributed to the conditions that resulted in, the premature termination of a life, it was hard to imagine that they themselves had never "murdered" someone in their heart in the same way they might have "committed adultery" by "looking lustfully" at whoever might have been their object of fascination. Those who were standing at attention with stones that were ready to fly were thus probably guilty of being phony doctors on the one hand and hypocrites on the other.

According to Mjomba, there were all sorts of people who loved to criticize individuals who sought and procured abortions for one reason or another, and called them murderers, while they themselves openly supported other types of "murder" and, for instance, saw nothing wrong with embargoes that resulted in the death of thousands of children, the elderly and others, or the needless deaths that resulted from expansionist policies of governments around the world.

With regard to being phony or "quacks", it was not that the right medication prescribed by the Doctor was unavailable. But even though the medication was available and at little or no cost, it has always seemed practically impossible for humans to follow the correct procedures in administering it, and above all administering it in the right doses. The solution to that problem, according to Mjomba, lay in the Doctor who "discovered" and pioneered the cure making

Himself available full time and everywhere to administer the concoction personally every time.

The simple fact of the matter, Mjomba went on, was that, present or not, the Doctor had never really been recognized for what He was or came on earth to accomplish. His presence in flesh and blood (outside of the blessed Eucharist) wouldn't have made much difference. That is because He would Himself not only run the gauntlet of being accused of being a phony, but also of being falsely diagnosed as one of those who needed treatment - He would be told He was Himself sick in the same way He was accused of being a sinner by association the last time He was around. And, labeled a dangerous phony, He likely would be matched off to Calvary one more time by the very people who now claim to be sinless almost as a matter of fashion, and made to suffer the exact same fate He suffered two millennia ago in a macabre repeat of history!

Mjomba suggested that the Deliverer, if He were here in person today, would be as popular as Nelson Mandela had been while he was incarcerated on Robben Island when it appeared as if the reign of apartheid in South Africa would never come to an end, or as popular as Martin Luther King had been in the Deep South before the passage of the Civil Rights legislation. And even that would be a gross understatement obviously; but may be the point is made.

Mjomba wrote that it did not surprise him that those sections of modern society that were always trying to claim a monopoly over justification were actually the ones where egotism and above all intolerance seemed to flourish most. He wrote that studies were not needed to establish the correlation between self-righteousness and intolerance in particular. He claimed that the correlation was just as obvious in these times as it had been in times past. Mjomba commented that as far as human nature went, it did not appear to have changed an iota; and that was not just in the two thousand years that had elapsed since the Deliverer returned to His Father, but since the time of Adam and Eve.

The Church of Rome...

Asking to be excused for diverting a little from the matter at hand, Mjomba wrote that it would not surprise him a little bit if some inside and, may be also, outside the Church found the material in his thesis ill-suited to their purposes and decided on that basis to roundly denounce his thesis in its entirety (or, if he was really lucky, only in part) as apostasy. There were so many things in his thesis that were at variance with what one found in the Catechism, like the blanket statement about "murder" and "adultery" being sinful independently of the "intention" to commit sin.

Mjomba's position, at least up until that point, was that "murder" and "adultery" could only be sinful if they were committed by creatures that possessed both reason *and* free will in the first place; and in their commission, "intention" automatically came into play and determined whether to proceed with the "illicit act" or not. It was Mjomba's opinion that in countering the position of those who advocated situational ethics, the theologians who framed the Church's official teachings, perhaps without intending it, occasionally themselves went overboard after proving too much. Quite a serious thing to do when one was speaking officially for Holy Mother the Church.

A much worse thing, of course, was using their positions in the Church to promote their own agendas, and doing so under the guise of protecting orthodoxy. These guys, Mjomba wrote, were human too. After all, even they themselves needed forgiveness "seventy times seven times a day" like everyone else.

And the "Holy Father" - wasn't he human too? Of course, he was. The difference between the pope as the Vicar of Rome and successor to Peter and the rest of the Church's prelates lay in the fact that the Deliverer, addressing Peter, had solemnly asked the fisherman: "Peter, Simon Bar Jona, do you love me?" And not once, but three times in succession! And, with Peter protesting that the risen Deliverer knew him all too well and did not need to doubt Peter's undying love for Him, the Son of Man and High Priest, and now alas also Judge who sits on the right hand of the Prime Mover, exercising His power as the Head of the Mystical Body, had declared thusly for the whole world to hear: "Feed my sheep!"

And while the Pontiff of Rome was infallible when speaking *ex cathedra* or guiding the flock in his capacity as Peter's successor, there was nothing in the Church's teaching that said that these other guys couldn't let the Church and their own consciences down by indulging in things of that nature! Whether you called it the human factor or something else, the fact that members of the Church's hierarchy were not sinless (just like other members of the Mystical Body of Christ), left wide open the possibility that any one of them, while purporting to speak and act under the inspiration of the Third Person of the Blessed Trinity, could in fact be pursuing an ungodly agenda, Mjomba asserted.

Would members of the Church's hierarchy who misused their positions and authority also have to provide an accounting for their actions? No doubt, Mjomba wrote. They all would have to give an accounting for the way they used their authority and power. Moreover, added Mjomba, from whom much was given, more would be expected! But - Mjomba quipped - the reward for good stewardship would certainly be well worth the effort that went into it.

History, Mjomba went on, had shown that, far from being smooth and trouble free, the road along which the Church travelled could be pretty bumpy, owing in part to the shortcomings of its functionaries, the successor to Šim`ôn bar-Yônâ or "Holy Father" himself included.

Mjomba tried to remember from his Church History class if the Church's rebuttal of Galileo's theories had been incorporated in the Catechism at any time and, if so, when it had been expunged. His efforts at recall merely established that the astronomer was born exactly one year after the first Church-wide Roman Catholic catechism, commissioned by the Council of Trent, was published, and did not otherwise bring any results; and, like any good and well-meaning Catholic, he hoped and prayed that the zealots in the Church did not blunder to that degree. The resulting embarrassment to the Church of God would have been quite unimaginable.

But, as it was, the embarrassment from the Galileo affair and other similar "affairs" in the course of the Church's history not only had been bad enough, but had given the Church's foes, many of whom were men and women who were morally bankrupt, grounds to do things that had made the Church's work of evangelization much more difficult than it needed to be. Recalling the time in history when a pretender occupied the Holy See while the real successor to St. Peter "languished" in exile in France, Mjomba wrote that it must have been a very difficult time indeed for the Church of God.

He added that, in circumstances like those, one was tempted to ask if these sorts of things did not constitute a valid reason for folks outside the visible Church, particularly the good folks, to write off the papacy and the organization over which the popes presided as the work of the Antichrist or even Beelzebub! But Mjomba quickly corrected himself again and wrote that that was the wrong question to ask. He suggested that it was more appropriate to ask how, despite the denials of Peter, the murders committed by Paul, the scandals in the Church, and the intransigence of men, including those of his own generation, the Spirit still managed to stay in the business of saving souls.

The answer Mjomba volunteered itself bordered on the ludicrous. It wasn't that we *didn't* know the answer to that question - we *couldn't* possibly know it! And the reason! We didn't understand how God, who was not simply good but goodness itself, was good to us; and presuming to understand how God, who did not just act but was activity itself, operated was hardly the proper thing for us to do. That question was the big question the answer to which only God knew, Mjomba wrote. To try to understand how the Prime Mover worked to implement His divine plan notwithstanding the "human factor" and the inclination to what was base implied a presumption that we could also grasp His ways in the face of the original sin committed by the first Man and the first Woman.

Around the time he was writing his thesis, Mjomba had told a stranger he had met while travelling on a bus in jest that arguing in that fashion was a manoeuvre that was typically "Catholic" and intrinsically fraudulent! He had added, still in jest, that it was still a wonderful ploy which, in this case, left the main question unanswered, while shielding defenders of the papacy (or "popery" as it was referred to by protagonists) from the obligation to defend their claim that the papacy was divinely instituted.

The stranger, a non-Catholic who did not know Mjomba's religious affiliation, had offered a rejoinder that made Mjomba wilt: "When it suits them (Catholics), they start talking about 'humanly speaking' this and 'speaking *ex cathedra*' that! When they are about to be cornered in an argument, they always change, and begin to speak in code. Still, one has to give them some credit - they start out by having their priests-in-training master Philosophy; and it is only after the seminarians, as they are called, become well versed in the sophistry of argument that they are introduced to biblical exegesis - which they then can manipulate according to their whims! Clever louts!

"A former member of the seminary brotherhood once bragged to me he could prove that there was God in seven ways. But then he added that he could also prove in as many ways that God wasn't there! And he went on to boast that, after his first year of Philosophy studies, he could prove that a sin was not a sin..."

Mjomba treasured memories of that encounter, and thought the exchange had left him with a better appreciation of the views of non-Catholics in general and anti-Catholics in particular.

Perhaps with that encounter in mind, Mjomba wrote that the return of the Vicar of Christ from Avignon to the Vatican was a turning point in the history of the Church, and one that was also pregnant with meaning. Noting that it, perhaps, wasn't entirely a coincidence that the "Great Schism", the "Black Death", and the European Wars of Destruction, and the fall of Constantinople almost all occurred at one and the same time, Mjomba suggested that the end of the Great Schism was really the beginning of a new type of schism.

From that point on, physically taking over the Vatican would no longer be regarded as essential for a schismatic movement to establish its credibility. Indeed, after a while, it wouldn't even be necessary for a movement to set itself up as an offshoot of the Catholic Church to stay in business. Very soon, things like apostolic succession, the apostolate as an office, and their importance for a valid ministerial priesthood would, in short order, all cease to matter.

The time would soon come when, armed with a bible, anybody could start a ministry - namely, take upon oneself "the task not only of representing Christ, Head of the Church, before the assembly of the faithful, but also of acting in the name of the whole Church when presenting to God the prayer of the Church". Instead of being anathema, it would become fashionable, in the new Age of Enlightenment, to "start one's own ministry" - which would be synonymous with "founding one's own church"! And even bashing the "traditional" Church would begin to rate as a heroic "Christian" act.

Mjomba wrote that the flowering of these ministries or "churches", led by individuals who acted as virtual "popes" but preferred to call themselves "Apostle", "Pastor", "Prophet", "Prophetess", "Bishop" and things like that, while perhaps not the best thing, would have a good side to it. Thus, instead of just the one individual in the New Testament who was not one of the twelve but was going around casting out devils in the Deliverer's name all the same, there would be a countless number of such individuals to the consternation of the successors of the apostles!

Mjomba even supposed that the people setting up the churches - which would effectively be in competition with the One True Church founded by the Deliverer - by and large would be doing so in good faith. This would be the case even though they might be entirely misguided. But it would be an unanticipated development that the Church's hierarchy would try to ignore for a long time, according to Mjomba's thesis. Mjomba would explain during his oral defense of the thesis that it was not for him to say whether or not leaders of the new brand of ecclesiastical institutions in fact wielded power over the devil as they claimed, or whether the exorcisms were for real.

Mjomba also claimed that these developments would inevitably lead to a totally new approach to the study of the sacred scriptures by those who regarded them as the only source of revealed truth, and to completely new concepts of terms like "*ecclesia*", "*fides*", and even "commandment".

The upshot of all this was that the Church of modern times found that it had now to walk a tight rope. It could not condemn those Christians who operated outside its authority outright.

Condemnation would imply that they cease their activities and any good work they were doing. In any case, the alternatives for all those "Separated Brethren" who participated in good faith were imponderable.

And the Church could not openly endorse them either, even though it had an obligation to "bear witness to Christ together with all Christians of every church and ecclesiastical community". Because endorsement would undermine its own authority, it was out of question. The historical rivalries between these groups and the Church did not help the situation; and much less the scandals, past and present, perpetrated by individuals in positions of leadership in the Church.

Mjomba wrote that while the scriptures and tradition attested to the fact that the Church, under the leadership of the Pontiff of Rome, derived its authority directly from the Deliverer, the fact that it had succeeded in weathering what often looked like insurmountable obstacles since its inception, including internal scandals, also constituted additional and rather compelling evidence in support of that contention.

Mjomba hoped and prayed that his own thesis would never embarrass the Church in anyway. And by "Church" he meant the *Mystical Body of Christ*, not just those other people in leadership positions who frequently did not have the interests of the Church at heart. Again, rather naively, he dreamed - quite often as a matter of fact - that his thesis would be a special instrument of God's grace by which thousands of souls in far flung places would come to know that He loved them.

Mjomba wrote that all he himself was doing, anyway, was attempt to apply what he dubbed the "Mjomba Method" (as opposed to the Scholastic Method) to the matter at hand, and then compare the results to the conclusions in Thomas Aquinas's Summa Theologiae. This was even though he himself didn't have any clue as to what the words "the Mjomba Method" which kept recurring throughout his thesis meant.

His point nonetheless was that, while engaged in that "speculative" exercise, he did not regard himself as a spokesperson for the Church, but as a scholar who, theoretically, could end up having it all wrong! He, for his part, would be more than satisfied if his "thesis" became required reading in seminaries so students could dissect it and proceed, with the help of their professors, to shoot as many holes in it as they could. And this, even though his thesis read like some fairy tale and did not bear the slightest resemblance to an academic paper.

But, like any other naive seminarian who was beginning to delve in the mysteries of theology, Mjomba was also dreaming that his thesis might one day become the standard companion to the Holy Bible - or something close to that! He could not imagine a neater way of "raking in souls", as he liked to put it, than writing a thesis that would challenge the minds of its readers and lead them, at their own pace, to the truth - and especially since the harvest was ripe.

After that diversion, Mjomba continued that, since there could really be only one Prime Mover, you would not expect to find opposing groups of humans (all of whom belonged to the specie known as *animal rationale*) locked in mortal combat with each group simultaneously proclaiming that it was doing the bidding of the Prime Mover! It was also very unrealistic, Mjomba wrote, to expect members of the feuding groups to heed the invitation to be one with the Deliverer and High Priest unless and until they were reconciled to each other!

As it was, people of different faiths were locked in mortal combat with each group asserting that it was the true religion. And they were, of course, far from being reconciled to one another. It was a situation that was really strange, and which also said plenty about the legacy of original sin, Mjomba wrote.

Murderous humans...

Mjomba suggested that just as a certain breed of whales had earned the title "killer whales" and a certain breed of bees had earned the title "killer bees", humans had definitely earned for themselves the title of "Killer Humans"! He added that some humans, after making it their business throughout their lives to make the lives of others a living hell - and after being accustomed (almost as a practical joke) to killing or otherwise curtailing the civil liberties of those they chose to dislike - became the most vocal in decrying the "absence of justice" when the tables became turned and they suddenly found themselves at the receiving end.

Noting that the lower beasts killed to survive, Mjomba wrote that, with a few exceptions, humans essentially killed for the fun of it, there being no good reason for it; but, unlike beasts, they even slaughtered their own. Mjomba theorized that those humans who saw nothing wrong with terrorizing and slaughtering their own did so because they thought that they felt they were - as he put it - "more equal than others".

He explained that while it appeared on the surface as if the murderous conduct was motivated by feelings of superiority, what drove people to harm others was actually the opposite, namely an inferiority complex. And it seemed to go hand in hand with stupidity, because, according to Mjomba, murderers thought that some human lives were worth more than others! Mjomba accordingly regarded anyone who promoted things like apartheid, racism discrimination on any grounds as potential murderers.

The fact that humans, like other earthly creatures, had but one lease of life whilst here on earth was one reason murderous conduct was so despicable, according to Mjomba. But it was also abhorrent because intentionally cutting short the life of another human in this world represented an attempt to thwart the divine plan and interfere with Providence.

The taking of a life was the height of what Mjomba called pretence - pretence to having mastery over everything in the universe including life. He argued that it was pretence because if they had power over life, they would also have power over death - the power to restore life - be it their own life or that of other humans - after they had done away with it.

Mjomba quipped that the life he was referring to was not even the everlasting life with which humans had an appointment in the after-life. It was just the mortal earthly life or the pep of a human body while it was still capable of being informed by the indiscernible spiritual essence or soul. He hypothesized that they were in fact incapable of restoring it for the simple reason that, in so far as their own existence on earth was concerned, they themselves were essentially on life-support that could be removed at any time at the Prime Mover's pleasure, and would, indeed, be removed in due course!

The one thing they were really good at was to rationalize away personal responsibility in each and every individual instance in which they committed murder; and it was in the exact same way in which they rationalized away their responsibility when they chose to be irresponsible by misusing their rights and privileges, Mjomba wrote.

The Deliverer's admonition to humans that they should not fear those that can destroy the body but the Judge who can cast the soul of the wayward into hell represented not only a powerful rebuke to those who played roles in dispatching fellow humans to their premature demise but constituted at one and the same time what Mjomba described as indescribable words of consolation for the hapless victims.

Mjomba went out of his way to emphasize what he meant by "playing a role" in the taking of a life. He did not just mean the part played by the executioner. In his view, a string of people were culpable - those individuals who inspired the evil deed at its inception; and all those who subsequently facilitated it by their deed or omission; those who acted as cheer leaders while the evil deed was being perpetrated; and also those who could have done something to halt the evil act, but decided, for one reason or another, to play it safe and look the other way. Also included in the censure were those who sanctioned or participated in the acts of revenge; because, according to Mjomba, the Deliverer's injunction that humans leave revenge to the Prime Mover was very clear and unequivocal.

Mjomba wrote that humans were enjoined by the Deliverer, and constantly reminded by those who were called by Him to be His apostles, to pray for their persecutors. Mjomba commented that even then, the act of "praying" for enemies itself often amounted to a disingenuous expression of contempt directed at the offending party. Hardly what the Deliverer had in mind. But also not surprising, since it was not just the upright or spotless that were exposed to harassment and persecution, but those who belonged to what the Deliverer termed "this sinful generation" as well!

Before commenting on that last category, which according to him, pretty well encompassed everybody with the exception of the Deliverer Himself, His blessed mother whose conception was immaculate and not tainted by original sin, and those counted by the Deliverer (and subsequently by the Church he founded and authorised to continue His work here on earth) among the Innocents, Mjomba compared the abuse of prayer in that manner to the undisguised clamor for justice by those humans who were bent on revenge.

Curious as to whether mockery of something as hallowed as prayer was more or less odious in the eyes of the Prime Mover than the eagerness of many in society, particularly folks who had lost loved ones at the hands of criminal elements, to see the perpetrators made quick work of at the guillotine, in the electric chair, or in the gas chamber, Mjomba started the laborious task of tabulating the pros and cons. As he did so, he could not help noting that, odious as it was, making a mockery of prayer was infinitely worse than making a mockery of the concept of the church.

Mjomba, however, abandoned the exercise not long after, when it became clear that there was no significant difference between the two positions. But by that time it was also obvious that those two positions (the position of the prayerful hypocrite and that of the death penalty advocates) entailed deeply ingrained attitudes that, quite conceivably, were more difficult to uproot than the shortcomings of the prime offenders who were waiting in line for execution.

More often than not, those shortcomings, according to Mjomba, had their origins in habitual deprivation and institutionalised social injustice, and were in that sense the product of the very society that now sought, for obvious reasons, to dissociate itself from them.

The similarities to the case of the good thief who had been condemned to die on Mt. Calvary alongside the Deliverer were so evident they really could not just be dismissed as contrived, Mjomba wrote; adding that it was also a very sad commentary on modern society that has always generally favored things like the death penalty over mercy, the incarceration of so-called criminals over treatment and/or rehabilitation. According to Mjomba, the fact that the so-called "criminals" in many cases were either the victims of profiling so-called, or people who, because of their social circumstances, had automatically been denied due process that was available only to the moneyed made the situation more not less lamentable.

Obstacle race...

Touching on a subject he would return to on numerous occasions in his thesis, Mjomba wrote that doing anything right in the aftermath of the Fall of Adam and Eve from grace seemed patently elusive for humans in general; and he added that any claims to the contrary, if divine grace was excluded from the picture, were decidedly vain. He went on that there was little doubt that, left to their own devices, humans were inclined to sin as opposed to doing what was honorable.

Human nature had obviously been corrupted to at least that extent by the temporary, but nonetheless serious and wholly inexcusable, lapse in judgement of humankind's first couple. But that ill-omened disposition, far from forming grounds for absolving humans from the obligation to uphold honesty and virtue in the highest regard and from keeping the ten commandments in the process, had only caused the Deliverer to remind us that it was not those who hailed Him constantly as their Lord who would be saved, but those who did His bidding.

Mjomba noted in passing that it would have been a chaotic situation indeed if no Redeemer had come to the rescue of humans in the wake of the rebellion of Adam and Eve. Instead of throwing up their arms in utter despair, humans - all humans, including the compatriots of Noah who had not been able to get aboard the arch and had perished in the flood - could now brag that their brother and Deliverer, who was none other than the Word-become-flesh, was seated at the right hand of God the Father. They could also take comfort from the fact that all their concerns were known to the Father who was determined to see them through their hazardous passage on earth in as much as He was determined to ensure the well-being of birds of the air. They could likewise take solace from the fact that all that was required of them now was to become like little children. On shedding their egotism and the trappings of power in that second childhood, humans would not only be relatively safe from the wiles of the devil, but they would be in a position to enjoy a fresh start in which compliance with the intimations of divine grace would be possible once again.

For those with truly forgiving hearts, Mjomba continued, the wrongs they suffered at the hands of fellow humans were akin to obstacles or hurdles in an obstacle race. Without them, the race would cease being what it was supposed to be - an obstacle race. And these being obstacle races in which the individual contestants were pitted against themselves, when the outlines of the white finish line loomed in the distance as the race neared its conclusion, that also marked the time for receiving the medallions and for the induction into halls of fame for the victorious on being ushered into the appropriate mansion in heaven. Which was not to say that the obstacle races were not trying, Mjomba wrote. For if they were not, the scriptures would not have contained any references to dire times that befell the Lord's people from time to time, or to the fact that the Lord was moved by the sight of human sufferings.

Mjomba conceded that there were indeed times when the obstacle races were more than just obstacle races - when the contestant, even though entirely innocent, appeared to be provoking a party or parties for whom things like consciences and natural justice did not appear to have any meaning. In the event, the contestant's life, according to Mjomba, frequently became transformed into a veritable nightmare, or even a living hell with no place to run; and with a tight noose as it were in place around his or her neck, so that any natural defensive move only made the already perilous situation that much more hazardous. Mjomba went on that it was precisely in the midst of situations of this type that, defenseless and utterly helpless, miraculous solutions came to the rescue; often turning the most hopeless predicament into one that was full of renewed hope for the contestant and, frequently also, the contestant's oppressor.

In a move that smacked of back-peddling, Mjomba went on that it was not just the innocent or the so-called men and women of good will who suffered in that particular manner and were then rescued and rewarded by the Deliverer; but everybody, including the perpetrators of injustice.

It would come as a surprise to Mjomba during his oral defense of the thesis that this was one of the positions that came under attack from all corners, and which he found himself having to defend with extra care. His response to the criticism that sinners could not possibly be in line for such undeserved largess was that the Deliverer had come so that Adam and Eve, and all their descendants without a single exception, "might have eternal life". The Deliverer being the New Adam, no member of the human race, provided he or she played his or her part, could be precluded from getting his or her share of the inheritance he merited with His death on the tree.

Clearly no individual, not even the most reprehensible - and not even Judas who kissed the Deliverer on the cheek to signal to the High Priests and the Sadducees that they could finally pounce on their man - was about to be discriminated against; and certainly not by Him who was not only the Word who became flesh, but the Word through whom all things were made. A true brother of mankind who had sacrificed Himself so we could be welcomed back in our Father's household like the prodigal children we were, He was not about to be the one to break His word, and discriminate against some of His fellow humans on any grounds. And it was imperative, Mjomba wrote, that humans took the cue from this - the reason the Deliverer could not discriminate was not because He was a "good human". It was because He was divine.

It was not in dispute, on the other hand, that humans, exercising their free will or freedom to choose, could decide on their own, to reject the offer - just like that servant in one of the New Testament parables who was disgusted that he had been given only one talent and who accordingly decided to bury it, saying "Bye, Bye" to his inheritance thereby.

As far as the Deliverer was concerned, all of His fellow human brothers and sisters were eligible for a piece of the hard-won inheritance. But, in everything He did, He did not look like the sort of character who could turn around on an impulse and begin practising any kind of apartheid - and this especially after He had earned the right to sit at the right hand of the Prime Mover by spilling His precious blood. Mjomba had accordingly suggested that even hardcore sinners were liable to be visited by calamities only to be rescued and rewarded in the exact same way those who were not as reprehensible were permitted to suffer before being rescued and rewarded. Indeed, if not sinners, who else? It was, after all, sinners whom He came to save, not those who were justified!

Later, during his oral defense of the thesis, Mjomba would comment that one of the legacies of original sin was the perennial tendency of humans to never see evil in themselves, and to see nothing good in other humans - especially those who were different from themselves in some respect. Humans, with the exception of the Deliverer and His blessed mother Mary, seemed incapable of seeing the sometimes glaring and all too noticeable moles in their own eyes, but were invariably bothered by the tiniest specs in other peoples' eyes, according to him.

Intercession of the ancestral spirits...

Talking about the faults of others, Mjomba had never stopped being amazed by the ridiculous labels that Westerners were always so eager to use when describing the cultural traditions of non-Westerners, and by the offhand way in which they downplayed the negative aspects of their own customs and traditions. In the course of defending his thesis, Mjomba caused eyebrows to be raised with his suggestion that the

Church hierarchy was wrong in labeling the symbolic actions that traditionalists in African societies used to give expression to the respect they believed their ancestors were due as "ancestral spirit worship" and "animism", and in dismissing those long established and also deeply cherished customs and traditions as evil and satanic.

Mjomba commented that there were some in African societies who exploited the fact that the spirits of ancestors were capable of interceding with the Prime Mover on behalf of the living in good as well as in hard times for their own personal gain, and others who were driven by their scrupulosity to expect what amounted to miracles from such intercession. But such actions were really no different from the actions of many in Christendom who exploited religion for their own personal gain or were driven by their scrupulosity to engage in excesses, or to wallow in activities that were "unorthodox". Mjomba argued that, if the actions of fringe groups in Christendom did not justify the rejection of Christianity *carte blanche* by its critics, similarly the actions of extremists in traditional African societies did not constitute a valid reason for the wholesale condemnation of African customs and traditions by any member of the Church's hierarchy.

What, after all, was wrong with the practice of asking the spirits of ancestors, particularly those who had been noted for their outstanding contributions in strengthening the moral fibre of members of the community and ensuring that the youth in society grew up physically and spiritually healthy, and unsullied by moral degradation of any kind, for their intercession with the Prime Mover! Or...with seeking to make amends and peace with the Divinity, regardless of the language used to describe Him. And what about the Catholic practice, now codified into Canon law, which requires that two miracles, attributed to the intercession of its candidates for sainthood, must be performed and recognized by the Sacred Congregation of Rites as a condition for the canonization of the candidate by the Pontiff of Rome! Mjomba argued that anyone who found fault with Africans for acknowledging that their ancestors, even though long dead and buried, still live on in their afterlife was therefore either a monumental ignoramus or a racist or both!

And if the only people who went to heaven were members of the "Visible Church" as the prejudiced views of many a Westerner implied, and if it was a waste of time for Africans to seek their ancestors' intercession with Mungu, Mulungu, Ngai, Olodumare, Asis, Ruwa, Ruhanga, Jok, Modimo, Unkulunkulu, Nyamuhanga, Imana, Katonda, Chi, Ngewo-Wa, Rugaba, Njambi, Wele (also known as Khakhabaisaywa), Qamata (also known as Quamta), Fa, Sakarabru, Omumborombonga, Bumba (also known as Mbombo), Waaqa (also known as Waaqa-Tokkichaa), Ngai, Tsui-Goab (also known as Dxui), Abassi, etc. then the Deliverer's mission of redemption was far from the success the Church's own Catechism trumpeted.

Mjomba wrote that Lazarus, walking tall among his compatriots in Bethany - some of whom had probably already written him off as history as is common in the West after someone passes on - was a living testament to the fact that the spirits of the dead remained very much alive even after the individuals had "passed on". It was, accordingly, imperative that the spirits of ancestors were accorded the full respect that was due to them, he went on, adding that his African ancestors, in league with St. Peter, would in all likelihood demand an apology from Westerners who derided the reverence accorded to the spirits of ancestors on that continent as "witchcraft' before they let them through the gates of heaven!

By causing the "dead" Lazarus - whose body had already started the process of returning to the dust from whence it came - to walk and get about again and interact with the living, the Deliverer and Author of Life himself let it be known that once in existence, humans, among whom He himself now also numbered, lived even in death, Mjomba wrote. And would He have raised a beast from the dead, asked Mjomba? He likely would not because, according to Mjomba, when the lower creatures died, unlike humans, they actually died and passed on in the real sense.

Mjomba supposed that the reason the Deliverer, who knew that Lazarus was mortally ill and "dying", did not appear to be in a hurry to get to Bethany was the fact that "death" was the gateway to the real life - the lasting, or even more appropriately, the everlasting, life! Thus, long before the "advent" of missionaries, the "Animists" recognized that there was such a thing as heaven - the place where "life" actually originated and where it was eternal - things that Westerners apparently found hard to accept even after the Deliverer and Author of Life had Himself come down from heaven, Mjomba asserted.

According to Mjomba's thesis, by allowing Lazarus to pick up where he had left off during his sojourn on earth, the Deliverer provided the best evidence yet that "death", which represented the wages of sin, was suddenly on the verge of losing its sting. But it also went to reinforce the fact that spiritual man, unlike the common beasts of the earth, remained very much alive and kicking even after the human body lost its capacity to sustain the soul. During the oral defense of the thesis, Mjomba emphasized that the problem at death was not the spirit - which just "went matching on" as he put it - but the body which ceased to be a suitable abode for the soul or whatever different people liked to call it.

Noting that the practices of worshipping idols carved by humans hands out of stone which distinguished ancient Rome and Greece from other centers of civilization of the time was the lowest humans could go in denying the Prime Mover His rightful place in the universe, Mjomba caused even more raised eyebrows when he went on to suggest that the practice of making libations - in the course of which individuals in society were forced to part with poultry, domestic animals, brew and other valued property - likely had their origin in the old testament practice of making burnt offerings to the Prime Mover in line with His injunctions which were communicated to the world through messengers like Moses and other prophets.

Mjomba was himself quite surprised that his audience appeared confounded and speechless when he claimed that idolatrous practices in Western societies had crept into and been incorporated in "Christian traditions". His surprise stemmed from his belief that there was a lot of evidence to support that contention. Mjomba was also astonished that the Church's clergy showed such little interest in the fact that if a catechumen could not appreciate his or her own cultural traditions, his or her practice of Christianity likely would be empty at best and radically flawed at worst.

Mjomba was almost eaten alive when he said that there had to be something the matter with a system that recognised and held up for emulation the heroic deeds of Westerners almost exclusively, and for the most part ignored the forbearing, long suffering and valiant struggles of Russians, Japanese, Indians, Pakistanis, Indonesians, Chinese, and Africans amongst others! And he was nearly lynched when he added that it seemed unlikely that those "wrongs" would ever be righted because the system in place assured that the curia in Rome which played such an important role in determining trends in the Church's liturgy and in other areas of Church endeavour remained under the domination and control of the most conservative members of the Church's hierarchy.

The African "connection"...

In the short term, according to Mjomba, focusing on the negatives invariably seemed like the right thing to do, because the number of African converts usually picked up and church attendance, even though largely fuelled by sentimentality and sometimes curiosity, also rose. In the long run, however, because of being built on a shallow foundation which ignored the fact that African Christian men and women, like their Western brethren, needed to be healthy members of society who were proud of their heritage, these converts drifted away from the Church and carried on their search for ideologies that could satisfy their craving for spiritual as well as social needs.

But some ended up paying a very heavy price for allowing themselves to be persuaded to abandon their social roots. According to Mjomba, they ended up as rank materialists wallowing in excesses that would have been unthinkable if they had rebuffed the approaches of the missionaries and refused to be proselytized by those zealots among the Church's clergy in the first place. According to Mjomba's theory, when an individual lost his or her culture in whatever manner, his or her life and existence lost meaning, and that individual's craving for social and spiritual fulfilment easily translated into a craving for short term material pleasures. For Mjomba, it was completely unimaginable that the Church's clergy, whose job was to alleviate those types of situations, quite conceivably were having a principal role in precipitating them.

Referring to the journey Joseph and Mary made to Africa, home to the so-called Animists, and also the home of the pyramids which the Egyptian pharaohs built as an eternal monument to humans who had already made the transition to the afterlife, Mjomba suggested that the holy family's visit had more to it than just to escape from Herod Agrippa. He wrote that the danger Herod posed to the Deliverer, while genuine, also provided Joseph and Mary the excuse to visit the continent that was home to the original Garden of Eden, and also to meet with those whose devotion to the afterlife and the celebration of animism - or, more appropriately, the human spirit - had never faltered throughout the ages.

This was after all the land of the pyramids - the unchallenged wonder of the world attributable to Man's ingenuity. Mjomba added that unlike other wonders of the world like the Acropolis which had been built as a monument to false gods, or the Roman amphitheatre where the most atrocious things took place in the name of sport, the pyramids had been built solely to honor those who, along with Adam and Eve, were in Gehenna awaiting deliverance by the promised Messiah from the clutches of death.

Joseph and Mary, Mjomba wrote, had made it their custom as a family to implore the inspiration and guidance of the Holy Spirit in whatever they did, and their flight into Egypt was no exception. It would have been very uncharacteristic of them to base their decisions on fear. And, in any case, the mother of the Deliverer and the man who had agreed to be their earthly guardian were not afraid of dying. The baby Jesus Himself wasn't aware of any danger. All he was aware of was the dedication of His blessed mother and of Joseph for His wellbeing and that of all humankind who lived under the shadow of death.

Encamped on the banks of the River Nile not far from the tall pyramids, Joseph and Mary could not help reflecting, as they drank of the waters of the Nile and used it to bathe the child Jesus, on the fact that they came all the way from the Mountains of the Moon on the Equator and site of the Garden of Eden and of creation. As Mary would explain to the child Jesus, the source of the Nile was also the place where Adam and Eve had lived and died, and also where Cain had visited death on his brother Abel in breach of the commandment that humans love their neighbors as themselves, and the Prime Mover above all else.

The child Jesus would also hear first-hand from Egyptian neighbors the folklore that went back many generations, and that had "little men from the land of trees and spirits", a place they had dubbed the "Cradle of Mankind" and which they also considered to be the source of the waters of the River Nile, to found the Egyptian civilization! As the folklore had it, the Pygmies from the "Mountains of the Moon" initially worshipped a God known as Bes, who nevertheless transformed in time to become the God of Gods in whose honor King Khufu built the Great Sphinx that was visible from their modest hamlet on the river's banks.

According to Mjomba's thesis, with life so hard and complicated, it wasn't surprising that there were things like the "dark night of the soul". Like Adam and Eve, humanity was after all still on trial. But, Mjomba went on, even though life could be really hard, for humans with forgiving hearts, all calamities were God-sent challenges regardless of whether the misfortunes befalling them were traceable to ill-intentioned acts of fellow humans or what he termed "acts of God".

Mjomba argued that they were God-sent in the exact same way the good things humans in their ignorance attributed to "good luck" were, because the primary purpose of adversities was to provide the Prime Mover a basis - or rather the excuse - to reward humans not just in a spectacular way but in a really extra-special way.

Mjomba would elaborate, during his oral defense of his thesis, that humans with a forgiving hearts and humans who were prepared to suffer martyrdom for their religious convictions were motivated by the same thing, namely the belief that their fate was in the hands of the Prime Mover. Wishing one's enemies well, including those responsible for cutting short one's existence on earth, on the one hand, and braving an uncertain future in this *Valley of Tears* where the pressures exerted to induce one to compromise his or her religious beliefs were immense, amounted to one and the same thing in Mjomba's view. Both actions, according to him, stemmed from acceptance of the fact that humans only needed to look to the Prime Mover for the fulfilment of all their needs, material and spiritual.

In the first of these situations, that acceptance translated in the recognition that the Prime Mover, having given the gift of existence to humans, also had the right to expect the recipients of that largess to exist or live as befitted their nature which was fashioned in His own image and likeness. And with regard to their earthly existence, the breath of life which made their bodies tick was something He had given humans under His divine plan, and it was also something He could take away at any time and in any manner He pleased.

Clearly, regardless of what it took, doing the will of the Prime Mover was not something that was negotiable between humans and the Prime Mover. The only hope they had of finding genuine fulfilment was carrying out that will. And hence the Deliverer's admonition that humans, among whom He now also numbered, take up their crosses and follow Him who not only was the Son of the Most High and the Word through whom everything, themselves included, were created, but also a human Brother whose Heart was the very epitome of forgiveness.

In the second situation, instead of the gift of life, it was the gift of faith or the invitation the Deliverer extended to humans that they sell all, give everything to the poor and follow Him. Humans responding to the invitation to leave everything and follow Him were in addition expected to be ready to face all sorts of inconveniences for His sake, including persecution. Acceptance of that invitation translated in the recognition that the Deliverer, anticipating that those who did His bidding would be rejected and in some cases even suffer martyrdom, was going to be there at all times to deliver them from the one and only thing they needed to fear, namely Gehenna or spiritual death. The bottom line in both situations was a readiness to follow in the Deliverer's footsteps.

Referring to life as a gift, Mjomba wrote that abuse of the gift of life and of the Prime Mover's other gifts to humans was sometimes on a scale that was so boggling to the imagination there were no words to describe it.

It was bad enough that the first thing humans tended to do, as they progressed from their original states of innocence, continence, virtue, modesty and decency, to a state of naiveté, feculence and artificiality, was to pretend that they had all the erudition and knowledge they needed for anything. That was clear from the unyielding attitudes and stubbornness that they exhibited around the time they committed their first serious misdeeds in life. On the evidence, humans had degenerated into a new breed that, for sure, was not normal. A weird breed! They were out of control and they bragged about it.

As an example, Mjomba cited the fact that outrageous violations of moral law and the law of natural justice continued to be committed even as those responsible for past violations of the same codes were being apprehended and brought to justice. Generations of evildoers succeeded other generations of evildoers so routinely, Mjomba wondered if humans were capable of learning from their own experience anymore!

Everybody is infallible...

Mjomba added that one of the weirdest things he had noticed about humans was the desire to show that everybody, not just the Pontiff of Rome, was infallible. Realising that someone had to be infallible for religion to be credible, everybody all of a sudden became infallible overnight. Even those who officially subscribed to Scepticism were certain that their tenets represented the only authentic system of belief! And, of course, all who doubted the doctrine of infallibility also did so infallibly!

If the problem was that someone had laid claim to being infallible, that problem had now been effectively compounded by those who thought they had found a solution. For everybody, without exception, now claimed to be infallible!

Mjomba devoted three entire pages of his one hundred and twenty or so page thesis to the relationship between the sacred scriptures - and specifically the New Testament - and the *Magisterium* or teaching authority of the Church as exercised by her since Pentecost Day on the one hand, and the relationship between the scriptures and the Deliverer's own personal witness on behalf of the Blessed Trinity. Mjomba started by noting that he himself was not particularly bothered by the fact that there were many religions and "churches"!

He would later defend that rather unorthodox position by arguing that, in the after-life, there were after all no "churches" there just as there were no state governments, empires, kingdoms, sultanates, chiefdoms, principalities, or even "households". There was after all no such a thing as the "Catholic Church"! But, as the Nicene Creed correctly put it, there was "one holy catholic and apostolic Church". Mjomba would also elaborate that "church" was a useful idea only to the extent to which it signified collective human efforts led by the individuals who could claim to be the authentic successors to the twelve apostles, and to the extent those efforts were devoted to the return of mankind to the fold as envisioned by the Deliverer; and, Mjomba would add, only to the extent those efforts were guided by the "Advocate" or Holy Spirit the Father sent down on the Day of Pentecost.

As far as Mjomba was concerned, "Church Triumphant" was really just another phrase for "heaven", the place where people of good will, drawn to their Maker in a variety of ways according to their circumstances by the graces merited by the Deliverer and Brother Human, became reunited with Him. And, while good folks, Israelites and non-Israelites, who passed on before they had an opportunity to be "baptised and become a part of the Pilgrim Church" technically were neither headed to heaven or hell, but "elsewhere" because the Deliverer (in the words of the catechism) has bound salvation to the sacrament of Baptism, the fact was that the Deliverer Himself was not bound by the sacraments He instituted; and He died for all humans; and all humans were called to one and the same divine destiny. But there was also the fact that the Deliverer was a member of the Godhead, and the ways of God were incomprehensible to humans. Therefore humans, according to Mjomba, could not but assume that all good folks in fact went to heaven.

It had to be supposed that they would have *desired* Baptism if they had known of its necessity (as well as membership in the one true Church if they had been in a position to obtain it). In fact Mjomba went as far as suggesting in his thesis that any human who regarded him/herself as saved, and who explicitly dared pronounce others as unsaved and damned, was probably guilty of presumption, and possibly also of pretending to understand the ways of the Prime Mover which were incomprehensible to men.

With the case of Cain who committed the first ever recorded murder, but subsequently repented and was now presumed to be in heaven, in mind, Mjomba was at first inclined to think that perhaps the case of the Deliverer's betrayer was similar. He even initially thought that it would amount to recklessness for any human to suggest that Judas, who died within hours of partaking of the body and blood of the Son of Man (as He referred to Himself) under the species of bread and wine at the hands of the Son of Man Himself,– the body that would be broken and the blood that would be poured forth on Calvary for the salvation of humans – and who was seemingly full of remorse when he put that noose around his neck in despair, was languishing in hell! Mjomba even supposed that everyone would be thinking the same about Cain if the scriptures had not expressly stated that he came round and not only regretted that "unforgivable" act, but explicitly sought the Prime Mover's forgiveness and went on to do penance for murdering his brother.

In the case of Judas, Matthew had written that after Judas, who had betrayed the Deliverer, saw that He was condemned, he (Judas) was seized with remorse and returned the thirty pieces of silver to the chief priests and the elders. "I have sinned in betraying innocent blood. But they said: What is that to us? look thou to it. And casting down the pieces of silver in the temple, he departed: and went and hanged himself with an halter." (Matthew 27:3-6)

After making that valiant effort at being magnanimous, Mjomba stepped back and begun wondering how anyone could construe the actions of the man who betrayed the Son of Man with a kiss as amounting to anything other than the pursuit of his own selfish ends while chucking aside the cross he was himself expected to take up and carry! The episode in which Judas is depicted as remorseful came after Judas had, with full knowledge and evil intent, colluded with the chief priests and the magistrates to thwart the ministry of the Miracle Worker behind His back as described by Luke: "And Satan entered into Judas, who was surnamed Iscariot, one of the twelve. And he went, and discoursed with the chief priests and the magistrates, how he might betray him to them. And they were glad, and covenanted to give him money. And he promised. And he sought opportunity to betray him in the absence of the multitude". (Luke 22: 3-6)

And so, there was Judas going off and hanging himself when his erstwhile friends and co-conspirators (the chief priests and ancients) let him know to his face that they were even more sleazy than he himself – that if he thought that he was capable of being "bad", they were capable of being even "badder" - and that he was really dumb to have hopped back into their presence with the blood money he had gotten from them in return for his "services"!

For anyone with a conscience, let alone someone who had had the privilege of calling the Miracle Worker "Master" over the period of three full years, and who not only witnessed all the miracles wrought by the Nazarene but who was also on hand as the promised Messiah taught the multitudes and counselled his would be disciples, and for someone who, above all, was not just one of the twelve specially chosen "apostles", but also drunk wine from the same cup as the Nazarene, the build-up of the events that followed the infamous betrayal of the Messiah of Mankind with a kiss and what followed – the kangaroo trial of the Miracle Worker before Annas, Caiaphas, and members of the Sanhedrin, followed by the events at the courts of Pontius Pilate and Herod Antipas, the scourging and the humiliation, and even the denial by Simon Peter, culminating in the crucifixion, death and the resurrection, and the aftermath of all of those events to which Judas was privy – constituted more than a betrayal. It wouldn't have been any different if that only son of Simon Iscariot and Cyborea Iscariot, a well to do family in Jericho, who had accepted the call to be one of the twelve apostles, had taken a kitchen knife and stuck it into the back of the Nazarene in broad daylight and then attempted to flee!

The Deliverer had cried out in a loud voice one more time before giving up his ghost, and the curtain of the temple was torn in two from top to bottom thereupon. The earth shook, the rocks split and the tombs broke open. Many bodies of the saints who had fallen asleep were raised to life. They came out of the tombs after the Deliverer's resurrection and went into the holy city and appeared to many people. (Matthew 27:50-53).

Mjomba had always been interested in the fact that the messages put out by the different religions and "churches" were contradictory in many respects; and he was very curious about the effect of that on the Deliverer's work of redemption. And it was this which led him to raise what, in his view, was a very fundamental question. The question pertained to the relative importance of the Messiah or Deliverer vis-à-vis the Church as an institution and along with it the Church's traditions dating back to the first day of its existence on the one hand, and also vis-à-vis the collection of the written testimony of the "saints" known as "Books of the New Testament" that, along with the Books of the Old Testament form what is known as the bible on the other.

It was pretty obvious, Mjomba wrote, that the personal witness of the Deliverer was the more important of the three, and that it would still have occupied that position even if the writings of the Old Testament by inspired writers, forecasting his coming, had not been available. And, what was more, it wasn't just a matter of the Deliverer being a witness to anything. As the Son of God who was sent to earth by His Father with a mission of reconciling humanity with the Creator, and who rose from the dead and was now seated at His Father's "right hand", He simply was in a class of His own.

Mjomba suggested that, in order of importance, the *ecclesia* or "church" which the Deliverer established on a "rock" came second. According to Mjomba, the Church was in all probability a close second, because it was somewhat difficult to distinguish the Church, defined as the Mystical Body of Christ, and what Mjomba referred to as the concomitant role of the Holy Ghost in it, from the Deliverer. Perhaps it even came down to semantics, Mjomba wrote, because of the continuous role played in it by the Deliverer both before and after its institution. And then, while it was the priesthood of the Deliverer in which those who ministered to the spiritual needs of the faithful shared, the Eucharistic presence inaugurated in the Upper House on the night before He laid down His life for humans left absolutely no doubt about the pre-eminence of the Church and its teachings over the bible. And that was not mentioning the role of sacramental grace in the life of the Church.

Mjomba wrote that the authors of the New and Old Testaments had as their guide the same Spirit that guided the *prophets* whose activities were recorded therein. In the case of the New Testament, the "prophet" was the Son of Man; and the writers, the evangelist John for example, acted with inspiration from "above", just as the prophets did. Mjomba supposed that it did not really matter if their inspiration actually originated from "above" or from their inner core where the Prime Mover dwelt, because that too was essentially semantics.

A critical aspect of the conversation relating to the scriptures, particularly for the majority of humans who did not have the privilege of being chosen and sent out to the world as the Prime Mover's special envoys or "prophets", was the role of the authority of the Church in determining whether the writings in question were inspired in the first place and also which ones. It was a responsibility that was one of many that were intrinsic to its evangelizing or teaching mission. And that mission was spelled out

by the Deliverer when He said to Peter: " על, אתה פיטר ‏
‏לבנות יהיה אני, סלע זה ס שלי הכסייה" (translated: *"You are Peter, and upon this rock, I will build my Church"*).

And, even though it was a church or institution that He was entrusting to the likes of Peter (a mortal erring human), it was still going to be an *ecclesia* church against which the gates of hell would never be able to prevail. And it was obviously "someone" who Himself had already prevailed against the powers of hell who could take that kind of action, and also make that sort of promise.

And may be it was not entirely coincidental that Peter was already on record as doing what was very close to the opposite of the role he was expected to play in the *Ecclesia* which the Deliverer was establishing, namely making moves to stop the Deliverer from proceeding to Jerusalem and his ignominious death. Not long after, Peter would maim and nearly kill a member of the militia that the high priest, Joseph ben Caiaphas, had dispatched to arrest the Deliverer and his devotees, slicing off the man's ear. That was because he (Peter) was slow in accepting that, even though the Deliverer had come to earth in fulfillment of the scriptures, His kingdom was not going to be of this world.

And, indeed, when push came to shove, Peter would act exactly like the Israelites who had walked away from the Deliverer when they heard Him state that His flesh was food indeed, and His blood drink indeed, and that He was inviting all His disciples to feast on them! Id'd by the alert page (who herself was clearly one of the breakaway members of the emerging "Christ Fellowship"), Peter would promptly and completely forget his own earlier avowals to the effect that the man who had been apprehended and was now being arraigned on the serious charge of declaring to the world that he was the Messiah the Israelites and the rest of mankind had been waiting for was what He claimed to be. He would disown the Messiah of the world in the clearest terms.

There, in the courtyard of the high priest's residence where the Deliverer was taken after being apprehended, an alert servant girl would recognise Peter as a confidante of the self-proclaimed Messiah of the Jews in the firelight and, after looking at him intently, venture: "This man was with him." Obviously caught off guard, the fisherman's response simply went: "Woman, I don't know him." And when a little later someone else saw him and said, "You also are one of them", a totally flabbergasted and also flustered Peter would reply: "Man, I am not!" But, then, an hour or so later another bystander would assert: "Certainly this fellow was with him, for he is a Galilean." Peter knew by then that Providence clearly wasn't treating him kindly at all now. He saw that there wasn't going to be any escape route given the cavalcade of witnesses to his dalliance with the Nazarene. A mere fisherman, there was no way he, Simon Peter, was going to be able to stand up to the priests and Pharisees - certainly not after they had the Nazarene in chains and were clearly determined to do away with Him.

Peter had, of course, witnessed the innumerable miracles and acts of wonder wrought by the Nazarene; and, like everyone else who was there in Bethany when the Deliverer got Lazarus to come back to life and pick up where he had left off, his awe at the Nazarene's power over death was real. But in the last analysis he was a simple man and a fisherman at that who had been brought up to look to the priests and Pharisees for guidance not just in matters of the spiritual, but in all matters pertaining to the destiny of Israel as the chosen race.

Peter was at wit's end; and, like someone who was about to lose his mind, he had replied: "Man, I don't know what you're talking about!" And, of course, just as he was speaking, the rooster had crowed. And to make things worse, the Son of Man, whom Peter as the first Pontiff would quote ever so many times in the years following that episode as he labored away in the fields that were ripe for the harvest, now turned and looked straight at him (Peter).

The "unforeseen chain of events" that occurred in front of the crowd that included Jerusalem's press corps actually wasn't quite so unforeseen. Not long before, after the Deliverer had inaugurated the Sacrament of the Eucharist, He had said to the twelve: "All you shall be scandalized in me this night. For it is written: I will strike the shepherd, and the sheep of the flock shall be dispersed. But after I shall be risen again, I will go before you into Galilee." Peter, answering, had said to the Nazarene: "Although all shall be scandalized in thee, I will never be scandalized." The Deliverer must have had the sins of all frail mortals in mind and the Prime Mover's response to all human acts of betrayal, when he said to Peter: "Amen I say to thee, that in this night before the cock crow, thou wilt deny me thrice." Peter, representing all sinful and sinning humans, then saith to Him (as described in Mark 14:27-31, Luke 22:31-38, John 13:36-38 and Matthew 26: 31-35): "Yea, though I should die with thee, I will not deny thee."

The "Logos" through Whom all things were made and without Whom was made nothing that was made, and in Whom was life - the life that was the light of men, the light that shineth in darkness, and the darkness did not comprehend it (John 1:3-5) – must have addressed those words to Peter in the same vein in which He would address the throng of women, who would bewail and lament Him as He bore His cross on the road to Mt. Calvary with the words: *"Filiae Hierusalem nolite flere super me sed super vos ipsas flete et super filios vestros quoniam ecce venient dies in quibus dicent beatae steriles et ventres qui non genuerunt et ubera quae non lactaverunt tunc incipient dicere montibus cadite super nos et collibus operite nos quia si in viridi ligno haec faciunt in arido quid fiet."* (Daughters of Jerusalem, weep not over me; but weep for yourselves, and for your children. For behold, the days shall come, wherein they will say: Blessed are the barren, and the wombs that have not borne, and the paps that have not given suck. Then shall they begin to say to the mountains: Fall upon us. And to the hills: Cover us. For if in the green wood they do these things, what shall be done in the dry?) (Luke 23:27-29)

Following in the example of those who had opted to go back to their old ways and continue living out their lives the way they had been doing before, he (Peter), also nicknamed the Rock by the Deliverer, had in that moment essentially quit the fellowship or the *Ecclesia* the Deliverer was in the process of launching. Caught in between a rock and a hard place, Peter now flatly averred that he too had already cut off all his links to the Nazarene in the same manner that so many other Judeans and Galileans (who presumably had been initially tricked by the smooth speaking Nazarene into becoming His devotees or disciples) had done. Hopelessly cornered and desperate, there was nothing the fisherman wanted more than to be left alone. But now, unable to avoid the gaze of the Nazarene, Peter remembered the words of the Lord: "Before the cock crow, thou shalt deny thrice!" Peter knew with unwavering certainty that his desire to be left alone was not going to be granted; and, going out, he wept bitterly. (Luke 22:54-62; Matthew 26:69-75; Mark 14:66-72; and John 18:15-18).

While stressing that the importance of these writings could nonetheless not be downplayed, Mjomba thought it was noteworthy that the writings of the Old Testament, while loaded with prophecies relating to the Deliverer, did not forecast that there would be authoritative books of the New Testament to guide those who would choose to follow in the footsteps of the Deliverer.

It was also noteworthy that even though the Deliverer Himself made numerous references to divine promises contained in the Old Testament, He apparently did not make any direct reference to the authoritative body of writings that we now know as the New Testament; and it was nowhere on record that He ever suggested that this authoritative body of writings would replace Him or, for that matter, His Church as the sole authoritative source of the message of redemption upon His ascension into heaven. Mjomba suggested that even if the Deliverer had personally made some reference to the forthcoming books of the New Testament, it would be difficult to imagine that He would subordinate the Church he had established (and metaphorically constructed on the rock by the name of Peter) to the writings in question, regardless of their importance.

Mjomba had no doubt that the collection of inspired writings, which came into existence after the Deliverer ascended into heaven, derived their authority from the Church. The fathers of the early Church - including the apostles - evidently understood that committing something to *writing* was an accepted and certainly practical way of preserving and passing on to believers in distant lands and also to future generations the teachings of the Deliverer. And a lot of the material they *passed* on to Mjomba's own generation was corroborated by historians of the time. But it obviously needed the Church to authoritatively declare through its hierarchy that what was being passed on was not just authentic, but produced *under inspiration*.

Mjomba consequently argued that statements like "the Bible says", "the Church says" or "the Deliverer says" had to be seen in relation to each other, and that there was no logic to the idea that the bible could contradict the Church or vice versa. Certainly, the Church established by the Deliverer could not contradict Him and still remain His Church. And the books of the New Testament, which could not have been written if there had not been an institution established by the Deliverer and informed by the Spirit in accordance with the will of the Prime Mover, not only had to be jealously guarded by "the Church" but could not possibly contradict the Church's teachings and vice versa.

While orally defending his thesis in that regard, Mjomba asserted that the bible did not write itself and, having no legs or wings, did not go hopping or flying around on its own on evangelizing missions. The bible was, in his words, "the fruit of human labor that was performed under the guidance and with the blessing of the Holy Ghost, the laborers being folks like Peter, James, John, Matthew, and Mark whom the Deliverer had personally tasked to go out and be fishers of men, Luke who was an operative of the infant Church and a confidant of Mary, the blessed mother of the Deliverer, and others like Paul and Timothy who had been inducted into the ministry with the laying on of hands by the original apostles".

The bible, Mjomba added, did not - could not - authenticate itself and much less interpret itself; and that there was no way in which any entity outside the Church that the Deliverer had established could certify books of the bible as being authentic or guarantee the correct interpretation of books of the New Testament or even the Old Testament. In other words, the books of the New Testament, inspired by the Holy Ghost, were the work of a Church - the Mystical Body of the Deliverer - that had been established by the Second Person of the Blessed Trinity and was informed and sustained by the Third Person of the same Holy Trinity.

That infant Church, established on the equivalent of a rock (*tu es Petrus, et super hanc petram, ecclesiam meam edificabo*), and informed by the Holy Ghost at the behest of the risen Christ, was an outfit that had nothing in common with the scores of so-called "churches" or "ministries" that had been started by misguided humans, and whose existence was such a salient reminder of the frailty and fickleness of the poor, forsaken descendants of Adam and Eve.

But, according to Mjomba, the existence of these churches or ministries was by no means the only problem that the Church had anticipated facing. The Church of the Deliverer had anticipated facing other problems as well. There was the fact that Peter - poor Peter - had denied his Master three times within the space of an hour despite having solemnly sworn that he could never do anything like that. And then there was Paul, the self-styled "Apostle of the Gentiles", who had participated in the murders of followers of the Deliverer before he was called to join the band of apostles, and who was probably shirked by some members of the Christian community to the end!

Mjomba wrote that the Church had major problems from Day One - problems that would have crippled it were it not for the manifestly critical role played in it by the Holy Ghost. Those problems, he asserted, did not go away. He went on that the work of the Holy Ghost was still at play centuries later when members of the Church's clergy, who should have extolled virtues of St. Joan of Arc and others like her, turned on them and murdered them! Mjomba had no doubt whatsoever in his mind that Methodists, Baptists, Calvinists, and others outside the "Church" had suffered "martyrdom", just like Joan of Arc, at the hands of the Church's operatives! But can it really surprise anyone in this God-forsaken-world that many "churchmen" who should have shown that they indeed were the salt of the earth, like Judas, hadn't lived up to expectations?

But an even bigger problem faced by the Church would be acceptance, and the Deliverer had accordingly warned his "workers" that they would occasionally have to dust the dust they picked up along their route as they entered some cities from their feet and move on because there would be no one there prepared to listen. The "Comforter" therefore had His work cut out for Him from the very beginning, and His work of necessity would start with

210

those who, like poor Peter and poor Paul, would be called to be "other Christs" or apostles.

How the Holy Ghost would remain in the business of saving souls in those types of situations would obviously remain a mystery - as would also the particular manner in which He worked with the frail humans He selected to be vessels of grace. Mjomba wrote that he was quite fascinated by the fact that Peter, Paul and other mortals who were struggling to remain afloat themselves and not sink under the load of their own sins (as Ananias of the Acts of the apostles did), were out there preaching to crowds that included thieves, murderers, and what have you!

Some of those who had murdered would not be content until they had sought out and found "clergy" who could stand by them as they publicly thanked the Prime Mover for their murderous exploits! Then, the crowds they preached to would also include people who would have no scruples in turning the good news and the word of the Prime Mover as it was expressed in the bible into profitable ventures in the worldly sense.

And in the meantime Diabolos, equipped with the knowledge that the apostles themselves, however holy, would (as the Church itself taught) remain exposed to his temptations until the time when their trial on earth came to an end and the results of their performance on the Church Triumphant Entrance Test (or CTET) were called in, would not just be there *observing* the proceedings idly from a distance. According to Mjomba, Satan had to be working overtime - a lot of it and with a lot of success no doubt - to create as much confusion as possible.

There was ample evidence that the devil had actually "struck back" viciously and with surprising success, even though he could only hurt the Church by enlisting the help of humans, Mjomba wrote. And Mjomba readily admitted that as someone who "committed sin seventy times seven times a day", he could not exclude himself from those who were subject to manipulation by the notorious Diabolos. He had indeed admitted as much when he wrote that he might be getting ideas or inspiration from the devil for his thesis!

And besides, here he was, suggesting in his thesis - despite everything he had said or would say about membership in the "invisible Church" or Mystical Body of the Deliverer and the Church Triumphant Entrance Test (or CTET) that everyone, Catholics included, had to pass to gain eternal life - that the devil had a hand in the formation of the splinter Christian churches! And he was making that suggestion at a time when, increasingly, representatives of those churches were themselves openly suggesting that the Catholic Church headed by Peter's successor, was the work of Satan! The evidence for that "outrageous" claim included the Church's use or (as they characterized it) abuse of icons of the Deliverer and the saints, icons that it employed as aids in religious instruction.

Challenged by a fellow student when he was orally defending his thesis in front of a panel of professors, Mjomba would respond that the "arguments" of the Church's adversaries both inside and outside it were really self-defeating, adding that they claimed to be knowledgeable about the "Word of God" after "studying" the sacred scriptures and then having a go at "interpreting" them from scratch and "correctly" while ignoring the institution that was the guardian of the self-same. According to Mjomba, those people "forgot" that it was not just the pictures and statues that were icons, but church buildings and even the "Church" itself were all icons that were not to be desecrated.

The same in fact went for the Deliverer's body and sacred blood, the cross on which he suffered and died, and the Shroud of Turin provided it was not a fake. After all some of the sick who touched the garments worn by the Deliverer received healing (even though it was because of their faith in Him and not so much because they had reached out and touched His cloak). And they also forgot that the book they waived about and on which they "relied" to attack the Church - the "bible" - was also an "icon"!

Mjomba asked if these people learned anything from the account in the gospels describing an irate Deliverer chasing merchants out of the temple in Jerusalem even though it was only weeks away if not days before the veil in the Holy of Holies was going to be torn asunder, signifying the fulfilment of the Prime Mover's covenant with Adam and Moses, and start of a New Order based on a new covenant. That "incident" in the temple was pregnant with meaning, according to Mjomba. Even though mere icons, the temple, churches, and other visual representations of the sacred and the divine such as pictures of the cross and pictures of saints, just like the Deliverer's own body before and after His resurrection, had a very important place in spiritual life and could not be belittled.

Mjomba also read something else from that incident in the temple in Jerusalem - the earthly Jerusalem, and it was that the Deliverer was prepared to openly and in front of witnesses cut off His relationship with any individual who had the audacity to use His Church for doing business or commerce. While this applied to those who took advantage of people's ignorance to misuse religious icons, it obviously applied even more to those who were prepared to challenge the authority of the Church in which He had invested so much. Just as He picked up a stick and chased the merchants out of "his Father's house", there was no doubt whatsoever that he would deal similarly with anyone who dared to employ His Church for conducting commerce.

It was Mjomba's view that, used in conjunction with the Deliverer's other promises to the apostles at their "ordination" - that he would send down the Holy Ghost upon them and that whatever they decided to keep bound or to loosen on earth it would be bound or loosened in heaven - the Deliverer's action on that occasion provided justification for the Church's actions in keeping out or excommunicating individuals from the "visible" Church.

Another lesson, according to Mjomba, was that you were free to bash the Church as much as you liked by attributing to it all manner of evil, but only up to a limit if you wanted to remain connected to the Mystical Body of Christ. And that, just like the body of the Deliverer (which was informed by the Holy Ghost and was effectively a temple or house of His Father), no amount of bashing or assault on the Church (which was also informed by the Holy Ghost) would ever prevail against it in the final analysis.

The final lesson, according to Mjomba, was that the Triune Divinity comprising the Prime Mover, the Word and also Deliverer, and the Holy Ghost and also Comforter, operated in mysterious ways. That being the case, appearances were very misleading, and what seemed impossible to man was not impossible for the Omnipotent One. It would, in any event, be naive to think that someone wanting to become a follower of the Deliverer and a member of the Church the Deliverer commissioned to take the message of salvation to the ends of the earth wouldn't be scandalized by that state of affairs.

Mjomba supposed that there wasn't anything that could be more thrilling to Diabolos than a situation in which members of the Mystical Body of the Deliverer referred to each other as lackeys of the Evil One in the same breath in which they said they were fulfilling the Deliverer's sacred mission of evangelization.

Mjomba noted that, by the same token, nothing could be more offensive to the Holy Ghost than the sight of creatures (the Prime Mover so loved that He gave His only son so that those who believed in Him might be saved) turning around and frustrating the work of the Church that His son (and their Deliverer) established (in accordance with His divine plan) to facilitate their salvation! Spiritual lepers, when they were not using the Deliverer's name in vain, they acted as if they had no need whatsoever for the graces He had merited for them with His death on the cross, or for the Church He had established for the purpose of dispensing His sacramental grace in His infinite wisdom!

Mjomba went on that if only humans could learn to be meek and humble of heart like the Deliverer, the Holy Ghost who informed the Church would take care of the rest. The problem was that humans - all humans - appeared unwilling to act like the creatures they were and give the grace of the Prime Mover a chance. After attempting in vain to be like the Prime Mover, they now wished to be their own Deliverer!

Pressed by members of the panel who were examining his thesis to say if those separated brethren who held the view that the Church was the work of Satan were hell-bound or not, Mjomba conceded that for all he knew, they could be saying what they said out of ignorance. These people were probably members of the invisible Church and did what they did unwittingly. This was even though their actions hurt the Church.

But so did the actions of many Catholics. Mjomba declared that, even though those Catholics were members of the visible Church, it was not beyond the realm of possibilities that they might not be members of the invisible Church. While admitting that as a human he was really not in a position to judge other humans on that score, Mjomba supposed that instead of waiting on the bridegroom with lit candles in hand, Catholics could choose to go off on other errands and show up after the wedding guests were seated and the doors of the banquet hall were closed. And that suggested, in theory at least, that someone could be outwardly a Catholic and yet miss out on something that really mattered, namely membership in the invisible Church.

To the charge, levelled by a fellow student, that he was making assumptions about the separated brethren being ignorant when he himself could be more ignorant, Mjomba's stock response was that he was not the pope and could not pretend to be infallible for that reason.

Concluding his discussion of the relative importance of the personal witness of the Deliverer vis-à-vis the Church on the one hand and the bible on the other, Mjomba wrote that it was not at all out of the ordinary that it was this Church that, as official guardian of the sacred scriptures, could certify if this or that piece of writing belonged to the official body of writings known as the bible or not. That was also why the bible had never contradicted the *official* teachings of the Church - the truly "anointed" of the Holy Ghost - and *vice versa*. And perhaps that also explained why, in contrast, individuals who walked away from the Mystical Body of the Deliverer soon enough begun contradicting themselves, increasing the prospects for divisions in Christendom.

According to Mjomba, the case for the so-called non-traditional "churches" which claimed the bible as their sole authority to the exclusion of Church tradition, but which themselves had a tradition of contradicting each other on important doctrinal matters, fell on that basis. And, in any case, how could anybody in those "non-traditional" churches or ministries claim to speak authoritatively on behalf of the apostles while at the same time deriding any connection to the "traditional" Church? Any claims to being "specially anointed" of the Holy Ghost or inspired by "ministers" in those churches remained just that - claims to personal inspiration and/or spiritual anointing and unauthenticated ones at that.

Mjomba went on that, for all he cared, so long as he himself wasn't propagating anything that went counter to the Church's teachings, even though the devil might be working overtime to trip him up, he too could claim to be laboring under inspiration from above as he worked on his thesis. And, as far as he was concerned, the thing that differentiated his thesis from the writings of the evangelists was the fact that the Church had declared the former as the "word of the Prime Mover".

Declaring that no one outside St. Augustine's Seminary was ever likely to hear about and even less read his thesis, Mjomba went on that the chances of his ever being declared an inspired writer by any one inside or outside the Church - regardless of the content of his thesis - were really slim.

Virtual "human devils

In spite of the confidence and self-assurance with which he had reached his conclusions, Mjomba was nagged by the feeling that he could be completely wrong - that there was just no way the devil could score any points in misplaced attempts to derail the divine plan; and that any research that resulted in some "human devils" being cast as more acceptable to the Prime Mover on the basis of "appearances" - including religious affiliation - was just misguided. It was typical of humans with their "small minds" to talk about the Prime Mover as if He were something they could comfortably tuck away in a pigeonhole, and he was quick to admit that he was one of them. Because they themselves were chatter boxes, they couldn't resist the temptation to claim that He (the Prime Mover) said this or said that - as if there was any human who had met or confronted the Prime Mover in person and lived to tell any tales regarding the encounter! There was no question but that the Prime Mover, after casting Beelzebub into hell, was now using the enemy to bring His divine plan to fruition.

Now, if Satan could not prevail against the Prime Mover, it was certainly also the case with humans. The extent to which humans were misguided and had become "devilish" was completely immaterial when the issue was implementing the divine plan. Mjomba conceded that even if all humans opted to become "little devils", the Holy Ghost - the third person of the Blessed Trinity – would definitely have a way of bringing redemption to any human "devil" who wanted to change and become a human "angel". The Holy Ghost and the Church established by the Deliverer (and which was informed by the Holy Ghost) would not even be deterred if the Pontiff of Rome opted to join hands with the Antichrist! That was not to say that the Holy Ghost was going to let that happen. Even if he didn't, there were already hordes who were convinced that the pope was *the* Antichrist anyway, and *that* was unlikely to affect the divine plan as well.

Mjomba easily acknowledged that he was one of the "virtual" human devils, noting that it would be wise for him to continue doing so until he was certain that he had received a pass on the Church Triumphant Entrance Test. Yes, virtual human devils who started by attempting to defy the Prime Mover and steal fruits from the Tree of the Knowledge of Good and Evil, failing which they tried to rid themselves of His only Son and also their Deliverer by stripping Him, scourging Him, mocking Him and crucifying Him on a cross; and who now seemed determined to exploit the bible - the word of the Prime Mover - and the *Sancta Ecclesia* to the max and also to the end just as the Law and the temple were exploited to the max and also right up until the Prime Mover's covenant with the people of Israel came to an end two thousand years ago!

Yes, virtual human devils who had abandoned the principles of sisterhood and brotherhood that were supposed to govern relations among humans, and had embraced a system under which entire populations were now enslaved to exploitive government bureaucracies and corporations for which they had to work a minimum of five out of seven days a week for a pittance. Yes, virtual human devils that operated prison systems and torture chambers, not for the purpose of curtailing the civil rights of some aliens, but of fellow human kindred. Virtual human devils who were not even ashamed to confine fellow humans in cages on "death row", and who even kept electric chairs, guillotines, and gas chambers oiled and ready for periodic use in nipping the lives of the condemned men, women and children including the mentally ill - condemned not by some aliens but by their own fellow men - in the bud.

Virtual human devils who invested in the development of killer viruses and germs, as well as biological and chemical weapons in publicly funded facilities alongside other weapons of messy human destruction, and who did not hesitate to use them on their fellow men! Yes, virtual human devils that were so blind that they saw nothing wrong with the fact that they were attempting to show other blind folk the way in pitch darkness without the help of a light.

Mjomba recalled the response of the Deliverer to the statement by an admirer in the crowd to the effect that He, the Deliverer, was good. The response of the Son of Man had included the words "Only God is good!" Now, that was a very "surprising" response by the one who was the

Second Person of the Blessed Trinity. Mjomba supposed that even though humans did not think so, it definitely *had* to be surprising that any of them could presume to be good at all.

And, more often than not, it was the most egregious offenders and hypocrites who balked at being lumped together with other humans as *virtual devils*, never mind that they all appeared seemly, gleaming and beautiful on the outside - like marble tombs - when, as the Deliverer put it, everything inside was rotting and ugly! Well, as far as Mjomba was concerned, it wasn't any wonder at all that the Deliverer actually taught that only God was good!

For his part, Mjomba had always had the feeling that, if he were given an opportunity to exercise rule over some unfortunate humans in some corner of the globe, he could very well end up making the most power hungry, repressive, cruel, corrupt, morally bankrupt, depraved, and baddest dictator - or the most unworthy pope for that matter if the Holy Ghost were to make the mistake of getting him (Rev. Mjomba) appointed bishop of the Holy See!

And Mjomba imagined that if he were president of the United States, perhaps he would end up as a neo-conservative *par excellence* who would expand the "axis of evil" to include even the Vatican if it did not "toe the line". Mjomba shuddered at the thought that as the incumbent in the White House, he might be tempted, in his pursuit of the policy of regime changes, to openly demand that the College of Cardinals elect as the next pope a "Prince of the Church" who not only was American, but one who also subscribed to the neo-conservative doctrines! He had no doubt that it would also be the surest way to earn an "F" on the CTET!

Even if a part of him did not like it, another and evidently more dominant part of him insisted that he, Mjomba, was closer to being a "human devil" than he might be prepared to admit. After all, here he was - a mere seminarian - presuming to be able to tell the world what being virtuous in the original sense meant. Mjomba wondered what would happen if he were ordained a priest with power to forgive sins and to deny forgiveness in the Deliverer's name. It was, of course, the Deliverer Himself who had given his apostles and their successors those powers - powers to effectively determine which sinners were truly penitent and deserved a second chance, and which ones looked like they were hell-bent, and deserved to end up in the Pit of the damned!

But if Providence were to make the mistake of getting him ordained a priest with powers to administer sacraments including the sacrament of penance - and it seemed like Providence was about to make that mistake - the way things were going, as *Father* Mjomba, he patently would be more inclined to use those powers to consign souls to hell and eternal damnation rather than to heaven and eternal life! Mjomba, who did not regard himself as someone who was "specially anointed" in the same way some preachers claimed to be, expected it to be a classic case of a blind man leading other blind men - unless the Holy Ghost intervened to rescue those who would be unfortunate to be counted among his parishioners, flock or whatever.

And He would have to act without any delay and quite fast after he received his holy orders - or so Mjomba thought! He told himself that he would hate to mislead multitudes who would flock to him for spiritual guidance - just as all those preachers out there who contradicted each other, and even themselves, all the time were doing without any shame or scruples.

Mjomba felt uneasy about the fact that he was passing criticism on other humans in the moral arena in the course of writing his thesis, and that it appeared unavoidable. It really couldn't do to criticize anyone with respect to anything, and *especially* if the criticism pertained to people's religious affiliation! He could not claim that he himself was good! It was only the Prime Mover who was good. The Sacred Scriptures were pretty clear about that. (Mark 10:18). And, He incidentally also retained the prerogative to avenge sinfulness and to critique humans on moral grounds. Doing so, after all, required the ability to discern inner thoughts, something only He could do. Mjomba also noted that if he were to become head of state of some nation or pope, the power he would wield would be from *above*. It would be completely immaterial whether he wielded that power wisely or foolishly. The fact he was receiving that power from above would automatically mean that he was being used by Providence for His own ends. It might not occur to him that this was the case, and that too would be immaterial.

Clearly therefore, regardless of what some humans did with the bible by way of interpretation, or even if they just used it to hoodwink the gullible and the-not-so-gullible in order to line their pockets, Providence would have its way. It occurred to Mjomba that even if humans went to war today and used nuclear and hydrogen bombs as well as other weapons of mass destruction on each other, even if entire continents were erased from the map and those that were not were left with populations that were permanently scarred and unable to take care of themselves, that would not of itself cause the world to come to an end.

It would, after all, not be the first time that weapons of mass destruction were used on the battlefield. There was no death of warmongering nations; and, from the perspective of those at the receiving end, deadly weapons of mass destruction were being employed by some bloodthirsty demagogues in some corner of the world to sniff out lives of their fellow human each passing hour! When only one nation in the world possessed nukes, that nation did not hesitate to use it. With so many nations possessing nukes today, the chances of these apparent weapons of choice being used again on a massive scale was also now much greater.

But Mjomba did concede that residents of Hiroshima and Nagasaki must have been convinced that the end of the world had come when the

Americans dropped their nukes on those cities! In a sense, anyone who was at the receiving end of violence of any sort, particularly violence that was uncalled for, could be excused for believing that their world was coming to an end. But Mjomba also supposed that humans who allowed themselves to become "virtual devils" presumably also were clear about the fate that was in store even for devils.

The "Talking" Book

Mjomba wrote in his thesis that establishing the relative importance of the "players" - the Deliverer and His personal witness (and not any deliverer', and certainly not the funny "deliverer" whose spots changed with time or depending on the mood of self-appointed "apostles", but the Deliverer who said (in John 6:51): "I am the living bread which came down from heaven. If any man eat of this bread, he shall live for ever; and the bread that I will give, is my flesh, for the life of the world"; vis-à-vis the Church (and not any church, but that Church which could demonstrate beyond any reasonable doubt that it was the lawful successor to the Church the Deliverer established on a rock called Cephas); vis-à-vis the contemporaries of the Deliverer who referred to each other as saints and their written testimony of the events surrounding the advent, life, death, resurrection, and ascension into heaven of the Deliverer - was just one question.

A different albeit related question, according to Mjomba, pertained to the statements "The Deliverer

says..."; "The Church says..."; and "The bible says...".
Those were all very much incomplete statements, he
wrote. Mjomba supposed that if the divine plan had
called for the appearance of the Deliverer in person
every once in a while, there was little doubt that there
would be all sorts of people turning up in different
places, and may be even in the same place at the
same time, claiming to be the Deliverer, and vying for
attention and an audience!

The Church, established by the Deliverer two
thousand years ago, and expected to be around at
least until the end of time, was in a slightly different
situation. Perhaps not entirely unexpectedly,
"churches" of all stripes and sizes had been turning
up all over the place all the time, each one of them
claiming to be the one true holy Church. As if that
was not bad enough, in addition to the two hundred
and sixty-six occupants of the Papal Chair beginning
with Simon Peter, historians have counted no less
than thirty pretenders to the Papal Chair to date!

The literature that comprised books of the New
Testament and the Old Testament, because they had
been around all the time and would so continue to be
until the end of time, had suffered a fate that was
very similar in many respects. When people did not
come up with apocryphal material which they sought
to include in the body of works that are referred to as
the "sacred scriptures", they were turning up in
droves and declaring that the bible said this or said
that *according to them.* And again, as expected, to
back up their claims, they usually went on to assert

that they had received revelations to the effect that they were not just the anointed of God, but His special messengers whose testimony was as good as that of the apostles.

But if the teachings of those newly anointed folks and their interpretation of the bible, if the bible according to them was markedly different from the bible according to the traditional or apostolic Church - and, again, not any traditional apostolic church, but the one against which "the gates of hell will not prevail" - one had to ask what the authority and credentials of these "saints" were, and where they had been up until now.

Mjomba wrote that the bible typically said one thing to Preacher A, and another thing, quite often the very opposite, to Preacher B. There was of course no mystery about that. Different preachers wanted to hear different things; and the bible, being the truly wonderful book that it was, obliged! When the bible spoke to the presence of the Deliverer in the Eucharist, some people thus distinctly heard it say that the Deliverer turned his twelve apostles into cannibals by feeding them on His sacred flesh and blood, and then commanded them to carry on with the practice of "breaking bread" in the manner He had prescribed, namely by saying some words over bread and wine to change them into the "bread of angels" and then feeding on it along with the body of the faithful like it was some spiritual sustenance.

And, relating what the Deliverer did that evening to events that took place a few days later when, following His resurrection from the dead, the

Deliverer solemnly laid His hands on the Eleven in a ceremony during which He also formally commissioned His Church telling them to go to the ends of the earth spreading His message of salvation and doing what He had taught them, they also understood that to change the species of bread and wine into the body and blood of the Deliverer, one had first to be chosen and then initiated into a holy priesthood in a specific manner.

But others who were listening to the bible speak apparently heard no such a thing. All they heard was something about eating a meal - supper - from time to time in the Deliverer's memory!

And when the bible said something about the Deliverer constructing His Church on a rock called Cephas, some heard it merely mumble something about a "church" with no ordained priesthood or even a leader. Others heard something entirely different. They heard it say that the Deliverer took Peter aside, and told the fisherman that he would be the head of something he was referring to as *Ecclesia Mea* (my Church).

And they also heard the Deliverer (who had also promised Peter and the other disciples that the Spirit that united the Deliverer and His Father in eternal love would come down, as it subsequently did on the Day of Pentecost and inform His Church and continue doing so until the end of time) reassure the fisherman turned "fisher of men" that everything would be alright; that the devil and his truly dangerous mob of fallen spirits, while he wouldn't be exactly sitting back and enjoying a snooze as Peter and his comrades worked the fields that were ready for the harvest, would never be able to prevail against the enterprise over which He was installing the fisherman as Chief Executive Officer. Yeah, the vacillating fisherman who would not hesitate to slice off the ear of Malchus, the high priest's slave, with a sword at one moment, and who in a matter of hours would be denying his Master and swearing in front of Malchus's kinsman saying: "I know not this man of whom ye speak!"

According to others, some statements that are found in the Holy Book couldn't be taken literally. These included the Deliverer's promises to Peter in particular when He said: "And I say to thee: That thou art Peter; and upon this rock I will build my church, and the gates of hell shall not prevail against it. And I will give to thee the keys of the kingdom of heaven. And whatsoever thou shalt bind upon earth, it shall be bound also in heaven: and whatsoever thou shalt loose upon earth, it shall be loosed also in heaven." This stood to reason as, in their opinion, the church had actually fallen into apostasy by the time they themselves came along.

Others, who heard the bible "speak", went away believing that the "Deliverer" was actually an impostor who, instead of helping the Jews cast off the Roman yoke, was predicting that the Holy Temple and the City of Jerusalem itself were going to be destroyed! According to them, the proof was in the pudding. The self-proclaimed Deliverer had "fallen" and in that sense "capitulated" to the Romans and, therefore, could not possibly have been the promised Messiah.

There were indeed others who, on hearing the bible speak, merely concluded that even though it might be a proven fact that the Nazarene was a historical figure who lived two thousand years ago, He was really just a good swimmer who made it look as if He could walk on water! These same folks did not fail to point out that the Deliverer was also a terrific magician who could juggle pots filled with water, and some filled with wine, in the full view of guests at a wedding party, and hoodwink them into believing that they were now sampling a mysterious new wine!

Mjomba wrote that the phrase "the bible says" and its equivalent in other languages was probably the most abused phrase ever. It was that same phrase which was used by the priests and Pharisees to justify their actions aimed at neutralizing the very person who had been sent to the world to deliver humans from the bondage of sin! And if it hadn't been for that phrase, the Church's problems would have been immeasurably reduced. Mjomba wondered aloud if that phrase had no connection with the Deliverer's warning about the "gates of hell", and what they would be attempting to do to his Ecclesia.

It had all become very confusing, the business of saving souls. But Mjomba argued that it was all exactly as it was supposed to be, given the nature of humans and the legacy of original sin or, as he preferred to put it, the loss by humans of their "original innocence". The fact of the matter, of course, was that the operative phrase "the bible says" was itself incomplete.

To be complete, it also needed to take cognizance of what the bible itself said that it *did not say.* What was wrong with people, Mjomba asked rhetorically? To make it absolutely clear that what the bible said was not the whole story, towards the end of his "gospel", St. John wrote - in letters that were so bold and large they had not been missed by any translator or transcriber of the biblical texts in memory - that his writings contained only partial information on the deeds and signs (or teachings) of the Messiah.

According to Mjomba, it was noteworthy that St. John went to the extent of explicitly pointing out in his "scrolls" recounting the birth, life, death and resurrection of the Nazarene that many deeds and signs that He had performed in front of the apostles - which undoubtedly comprised the great bulk of the information knowledge to which members of the infant Church were already privy - would definitely not be found therein. It went without saying that the same would be true of the accounts of the life of the Nazarene that Matthew, Luke, Mark and others were compiling.

The seminarian was nagged by the implied suggestion that a book, a man-made object that was nonetheless inanimate, could speak! But it perplexed Mjomba even more that, in the age of Think Tanks, no one had succeeded in figuring out what was at play here, namely that it was not a "talking book" but human nature!

Of course, it wasn't the fact that the coming of the Deliverer had been *foretold* in Genesis 3:15 that *caused* Him to be born of a virgin as recorded in Matthew 1:18-25.

Or that *caused* Him, after He had spent the whole night on the mountain in prayer with His Father, to gather unto Him His disciples, and to choose twelve from among them (whom also he named apostles): Simon, whom he surnamed Peter, and Andrew his brother, James and John, Philip and Bartholomew, Matthew and Thomas, James the son of Alpheus, and Simon who is called Zelotes, And Jude, the brother of James, and Judas Iscariot, who was the traitor, as recorded in Luke 6:12-16.

Or that *caused* him to proclaim to Simon Peter no less than three times saying: "Simon son of John, lovest thou me more than these? ...Feed my lambs" as recorded in John 21:15-17.

Or that *caused* Him in response to Peter's statement that He, the Deliverer, was "Christ, the Son of the living God", to state categorically and unequivocally: "Blessed art thou, Simon Bar-Jona: because flesh and blood hath not revealed it to thee, but my Father who is in heaven", as recorded in Matthew 16:17.

Or that *caused* him to say to His apostles in John 15.26: "But when the Paraclete cometh, whom I will send you from the Father, the Spirit of truth, who proceedeth from the Father, he shall give testimony of me. And you shall give testimony, because you are with me from the beginning."

Or that *caused* Him to say to Peter in Matthew 16.18-19: "And I say to you that you are Peter, and on this rock will my church be based, and the doors of hell will not overcome it. I will give to you the keys of the kingdom of heaven: and whatever is fixed by you on earth will be fixed in heaven: and whatever you make free on earth will be made free in heaven: and whatever you make free on earth will be made free in heaven."

Or that *caused* Him, eight days following His resurrection from the dead (as stated in John 20.11), to reappear to the apostles and to say to Thomas who was also called Didymus: "Put in thy finger hither, and see my hands; and bring hither thy hand, and put it into my side; and be not faithless, but believing."

Rather, it was the *decision* of the Second Person of the Holy Trinity to take up His human nature that caused things to be foretold about Him, with *only some* of them being committed to paper.

And there was no doubt in Mjomba's mind that it was *human nature*, not a "talking" book, that got the better of humans and, starting with the issue of circumcision in the infant Church, made it necessary for Peter (as described in Acts 15.7), after there had been much disputing, to rise up and remind the sect of the Pharisees in the church and others saying to them: "Men, brethren, you know that in former days God made choice among us, that by my mouth the Gentiles should hear the word of the gospel and believe.   And God who knows the hearts gave testimony, giving unto them the Holy Ghost, as well as to us.   And put no difference between us and them, purifying their hearts by faith.   Now therefore, why tempt you God to put a yoke upon the necks of the disciples which neither our fathers nor we have been able to bear?   But by the grace of the Lord Jesus Christ, we believe to be saved, in like manner as they also."

The talking book, handicapped by the fact that its most important parts, namely those pertaining to the Deliverer's advent and ministry, His death on the cross, His resurrection and ascension into heaven, were still missing, wasn't capable of talking at that time; and that presumably stopped the sect of the Pharisees from proceeding with their attempt to "reform" the infant church.   And it also helped that Paul and Barnabas, who "had no small contest" with the sect of the Pharisees, had the presence of mind to seek counsel with the apostles and priests in Jerusalem concerning the issue of circumcision.

It also probably helped in no small way that the "Holy Father" was the fisherman who had been groomed for that post by none other than the Deliverer himself, and was revered by all of Christendom, including the Christians who belonged to the sect of the Pharisees.   And luckily there were no other issues like divorce in the mix!

Mjomba wrote in his thesis on Original Virtue that, instead of a "talking" book, there were a lot of talking humans and "talking heads" with a variety of motivations. For one, a "talking" book would by itself not have been able to usher in the so-called "reformation" in the Church. By definition, that reformation was aimed at activities by church functionaries that were allegedly inconsistent with what the *reformists* perceived as regular. The reformers were reacting against individuals with whom they did not agree.

But because they could not dislodge those with whom they were at loggerheads from their entrenched positions of authority and power in the Church, and were loath to submit to the Church's authority as exercised by their former friends now turned sworn "enemies", the only recourse they had left was to suppose that humans, however high placed in the church, could not possibly speak for either the "absent" Deliverer or the Comforter He had promised to send in the wake of His ascension into heaven, let alone possess and exercise the power to eject any dissenting individual from the *Sancta Ecclesia*. And since that included themselves, the only way to win the argument was to retreat behind the Book.

The scriptures that up until then had been quite silent were suddenly given voice as the reformers went on the offensive in an effort to deny the Curia in Rome the authority it had been wielding against them. And the refrain, from then on, was to be that salvation came by faith alone! Also, since the subject matter was the salvation of humans, how could there possibly be such a thing as a living authoritative human(s) with the last word in spiritual matters?

That, Mjomba claimed, was how the primitive parchments of the medieval times, with their stylistic hand-scribbled passages of the Old and New Testaments, came alive overnight and began talking!

But it could not be denied that the Book was even then talking only in a euphemistic sense. The fact of the matter was that the situation hadn't really changed one iota; and it was the same folks (who had already been formally "excommunicated" by then) who (not unlike the proverbial branches that had been cut off from the vine and were starved for sustenance) could now not help but grasp at anything that promised them salvation!

Still, it was some consolation for these "reformers" to be able to use the doctrinal position that hinged on the "Talking Book" to poke fun at the Curia in Rome by suggesting that they themselves were saved by faith alone through the twin doctrines of *sola fidei* and *sola scriptura*, and that their enemies were the ones who were in schism and for all practical purposes already lost by reason of their uncompromising dogmatism and obduracy!

After initially hesitating, the holy book, with some assistance from the reformers, stuttered and, Lo and behold, began to speak. The reformers were in fact able to give voice to the book's contents quite eloquently.

Following in the footsteps of the original reformers, the second wave of reformers also gave voice to the holy book's contents, except that the results, reflecting their preconceptions and personal biases, were not quite the same. The latter, just like the earlier reformers who based the reforms they were promulgating on the twin doctrines of *sola fide* and *sola scriptura*, believed that it was anathema to include both Tradition and the so-called *Magisterium* (or teaching authority of the *Ecclesia* the Deliverer had chosen to establish on the Rock called Peter) as authoritative sources of revelation. And as years and decades went by, the cacophony created by the conflicting reformed voices became bewildering with each sect claiming to represent the True Believers who were also faithfully interpreting the *infallible* Word of the Prime Mover.

Thus, as long as they were alive and still kicking, the apostles would not have countenanced anyone getting up and declaring that "the bible says...period" as if that was all there was to the message of the "gospel" which they not only had received and embraced, but had sworn to spread to the ends of the earth and were even prepared to die for.

And if that was valid and true in the early Church, what was it that could make it untrue or invalid in later times, including Mjomba's own times? The answer clearly was "Nothing!"

And this was so, not so much because John (and his fellow evangelists) produced and published their stories while under inspiration from above, as because common sense itself said so. If the phrase "the bible says" had been adequate, then the death of the Messiah, His repeated admonitions to the apostles to do this or do that in the way that the

Deliverer specified, the idea of a Church, the apostles and their successors, their blood and that of the many martyrs beginning with the Holy Innocents, were all wasted effort.

One could also accordingly downgrade the role of the Messiah Himself in the work of salvation because the only thing that really mattered was to get some willing humans to agree to scribble down the "message" of salvation while under inspiration from above. If the phrase "the bible says" was adequate, then the Deliverer's promises that he would be with his Church to the ends of time were completely hollow, and His prayer that "they may be one" was something He did in jest, as also were the Deliverer's actions in empowering the apostles with words such as "teach...", or "Whose sins you forgive are forgiven...", or "Go forth and baptize in my name..." – and so on and so forth.

Mjomba concluded that section of his thesis by arguing that it was precisely because the Deliverer anticipated the appearance of false prophets and the rise to prominence of self-appointed "messengers" that He had sought to reassure his handpicked apostles and their successors not only that the Holy Ghost would come down from heaven and be their guide, but that He Himself, even though He would be seated at the right hand of His Father in heaven, would also be with them in person in the Holy Eucharist until the end of time.

Casting the net for "humans"...

Elaborating on a statement he had inserted into his thesis to the effect that he was not personally bothered that there were many religions and even churches, Mjomba wrote that this state of affairs, while disappointing and far from the ideal, was not entirely surprising, given the backdrop of original sin. For one, humans now knew for a fact that the path to their heavenly paradise was not wide, but narrow – actually very narrow!

And, according to Mjomba, the Church's own liturgy not only recognized the fact of disunity in Christendom, but included special prayers imploring the Prime Mover not to begrudge His graces to erring Christians as well as others who did not even accept Christ. What was more - the Church's liturgy, using the words of the prophet Isaiah, even acknowledged that at the end of time there would be those who had not been told who would see, while there would be others who had not heard who would ponder!

Even though humans were still endowed with reason, which was in turn now reinforced by the Deliverer's redeeming grace, and had likewise been allowed to retain their freedom to choose, they now also had concupiscence that permeated both those faculties like an insidious cancer. The latter, also operating like a veil, made it much harder for humans to focus on spiritual things and so much easier to be blinded by desires of the flesh. And it also gave them a soft spot for the ploys of the devil, Mjomba wrote.

The upshot of it all was that humans let their likes and dislikes, not reason, dictate what they ultimately chose to do.

Thus, some humans, seeing some things about the Deliverer which they liked, had elected to adopt Him simply as an icon, but not to carry out his bidding by openly throwing in their lot with the apostles and their successors in the Church he had established and following the Church's teachings. Others saw something about the Church which they liked and so became nominal members without a commitment either to its teachings or its official interpretation of the sacred scriptures. There were others still who found only some of the Church's teachings and injunctions to their liking, and who then proceeded to structure their religious beliefs accordingly.

And many, propelled on by the rampant scandals that had bedevilled the Church since the days of Judas and Ananias, some of those scandals even involving the misuse of Church facilities in much the same way the temple in Jerusalem was used for commerce instead of the original purpose for which it was built, had opted to continue doing their thing as if the Church did not exist. But the one thing that did not surprise Mjomba was that the world was now packed with so many feuding church organizations, each one claiming to be the Church that was originally established by the Deliverer and rendering the evangelizing mission of the apostles and their successors humanly speaking impossible.

Mjomba added as an aside that if he had not been brought up in the Christian faith, the odds were that he would never have seen the inside of a church, Catholic or otherwise, for that reason alone! Mjomba wrote that a leap of faith, not just reason, was needed by a modern gentile to find his or her way into the Catholic Church - and that was even before he/she had a chance to receive that faith! He added that this was a legacy of individuals in the Church since its inception not living lives that were truly Christ-like, and they ranged from ordinary members of the Church's laity to members of the clergy, including the so-called "princes of the church", to the successors of Peter!

Disunity in Christendom undoubtedly came with a price, Mjomba wrote. The constant prayer of the Deliverer to His Father that "they may be one" was, Mjomba asserted, an explicit acknowledgement of the heavy price which selfishness in the human family, and above all hatred, would exact from the beginning. Mjomba also suggested that the agony of the Deliverer in the Garden of Gethsemane had everything to do with that aspect of human frailty just as it had everything to do with the other sins for which the Deliverer came on earth to atone.

The invisible dimension...

It was during Mjomba's discussion of the subject of the Church that he decided to touch on a related subject, namely the Sacrament of Baptism.

Baptism, whether it was baptism with water or baptism with fire or the simple baptism of desire, was somewhat analogous to the notion of "church". He supposed that this was, perhaps, something to be expected since baptism delineated members and non-members of the Church the Deliverer established.

And, according to Mjomba, "going to heaven" - which, alternately, could be described as being in direct communion with the Prime Mover while unimpeded by the limitations of physical bodily matter, or the beatific vision enjoyed by holy souls in the afterlife - was something that was directly related to the notion of God's Church on earth.

Defined as the Mystical Body of Christ and comprising a visible Church as well as an invisible one, the exact makeup of the Church's members was really unknown to humans precisely because of the mysterious way humans as a whole received baptism and joined those who were saved by the blood of the Deliverer in the Church. Mjomba suggested that humans were not privy to the exact qualifications for being ushered into heaven, which was itself analogous to holy Mother Church on earth.

Mjomba wrote that baptism, while it was a necessary condition for the salvation of sinners, was not sufficient. But, even assuming that all the other conditions were satisfied, not knowing how the Sacrament of Baptism really worked and relying on human ingenuity alone, it was not really possible to tell from a line up who was slated to go to heaven and who was not, just as there was no way of determining that an individual who did not belong to the visible Church was not a member of the invisible Church.

Mjomba wrote that it was not just revelation but also reason which attested to the existence of that place, midway between earth and heaven, where those whose disposition and integrity were not ship shape enough for their encounter with the Deliverer and Judge, His Father and the Spirit which united them in everlasting love - but not so wanting as to qualify them for permanent banishment from the face of the Prime Mover, just like happened to Lucifer and his legion of rebellious spirits - ended up.

It was in Purgatory, Mjomba wrote, where souls in transit to heaven spent time being adequately prepared and purified, so that they would be able to withstand the radiance and glow of the Prime Mover and his company of pure and spotless souls, luminous and comely choirs of angels, and shimmering hierarchies of Cherubim and Seraphims. This would also ensure that they would feel at home and not be like strangers in heaven.

But what human, besides the Deliverer, was in a position to say who was where at what point in time by just employing his or her reason! Mjomba suggested that it was an area where the new knowledge about genes and genomes was absolutely useless.

There was a direct connection, according to Mjomba, between the fact that some things were invisible, like the Mystical Body of Christ or the invisible Church so-called, and grace which itself operated in mysterious ways on an invisible level. And, consequently, since the subject in which grace worked (or, rather, was intended to work) was Man, as far as Mjomba was concerned, that removed any remaining doubts about the existence of the "invisible Man" who remained alive and well even after the time of his visible self on earth ran its course and his earthly existence came to its terminus at death.

Mjomba explained that, if sin had not come into the world, the exit from this world would undoubtedly have been the diametric opposite of death and would have translated into a delightful and glorious homecoming by steadfastly loyal but free and also exceptionally endowed and resourceful creatures. Having opted for loyalty to the Prime Mover over rebellion, humans would also have been in a position to lay claim to notching a pivotal, irreversible and crowning victory over Satan and his legion of mutinous spirits earning themselves a double crown in the process.

This would have put to even greater shame the fallen spirits, free and rational beings themselves who elected to seek adulation in their individual selves rather than in the Prime Mover, while knowing full well that their sacrilegious and unpardonable act would earn them instant banishment from His face once and for all - as it did, indeed, come to pass - and who now sought to frustrate the divine plan out of pure malice and by any means!

A holy priesthood...

And that, Mjomba wrote, brought him to the matter that was at the center of his thesis, namely the priestly vocation. Given the role of the Church in the divine plan and specifically the manner in which the Deliverer got together his band of apostles, the way he sent the Spirit upon them, the authority he imparted on them, and the manner in which he ordered them to go out in the world to do his bidding, anyone seeking ordination to the priesthood had to know that the calling to be a priest was a very special one.

Mjomba commented that if there was anyone who knew anything about vocations, it was the woman whose famous *Fiat* paved the way for the arrival on Earth of the Deliverer. Her calling was even more special than the calling to be a priest. What indeed could be said, Mjomba wrote, of someone for whom messengers from on high employed expressions like "Hail!", "full of grace", "the Lord is with you", "blessed are you among women", and "blessed womb" in their address! And, even while an awesome title such as *"Mater Dei"* (Mother of God) could be used in addressing her, it had to be a very humbling experience for a human to be so addressed, Mjomba added.

Her human body, ordinarily a temple of the Prime Mover like any other human body, additionally became a tabernacle in which God dwelt verily for the space of nine months, Mjomba wrote. Through her

"Fiat" communicated to the Prime Mover through the angel, she consented to be the vehicle by which the Word, through Whom all things that are created came into being, Himself came into the world; and, like Him, she saw everything in its proper perspective, including the delineation between an earthly existence and the after-life that awaited humans when they passed from this world.

It was, Mjomba wrote, her *fiat* that the Prime Mover transformed into the living Christ in a transubstantiation of sorts, a precursor to the Sacrament of the Blessed Eucharist - the "unending sacrifice" the true and eternal priest would establish on the night before He gave up His life for humans. And, of course, Mary's *fiat* highlighted the role which the apostles - and those who would be called to be members of the priestly order after them - would also play in the administration of the Sacrament of the Eucharist in particular and in the salvation of their fellow men in general.

And indeed, to underline Mary's role in the work of salvation, before breathing His last and delivering up His ghost, the Deliverer and Author of Life had commended humanity to her spiritual care with the famous words he spoke to John, representing all humans, and to the woman whose seed was about to triumph over evil in turn: "Son, behold your mother" and "Mother, behold your son"!

Mary, who came into the world without original sin like Adam and Eve, but who (unlike them) would never once risk severing the communication lines between the Prime Mover and herself by even once betraying Him, had continued to be "full of grace". And the Prime Mover, ever faithful to His word, had continued to be with her all through her motherhood and during her period of sorrow. A "Virgin Mother", she had become a truly "Sorrowful Mother" who found herself, for no fault of hers, standing at the foot of the tree from which hung her divine son.

Mary found herself sandwiched between the murderous descendants of Adam and Eve for whom concepts of love, justice and faithfulness had lost meaning, and an eternally faithful, loving and above all merciful Prime Mover! And would it be any wonder that the Church, guided by the Spirit the Deliverer would send in the wake of His own ascension into heaven, would declare her *Regina Coeli* (the Queen of Heaven)!

Unfortunately, many of those who advocated the ordination of women usually were also the very ones who, according to Mjomba, tended to believe that the praises heaped on Mary by the Church were too many and also undeserved. But it was perhaps not entirely surprising that, in this "Valley of Tears" which the former "Garden of Eden" became when humans revolted against the Prime Mover, some found themselves scandalized and outraged by the fact that Mary, a fellow human, had found herself in a position to intercede for other humans with her son, a human who also happened to be the Second Person of the Holy Trinity! This was despite the fact that Mary did not herself choose to become the mother of the Deliverer, but agreed to become the Mother of a divine essence only after receiving a "call" from above to fill that exceedingly elevated role!

It did surprise Mjomba, however, that those who doubted Mary's elevated position among humans included persons who showed that they had an impressive grasp of the scriptures, and that they did so despite the clear reference in the Book of Genesis to the enormous power she would be capable of wielding. According to Mjomba, that reference was contained in the words: "And she will crush the serpent's head!"

For his part, Mjomba could not help making a direct association between the power of the Deliverer's mother and the fact that she led a humble life devoid of self-indulgence in as much as it was full of sorrows. According to Mjomba, Mary was, along with her son, the perfect embodiment of the truly spiritual human; and she also was the best role model among the descendants of Adam and Eve, aside from her son who, of course, was in a class of His own because he also happened to be divine.

Citing St. Francis of Assisi as an example, Mjomba wrote that saints "ran away from priesthood", because they saw it as a calling that was so elevated, they felt they themselves were unworthy to aspire for it. To be a priest after all was to be an *alter Christus* he went on. Then, noting that it was an "apostle" and a candidate for the priesthood (Judas Iscariot) who committed what might be said to be the most overt act of betrayal, and that he was in fact only days away from being ordained a priest and a bishop simultaneously along with the other apostles, Mjomba commented that it did not mean that the remaining eleven candidates were perfect by any means.

He wrote that Paul had murdered, even though perhaps only through surrogates; and Mjomba did not fail to make a reference to the legend which said that Peter, after denying the Deliverer on so many occasions, had afterward shed so many tears that he was easily recognizable, everywhere he went by the deep grooves the tears left as they trickled down his face. Mjomba wrote that a repentant Judas would probably have made a spectacular man of the cloth and probably also an eminent father of the infant Church.

Mjomba concluded from these and other cases he had studied that the calling actually did go to mortal human beings, and very frail ones at that, a clear sign that it was the grace of the Prime Mover working through men which saved souls and those ordained priests really only served as vessels of the grace which came to the world through the Deliverer.

The key to achieving a happy medium between a finite bodily existence and an immortal spiritual existence, on the other hand, was leading an upright life. Which is just as well, Mjomba wrote, since the soul which informs the body over the duration of one's earthly existence, because it is as much a spirit as any other created spiritual essences - the heavenly hosts and the fallen angels for instance - cannot escape accountability for its actions once it shed that body.

The human paradox...

Mjomba supposed that there was some merit in discussing the question of identity in that particular regard, and so he went on that the real identity of humans was not even close to the reflection that appeared in a mirror! If it were, it would be possible to argue that the back of the head or the crown, or any part of the body including internal organs for that matter, rather than the face (with or without goggles), represented a true picture of what humans really looked like.

The true identity of humans, Mjomba suggested, was spiritual and not physical, the fact that the human constitution consisted of a soul (which was invisible to the naked eye) and a body (which was visible) notwithstanding. Admitting that he himself could not pretend to know exactly what a human's true identity was like, Mjomba still proceeded to provide what he said were his strong suspicions in that respect. The situation of humans, he went on, was similar to that of angels, and the state of their morality or relationship with the Prime Mover defined the identities in both cases. Which was just another way of saying that a human - or an angel - created in the image of the Prime Mover, looked a little like Him, Mjomba concluded.

Mjomba wrote that during their early years, while they were innocent and childlike, humans appeared capable of knowing and accepting their limitations - that they did not at all elect to come into existence and much less that they themselves chose to be humans rather than some other creature; that they did not choose to come into the world male or female, blond or auburn, Mongoloid, Caucasian, Negroid, or something else. As they outgrew their childhood and innocence, just when you were starting to think that they were maturing and growing in common sense, all humans almost without exception apparently went nuts and begun to act as though they could have affected the course of those events!

They smarted so very much when they made mistakes and were being corrected on the one hand, and then they became so enraged and were almost prepared to kill at the sight of other people making identical mistakes, you would think that they themselves were "saved" (as they say) even before deliverance visited them so they could become saved. And may be they were right because it was, after all, when they were still childlike and guileless that they were vouchsafed with grace and were really saved. Meaning they got lost when they started to proclaim that they had been delivered and were finally saved!

The idea that they might owe anything to a Prime Mover or any such entity became not just the most elusive but seemingly also the most offensive to boot almost overnight, Mjomba decried. He suggested that it was a syndrome that fully merited the title "the Human Paradox"!

Mjomba even volunteered a definition for "Losing Innocence": Doing things humans ordinarily would not have brought themselves to do out of respect for and deference to the Prime Mover. In the course of losing innocence, humans, who until then were completely at home trusting in the Prime Mover, perhaps as a direct result of the unavoidable feelings of guilt, gradually took to trusting either in themselves or in fellow humans, effectively "losing" themselves in the process, Mjomba wrote.

Mjomba called it the big lie, and it concerned the question of human mastery over nature and ownership. Mjomba wrote that humans had somehow succeeded in convincing themselves that nature itself was subservient to them, and that they had complete mastery over it, including whatever made up their own constitution; and he claimed that it was what the sacred scriptures referred to as "vanity of vanities" and "vanity of the eyes"!

What was it that made a human being tick? Not the physical body or its parts (which, according to Mjomba, were all essentially expendable, even though some more easily than others) but the spirit (which, according to him, once brought into existence, did not expire) and the spiritual faculties that were the guiding force behind the actions of a human. And then, belief in a Supreme Being or Prime Mover, when not completely diluted by the irrational notion that things evolved out of nothing over time following the so-called Big Bang, had degenerated into sentimental feelings that had them worship an equally strange Omnipotent Being who was nice and forgiving to the 'faithful', but was utterly merciless to any so-called 'unbelievers' who did not belong to the 'fold'.

The spirit, Mjomba noted, was invisible. And that, Mjomba claimed, was what provided humans the excuse to act as if the spirit was an imaginary thing; that it only existed in ghost stories, and that no spirits existed in reality. Using the excuse that spirits could not be seen, touched, smelt, heard, or be tasted (as if it were some delicacy), they even tried to convince themselves that the body did not really need the spirit to inform it, but was self-sustaining, like the bodies of the lower beasts which acted on instinct and did not possess the spiritual faculties of reason and free will.

Mjomba added that humans were in denial in this regard, and their state of denial caused many a human to live as if the spirit did not survive the body (which was itself corruptible) to live on in the nether world. He wrote that humans used the fact that things that belonged to the spiritual realm were invisible to the naked eye as an excuse to live lives that fell short of upright. They conveniently - very conveniently - forgot the fact that the Prime Mover dwelt at the core of their being such that humans, in acknowledging that they existed, *ipso facto* paid tribute, albeit reluctantly, to the existence of the Supreme Being at their core who actually made them tick.

Mjomba suggested that humans were so preoccupied with material things that could only be seen (like a house, an automobile, a fur coat or a television set), be heard (like chamber or rap music), be touched (like money or jewellery), be smelt (like scent from roses or artificial perfume), or tasted (like roast beef or wine) that spiritual things were now almost completely lost on them. He wrote that when they were not claiming to be automatically and irrevocably saved, and thereby abnegating individual personal responsibility for their actions, they were invariably asserting that spiritual things were for the imbeciles, simpletons with backward mentalities, and others like them in need of something of that sort for emotional support.

Mjomba wrote that all grown-up humans without exception started out as little innocent angels. The turning point seemed to coincide with their ceasing to rely on all fours to get about, and their mastery of the skills for standing upright and walking unaided. That was when they apparently started to believe that they were really not humans but small gods, and ended up deceiving themselves that they could actually be complete masters of their own destiny.

And soon enough they began behaving as if they could have elected to walk on their heads instead of their feet, or to breathe with their ears instead of their noses, to sleep while standing upright on one foot like a crested crane instead of while lying prostrate on a flat surface, etc. Worst of all, they begun to act as if they themselves chose to be who they were, to have two rather than one eye or none as is the case with a certain snake specie, to walk on feet that have five toes each rather than one or two, to feed with the mouth instead of some other way, and so on and so forth.

It was all exactly as the inspired author had observed: Vanity of vanities! And it was irrational. And not because the holy book said so, but because the physical human frame - the center of the self-deception - must disintegrate into the dust (from which it originally came in any event) in due course, Mjomba wrote. For humans to claim that they owned anything at any time when the very next moment it could all be taken away with the humans concerned having no option but to accept the result was, Mjomba wrote, presumptive and tantamount to living in an imaginary world. Mjomba suggested that humans did not in fact own even their own lives.

Humans did not stop at pretending that they were capable of doing what was essentially impossible, namely give what they themselves did not have! But they even pretended that acceptance of their true nature, namely that they were creatures who just happened to be blessed in a special way, made them less human. And they ridiculed the few amongst them who eschewed such idiotic behavior.

In the process of trying to keep up with the Joneses, humans went to some surprising excesses. The young-blooded, for instance, strove to acquire fast autos and other means that might speed up their exit from this world. Those who were older and had the means resorted to acquiring single engine airplanes that they promptly converted into toys. Others took to bungee jumping with the obvious intention of testing the strength of nylon cords. Still others found all sorts of ways to make their already short life spans shorter. Those who found themselves occupying seats of power begun courting wars as if they had to do something to break the boredom engendered by the modest intervals of peacetime.

But it was both a telling and implicit acknowledgement of their total dependence on the Prime Mover, he wrote, that when the diehards among humans clambered aboard their Leer jets to enjoy the feel of being as free as birds of the air, they did so with parachutes under arm. They made sure that their fast autos were equipped with air bags when they jumped into them to test the maximum cruising speeds of the machines and to enjoy the excitement of living on the edge in the process. And they had helmets handy when they hopped onto motorbikes and used them to perform daredevil manoeuvres. But any investment in insurance aimed at postponing the inevitable, even though useful in the short run, always proved inadequate in the long run, Mjomba wrote.

The list of insane things humans did was endless, Mjomba wrote. And to compound the problem, they seemed so helpless as far as action to pull back or reverse course went. They reminded Mjomba of speeding autos that were unable to stop because the accelerators were jammed and stuck to the floors of the vehicles, and of runaway rollercoasters that had gotten out of control. And yet all humans needed to do, like the prized creatures of the Prime Mover they were, was to accept that they were recipients of the Prime Mover's strikingly exceptional largess; and then, like princes and princesses, settle back to enjoy His unfathomable bounty in His everlasting kingdom. As it was, the only thing humans liked to do seemed going out and trying as hard as they could to reverse their good fortune.

All this contrasted so much with true deliverance that, according to Mjomba, consisted in the passage from this life to the afterlife whilst on good terms with the Prime Mover. It was paradoxical, but the fact remained that to die to oneself whilst in this life, and above all to lose one's life while in the Prime Mover's service, was what constituted deliverance of a human! Coming into this "world" at birth could thus be likened to being allowed to set one's foot at the gate of heaven and dying was equivalent to heading off to be united spirit to spirit with the Prime Mover.

All of which reminded Mjomba of Judas, the apostle who had come to personify "betrayal" in the eyes of most.

PART 4: THE BETRAYER

Referring to the expression "It were better if he had not been born", Mjomba noted that all the descendants of Adam and Eve, with the exception of Mary and her son, had also been betrayers at one time or other and were to that extent like Judas. He believed that the Deliverer's words, even though addressed to Judas, applied to all humans to the extent to which they resembled Judas or were betrayers.

Quoting liberally from the Canadian Scrolls, which scholars unanimously ascribed to a friend and contemporary of the apostles who went by the name of Josephus, and which appeared to have been intended as a companion to what was now known as the Acts of the Apostles, Mjomba wrote that Judas apparently harbored a great dislike for Peter, and that the apostle who would subsequently gain notoriety as "Betrayer of the Deliverer" had hated Peter's guts from the moment he heard the Nazarene pick out the fisherman from His audience during an address He gave at a popular beach spot along the shores of the Sea of Galilee and tell him in front of everybody that he was the equivalent of a rock, and that it was upon that "rock" that He intended to establish His "Church". This was even though Judas thought that the Deliverer had to be cracking some sort of joke!

The Deliverer's exact words were as follows: "You are blessed, Simon Bar-Jona. I tell you Peter -

you, whose name coincidentally means 'rock'! In front of John, Judas and all these others, I am saying to you here and now: You are the rock on which I am going to build the New Jerusalem - or my 'Church' as it will be known. My Church is going to be universal, and it is going to have you, Peter, as its main cornerstone..."

And, as Peter protested that he was only a fisherman who was a vacillating schnook and a weakling by nature, and retorted that it would be too risky for the New Jerusalem to have him as its hinge, the Deliverer had pursued: "Tut, tut, tut! You are Peter and also the rock I am talking about; and it is you I have chosen - not your brother James here, or Judas or even John who also happens to be my own blood relative - to be the rock upon which I will build my Church. And, take my word for it, Peter - the gates of hell shall not prevail against it. All this means that I am going to give to you the keys of my celestial kingdom. And, mark this! Whatever you will hold bound on earth, will be automatically bound also in heaven above! And whatever you will loosen and free down here on earth, it shall be loosened and freed also in my kingdom in heaven above. This is my covenant to you and whoever will succeed you as the '*papa*' who oversees my flock in this 'Valley of Tears'."

Judas had at first tried to pretend that, even though he was standing right there by the Deliverer's side, he hadn't heard anything. But seeing that he was just making a fool of himself, he had decided that, even though he had never heard the Deliverer speak frivolously and indulge in cracking jokes, He had to be breaking that rule on this occasion. He simply had to be joking! Judas had felt almost as if the Deliverer had told him: "See this fisherman? He is my Eliacim. I will place the key of the house of David on his shoulder; and he shall open, and no one shall shut. And he shall shut and no one shall open! And you - Judas: you are like the worthless Sobna. That is why I am choosing to invest the office of 'Papa' in Peter and not in you!"

Citing new evidence Mjomba claimed was contained in the recently unearthed Canadian Scrolls, he wrote in his thesis that, when interviewed by the Evangelist Luke, witnesses to the incident had described the reaction of Judas as uncharacteristic of someone who was a member of the Deliverer's inner circle. He had murmured: "Jees! Not Peter of all people! Not that blockhead!" And then Judas reportedly had added rather ominously: "Master, this you will regret, I promise you!"

It was may be three months later that Peter, who was unaware of the dislike Judas harbored for him, ran bubbling to the comrade from Jericho that John, his own brother James and himself, while on a mountain top with the Deliverer, had been treated to something entirely out of this world. It annoyed Judas even more that Peter, after saying that the instructions they had been given were that they not mention the incident to anyone, was unable to find words to describe what had transpired, and just managed to blunder his way through the word "transfiguration"! This had also given Judas a basis to conclude that Peter was a blithering idiot who could not even be trusted to keep a secret.

According to Judas Iscariot, the only time that Peter got anything right was when the Deliverer told them that he was making his way to Jerusalem where he was going to suffer greatly from the elders, the chief priests, and the scribes, and be killed. The Deliverer had added something totally incomprehensible, namely that on the third day he was going to be raised up! That was so ridiculous - deliberately giving the priests and Pharisees an opening to do their worst, and then trying to reassure them (his disciples) that everything was going to be all right. No one in his right mind could do such a thing!

And if Peter had not taken the Deliverer aside to rebuke him saying "God forbid, Lord! No such thing shall ever happen to you," he, Judas Iscariot (perhaps even John, if he himself didn't react fast enough) would have done it. Judas interpreted the harangue the Deliverer gave them in the aftermath of Peter's "righteous" explosion, about thinking as the Prime Mover did instead of as humans did, as further evidence that the people of Israel might as well just forget and abandon their hopes for deliverance from the bondage of the Romans, and from their erstwhile allies, namely the self-centered and evil clique that controlled the Sanhedrin in Jerusalem!

The real Judas...

Judas, who had been one of the very first people to join the ranks of the Deliverer's disciples and who had done so by ingratiating himself with the youthful John whom he knew to be very close to the Deliverer by virtue of being a relative of the Deliverer's mom, was certain from the beginning that he was destined to play an important role in the "Christ Fellowship" as he himself liked to refer to the work and mission of the Deliverer.

He did not conceal the fact that he thought highly of John from the beginning, and he even went to the extent of calling him very intelligent in public. In private, around the time that the Deliverer's immediate deputies - or "apostles" as they had already been nicknamed by the crowds which followed them everywhere - reached the magic number of twelve, the disciple from Jericho had pulled John aside to discuss what he said was a very important matter. Judas had noticed that many people in the crowd, after they witnessed the Deliverer's eloquence and were moved by his discourses, frequently reached into their pockets and took out *denarii*, and sometimes pieces of silver, which they then sought, albeit always in vain, to present to the Deliverer for keepsake. His immediate aim was to become the Deliverer's purse holder, but he also had other things on his mind when he asked John to step aside for the private session.

Judas persuaded John that they needed to start thinking big and to approach everything they did from then on systematically, and that if they did not do that, absolute chaos was going to result, especially given the growing popularity of the Deliverer. Recalling the events of the afternoon not long before when the Deliverer miraculously multiplied the five loaves and two fishes into baskets upon baskets of food, Judas said that, because there was no organization, the starving multitudes had initially surged forward for a free helping, much to the disadvantage of the children and the feeble as well as the women who were just as hungry but could not muster the strength to join the unruly rabble.

For starts, Judas explained, they needed to draw up an organization chart that would facilitate coordination of activities and the allocation of tasks among the twelve. He claimed that these things were of critical importance now that people were being attracted in large numbers every day to the Fellowship. If they did not act, Judas told John, the new catechumens would soon be disenchanted with them and would actually walk away.

He told John about the donations, and said he was already in the process of drawing up a plan to take care of that. He confided to John that, under the plan, trusted assistants reporting directly to him would mill in the crowds, armed with the baskets, to ensure that the voluntary offerings were all gathered in efficiently and were safely tucked away.

Judas suggested that a committee preferably consisting of Matthew and Mark, both of whom seemed to be good with the quill, meet under John's chairmanship and begin the all-important task of drawing up the Fellowship's mission statement and a constitution. To get anywhere, they needed to register the Fellowship with the Roman authorities. Such a move, Judas added in a whisper, would put the nervous high priests and other members of the Sanhedrin and the Roman prefect off the scent by making it appear that there was nothing for them to be worried about with respect to the Fellowship's activities.

Judas went on that they needed to move quickly to set up a security detail to protect the Deliverer from any possible harm. The growing belligerency of the high priests highlighted the importance of taking such a step, he said. Judas suggested that John himself be in charge of the security detail.

Judas had even mentioned something about having someone reliably document all the miracles that the Deliverer was performing, with special care being taken to record the exact phrases used by the Deliverer - just in case those phrases contained formulae that might require more time to decipher! In the case of miracles of healing, the log would also include the names and addresses of those healed, as well as a short description of the ailments that had afflicted them. But it was important that the log also include a synopsis of the Deliverer's addresses to the crowds. For, as Judas kept repeating to John and others, there was no doubt whatsoever that they were living at a turning point in the history of mankind; and the way the twelve who surrounded the "Teacher" and "Miracle Worker" conducted themselves was going to affect generations to come.

Now John had never been enamored of strangers, especially fast-talking strangers, and initially lent Judas only half an ear. Besides, a lot of what Judas was saying only struck the wrong chords in him. Big organization, money, etc. were completely novel things to John. These things smacked of greed - organized or what today would be called "corporate greed"!

But Judas, who had anticipated all that, was easily able to read John's thoughts even before he spoke. And so, cutting in, he had added piously: "The Deliverer is here at long last, John. With His help we can channel the ill-gotten gains of the moneyed, who cannot even leave the Deliverer alone, to the poorest of the poor in the Nation of Israel!"

And because he also enjoyed exaggerating things, he had continued that they had a lot of work to do given the number of those who were even then displaced as a result of the Roman occupation.

According to Mjomba, Judas succeeded brilliantly in concealing behind a series of platitudes his real intention of using the Deliverer to establish what would essentially be a corporate entity complete with a separate personality. Once on-going, the corporation under his direction would in turn reward him generously with the equivalent of stock options, magnanimous living allowances equivalent to a fat salary, and a severance package that would be the envy of everyone including the Roman Prefect!

Finally persuaded, John commended Judas for thinking ahead, and even confessed that, up until that moment, he himself had been moving along blindly with the crowd so to speak - as if they owed it to Providence to take care of everything, including taking steps to ensure that no harm befell the Deliverer! In short, John was in total agreement with the proposed plan of action. And they both agreed that, acting jointly, they would arrange for all the twelve to meet in conclave as a matter of urgency. At that meeting, the necessary resolutions legitimizing what they had discussed would also be passed.

After a further exchange of ideas regarding the post of Secretary/Treasurer that, according to Judas, needed to be filled expeditiously, John promised that he would nominate Judas to fill that key position at the upcoming conference.

As expected, the conference, which was convened shortly after the "Sermon on the Beach", appointed Judas to the glamorous position of Secretary/Treasurer of the Christ Fellowship, while the position of Chief of Security went to John. Judas meanwhile derived secret pleasure from the fact that his rival, Peter, had been passed over when appointments to all the other important positions were being made, and that Peter, who clearly showed at the meeting that he could not even address an audience of eleven people, only succeeded in getting himself commissioned, along with his brother James, to form the first line of defense around the Deliverer.

Citing evidence in the Canadian Scrolls, Mjomba wrote that Judas was always elated and smiling whenever he wandered upon Peter or James, because he was sure - or so he thought - that, with just daggers in their arsenals, the duo would be mincemeat when confronted by members of the Jewish constabulary or Roman foot soldiers, not to mention members of the Roman cavalry.

A disciple of the Deliverer and also a candidate for the holy priesthood, Judas was still not really prepared to defend the Messiah to the death as the apostle Peter and the others were despite his avowal to that effect. To be prepared to sacrifice his life for the Deliverer was the last thing on Judas' mind! This was even though Judas, who still "loved" the Deliverer very much, albeit for the wrong reasons, enjoyed very much being the busiest body around Him.

Judas' personal attachment to the things of this world and above all gold or "mammon" (he must have known its worth since he was the fledgling organization's Chief Accountant and Financial Controller) would result in the unsavory situation in which a confidante of the Deliverer ended up betraying Him and then taking his own life shortly afterward! For the right price - and perhaps even the promise of a unique place in history for being the one who would help put away by far the most popular claimant to the title of Deliverer up until that time - Judas was prepared to do the unthinkable, namely send a wholly innocent and just man to His ghastly death on a tree!

High-stakes diplomatic gamble...

In Mjomba's view, the traditional image of Judas as someone who was dumb and short sighted - someone who easily fell for get-rich-quick schemes one moment and who was rushing to cut short his life in despair the next moment - was well off the mark. Arguing that nothing could be further from the truth, Mjomba wrote that the betrayer was in fact a very farsighted and brilliant individual, and almost certainly the brightest of the twelve apostles.

In contrast to Judas, Peter and his brother James (along with their mother) wondered why - since the mission of the Deliverer clearly was not to drive the Roman imperialists out of the promised land as some folks thought - the Messiah, if He was indeed the promised Messiah, did not just "do it", by which they meant whisking them off into heaven and into the company of Moses and Elias, and out of reach of those imperialists!

Following in the footsteps of the first century historian Josephus, Mjomba contrasted Judas to the constantly "bumbling" Peter, a fisherman by trade who seemed a little tardy when it came to learning and had to take his time to decide if dying for the Messiah was actually worth it or not. Mjomba supposed that, in the betrayer's eyes, Peter must have stood out as one of those individuals who generally tended to have an excess of brawn power and a deficiency of brainpower.

Mjomba went on to suggest that Judas was ahead of his time in discerning the winds of change, and the direction in which they likely would blow. According to Mjomba, the Apostle from Jericho therefore clearly understood that the movement the Deliverer was leading wasn't going to go away. If anything, after seeing some of the miracles wrought by the Nazarene, Judas calculated that if he positioned himself strategically inside the movement, he stood a good chance of achieving his ultimate goal of becoming the Deliverer's undisputed deputy, and guaranteeing himself considerable material rewards in the process.

The fact that he had already been appointed Financial Controller and Chief Accountant was clear evidence that the Deliverer would not be in a position to personally oversee His empire as it spread beyond the borders of Palestine and conceivably even supplanted the Roman Empire as the unchallenged world power. Judas was prepared to play his part to bring about the new order and help the Deliverer realize His own dream of dominating the world!

But, while he was a topflight manager with the kind of vision that entrepreneurs prized, the betrayer was a very practical man at the same time. Mjomba wrote that the cunning Judas also believed that there was an acute shortage of diplomatic skills in the upper echelons of the movement's leadership, and he thought that he himself could easily remedy that unsatisfactory situation. One way of doing that was to forge secret connections with the members of the Sanhedrin and eventually also with members of the Roman governor's inner cabinet. That had one special advantage: he, Judas, would always be in the know and, for one, could jump ship early in the unlikely event that the movement's fortunes did not quite meet his expectations and thereby avoid the harsh consequences of promoting a rebellion.

As a young man, Judas had been enrolled by his wealthy parents in an elite academy in suburban Jericho. His major, Management, had included everything from Philosophy, Commerce, Astronomy, International relations, History, and Anthropology to the Scriptures. Although locally owned and managed, the academy also enrolled young Romans whose parents were top brass in the garrison in Jericho. Having rubbed shoulders with the cream of Romans and Jews alike in those formative years, Judas was bursting with confidence that he could dabble in the shady deals that would be the normal fare for him as a double agent and spy, and still successfully cover his tracks.

And so, whereas ordinary folk, unschooled in the ways of this world, would easily be vulnerable, he had no doubt that he was in a position to handle any situation that would threaten to compromise his safety in his wheelings and dealings with the crooked high priests and cunning Romans.

Deep down, Judas actually scorned the high priests and considered them a dumb lot for failing to realize that the Deliverer could not be stopped if for no other reason than that he could actually perform miracles. In his view, people had to be real ignoramuses not to weigh in that fact when choosing sides in a contest and this one in particular. Judas held them in such contempt he was in fact prepared to double cross them too if a suitable opportunity ever came along.

On the strength of the miracles he had personally witnessed first-hand, Judas, who was quite capable of distinguishing the "good guys" from the "bad guys", was convinced that the best thing for now was to hang in there with the rest of the followers of this miracle worker. Here was, after all, a leader who, in addition to being eloquent, could calm rough seas and walk on water at will; he could tell, using divination that was beyond the reach of even the smartest magicians, where to cast nets for the biggest haul of fish; here was an individual who could multiply loaves of bread, and who could read people's secret thoughts; and he could also cure diseases, and above all, raise up the dead!

If he could do these things, he definitely could also strike terror in an enemy force of any strength by, for instance, causing the enemy's provisions and ordinance to evaporate into thin air, or by simply rendering his own troops and those of his allies invulnerable in the face of any kind of enemy assault. He could, if he chose, knock enemy troops off their feet just by poisoning the air they breathed from a safe distance, or he could induce the enemy to surrender by threatening to unleash at a command a deadly virus or some other such calamity on the hostile forces and, if necessary, on their beloved ones as well. Judas had concluded - correctly - that this person, far from being just human, was something else completely. And it was not just a case of "heaven walking on earth" in the manner of Shakespeare's character (Olivia). Judas, despite the soft spot he had for the good life, had absolutely no doubt that this was a case of *God* Himself walking on earth! The Deliverer was divine.

For their part, the priests and Pharisees despised Judas and regarded him as a small-time cheat and scoundrel even as they sought to use his services to achieve their own ends. And they were, accordingly, prepared to blackmail him at any time if they found it in their best interest to do so. And so, when Judas came to the temple in the dead of night to apprise members of the Sanhedrin of the Deliverer's next move, the high priests decided to do precisely that.

Judas had no sooner been ushered into the council chamber where the high priests were still meeting in spite of the fact that it was the day of the Passover than they began berating him for being in league with what they termed "enemies of the Nation of Israel", and an active member of an outlawed movement, to wit. Charging him with participating in an illegal gathering on such a solemn day without special dispensation or a permit, they pressed him to confirm or deny that the gathering in the Upper House, ostensibly to celebrate the Passover, was not for the purpose of conspiring to further sour the relations between the Roman authorities and the Sanhedrin!

The strategy adopted by the high priests played right into the hands of Judas. He only needed to suggest that the Deliverer was up to something very special just on that very night to make any information he might be bringing along seem very important and critical to the success of the plans of the high priests to rein Him in, and Judas did just that.

Saying just enough to alarm the Pharisees and Sadducees without giving away too much and thereby diminishing his usefulness, the betrayer recounted how the self-styled Deliverer had inaugurated the Sacrament of the Eucharist in the Upper House, adding that the Nazarene had also urged them to continue with the practice of "breaking bread" together in His memory. Describing the Deliverer as suicidal, Judas had the members of the Sanhedrin begging for more by merely hinting without providing any further details that the son of the carpenter had served them with His own flesh and blood during that ceremony!

Seeing the utter confusion the information he was volunteering caused his erstwhile friends, Judas knew he had them. He also knew how to add to the terror that was clearly starting to grip them; and he proceeded to provide additional hints relating to other "bizarre" events that had unfolded behind closed doors that evening in the Upper House, including the ritual washing of the feet by the Deliverer!

It gave Judas enormous satisfaction to observe the rising level of apprehension blended with fear in the eyes of his audience as he went on to suggest that the Nazarene was a man on an unstoppable mission; that He had real psychic powers, wielded the equivalent of supernatural powers, and was determined to prosecute His war on the Powers of the Underworld so-called not just religiously, but with certainty that His enemies were already doomed and victory was going to be His. To ensure that he left the high priests and Pharisees totally confused and mystified, the cunning Judas had added something to the effect that the Nazarene had no interest whatsoever in material things, and also that the kingdom He sought to establish was not of this world! The high priests were seething and up in arms as the betrayer, quoting the Nazarene, made a reference to days soon to come when "the temple would be no more"!

Mjomba wrote that the members of the Sanhedrin did not wait for the betrayer to finish before withdrawing the accusations they had just levelled against him; and they even apologized profusely for their rash action which, they now claimed, had been motivated by their zeal for preserving public order and the lofty sense of duty that governed the Council's actions. But their apparent "rush to judgement" had already exposed them as double dealers who could not really be trusted. And their offer to pay Judas whatever sum he demanded (so long as the amount was within reason) for helping them to neutralize the "blasphemer" and his misguided followers (before "that pack", as they referred to the Nazarene and His followers, had done too much harm to the good relations between the Sanhedrin and the Roman occupiers) only confirmed the poor man's worst fears!

In Judas's words, these people were "vipers" with whom one could not conduct business of any sort. He saw that he had made a serious mistake by becoming involved with them, particularly given his aspirations for the position of Chief Executive Officer in the Deliverer's organization. He had no doubt that, after "neutralizing" the Deliverer, they would spare no efforts to neutralize everyone else who was remotely associated with Him.

As Judas left the temple, he was telling himself that if his fellow Israelites could be so callous and could not see any good in having someone who was as admirable and commanding as the Nazarene around (someone who looked like he might even be the awaited Messiah), and if they were so determined to be rid of the Deliverer for no real good reason, it would be bad news indeed when it came to the Romans and especially an individual as morally bankrupt and wily as Pontius Pilate!

Foolishly the betrayer continued to kid himself with the thought that his bold move to play the diplomatic card had paid off. He even told himself that if he had not gambled, he would never have been able to know how bad and dangerous the Pharisees and Sadducees really were! According to Mjomba, Judas was too proud to do otherwise. It would only be after he had finally been stung with a terrible sense of guilt for his part in bringing down the downfall of the Deliverer and Author of Life, and after he had attempted, on second thoughts, to return the blood money that Judas would realize the hopelessness of his own situation.

Essence of being a disciple of the Deliverer...

The betrayer had no doubt in his mind that, with the exception of the Deliverer's immaculately conceived Blessed Mother and a few other individuals like Lazarus whom the Deliverer had caused to live again after he had been dead a while, it was he himself (Judas) who, more than anyone else, grasped the fact that the appearance of the Deliverer was the greatest event since the creation of the world. Even though he had not been present on the mountain with Peter, James and John when the Deliverer became transfigured and appeared to the trio in the company of Moses and Abraham, he certainly had seen and heard enough to convince him that this self-styled "Son of Man" was both *from* and *of* God. Judas certainly knew that, as one of the twelve, he was privy to far more than any of the priests and Pharisees. Judas regarded them with disdain because they were the very people who ought to have been in the forefront welcoming the Deliverer, and also advising the Israelites to prepare themselves for the new order and the "New

Testament" that was going to see the descendants of Adam and Eve reconciled with their Maker!

And so, when Judas finally came to the realization that he had gambled away his chances of being heir apparent to the Deliverer, and of being in a position to benefit from the miracle worker's protection, he could not stand the thought that the "stupid" Peter - the betrayer was so biased against the fisherman, he never thought of him without that pejorative term - and the Deliverer's other disciples whom he likewise regarded as dimwits, were now in a far more secure position than himself vis-à-vis the Deliverer. That was also when Judas literally began seeing red. Suffice it to say, Mjomba wrote, that after Judas started losing control, his pathetic slide into the abyss became a virtual certainty from there on.

Whereas the essence of being a disciple was to learn to deny oneself in order to focus on the hereafter, Judas was still having the blues and unable to get over the fact that he could not lay any real claim to owning anything in this world - not even his own earthly existence which was in every sense a passing existence. The world, of course, needed a Judas to hand the Judge to his judges. Otherwise a critical phase in the work of redemption would not have taken off. In the divine plan, Judas clearly had a distinctive role to play - just as all the other humans have their distinctive roles to play. And if there had been no betrayers, the Son of man, had He decided to come down to earth from heaven all the same, would not have needed Judas to play the role he played.

The roles humans play in the divine plan are all distinctive and important even though humans shun the responsibilities associated with those roles and are, therefore, reluctant to acknowledge that fact. Had the role Judas played been unnecessary, the very idea of a betrayer would have been superfluous! Now that scenario was not in the divine plan, but it would without a doubt have been a much better scenario from the point of view of law and justice.

According to Mjomba, the words "It were better if he had not been born" did not apply to Judas alone, but equally to all humans who ever sinned. The problem with humans, Mjomba wrote, was that they loved to point fingers and even shied away from everything that was likely to trigger their own individual feelings of guilt. Claiming that a re-enactment of what happened was invaluable in establishing that all sinners were as much betrayers of the Deliverer as Judas, the son of Simon Iscariot, Mjomba as usual launched into a detailed and somewhat graphic account of the events that led up to Judas' ignominious end.

Mjomba wrote that, with "Pentecost" and the outpouring of the Holy Ghost that would accompany it along with the calming presence of the Comforter still in abeyance, the Messiah was having a very hard time restraining the eleven apostles. Judas realized that if it were not for the man the group had come to know as "Master" - the very man Judas had just betrayed - he, Judas, was dead meat. It became clear to Judas almost immediately he let go of his embrace of the Deliverer that he faced a certain lynching by the eleven. All of them, not just Peter, were in a foul mood. Judas realized that only a miracle could save him when he saw the eleven closing in on him.

And it was another miracle yet that the betrayer witnessed as the Deliverer, without uttering a word to the eleven or even as much as raising a finger urging them to move away, saved his life just like that. According to Mjomba, it was appropriate to credit the Deliverer with halting the lynching of Judas, which had been imminent in the same way that it was appropriate to credit Him with stepping in just in the nick of time and saving the life of the Roman soldier whom Peter had begun to hack to bits with a butcher's knife! When the Deliverer ordered His disciples to put away their weapons, Judas had already been pinned down and a couple of his former buddies, with Peter at the helm, were preparing to make mincemeat of him.

Mjomba wrote that Judas did not at first understand the action of the Deliverer in stepping in to save his life. Anyone could have told that his act of betrayal was a vile deed indeed, which was made infinitely worse by the fact that he, Judas, had betrayed the miracle worker and Master with - of all things - a kiss! And that was in addition to the fact that hardly four hours earlier, as they celebrated the Pascal feast in the upper house, he not only had had the honor of occupying the most favored seat - immediately to the right of the Deliverer - but he and the Nazarene had in fact shared the same chalice when the wine was served.

It was not as if he did not know that the Nazarene was the long-awaited Messiah. He had never doubted that. But instead of struggling to learn how to pray and mediate with the Deliverer as the "stupid" Peter and the other disciples did, Judas had grown more and more absorbed with material things, including worldly power, he was certain were going to come his way as a result of his association with the miracle worker. Quite a different kind of sin, Judas now acknowledged, from the original sin committed by the first Man and Woman; and his sin typified the sins of his generation that were not really dissimilar to the sins of the immediate descendants of Adam and Eve, focusing as they did strictly on the temporal!

Judas was a very intelligent man who knew without a doubt that the "Miracle Worker" was going to be ridiculed, despised and spat upon. And he had no doubt whatsoever in his mind that a certain and quite gruesome death on the cross awaited the "insurgent", even though He was completely innocent of the false accusations which the priests and Pharisees were preparing to level against Him.

According to Mjomba, Judas, who had decided to pass up the opportunity to be an apostle and a "father of the Church" along with Peter, John and the rest of the twelve because he was not prepared to serve under Peter (the Rock), knew that the "insurgent" and "terrorist", as members of the Sanhedrin consistently referred to the Deliverer, was not really going to do a vanishing act. The "betrayer" knew that his quarry was going to continue going about His Father's business in the open until all the prophecies about Him had been fulfilled.

But, in his greed for money and his craving for power and influence, Judas had gone out of his way to depict his Divine Master as a crafty felon who was likely to disappear in Galilee or Judea after the feast of the Passover, and that he (Judas) was in a position to help the priests and Pharisees capture the insurgent and terrorist before He vanished into thin air - if they coughed up a minimum of thirty pieces of silver. That was even though Judas knew that the real reason the priests and Pharisees were after the Deliverer was the fact that He had interfered with their practice of using the grounds of the temple in Jerusalem and its adjoining facilities for their worldly ends.

That was how Judas, who was bitter with the Deliverer for promoting Peter over him, planned to get even with Him. But that was also the man (Judas Iscariot), at once a betrayer and also an infernal liar, who would forever serve as the role model for all traitors and weasels, despite their lip service to the cause of justice in the world.

Could it really be that it was the Deliverer's desire that he, Judas, should continue to exist even after he had committed that dastardly act of betrayal, just like Lucifer and his minions after they had committed their own flagrant acts of disobedience to the Prime Mover? Judas Iscariot was intrigued. That latest "miracle" seemed to imply just that!

Judas thought about Lucifer and his fellow devils - perhaps their numbers boosted by some human "devils" by now - roasting in hell for eternity, and wishing in vain that there was some way these damned spirits could end their miseries! Yes, wishing in vain that they could above all wipe their guilty consciences clean causing their *"esse"* to evaporate into the nothingness from which they originally came! But Judas appreciated the fact that this was not possible for the simple reason that fallen angels *and* damned humans had been created in the image of the Prime Mover!

But that "miracle", real or imagined, combined with the devastating thought that there was no way in which creatures that had been fashioned in the image of the Creator could escape "judgement", brought Judas back to his senses, according to Mjomba thesis. And it now took the betrayer a fraction of a second to embrace a simple truth the Messiah had tried unsuccessfully over a period of three whole years to drive home to him. The truth in question was that humans were on borrowed time during their sojourn here on earth. Judas also immediately made the connection: even if the Sanhedrin had quadrupled the compensation it had paid him for the pivotal role he played in the arrest of his Master and self-proclaimed Deliverer (who was by all counts quite a "strange" fellow for not heading his advice to stay away from Jerusalem), he, Judas, would not have been able, if the lynching had been successful, to take any of those pieces of silver along with him to his grave!

According to Mjomba's thesis, Judas now clearly realized above all that it was completely unacceptable and disgraceful for humans to be brought into existence out of nothingness by the Prime Mover, and to be promised an inheritance in eternity worthy of celestial princes and princesses, only to turn around and try to claim for themselves prerogatives that belonged to the Prime Mover and Him alone. Judas saw that, in the circumstances, it would have been far better if all humans who had ever offended the Prime Mover, himself included, would not have seen the light of day. It was that simple: if sinners had not come into existence as a result of the gratuitous act of the Creator in the first place, the question of them doing anything contrary to the divine plan - or "sinning" if you will - could never have arisen!

In that moment, Judas would have voluntarily committed himself to a monastery that espoused the most rigorous and severe rules for penitents; but he knew that no such place existed. And so, he rushed back to the temple where the Sanhedrin was still in session, and offered to be put to death in place of the man he had falsely accused. But the high priests informed him they would brook no such nonsense from a person of his intelligence, and they told him to get the blazes quickly out of the august chamber and out of their sight with his tripe. They even let him know that they were so busy they had neither the time nor the resources to devote to a suicide watch in his behalf!

It was at that juncture, Mjomba went on, that Judas saw that all the exits were blocked. He made his situation worse by emptying the silver coins the priests had used to bribe him at their feet before scrambling out of the chamber and the temple. Like someone who had been transformed into a zombie, he hurried away from the imposing structure and headed blindly for the forest located on the western slopes of the Mount of Olives.

A man beyond his time (Judas Iscariot)...

As he shuffled along mindlessly in the darkness, his fingers were busy, nonetheless; and the same went for his sharp mind, which had discovered what he thought was a "loophole" of sorts. He, Judas Iscariot, son of Simon, might not be able to end his existence, or somehow wipe his guilty conscience clean. But he damn well could end his own life and thus be a winner - even if only in the short term! Roman generals defeated in battle against the "barbarians" did it rather than live with the humiliation. So he was not going to be the only one who went that route.

The difference between himself and the Romans was that he was a Jew; and he felt terrible shame being the one who had been caught ostensibly betraying the Messiah - the anointed one whose coming had been eagerly awaited by generations before him, and who was the only reason he and his fellow Jews regarded themselves as special. Yes - a chosen people through whom the Son of the Most High and Redeemer, promised by Him-Who-is-Who-is to Adam and Eve after their fall from grace, was to be given unto the world!

The thought that the priests and Pharisees - the real culprits in his opinion - would still be running around scot-free made him seethe with anger.

But while Roman generals could be excused for not understanding that they had been created in the image of Him-Who-is-Who-is, and could not therefore dilly-dally with their lives in that fashion, the same could not be said for Judas and his fellow Jews. They had had the benefit of being admonished time and again by people like Moses and Abraham, and other messengers of Him-Who-is-Who-is, and could not be excused for not knowing that it was wrong to take away one's own life. And certainly not he, Judas, who not only had been honored with being a contemporary of the Messiah, but was one of the twelve whom the Son of Man, as the Deliverer called Himself, had hand-picked to be "apostles".

But, looked at from a slightly different angle - the angle of a recalcitrant sinner who chose to pursue selfish worldly goals that, taken together, did amount to betrayal of sorts - the shame was just too much to bear! He had cut off his ties with the so-called teachers of the law and the leadership in Jerusalem who were bent on liquidating the Deliverer, and had been trying like mad to find evidence to use to convict Him of everything from disturbing the peace to blasphemy. As far as he (Judas) was concerned, the only evidence they would have against him was the satchel. But it was empty now; and by the time he would be done, it wouldn't even look like one. Most importantly, he could no longer be held to account for the measly thirty pieces of silver that were back in the hands of those who were out to get the Nazarene by hook or by crook.

They were free to use the money as they deemed fit. They were free to use it to buy off people who would spin lies about him in the same way they had tried to buy him off to lie about the Son of Man. The only thing that now bothered the apostle from Jericho was that, before becoming involved with the priests and Pharisees, he had the extraordinary opportunity of learning directly from the Son of Man Himself how to live aright, but had now forfeited it with his reckless gambit.

Judas thought of the countless generations that had gone before his own generation - not to mention the countless humans who had come and gone - since that day in the Garden of Eden, the primeval home of humankind, when the Prime Mover promised the penitent, but still spiritually indigent, Adam and Eve that He would send a Deliverer; and Judas could not, of course, help noting that it was during his own generation that the Prime Mover's promise was being fulfilled. And then, to cap it all, he was one of the chosen few who was allowed by the invisible army of guardian angels that surrounded the Deliverer at all times to get so close to the Author of Life that he could have gotten any of his own questions answered - questions concerning things like the mystery of pain and suffering and the reason good people suffered, the reason birds could fly in the air when other objects were subject to the pull of gravity, and so on - by the Nazarene Himself. This could not be just a coincidence.

He, Judas Iscariot, a Jew and a native son of Jericho, a city that was not even a half-day's walk to Nazareth where the Deliverer grew up, was also one of the Deliverer's twelve apostles! And he had personally heard the Deliverer say so many things that should have been music to the ears of his compatriots, but had clearly fallen on deaf ears.

He had heard the Deliverer say things like "I am the light of the world; he who follows me shall not walk in the darkness, but shall have the light of life…I am the light of the world: he that followeth me, walketh not in darkness, but shall have the light of life…Although I give testimony of myself, my testimony is true: for I know whence I came, and whither I go: but you know not whence I come, or whither I go. You judge according to the flesh: I judge not any man. And if I do judge, my judgment is true: because I am not alone, but I and the Father that sent me…You are from beneath, I am from above. You are of this world; I am not of this world. Therefore I said to you, that you shall die in your sins. For if you believe not that I am He, you shall die in your sin…I go, and you shall seek me, and you shall die in your sin. Whither I go, you cannot come…Neither me do you know, nor my Father: if you did know me, perhaps you would know my Father also...I have not a devil: but I honour my Father, and you have dishonored me. But I seek not my own glory: there is one that seeketh and judgeth. Amen, amen I say to you: If any man keep my word, he shall not see death for ever...Amen, amen I say to you, before Abraham was made, I am."

But it was what the Deliverer had said to the adulterous woman - after the scribes and Pharisees, who had brought and set her in their midst with the intent of using her to entrap Him, went away one by one beginning with the eldest - that had been the most touching of all. In response to her statement that her accusers had all left without condemning her, He had simply said: "Neither will I condemn thee. Go, and now sin no more."

The whore, Judas noted, was a fickle human, and she was inclined to sin like all humans, he himself included. On her own she undoubtedly was going to revert to her life of sin. But here the Deliverer was, looking her in the eye, and telling her to "go and sin no more". There was one thing the Nazarene certainly wasn't meaning in a literal sense. Even though He was using the word "Go", Judas understood that as meaning "Take care and don't you forget who is addressing you!" For this woman not to revert to her adulterous life, she had to stay quite close to the Son of Man and Deliverer of Humankind, who had taught His disciples that He was also the fount of the grace humans needed to stay upright.

That, quite obviously, was a testament to the Deliverer's divinity. But what still eluded Judas Iscariot was how exactly this would work. Judas Iscariot had ruled out the possibility that the Deliverer needed to suffer, and perhaps even sacrifice His life, like a lamb lead to the slaughter, to merit the graces that humans needed for their redemption. That was completely out of question in Judas's view. The Nazarene was not just from God. He was God - period. And that meant that he couldn't wage a losing battle against Evil by allowing Himself to die or perish - as would have been the lot of humans in the absence of the promise of a Deliverer!

It did not strike Judas Iscariot that, because the Deliverer had two natures, namely a human nature and a divine nature, what he regarded as impossible and completely improbable was in a fact quite feasible. But even then, Judas Iscariot could not have imagined the miracle worker and His Savior humiliating Himself to that extent. As Judas Iscariot saw it, if the Deliverer allowed the priests and Pharisees to triumph over Him, it would not just be tantamount to an acknowledgement that He had suffered dismal defeat at the hands of wicked humans, but to a statement that the rule of Evil on earth was going to continue as if the Messiah, who had been foretold, had not come! If He did that, He would be betraying them (Judas and the Deliverer's other disciples)!

Thinking about the adulterous woman, Judas Iscariot knew that his own dilly-dallying with the priests and Pharisees represented questionable actions and probably unconscionable given the motivations behind them; and he knew that they were in fact scandalous, given his position in the Fellowship or movement the Deliverer had been laboring to establish over the three year He had been criss-crossing Galilee, Judea and Samaria. But even though Judas Iscariot now heard those same words of the Deliverer ringing in his ears as never before, and knew the disposition of the Deliverer to human weaknesses, failings, imperfections and sins of omission and commission, he had already decided that he was completely undeserving of God's mercies.

He, Judas Iscariot, wasn't a tax collector or a highway robber, and certainly no murderer. But he still knew deep down in his heart that it was his greed that had been behind his desperate hope that the priests and Pharisees would see light and join the Fellowship; and it was also that same greed - coupled with his displeasure at having to answer to Peter, the "Rock upon which the Deliverer was going to build His church" - that had resulted in his realizing too late that his actions had given the priests and Pharisees everything they needed to liquidate the Deliverer, namely the one "witness" from the inner circle of their Public Enemy Number One!

But he was a witness who, if not handled properly, could expose them and threaten their own positions, and who could poison the relations they had hitherto enjoyed with the Cæsar, or "the Great Satan" as they surreptitiously referred to the Roman emperor. Even now, Judas Iscariot suspected that agents of M1, as the dreaded secret police were known, were on his trail; perhaps watching and observing his every move. Their mission: to seize him and, after wringing more "voluntary confessions" from him using water boarding and their other methods which of course amounted to torture, present him as their star witness at the kangaroo trial of the Deliverer.

Judas, who had been the *de facto* major-domo in the organization of the Miracle Worker and self-proclaimed "Son of Man", wasn't going to let them. He preferred to kill himself, especially as he knew that the priests and Pharisees would in any case find a way to make him "disappear" as soon as he had served their purposes. He was not going to let those crooks use him in any way - period! He had no doubt that he, Judas Iscariot and son of Simon, was a particularly important "catch" in their eyes - even more so than Peter or Simon Bar-Jona who had been designated by the Nazarene as the rock on which He was going to construct His church, and also as the recipient of the keys of the kingdom of heaven, so that whatever he would bind on earth would be bound in heaven, and whatever he would loose on earth would be loosed in heaven!

There was one thing about the Deliverer and his relationship with the rulers and elders and scribes that really thrilled Judas Iscariot. This was the courage coupled with the Deliverer's extraordinary self-effacing approach in his dealings with the scribes and teachers of the law, and the forthright manner with which the Nazarene was able to tell the priests and scribes to their face that He was the Truth and the Light. From the day Judas Iscariot was inducted into the ranks of the apostles, Judas had marvelled at the extreme care, respect and tact that characterized the Deliverer's dealings with the scribes and teachers of the law.

It was obvious to Judas Iscariot that the Nazarene, who could read minds, did everything according to script from Day One, as "He went about His Father's business". He had left no doubt in the minds of His twelve apostles that He recognized the elders and the priests and Pharisees as the lawful successors of Moses and the other messengers whom the Prime Mover, His Father in heaven, had employed in guiding the twelve tribes of Israel from Egypt into the Promised Land in anticipation of His own coming. He had accordingly engaged them from very early on, as it was incumbent upon these people as the leaders of the people of Israel to establish contact with Him, and place themselves at His service during the pivotal transition from the Old Order or Testament to the New Testament. But it had soon become very clear that those poor forsaken children of Adam and Eve were going to do no such thing!

Judas Iscariot had also noted that, unworthy though the leadership in Jerusalem was, it deserved the prayers of all people of good will, starting with the Deliverer Himself; and it did not surprise Judas Iscariot that the Son of Man, leading them by example, constantly had the scribes and the teachers of the law in His prayers. It was clear to the Deliverer's Purse Bearer and to the other apostles that the Deliverer had all the Jews and their leaders very much in mind when he taught them to pray to His Father in heaven.

But the Deliverer spent a lot of time praying for all the descendants of Adam and Eve as well as for themselves as his chosen apostles. For instance, before formally appointing them as His disciples or "apostles", He had formally invited them individually by name to join Him on His trek to the top of Mount Tabor in Galilee. And once there, He had prayed over them, and had solemnly laid His sacred hands on them, and beseeched forgiveness for their trespasses personally from His heavenly Father, praying that they would each individually have the strength and perseverance which they needed to carry out the work He was entrusting upon them as His missionaries.

It was not until each one of them had voluntarily taken turns to recite the "Our Father" and do so accurately and with due solemnity that He gave them the authority to cast out devils. Judas Iscariot recalled how hard it was for him to understand the full significance of the words "The light shines in the darkness, but the darkness has not understood it. I am in the world, and though the world was made through Me, the world does not recognize Me"! But Judas Iscariot was not at all surprised when it took Peter so much longer than everyone else to just understand that "the light" signified "the Deliverer'!

Now, it didn't take long for Judas Iscariot and his buddies in the Deliverer's inner circle to see that the scribes and the teachers of the law just weren't going to get it. It was always as if these folks and the Deliverer were speaking in two completely different languages! To take just one example, the Deliverer, who must have known that He didn't have a whole lot of time, was in the temple courts long before dawn broke on one occasion, and he was surrounded by a large concourse of people who were eager to hear Him speak about the "New Testament" that He was ushering in.

He was speaking only a day after He had performed many miracles, and cast out the devils that had been tormenting so many souls; and He was expressing what the Purse Bearer thought was obvious, and saying to the gathering: "I am the light of the world. Whoever follows me will never walk in darkness, but will have the light of life."

But the Pharisees challenged him saying, "Here you are, appearing as your own witness; your testimony is not valid."

These people were clearly set against the Nazarene without regard to whatever His message to the crowd might be, and had their own fixed ideas concerning the redemption of mankind. But the Deliverer, ever meek and humble of heart, had answered, "Even if I testify on my own behalf, my testimony is valid, for I know where I came from and where I am going... But you have no idea where I come from or where I am going... You are from below; I am from above. You are of this world; I am not of this world…I told you that you would die in your sins; if you do not believe that I am the one I claim to be, you will indeed die in your sins."

"And who are you?" they growled?

"Just what I have been claiming all along," the Deliverer answered resolutely; "When you have lifted up the Son of Man, then you will know that I am, and that I do nothing on my own but speak just what the Father has taught me. Then you will know the truth, and the truth will set you free."

That caused the priests and Pharisees to scream: "We are Abraham's descendants and have never been slaves of anyone. How can you say that we shall be set free?"

The Nazarene said calmly in response: "I tell you the truth, everyone who sins is a slave to sin. Now a slave has no permanent place in the family, but a son belongs to it forever. So if the Son sets you free, you will be free indeed. I know you are Abraham's descendants. Yet you are ready to kill me, because you have no room for my word. I am telling you what I have seen in the Father's presence, and you do what you have heard from your father."

"Abraham is our father," they hollered in fury.

Already at that point, Judas Iscariot and the rest of the twelve were worried that all hell was going to get loose, and had edged in closer to the Deliverer, not so much for the purpose of shielding Him, but because they themselves felt safer from the throng in His vicinity.

"If you were Abraham's children," the Miracle Worker continued, "then you would do the things Abraham did. As it is, you are determined to kill me, a man who has told you the truth that I heard from God. Abraham did not do such things. You are doing the things your own father does."

"We are not illegitimate children," they shouted while beating their breasts. "The only Father we have is God himself."

The Son of Man said to them, "If God were your Father, you would love me, for I came from God and now am here. I have not come on my own; but he sent me. Why is my language not clear to you? It is because you are unable to hear what I say. You belong to your father, the devil, and you want to carry out your father's desire. He was a murderer from the beginning, not holding to the truth, for there is no truth in him. When he lies, he speaks his native language, for he is a liar and the father of lies. Yet because I tell the truth, you do not believe me! Can any of you prove me guilty of sin? If I am telling the truth, why don't you believe me? He who belongs to God hears what God says. The reason you do not hear is that you do not belong to God."

The spokesmen for the Jews answered him, "Aren't we right in saying that you are a Samaritan and demon-possessed?"

"I am not possessed by a demon," said the Deliverer, "but I honor my Father and you dishonor me. I am not seeking glory for myself; but there is one who seeks it, and he is the judge. I tell you the truth, if anyone keeps my word, he will never see death."

At that the priests and Pharisees exclaimed, "Now we know that you are demon-possessed! Abraham died and so did the prophets, yet you say that if anyone keeps your word, he will never taste death. Are you greater than our father Abraham? He died, and so did the prophets. Who do you think you are?"

By that time Judas Iscariot, who had already lost his patience with the hostile crowd, was agitated and would have liked to see the Deliverer perform a sign that would cause the Deliverer's enemies to scatter before them in disarray. This was despite the fact that the Purse Bearer and the other apostles had been receiving instructions from the Nazarene for some time now as a part of their preparation for their roles as His apostles.

The instructions received by the twelve were always preceded by prayers led by the Son of Man, and by meditation in the course of which He always unfailingly reminded them of the fact that His Father in heaven so loved the world, that He gave his only begotten Son, so that everyone who believes in him may not perish but may have eternal life. Thanks to these instructions, Judas Iscariot and the other apostles were all on board, and understood that the Nazarene was indeed the Son of the Most High who had come down in fulfillment of the promise of a Deliverer which the Prime Mover made to Adam and Eve and their descendants in the wake of the fall from grace.

On this occasion just as on the other occasions when the teaching of their loving divine Master fell on deaf ears, the apostles were shocked to see the Jews reject the promised Messiah out of ignorance. But they also benefited from observing the persistence of the Son of Man for whom every human soul was priceless.

The hawkish Judas Iscariot was mollified just the same when he heard the Nazarene reply thus: "If I glorify myself, my glory means nothing. My Father, whom you claim as your God, is the one who glorifies me. Though you do not know him, I know him. If I said I did not, I would be a liar like you, but I do know him and keep his word. Your father Abraham rejoiced at the thought of seeing my day; he saw it and was glad."

Any observer could have told that the Deliverer's purse-bearer was thoroughly disgusted when one of the scribes, after briefly consulting with the other teachers of the law and speaking on behalf of all of them, retorted: "You are not yet fifty years old, and you have seen Abraham!"

Whereupon the miracle worker answered: "I tell you the truth, before Abraham was born, I am!"

At that, the concourse of people, led by the priests and Pharisees, picked up stones to stone the promised Messiah. The situation was very serious, and it was only the quick thinking of Judas Iscariot that saved the day permitting the Nazarene to slip away from the temple grounds. After whisking the Son of Man behind an enclosure, Judas Iscariot, with

John's help, had succeeded in disguising the Nazarene as a woman, thus enabling Him to avoid being apprehended by the infuriated scribes and teachers of the law.

It seemed to Judas Iscariot that the greater the unbelief of the scribes and Pharisees, the greater the zeal which the Deliverer put into efforts to help them see through their selfishness, and come to the realization that He *was* the promised Redeemer of humankind. In order to drive the lessons home to the leadership in Jerusalem, the Deliverer went out of His way to tell parables that left no doubt whatsoever that the intensity of their animosity for Him notwithstanding, it was incumbent upon them as the lawful representatives of the twelve tribes of Israel to own up to the fact that He was the long-awaited Messiah, or stand condemned for their unbelief.

In other words, He expected them to step up to the plate and provide leadership to the people of the Prime Mover who, like Simeon, had been waiting for their redemption for a long time. He did not beat about the bush, or disguise the fact that the salvation of their souls was at risk, as He told parables during the course of His teaching, and made it crystal clear that He was from the Prime Mover and not from the devil (as they would have liked to suppose) by performing many wonders to back up His claims to boot.

The failure of the compatriots of the apostles, led by the scribes and Pharisees, to recognize the Deliverer and Son of Man in the miracle worker from Nazareth was at first nothing short of a mystery in the eyes of Judas Iscariot and the other apostles. And it was only little by little that the twelve started to realize that it wasn't just the priests and scribes and teachers of the law who were thick skinned and totally blind when it came to recognizing the truth, but humankind as a whole, they themselves included. The apostles seemed surprised by the reticence shown by the Deliverer and the pains he took to avoid embarrassing the priests and Pharisees even as those zealots were as determined as ever to seize on every straw in their efforts to entrap the man of God.

Unaccustomed to the rough and tumble of the politics of the day, and the cloak and dagger intrigues and the outright lies that characterized them, the apostles were already worrying to death that the Deliverer was in danger of falling victim to the chicanery of the hypocritical priests and Pharisees when it became obvious that it was those supposed defenders of truth who were making themselves a laughing stock in the course of trying to malign the Savior of the world!

But this also coincided with the realization by the apostles that their own disposition wasn't all that different from that of the despicable priests and Pharisees. This was especially true of Judas Iscariot who started to acknowledge, deep down in his heart, that if push came to shove, he would have to admit that he was in the Fellowship or the Movement for the money and the prestige. This was even though he had no doubt whatsoever in his mind that the

Nazarene was the promised Messiah who had come to redeem humankind including himself!

It was as Judas Iscariot was following the incredible story of the miraculous cure of the man who had been blind from birth and whose sight was restored by the Deliverer on the sacred day of rest - and the equally incredible tale of unbelief demonstrated by the teachers of the law - that the betrayer came round and acknowledged his own precarious position. He could not at first believe that a person of his intelligence could knowingly turn a blind eye to sacred truths, and continue merrily along in pursuit of things of this world, in complete disregard of the overwhelming evidence in favor of a life of self-denial and a commitment to follow in the footsteps of the Anointed One and Redeemer of the World! Judas Iscariot was certain that all his fellow apostles, including Simon Peter whom the Deliverer had referred to as the rock that was going to be the bulwark or foundation of His *Sancta Ecclesia*, were in the exact same boat as himself if not worse. And whereas he himself was at least acknowledging that he was wanting as an apostle of the Son of Man, he recorded in the diary he surreptitiously kept that he hadn't seen any sign that the same was true with any of his buddies!

Judas Iscariot, who had nothing but disdain for the priests and Pharisees, thought that they quite often went completely overboard and, blinded by their rage and hatred for the man who was indisputably the Messiah of Israel and the Savior of the World, ended up making complete fools of themselves as they attempted to trip Him up in vain! He thought that the temple leadership had become like charlatans who actually found fun in twisting facts to suit any situation, as was evidenced by their jingoistic and at times wacky reaction to the miraculous healing of the man who had been blind from birth.

Like the Deliverer, Judas Iscariot did not question the fact that the priests and scribes were the true successors to Moses and also to Joshua, Moses' immediate successor whose name coincidentally meant "Jehovah is salvation", and was the same name as Jesus! Judas Iscariot nonetheless had an intense personal interest in building a case against the temple leadership – a case that would fault them for being morally bankrupt at a time when their positions as the spiritual leaders of the twelve tribes of Israel required them to be exemplars of virtue and wisdom in the same way Moses and Joshua were!

The betrayer and his fellow apostles had been privileged to hear first-hand from Mary, the Mother of the Son of Man, the events of that day years earlier when Joseph travelled with Mary for the consecration to the Lord of their month and a half old son in accordance with the Law of Moses. Mary had narrated to the apostles how everyone's attention had turned to Simeon and the song into which he burst upon taking the child Jesus in his arms. Simeon, who lived in Jerusalem and was just a few years short of his 100th birth day, had proclaimed aloud as all those who were present listened attentively: "Now thou dost dismiss thy servant, O

Lord, according to thy word in peace; Because my eyes have seen thy salvation, Which thou hast prepared before the face of all peoples: A light to the revelation of the Gentiles, and the glory of thy people Israel!"

Simeon's canticle echoed the words of an angel of the Lord on an earlier occasion to Joseph: "Joseph, son of David; do not be afraid to take Mary as your wife; for that which has been conceived in her is of the Holy Spirit. And she will bear a son; and you shall call His name Jesus, for it is He who will save His people from their sins."

And Judas Iscariot also saw a direct connection with Mary's account of the manner in which an entire choir of angels brought the good tidings to the shepherds in Bethlehem as the angels sang: "Do not be afraid. We bring you great joy for all the people: to you is born this day in the City of David a savior, who is the Messiah, the Lord!"

According to the entry in the diary of Judas Iscariot, the actions of the priests and scribes confirmed his conclusion that human history up until the advent of the Messiah represented an era of darkness and despair; and that, sadly, not all the people who walked in darkness would see the great light--the light that nevertheless was going to shine on all who lived in the land where, in the words of the Prophet Isaiah, "death cast its shadow".

And so, while Joseph, the shepherds, and Simeon saw that great light, the scribes and the Pharisees, for whatever reason, wanted to live on in darkness! For these people, it was anathema to accept that the prophecy of Isaiah was fulfilled in the birth of Mary's God child, the one who would be called "Wonderful Counsellor, Mighty God, Everlasting Father, and the Prince of Peace"! And to show that they meant business, they expelled the man who had been blind from birth, but now could see after being healed by the Deliverer, from the Synagogue and openly dared anyone else to try and align himself or herself with the Son of Man and Savior of Humankind! Judas Iscariot did not even know if the era of darkness was now really over or continuing!

After restoring the sight of the man who would subsequently be excommunicated by the priests and Pharisees from the Synagogue, the miracle worker used the occasion to emphasize that being in the world, He was de facto the Light that was shining in that dark world. That automatically signified that the elevated positions of the priests and Pharisees as "teachers of the law" notwithstanding, they in fact were children of darkness as well as liars and pretenders who, like the hired hands in the parable of the Good Shepherd, were liable to abandon the sheep and to flee at the first sign of a wolf!

And that also made one thing very clear to the betrayer (Judas Iscariot), namely that a hallmark of liars amongst humans was the eagerness with which individuals proclaimed that they were the standard bearers of truth. In other words, humans who laid claim to having a monopoly over truths were more likely than not to be purveyors of lies and masters in the art of deception and misinformation! And the sole exception to that rule was the Deliverer and Light of the World; and it was becoming clearer and clearer by the day if not by the hour that He was going to pay for that with His life! It was something Judas Iscariot now saw as inevitable.

And, as far as the apostle from Jericho was concerned, the exchange between the blind man from birth who went and washed the clay and spittle the Deliverer had rubbed on his eyes and started seeing again, and the bigoted, high strung priests and Pharisees who had gone out of their way to peddle lies about the Deliverer in their efforts to make the Roman governor side with them against the miracle worker from Nazareth, amply illustrated how the minds of pathological liars worked.

It saddened the purse bearer of the Deliverer to think that the world was a wicked place in which liars as a rule triumphed while those who held to the truth invariably lost out. And, seeing the death of the Deliverer and Son of Man coming, the betrayer expected the world to plunge into pitch darkness once again!

Like a pundit-cum-diplomat, Judas Iscariot had been monitoring the speeches of members of the Sanhedrin, and he had been utterly disgusted by the way they twisted the truth and lied about the opposition in order to win political points. And if there had been anyone willing to lend him an ear, he could have predicted from day one that the priests and Pharisees on the one hand and the Deliverer on the other were going to be the strangest of bedfellows.

But Judas Iscariot also knew that if anyone found oneself, wittingly or unwittingly, in opposition to that clique in Jerusalem, the clique that was the *de facto* ruling oligarchy in the Roman enclaves of Galilee, Judea and Samaria, that was for all intents and purposes tantamount to a kiss of death. Opposition was simply not tolerated; and, not surprisingly, not a soul in memory was known to have stood up against the establishment in Jerusalem and survived unscathed. This was also the reason there was ostensibly such harmony among the twelve tribes of the Chosen People.

It irked Judas Iscariot that the chief priests and the teachers of the law - the very people who should have stepped up to the plate and laid out a red carpet welcome for the long expected Messiah - not only had abdicated their responsibilities in that regard; but, following their gross betrayal of the trust of both the Nation of Israel and all the descendants of Adam and Eve, were now also guilty of what amounted, in his view, to a crime against humanity! But, as if that wasn't bad enough, led by Joseph Caiaphas and his father-in-law, Annas, the scribes and the chief priests, while quite capable of recognizing the promised Messiah in the miracle worker, even though they had eyes that could see, were unwilling to do so for the simple reason that His unheralded arrival threatened their livelihood!

As leaders of the twelve tribes of Israel, they should have recognized the Nazarene for what He was, namely someone in whom the Spirit of the Lord reposed as a result of being anointed and being commanded to take good tidings to the poor - someone who was sent to proclaim release to the captives and recovery of sight to the blind, and to let the oppressed go free as Isaiah had foretold!

It may be that, thanks to His virgin mother Mary's *fiat*, His advent, which had been foretold according to what they themselves taught, was already a *fait accompli*! It may well be, likewise, that He was the *Alpha* and the *Omega*, the beginning and the end, whose stated mission was to lead souls that were thirsty to the springs of the living water so they could freely drink. But that was no excuse for their unpreparedness which now made it look like it was the Messiah who, coming out of nowhere and blundering into their world, was threatening to render them jobless without even as much as a warning!

They still knew that God had spoken to Moses; and, as teachers of the law, their work was cut out for them. They were also no doubt still very conscious of the fact that everyone, male and female, young and old, with means or without, in good health or in bad health, looked up to them for guidance not just in matters of the spirit, but also in matters pertaining to the outer man. But then all of a sudden, feigning ignorance, they seemed quite happy to just remain Moses' disciples, and were not only unwilling to step into the role of welcoming the promised Messiah when He was finally showing up, but were out to stop anyone who did!

And for the past several months, those "teachers of the law" whom the Deliverer, not once but on many occasions, had engaged as he healed the sick and spoke to the multitudes about the kingdom of heaven, had mounted the dirtiest smear campaign imaginable to discredit the Deliverer - a campaign based on such naked lies, many ordinary folk could not help laughing at what they heard coming out of the mouths of the priests and Pharisees! The fact that the priests and Pharisees had not stretched forth their hands against the Deliverer in the days when the miracle worker had been daily with them in the temple initially had caused others, including Judas, to think that the elders of the people had to be joking!

But now that their evil intent had been unmasked, the Apostle from Jericho was livid, and wondered how those *ignoramuses* had gotten the cheek to say what they were saying about his Master and Rabbi, let alone their evident determination to see Him liquidated at any cost! Since he not only had been attempting to maintain a line of communication with them, but still believed that it was a good idea to remain in touch, given his position as the Deliverer's "treasurer-cum-corporate secretary', Judas felt genuinely betrayed. He could almost imagine the liars coming out, and bearing down on the miracle worker with swords and clubs - as though against a thief! These people were just so reckless and unfeeling!

In Judas Iscariot's view, this was just terrible, happening in these times when there was the ever present danger that the Roman occupiers who worshiped idols instead of the God of Abraham and Isaac, on an impulse could impose on the chosen people of the Prime Mover laws that were at variance with the faith of their forefathers. The twelve tribes of Israel, whose individual members had held fast to the Law of Moses while they waited on the Prime Mover for deliverance from the god-less Roman imperialists, deserved better leadership. Judas Iscariot was very disappointed that the scribes and Pharisees, who spent a great deal of their time teaching and explaining the law, and who were renowned for their sanctity and holiness, not to mention the great care they exercised in their observance of the smallest precepts of the law, were failing the nation of Israel in that fashion.

It was also the role of the priests and scribes to help their flock grapple and cope with blessings and especially with misfortunes in life one example of which was the blight of coming into the world blind. But here they were manhandling the poor chap who had been delivered from his infirmity by the Nazarene. He had done as he had been instructed by the Nazarene; and he had received healing thereby.

But they had instead thrown him out of the Synagogue and excommunicated him for bearing witness to the Nazarene and Messiah, arguing that he was "altogether born in sins" and yet was daring to show them the way to the promised Messiah! He was daring to suggest that his supposed "Deliverer", who did not observe the Sabbath, was someone from God; and this man who had been blind from birth even had the guts to stand there and argue with them regarding who was or was not a worshipper of God, or a doer of God's will!

In the view of the priests and Pharisees, this was unheard of; and it highlighted the importance of reigning in the Nazarene without delay to stop Him from confusing the people, and perhaps even instigating a rebellion against the authorities! In any case, the priests and Pharisees and the teachers of the law, who sincerely did not know whence the reputed miracle worker came from - and (as Judas Iscariot noted) didn't have any reason to care to know - could be excused for not having any time for the outsider and impostor!

But, Oh - Mama Mia! If the Deliverer and Son of Man, who had come down from heaven, had not only signified his willingness to suffer indignities at the hands of wicked humans, but had even revealed that these "teachers of the law and elders" were plotting to kill him for stating the unpalatable truth and refusing to betray His heavenly Father, they on their part surely could also have stepped back to see what was at stake here, and done a favor not just to the twelve tribes of Israel over which they presided but to themselves as well.

Even though Judas Iscariot was fully cognizant of the activities of Matthew and Mark with respect to the all-important task of keeping detailed accounts of the miracles and signs the Deliverer performed, and also of His exchanges with the teachers of the law, on papyri pursuant to resolutions that had been passed by all twelve apostles in conclave, he had been so moved by the confrontations he saw developing between the Deliverer and the priests and Pharisees, he had decided to keep his own independent record of the goings-on. This was in addition to his official responsibilities as the Movement's comptroller.

In his mind, there was simply too much at stake to leave that task to Matthew and Mark alone. Judas Iscariot nonetheless felt a sense of guilt and even shame for supposing that Matthew and Mark couldn't be trusted to do what they were actually well equipped to do. But those feelings of guilt and shame dissipated when Judas Iscariot noticed not long afterwards that John was doing the same thing, namely keeping detailed notes of almost everything that was happening. But even as Judas Iscariot was feeling vindicated, and was taking comfort of sorts from knowing that his own reasoning had been right on, his feelings of relief were suddenly overshadowed by something else.

This was the realization that his decision to keep a tab on the scheming of the chief priests and Pharisees and their determined efforts to try and ensnare the Deliverer into making a misstep, real or imagined, coinciding as it did with John's own decision in the same regard, pointed to an even larger issue. This, namely, was the determination of the scribes and Pharisees to stop the Deliverer at all costs. Although it was evident at every step that they were in the wrong and the Deliverer was in the right, that very fact was working against the Deliverer who consistently claimed that His kingdom was not of this world. That in turn caused Judas Iscariot to sense that the final battle lines had been drawn.

Judas Iscariot recalled that the Deliverer had told the priests and Pharisees to their face that he was going, and they would be looking for him, and they were going to die in their sin, because whither he was going, they could not go. He had let them know that they were from beneath and He was from above; and that they were of this world while He was not of this world. Judas Iscariot even found comfort of sorts in the fact that the priests and Pharisees seemed incapable of grasping how the Deliverer could call the Prime Mover his Father! Noting that they all were likely to bump into each other in hell, Judas Iscariot still managed to focus on just the priests and Pharisees, and he had hissed "Good riddance!" as if his own damnation did not really matter.

Judas Iscariot could not believe that, all through the time he had been a member of the Deliverer's inner circle, he had continued to maintain secret lines of communication with the despicable foes of his Master. When he started dillydallying with the scribes and the priests and Pharisees, it was not so much their role as the leaders of the twelve tribes of Israel, and as teachers of the Law, that was uppermost in his mind, as his own potential role as a power broker who in time might be pivotal in getting these successors to Moses and the prophets to accept the Nazarene as the promised Messiah! He was only focused on the potential influence he might wield in the Christ Fellowship, and he had realized too late that the priests and Pharisees and particularly the scribes were not the sort of people one could bargain with - and that he had been relegated to the status of a mole, and was just being used by them to monitor the Deliverer's activities!

Judas Iscariot was feeling much calmer now; and this was reflected in the things he started recalling from his vast store of knowledge of the things that characterized the life of the Son of Man from the time he himself had been called to join the Deliverer's fellowship as one of the twelve. He again recalled that the Messiah, or "Anointed One", had gone out of His way to teach him and the other apostles how to pray and how to meditate on divine mysteries, and above all how to serve, and eschew selfishness. Judas saw that he had squandered the chance of a lifetime!

But Judas could not stomach the idea of falling tummy first on-to a sharpened sword, and even less the thought of ending his miseries by sipping a drink laced with poison from a goblet. Again as a Jew, he preferred to go along with the common if unsubstantiated belief that taking a life - your own or someone else's - by hanging was a more "humane" way of doing it.

From the little Judas knew, even if Adam and Eve had not sinned and there was no need for a Deliverer, this man whom he had betrayed by continuing to "talk" to the priests and Pharisees - the Son of Man - would definitely have come down from heaven just to keep the family of humans company all the same! Observing the mien of the Son of Man from close quarters as He trudged up and down the hills of Galilee talking about His Father, Judas had come to the conclusion that this Man and His Father, united in the Holy Ghost, really loved the world. The world was, after all, their own creation!

It was clear to Judas that if He-Who-is-Who-is had been prepared to sacrifice His only begotten Son for the salvation of mankind from sin, and not allow Beelzebub to triumph, He would have had even more reason to send His Son to keep humans company in a sinless world - if only because humans, who one and all were created through the Prime Mover's self-same divine Son along with all things that He made, had been fashioned in the image! Judas was convinced of that.

And now the thought that the Son of Man, if there had not been any "sin in the world" - which was the same thing as saying "people like Judas who were prepared to betray Him-Who-is-Who-is" - would have come down to earth from heaven all the same to be with humans, in a glorious and triumphant display of divine love, and in complete safety from the likes of Judas, was just overwhelming. His fingers working very quickly, the betrayer had no difficulty converting the pouch he had used to carry the pieces of silver into a rope. That bag had been made of rugged fibre; and, consequently, the rope with which Judas was going to hang himself was also rugged and strong. Even though it was not overly long, he was sure it could do the job and he was quite happy with it.

Judas could not help recalling how, a couple of months earlier, the priests and Pharisees, incensed by the fact that the Nazarene and self-proclaimed Deliverer had restored the sight of a man who had been blind from birth on the Sabbath Day, had tried to arrest Him and failed miserably in their attempt. The miracle worker simply vanished from their midst. For a moment, Judas, John, Mark and the other members of the Nazarene's inner circle had no doubt that the priests and Pharisees, aided by the posse of Temple guards accompanying them, were going to vent their anger on them and ship them off to the torture chambers in the belly of the Temple!

Perhaps, to show that He hadn't abandoned them, the Deliverer, clad in His distinctive, seamless white cassock, had suddenly reappeared on the edge of the crowd that had gathered when word spread that the authorities had descended on the group with the intention of taking the miracle worker into custody.

The priests and Pharisees had obviously not yet recovered from the fact that their quarry could vanish from right under their noses as they were closing in on Him on the other hand; and His reappearance in the vicinity moments later apparently caused them to be seized with fright, so that, instead of the apostles taking off in all directions to try and avoid being taken into custody and everything that would have entailed, it was the priests and Pharisees who had scrambled to get the hell out of there with the Temple guards hard on their heels! It made for a very amusing sight as the excited crowd joined Judas and his buddies in clapping with joy and cheering them as they chanted "Good riddance"!

But this time around, the Deliverer, like someone who was suicidal, had journeyed to Jerusalem and into the hornet's nest so to speak against their advice and that of their well-wishers. And Judas was not one to be deluded by the passing and indeed short-lived welcome that the group had received as they entered Jerusalem. He had sensed, correctly, that the palm waving and delirious crowds could easily be infiltrated by agents of the Pharisees and Sadducees, and transformed into a mob that was screaming for their blood in the twinkling of an eye. It was indeed a wonder that this had not yet happened!

Anyway, Judas knew that the Deliverer, even though bent on courting death at the hands of his enemies, was totally innocent of any human frailty or sin, let alone being guilty of any breach of the law, be it Jewish Law or Roman Law or, for that matter, Divine Law. The only wrongdoing the Deliverer had been guilty of (if it could be called wrongdoing) was His decision to pass him over when choosing the "Rock" as He put it on which He planned to build His ecclesia! The Deliverer's purse bearer, who still had nothing but contempt for Peter, had himself always been inclined to see nothing but opportunity - albeit opportunity in the worldly sense - in being close to the preacher-man from Nazareth. The Nazarene, as it had indeed transpired, was not just some clever magician with a sly of hand that was unrivalled, but a miracle worker of the first order!

Shortly before the passing away nearly three years earlier of Joseph the Carpenter, whom everyone took to be the biological father of the preacher-man, the old man had summoned Judas and the other apostles the Deliverer had assembled, and had described to them in detail the events surrounding the birth of "the preacher-man" as they all referred to the Deliverer up until then, the family's flight to Egypt that Joseph, who was quite athletic and able-bodied at the time, made to save the child infant Deliverer from meeting his death at the hands of the murderous King Herod the Great so-called, and the slaughter that was taking place behind them of the hundreds of innocent babies the tyrant decided to target in hopes of nipping the idea of a Messiah in the bud.

Judas now wished that he were like one of those Innocents who met their fate as the squads of King Herod the Great roamed the countryside of Judea and Galilee in search of the "King of the Jews", and putting any newly born whom they could lay their hands on to the sword. Judas knew that he could easily have been one of the Innocents were it not for the fact that he was three years old at the time. He now wished that he too had come into the world about the same time as the Deliverer. That would have assured him martyrdom at the hands of the tyrant, and a place on the right side of Divine Law.

Judas acknowledged that, despite his exposure to all those sermons of the Deliverer, and being first hand witness to the innumerable wonders He wrought, deep down in his conscience, he was as materialistic and as unsaved even though perhaps not as bad as the priests and Pharisees - and Herod the Great! But, by the same token, being a practical man, Judas now had this gut feeling that there was no way he was ever going to succeed in explaining to the world, and even less to his former buddies in the Deliverer's inner circle, that he was innocent of the terrible fate that now hung over the miracle worker! This was unless the Deliverer changed his mind, wrestled free of his captors who would soon include the Roman governor who was backed by contingents of the Roman army, and retreated to some forest.

But Judas was convinced that this time around, even though He had the wherewithal to pull off such a feat, the miracle worker had made up His mind to let those evil people and sinners take His life. After all, addressing the crowds, He had made it crystal clear that an important goal of His mission as the Son of Man - if not the most important one - was to be a sacrificial lamb for the salvation of His fellow humans. And that was exactly the point. Just as no one, including Peter and the other apostles, was prepared to take the Deliverer at His word, and also just as everyone was almost certainly going to take flight as soon as the Nazarene is delivered by the priests and Pharisees into the hands of the Romans, it was completely out of question that any of these turncoats could change, and make an objective judgement on his diplomatic efforts to save the Deliverer's life!

He (Judas Iscariot) might not be all that innocent, but it was quite clear to him now that, in the rough and tumble of things, it was always the innocent who lost out. In the case of the Son of Man, this took on a completely different dimension, because He had freely chosen to be a sacrificial lamb. But the fact was that, in the current situation, he too now stood to pay a heavy price for the inability of human beings to weigh issues in the proper manner, and to render correct and fair judgements in situations where they were deserved.

Judas had seen the Deliverer come close to roughing up Peter when the fisherman jumped in front of the miracle worker and asserted that he was not going to let the Nazarene head to Jerusalem and to His certain death. And that had spelled the end of the hopes Judas had himself entertained of pulling off a diplomatic coup. His hopes of persuading members of the Sanhedrin that the individual they were hounding and wanting to liquidate was the promised Messiah, and that they direly needed His good offices if they hoped to rid the Nation of Israel of the yoke of the Romans, were now destined to come to naught. Judas had sought the opportunity to prove to them that it was going to work because the Nazarene was a miracle worker! But they had proved to be hardheaded and all too shortsighted.

He reminisced that he had been expecting a miracle when he lead them to the Deliverer that night in the garden of Gethsemane, and planted a kiss on the miracle worker's cheek. He had great faith, and had expected them to receive enlightenment even at that late stage, and had held out the hope that they would be converted and would seize the opportunity to acclaim the Deliverer as the awaited Messiah. He had held out the possibility even at that late stage that, instead of following through with their plans to hand the Nazarene over to the Romans for trial, they were going to hoist the Nazarene aloft and lead Him in triumph to the Temple on the eve of that august day for the purpose of formally introducing Him to the populace as savior in a spiritual as well as earthly sense. But he had obviously been seriously mistaken.

And now, to top it all, because of those same efforts, upon which he could not have embarked without summoning what clearly was uncommon courage, he, Judas Iscariot, was going to be adjudged by history as a selfish, money hungry betrayer of his divine Master! And this had come to pass because the "stupid" priests and Pharisees were determined to have their revenge on the Nazarene for perceived affronts, as when the Deliverer exposed their chicanery by scrawling their sinful dealings in the sand following the cure of the woman with the palsy.

The last straw was the widespread ridicule they deservedly garnered in the wake of their cowardly flight from the scene of the Deliverer's attempted arrest! And, if anything, Judas now realized, they had been even more determined than ever to try and destroy the Son of Man who had come on Earth to deliver the people of Israel from the bondage of sin and from the Romans! This was so they would remain unchallenged as the de facto rulers of Israelites. Judas told himself that his own conscience was clear, especially after dumping all thirty pieces of silver with which the priests and Pharisee, employing their surrogates, tried to bribe him there at their feet in the full view of witnesses.

And that was not the first time the chief priests and the Pharisees had tried to arrest or kill the Nazarene. On one occasion, using agents provocateurs whom they had planted in the crowds, they had tried to push Him over the cliff to His death only to see Him pass through the crowd and go His way. On another occasion, the temple guards who had been sent to arrest and detain the Nazarene had not just returned empty-handed, but they had told the chief priests and Pharisees to the latter's utter chagrin that they had never heard any one speak the way the Nazarene did, and that they were going off to become His disciples!

Consequently, Judas had not thought much of the assistance he had agreed to provide so that the one hundred strong Special Forces Operational Detachment made up of specially trained temple guards and soldiers (or "Delta 100" as the detachment's members referred to themselves) wouldn't nab the wrong person. This was even though Judas knew that the chief priests and Pharisees had already made the Governor, Pontius Pilate, aware of their intentions regarding the "dangerous rebel and criminal from Nazareth". Judas had even planned to use the thirty pieces of silver to boosts the week's collections. It was an amount of money that would have enabled the apostles to buy provisions for an entire week, and Judas had gone for it.

But it was blood money, as it had turned out; and, anyway, Judas had delivered all of it back to the faithless clique that occupied the corridors of power in Jerusalem and, he now realized too late, had no scruples whatsoever about using that power for their personal aggrandizement, and to utterly destroy any and all in Palestine who posed the remotest challenge their rule.

The one thing Judas had internalized above all else in the course of listening to the Deliverer over the space of three years was that humans could be really wicked. That was due to the fact that they were creations of the Prime Mover that were spiritual. But unlike the demons headed by Satan, their ring leader and also demon-in-chief so to speak, right up until they passed from this world and crossed the gulf that separated the living from the dead, humans could pull back and renounce their wicked ways and repent - just as he himself had done.

That was not something that the devil and the other fallen angels could do. Their fall from grace was a testament to the fact that at the point these spirits became evil intentioned or entranced with evil, they did not just become disposed to commit more and more evil acts, but the state of their mind programmed them to remain committed for all eternity to the cause of evil. And humans, because they too were spiritual creatures fashioned in the image of their Maker, could choose to act like demons; so that, instead of being merely in a state of sin and intent on wicked pursuits, they could additionally become evil-minded and evil-intentioned in the true sense and incapable of retreat - just like the demons!

That was the nature of things when a creature was a spirit. And it also spoke to the elevated status of creatures that were created in the image of the Prime Mover and were spiritual beings.

After observing the chief priests and Pharisees from close quarters as they plotted to liquidate the Deliverer, Judas had concluded that he was seeing humans who had transformed into human demons, and were of the devil just as the Nazarene has said in reference to them. Judas had no doubt in his mind that it needed demonic minds to be intent on doing what those folks were now clearly determined to do, namely destroy the living "Son of God"! Judas Iscariot had never imagined that he could live in a world in which such a thing could cross people's minds, let alone be pursued with such vigor and determination!

For the three years that he had been a confidant of the Nazarene, Judas had observed the other members of the Nazarene's inner circle from close quarters and felt that he now knew them as well as anyone else who was in a similar position was capable of knowing acquaintances. And knowing Peter as he did, he had no doubt in his mind that the fisherman especially was going to be the first to turn around, and not wish to be associated in any way with the Deliverer at the first sign that the priests and Pharisees had gotten their man and were well on the way to delivering Him to the Romans for execution.

Then the fact that it was Peter who was supposed to be the Rock upon which the Deliverer was going to build His *ecclesia* also signalled one additional thing, which namely was that the *ecclesia* itself was doomed from its inception. By being doomed, Judas meant that, even if the ecclesia (which, as far as he himself was concerned, was already floundering) miraculously survived the miracle worker's certain demise, the *ecclesia* or church would end up populated only with riffraff of Peter's mold; and those riffraff, taking after their leader (Peter), would turn into a miserable bunch of hypocrites and possibly even murderers.

Judas knew enough not to expect too much from those who would be flocking to a Church that had Peter as its head to worship the Prime Mover under the New Testament. No, he himself might have his disagreements with the Deliverer. Still, the fact remained that the future prognosis for a world without the Deliverer was not good at all. It was in fact so bad it scared Judas to death.

Judas did not have any delusions concerning the import of the events of the past few days that he had had witnessed. There was the Deliverer's triumphal entry into Jerusalem as the exuberant multitudes shouted: "Hosanna to the son of David! Blessed is the king who comes in the name of the

Lord! Peace in heaven and glory in the highest!" Unlike victorious Roman generals who rode into Rome riding chariots pulled by galloping horses, the miracle worker had entered the city riding a mule. But it became the talk of Jerusalem all the same, because it epitomized His triumph over the priests and Pharisees who were notorious for their scheming and underhand dealings!

And then there was the last supper! Judas had not only been honored to sit right there next to the miracle worker and Deliverer, but he had even shared the cup of wine with the Deliverer. Just to think that that "wine", according to the Deliverer's solemn declaration, was actually His own precious blood, the blood that He was going to shed for the sins of humans! Judas was well aware of his own propensity to impetuousness, not to mention his erstwhile obsession with money, and was relieved to know that his own sin of dilly-dallying with those deadly vices was also included. But he was grateful to God that the much talked about vice of procrastination was not one of them!

It was now approaching midnight, and Judas was not in any doubt regarding the fate that awaited the Deliverer. Before the sun set the next day, the Nazarene and son of David was going to be dead after being scourged, spat upon, and perhaps even mocked as the King of the Jews, and the Son of the Prime Mover! Instead of taking Him at His word that He had come to Earth at the bequest of His Father in heaven; and that - if it were not for the fact that he was permitting sinful and sinning humans to try to destroy Him in order that the scriptures pertaining to His death and resurrection would be fulfilled - legions of the biblical cherubim and seraphim would be on hand to stop the ill-advised assault on His person, the stupid fools probably would go as far as daring the miracle worker to try and escape after they had him "safely" surrounded by members of the Roman cavalry! But, as far as Judas himself knew, it was now a matter of hours before the Son of Man would be dead, albeit of His own choosing. The cunning priests and Pharisees would be in the thick of it, and making what was undoubtedly one hell of a gamble!

When speaking to the multitudes about death and the last days, the Deliverer had used the metaphor "thief in the night". Judas allowed that a week earlier, as he and the other apostles savored the limelight with the Nazarene as he rode victoriously into Jerusalem on the back of a colt and symbolically wrested the city from the power of the surprised priests and Pharisees without a fight, he would not have anticipated either the impending death in ignominy of his Lord and Master, or his own impending death by hanging! It was ironic that this was all taking place as Herod Antipas, the flamboyant "King of Galilee", had himself come to Jerusalem, ostensibly to take part in the Feast of the Passover, when the real purpose of his annual visit was to assert his power over the high priests and Pharisees, and particularly the affluent and aristocratic Sadducees who held high priesthood and the majority of the seats on the Sanhedrin!

The greatest losers were undoubtedly the elders and chief priests and scribes who not only should have recognized the promised Messiah in the Nazarene, but should have given Him a great red carpet welcome regardless of whether the Roman imperialists and their cronies in Palestine liked it or not! As Judas Iscariot saw it, the poor fools not only had no inkling that they were allowing themselves to be used by Providence, on the one hand, to cause the scriptures in which they themselves claimed to be experts to be fulfilled, but they did not know, on the other hand, that they were playing themselves into the hands of the very people who did not care a hoot about the temple in Jerusalem!

Still, the now almost certain fact that the Deliverer, like a lamb led to slaughter and like a sheep before shearers, was going to offer Himself to die for the sins of all men on the altar of the cross in a matter of hours, and Judas's own impending self-immolation by hanging from a tree, which he (Judas) equated to the "day of the Lord", had all verily burst in on him very much like a "thief in the night"!

The Deliverer had repeated to the apostles in the Upper Room, as they feasted on the species of bread and wine that He had mysteriously transformed into His sacred body and blood, that He had to die, but was going to overcome death and resurrect from the dead as prophesied. Judas was keenly aware that death was by no means the end. He did not doubt that he too was eventually going to rise up from the dead at the end of time. He too believed in the resurrection of the dead just like Martha, who had said: "I know that he (Lazarus) shall rise again, in the resurrection at the last day" when the Nazarene told her "Thy brother shall rise again" in the minutes before He raised Lazarus from the dead

It was Judas' humble prayer as he prepared to take his own life that, at the end of time, he too would be ushered, body and soul, before the throne of the victorious Son of Man in the presence of the heavenly host. After all, like the other apostles, he had left all to follow the Nazarene; and, as the Deliverer's purse bearer over the space of three years, Judas had developed a relationship with the Son of Man that was as deep and personal as any. And then there was the fact that, only a few hours earlier, he had been honored and humbled to receive "holy communion" from the hands of His Master.

When supper was over, the Deliverer had engaged them all in a long and solemn discourse that ended with all of the Apostles openly acknowledging and confessing any shameful deed that they recalled doing since they were small. Even now, Judas was still irked by the fact that the dissembling, cowardly and lying Peter, his face all wrapped up in "false humility" and speaking with a straight face, had said he was not going to allow the Son of Man to wash his feet! This was even though it was Peter who had started the argument about who among them would be the greatest!

But, the theatrics in which Peter had indulged aside, the air of foreboding had been ominous as the Deliverer completed the ritual of the washing of the feet and then allowed everyone assembled there, including Judas, to give Him a warm hug. Judas Iscariot, who was still clinging to the notion that his diplomacy could still save the life of the Deliverer even at that late hour, tore himself from the gathering and quietly slipped out of the Upper Room ahead of everyone else.

Judas had been drawn to the Deliverer by the total self-abnegation that seemed to be the Nazarene's hallmark, even as He showed that He had power over diseases and, indeed, over all creation; and Judas was justifiably frustrated - or so he thought - that he still had ended up with a bunch of people who were given to bickering and posturing on that scale!

He knew that the priests and Pharisees comprised a clique that was infinitely worse, and he himself had started to entertain doubts about the wisdom of confronting them the way he planned to do in his efforts to save the Deliverer's life and advance His mission of bringing hope to humans thereby. While he envisioned great things for himself if he succeeded in pulling this thing off and saving the Deliverer's life, he also had this idea that his own fortunes were completely intertwined with those of the Nazarene, and he therefore saw nothing but gloom and doom if he did not succeed in pulling this thing off.

It seemed unthinkable that Providence could allow his efforts to end in failure. It would be so terrible if the Prime Mover, who so loved the world that He gave His only begotten Son so that those who believe in Him might be saved, permitted such an eventuality. First, even though they were a crooked lot, the priests and Pharisees were the very ones who were expected to welcome the Son of Man. And, secondly, the plot those crooks were hatching – a plot in which they would try to present the Nazarene to the Roman authorities as the leader of a ring that planned to free the nation of Israel from their grip - was so perfidious and vile, Judas thought it was just the sort of crime that cried out to heaven for vengeance! The apostle from Jericho could not stomach the thought that the dissembling and hypocritical priests and Pharisees were bent on lynching the Son of Man in the name of the Prime Mover.

How in heaven and on earth could the Prime Mover allow things of that nature to continue happening now that the Deliverer had made His appearance on earth! And if the crooks would succeed in doing it to the Author of Life, King of Kings, and Lord of Lords, then who would be safe from the ill-intentioned and malicious with their never-ending scheming and intrigues. Judas had stuck with the Son of Man over the period He and the twelve had spent criss-crossing Judea, Galilee and Samaria precisely because here at long last was someone who could put a stop to the chicanery not just of humans but also of demons as well!

If they got away with it, it would, in his view, strike at the heart of the very notion of deliverance - deliverance from the evil that had been kick-started by the intransigence of the first Man and the first woman. The reign of evil in the world that had spread to every aspect of human life like a cancer would triumph, as also would Beelzebub, the father of lies! Judas had accordingly rationalized that it was fitting that the Deliverer was not just a miracle worker, but someone who had come down from heaven and shared in the divine nature of the Omnipotent.

It was, of course, an open secret that the prophet Isaiah referred to the priests and Pharisees when he said: "This people honors me with their lips, but their heart is far from me; in vain do they worship me, teaching as doctrines the precepts of men." But Judas expected that sort of behavior to come to an end with the appearance on earth of the Son of Man, and the ushering in of a New Testament.

Judas had visited with John the Baptist before that forerunner of the Deliverer was murdered at the bequest of the cowardly King Herod. And he distinctly recalled the son of Zachariah remind the crowds that, while he was a voice crying on the wilderness, they all needed to commit themselves to "preparing the way for the Lord", and "making His paths straight".

By that, Judas had understood that, under the New Testament that was being ushered in, chicanery and intrigues perpetuated in the Prime Mover's name were going to be things of the past! And he would not have thought that those who had succeeded Moses as leaders of God's people could dare make things difficult for the promised Messiah, let alone turn against Him. It was that frustration with everything that had caused Judas to lose his cool and denounce the members of the Sanhedrin in front of the temple guards before casting the blood money at their feet and making his hasty gateway.

Judas was a widower, having lost his wife just months after they had got married, and before they had any issue. He recalled how the Deliverer, addressing the multitudes one day, went out of his way to explain that while it was good to be married, it was much better to consecrate one's life to the Prime Mover by leading a celibate life.

The Deliverer had found it necessary to explain that statement several times over as the crowds and even some of his disciples seemed to regard the position the Deliverer had taken on that subject as being heretical, and were grumbling! Judas would always remember that "Sermon by the River Jordan", as it came to be known, because he had lost his temper and had to be restrained by the Deliverer Himself. He had lost patience with those who were grumbling not just because the Sermon by the River Jordan made a lot of sense, but he could not understand how those damn ignorant people could stand there and suggest that the Nazarene who had explained that he was a member of the Godhead and was therefore Knowledge itself was committing heresy!

For his part, Judas had taken the words of the Deliverer as a call to those among his apostles who were not burdened with family responsibilities to remain celibate, as that would enable them to devote their lives to the work at hand. The Deliverer had likened that work, namely going out into the world to spread the Gospel of Salvation to the ends of the earth as His "missionaries", to going out into the fields to rake in the harvest.

Judas was glad that he had heeded the Deliverer's call, and the fact that he himself, along with the other apostles who were still single, had vowed to remain chaste and poor and thenceforth to live like spouses of the Prime Mover. As he readied himself for what he saw as his own self-immolation, he told himself that he could go ahead with that scheme with a clear conscience. Ending his own life the way he proposed to do - which actually differed from the way the Deliverer was about to end His life only in methodology - was not going to be a burden to anyone!

He reflected on the fact that, by and large, he had been a faithful follower of the Deliverer, even though his motives had a tinge of worldliness about them. That was a definite and serious failure on his part; and, in his scrupulosity, he could not see how he could allow himself to continue on as if nothing had happened when the Deliverer, who was completely free from sin, was going to die. Understanding the purpose of the Son of Man's sojourn on earth as he did, Judas even commended his soul to Him, and prayed that he too would be a recipient of the mercies of the Prime Mover whose will the Nazarene was completely committed to accomplishing.

Judas acknowledged with dismay that his labors, since leaving all to follow the Nazarene, had ended up a total failure. And now, to make things worse, no one would ever know the true extent of his love for the Deliverer - love that had driven him to embark on his risky mission. It was clear that if he had not succeeded in making his getaway, after he thrust the thirty pieces of silver at the feet of the priests and Pharisees, they would have done everything in their power, willy-nilly, to compel him to testify against his "fallen Master" at the trial.

Judas was determined to deny them their wish. But he also knew that those cunning and lying "idiots" were even now not going to let him die in peace. They were going to try and depict him to the world as the apostle who turned star witness against his Master and betrayed the Deliverer's cause; and as the one who provided the inside knowledge about the Nazarene's determination to lead Judeans and Galileans - and may be Samaria as well - in rebellion against Rome! It would serve their agenda to do that, and Judas had no doubt whatsoever that they were going to do exactly that.

Those sell-outs and cowards were going to depict him as an insurgent in the tradition of James (Jacob) and Simon, the sons of Judas the Galilean, who tried to start a people's revolution against the Roman occupiers around the time he himself was a teenager. This was as one, Cyrenius (Quirinus), was conducting a census of the estates owned by locals in Galilee in preparation for levying taxes on them.

This all happened when Tiberius Alexander, son of Alexander the alabarch of Alexandria and nephew of the philosopher Philo, was Roman procurator of Judea.

Even though the revolt, which was put down harshly by Tiberius, took place when he himself was a teen, the visions of the lifeless bodies of his kin who had died by crucifixion being taken down from the crosses so they would be buried before sunset were still fresh in his mind. And, of course, his parents as he grew up had made a point of ingraining in him the history of that revolt with its fascinating details of how Judas the Galilean came close to ridding Galilee of Roman yoke, including the fact that Alexander succeeded in nipping the revolt in the bud and getting not just the two brothers but many other compatriots crucified with the collusion of some of the priests and Pharisees of the day. For all he knew, James and (Jacob) Simon and their brother Menahem, who became leader of the Sicarii (or "dagger men") for a while with a lot of success but was finally slain by the high-priestly party, were close kin given the fact that their father was also called Judas. Deep down, Judas Iscariot hated the priests and Pharisees for what he saw as a decided tendency to betray and sell out their own people.

Judas decided to allow himself an extra moment in which to marvel at the way in which Providence had arranged things before slipping the noose over his head; and, once the noose was tightly in place around his neck, he was going to jump from the bow of the tree so his ample frame would slide forward and start hurtling downward with the natural force of gravity. But then he had second thoughts.

Judas hesitated and wondered if he really wanted to die - at least just yet. He knew that the Deliverer, whom he himself had betrayed with a kiss, was a miracle worker, and could steam out of Caiaphas's house just like that and walk free. He could then warn his enemies to keep their distance if they wanted to stay alive; but that was if He wanted to. Judas, his face contorted in a grin, hissed: "It would be so satisfying to watch those crafty and shameless priests and Pharisees stricken with fear in the face of an invisible enemy and scattering in every which way while hampered as they run for their lives by those ridiculous gowns of theirs!" And, in his convoluted thinking, if things turned out that way, he, Judas, son of Simon Iscariot, would be fully vindicated for having placed all his bets on whoever would come out brandishing raw and uncompromising Herculean power!

The Nazarene was divine, not in the sense in which Roman emperors considered themselves divine, but in the real Judeo-traditional sense and in the true meaning of that word; and He was a Miracle Worker to boot! Depending on the signs, he (Judas) might himself have second thoughts about laying down His life for those idiots! Judas decided that he was going to bide his time for now and observe how things turned out over the next couple of days.

But even if this man, who had raised up Lazarus from the dead, was executed by Pontius

Pilate at the behest of the priests and Pharisees, since He was without any doubt a divinity, He just might have something else up His sleeve. Judas told himself that it perhaps wasn't such a bad idea to shelve the suicide option for now, and to take time to observe how things developed.

A New Era...

To be sure, the Son of Man, who was also the Author of Life, had made it clear that He had come down to earth at the behest of His heavenly Father to deliver humankind from the clutches of sin and from bondage thereof. In Judas' mind, the advent of the Messiah spelled an end to the reign of evil which started with the rebellion of Lucifer and the band of angels who joined him in refusing to go down on bended knee to worship the Almighty One and their Maker, and whose act of transgression had caused them to become transformed into demons. With their fall from grace, Adam and Eve had dragged humankind into the fray, and aligned humans with Old Scratch and his band of fallen angels.

The brazen act of rebellion of the first man and the first woman, and their outrageous attempt to be like the Prime Mover represented what amounted to an earth-based axis of evil that also militated against all that was good. The inclination of humans to sin effectively made them allies with Satan and the fallen angels in the ongoing battle between good and evil.

Judas had attempted unsuccessfully to persuade the priests and Pharisees that the Nazarene, the Anointed One whose shoe laces John the Baptist had been unworthy to untie, and whom they were bent on liquidating, was the awaited Messiah - a Messiah not just of the Israelites, but of all humankind! As he planted the kiss on the cheek of the Deliverer, a kiss he knew his fellow apostles were going to immediately interpret as a kiss of betrayal, Judas was still hoping for a miracle, namely a sudden and welcome change of heart on the part of the chief priests and scribes that would be followed by a proclamation that the deliverance of the people of Israel and of all humankind was at hand, and in its wake by a red carpet welcome for the Deliverer.

Judas was still clinging to the hope that his wish would be granted. He was hoping that, even at that late stage in the game, Providence was not going to allow the Savior of Mankind to suffer any harm at the hands of the Pharisees and Sadducees on the one hand, and the Roman imperialists who did not see any wrong in subjugating entire peoples and condemning them to slavery, or using torture to maintain their super power status, on the other. Judas had heard the Son of Man proclaim that the poor and the marginalized, and those who now wept were blessed; and He had given notice to the evil of heart with His proclamation that those who now laughed and were delighted in perpetuating the miseries of their fellow humans would soon find themselves weeping and gnashing their teeth.

But, even though, the Son of Man had also alluded on multiple occasions to His own impending rejection; and had taught His disciples that He had to go to the Holy City and, once there, suffer incredibly at the hands of the elders and the chief priests and scribes, and even be killed. Judas had refused to come to grips with the possibility of evil triumphing over good in any way, and certainly not when the Anointed One and Author of Life had deigned to come to earth in fulfillment of the promise of His father in heaven. And to top it all, the Nazarene had made the blind see, and the lame walk; and He had healed the sick and even raised Lazarus from the dead.

Judas believed that he was on firm ground when he took the Deliverer's references to His own suffering and death as a joke. If that happened, it would signal victory over the forces of good by the forces of evil! And, instead of pulling the rug from under the feet of the likes of Pontius Pilate, governor of Judea, Herod who was tetrarch of Galilee, Annas and Caiaphas who were the high priests, and the tyrant Tiberius Caesar, all of whom operated in concert with the Evil One, it would be tantamount to surrender! Judas' decision to leave all and become a disciple of the Nazarene and Son of Man had been prompted by his belief that, with the advent of the promised Messiah, humans at long last could take a breath and hope for better days in this god-forsaken world. Humans of good will were now poised to be redeemed from the earth-based axis of evil in the shape of human greed that was responsible for so much misery and suffering.

When good people fell ill, the Deliverer and miracle worker, who was also the Truth and the Life, was going to make sure that they were delivered of their infirmities. And if it happened that good people died, they too could count on their resurrection from the dead in God's time. Judas expected the Nazarene to cause the evils that plagued humankind to come to an abrupt halt. The Sermon of the Mount could not have come at a more opportune time; and Judas was very thankful to Providence for allowing him, unworthy though he was, to be a part of such momentous history.

The miseries of those who were poor in spirit, meek, or hungry and thirsting for righteousness were going to end, and they were all going to be fulfilled. Those who had a record of being merciful were going to be shown mercy by the Deliverer. Those who were pure in spirit were going to see the Prime Mover. The peacemakers were going to be called Sons of God and blessed. Those who were harassed by the evil-intentioned could even afford to turn the other cheek. And, just as the prophet Habakkuk had pronounced Woe upon Babylon, the Deliverer had pronounced Woe upon those who were knaves, thieves, war mongers, lying hypocrites, adulterers, and others who clung to the motto of an eye for an eye and a tooth for a tooth, and he had affirmed that they would not see the kingdom of heaven.

It came as a complete surprise to Judas that the Nazarene had been dead serious when He had asserted that He was going to Jerusalem to suffer and even be killed at the hands of the very people who ought to have been waiting in line to receive Him, namely the elders and the chief priests and scribes. But even if the Deliverer's kingdom was not of this world, it was just too much for Judas that the reign of evil was not going to be stemmed - a reign in which wars, imperialism, colonialism, militarism, expansionism, and all the other abominable isms, slavery, discrimination against minorities and against women, banditry perpetuated by conquering powers, and the unbridled greed of the ruling classes, and other evils were going to continue unabated!

But, with the blood of the Son of Man Himself on their hands, and flush from their ostensible victory over the Deliverer and Author of Life, the wicked of this world were in fact going to be emboldened. Judas could visualize the elders and the chief priests and scribes, along with the Roman imperialists and their stooges, combining forces with none other than Lucifer and his band of fallen angels to try and thwart the work of the *ecclesia* which the Deliverer had formally launched that evening as he supped with the clutch of followers who now consisted of just the twelve apostles.

The symbolism of that meal at which the Deliverer had changed bread and wine into His own body and blood, and then shared the "bread of angels' as he called it with them, was overwhelming. Judas could still hear the steady voice of the

Deliverer, as He commanded them to continue doing likewise, ringing in his ears. As the betrayer held up the noose and slipped it over his own head, he could almost hear, first the slow drum roll as the Son of Man and Author of Life was matched to Golgotha (or the Place of the Skull as it was called) bearing the cross on which he was going to offer Himself to His Father as a sacrificial lamb for the sins of humankind and as an unblemished oblation; and then the loud groans of the Son of Man as the crude nails were driven with force into His sacred palms and feet.

Judas reminisced that it was quite clear that the forces of evil were determined to stop the Son of Man from healing the sick and alleviating the sufferings of the poor and the marginalized. It was also very clear that tyranny and bigotry were going to continue as unchecked vices that would cause many a human to suffer as never before. And, instead of being driven by the love for fellow humans as the Nazarene had admonished in His Sermon on the Mount, and developing and putting to use the earth's resources for the common good of all humankind, the world's nations, under the rule of tyrants who would be masquerading as benevolent dictators as had hitherto been the case, would be seeking to gain control over those selfsame resources for their exclusive use, and angling for positions of advantage with a view to becoming entrenched as invincible super powers.

Anger welled up inside Judas at the thought that the great bulk of humans in their millions would be barely getting by, and surviving in conditions of extreme deprivation, while a greedy minority who claimed citizenship of the powerful nations would be obscenely rich. Others, oblivious to the fact that they were all descendants of Adam and Eve, and that the Prime Mover so loved the world, that he gave his only begotten Son, that whosoever believeth on him should not perish, would be acting just like the Pharisees and Sadducees were doing now.

The Nazarene, echoing the words of John the Baptist, His forerunner, had referred to them as a brood of vipers out of whose mouths nothing good could be expected to come. They were not going to escape being condemned to hell because, as the miracle worker had pointed out, it was upon them that all the righteous blood that had been shed on earth, from the blood of righteous Abel to the blood of Zechariah son of Berekiah who was murdered between the temple and the altar, would come. Some of the prophets and wise men and teachers who had been sent by the Prime Mover had been killed and crucified by them. And now, with his failure to dissuade them from their chosen path with regard to the Nazarene, they were set to commit the most abominable act of them all, namely to crucify and kill the Son of Man and Author of Life Himself!

Judas recalled the words of the prophet Isaiah who wrote that fools spoke nonsense, and that their hearts were inclined toward wickedness. The prophet had added that these fools would not just practice ungodliness and speak errors against the Lord, but they would keep the hungry unsatisfied, and also withhold drink from the thirsty! The prophet's words could only mean one thing, namely that, even though the Deliverer was bequeathing to the world but one *ecclesia* against which the gates of hell would never prevail, the same elders, chief priests and scribes, as a result of whose actions the Son of Man could already be said to be on death row for all practical purposes, were not going to stop there.

For one, they were going to persist in maintaining that, because they had Abraham as their father, they and not the apostles were the rightful messengers of the Prime Mover. But they would not just perpetuate the errors they taught against the Lord thereby. They would also continue to harass and even murder the remnants of the Deliverer's band of disciples in league with their Roman masters.

The betrayer thought about the Deliverer's choice of Peter as the rock on which he was going to establish His Church in those circumstances. That was such a poor choice in Judas' view. Well, instead of one church, several hundred thousand churches, all of them claiming to be the true Church founded by the Deliverer, would blossom as every Dick and Harry angled to lay claim to the prize!

"Yes, the prize", Judas hissed. As the Deliverer's purse bearer up until that moment, he understood very well that any church that succeeded in laying claim to some form of association with the Deliverer and legitimacy would be a moneymaker that was worth the investment. Judas had no doubt in his mind that there would be many shrewd and calculating humans on hand who would emulate the chief priests and scribes who clearly were now plotting to hijack the *qahal 'êdah* or church of the Old Testament; and, in his mind, he could see the clever louts proceed to set up and operate their own fake *ecclesiae* or church enterprises to exploit the gullible, spiritually starved masses by pretending that they were the rightful successors of the Deliverer's apostles!

And this would all be because of the Deliverer's stubborn refusal to head to Jerusalem against his advice, and to acknowledge above all that even a *Sancta Ecclesia* could use a few management skills. In Judas' estimation, if one was serious about going out into the ripened fields to "harvest souls", it wasn't good enough to engage the services of chaps who were just good at hauling in rich harvests of fish!

This in turn reinforced Judas's fears that the scheming by the chief priests and scribes and their ilk, which was now set to continue in the face of the virtual capitulation by the Deliverer and Author of Life, was going to cause unspeakable distress, pain and anguish endured by the innocent in the world! Their frustration and the miseries they endured as a result of the fall from grace of Adam and Eve were going to continue unchecked - as if the Savior and Redeemer of humankind had not come! It said something about evil and its continuing reign on earth.

After they had liquidated the Son of Man and Author of Life - which was in Judas Iscariot's view the ultimate sin that humans could commit - and gotten away with it, the elders and the chief priests and scribes were going to form an alliance with the Roman imperialists and, together, were going to try and pacify the rest of the world. Judas noted that neither those nominally "religious" leaders nor their Roman political allies, led by Pontius Pilate who had demonstrated that he did not have any conscience at all by his action in keeping the Deliverer and King of Kings under surveillance from the day He was baptized by the son of Zechariah, had any regard for human life; and he told himself that the take-over of the world by this evil alliance was going to be a very bloody affair indeed!

It was unimaginable that it was murderers and other evil members of humankind who governed the world! There was Herod, the self-styled Herod the Great and King of Judah, who had unleashed the unthinkable slaughter of the Innocents in his insane drive to find and kill the infant Deliverer and Author of Life. Then there was his son, Herod Antipas and Tetrarch of Galilee, who did not rest until he was presented with the head of John the Baptist on a plate, and who was now about to preside over the greatest injustice ever done to a human - the murder, most likely by crucifixion, of the Savior of mankind! And then there was the brutal, obdurate and completely selfish Pontius Pilate who, as Roman prefect of Judea, was notorious for his dreadful human rights record!

And as for the "brood of vipers", Judas had no doubt in his mind that those hypocrites had even now already made plans to silence him forever in the best way they knew, just because he had told them in their face that the Nazarene was not guilty of any wrong doing, and that he himself had no desire to have the blood of an innocent man on his hands! That had led Judas to stop tallying any benefits he previously hoped were going to accrue to humankind as a result of the appearance on earth of the promised Messiah.

As Judas saw it, from now on going forward, it would not be necessary for a human to make an explicit declaration that he/she was allied to liars and murderers to belong to that camp. From here on, everyone who did not live according to the principles of the Sermon on the Mount became an ally of haters of the Son of Man by default. One was either with the Deliverer - and prepared to sacrifice one's life for Him the way he (Judas) was about to do - or against the Deliverer! Positions of neutrality in the face of injustice were going to be out of question. That was because the humankind the Deliverer had come to save was one.

Judas was certain that, with the life of John the Baptist, the precursor of the Deliverer, snuffed out prematurely by Herod Antipatros to pre-empt what that demagogue saw as a possible uprising by the Galilean peasants against his evil rule, and the Deliverer Himself about to be liquidated, the world was doomed! If evil triumphed, as now appeared almost certain with the elders and the chief priests and scribes poised to join forces with the Roman imperialists to do away with the Son of Man and Author of Life, darkness was verily going to envelope the earth figuratively at any rate. That was because there wouldn't be anyone left in the whole wide world who was capable of telling the truth and shaming the devil the way those two had.

Judas was in total shock and angry as he reflected on the fact that, in the battle between the forces of good and the forces of evil, the side he favored was about to be dealt another devastating blow. After the Son of Man and miracle worker was liquidated, Judas did not see any force left that could take on the twin axis of evil consisting of the alliance between the Sanhedrin and the Roman imperialists on the one hand, and Lucifer and his band of rebel angels on the other!

Before jumping to his death, Judas mumbled aloud that he had no wish to continue living in a world in which the sort of injustice that was about to be perpetrated against the Son of Man and Author of Life could go unavenged as it most certainly would. He could not imagine himself living through just one day of the New Era that was about to emerge.

Not everything the Deliverer said - or everything the Spirit had taught the eleven and their successors since Pentecost Day - was in the Book, Mjomba argued in his thesis. He attributed a statement to the Deliverer to the effect that it would have been better from the point of view of law and justice if sinners had not been allowed to exist, not because they then wouldn't have had the opportunity to sin and so expose themselves to the wrath of the Almighty One, but because sin - all sin - represented a demonstration of the most flagrant ingratitude in the eyes of the Perfect One who was also Love personified. And Mjomba now claimed that this statement was one of those that were not in the Book! He did not explain how he had come by the statement in question. But he also hastened to add that the birth of sinners - which was allowed to take place nonetheless - was probably the best evidence humans had of the love, power and majesty of the Prime Mover. According to Mjomba, the fact that evil was rampant also argued powerfully for the existence of a loving Creator.

Commenting on the position of Adam and Eve which, according to him, explained the saintly life they chose to lead in the aftermath of their failed revolt, Mjomba wrote that they were apparently borrowing a leaf from one who was both the nonpareil of "Beauty" and whose titles included that of "Wisdom". Even though invisible, He had left mountains of evidence (which Adam and Eve in their time found impossible to ignore but many today had been successful in imagining away) attesting to the fact that, even though some of his works had a short lease of life, His was an Essence that transcended time and space, and that had freely chosen not only to bring creatures into being, but to allow these "beings" to share in its glorious "*Esse*".

Mjomba went on that the first Man and the first Woman had not been entirely blind to the lessons that could be drawn from the manner in which other earth-bound creatures - birds of the air, marine creatures, lions, elephants, gazelle, giraffe and the other creatures of the wild, reptiles, members of the insect world, microbes and other invisible organisms, not forgetting matter itself and the elements - passed their days while here on earth. Mjomba wrote that these other creatures spent all their time doing what they had to do in order to allow the brilliance of the Prime Mover shine in them and also to let the glory of "that greater than which cannot be conceived" become manifest in them.

And because, unlike humans and other spiritual essences such as angels, they do not possess an intellect and a free will - something that appears at first sight to put them at a disadvantage - they are not tempted to usurp any of the Prime Mover's prerogatives, including copyrights to the marvelous things He has designed and given an existence; or to act as if they were gods unto themselves, pretending that what they succeed in producing or achieving using their God-given talents - which often happens by chance - is purely their own invention for which they deserve original copyrights!

In illustration, Mjomba wrote that if lions had been endowed with a free will and an intellect, after falling from grace as angels and humans did, they would probably have tried - and perhaps succeeded - in passing themselves off as a superior race or something, or may be even as gods to whom the "lesser" beings that were not capable of subduing their prey with their bare fangs owed divine allegiance of sorts - or, at the very least, they would be worshipping idols that they themselves had fabricated. And they likely would be breaking all the other commandments (in addition to the commandment not to worship false gods) at the same time - just like humans and the fallen angels!

Talking about angels - Mjomba argued in his thesis that the Prime Mover's work of creation in the realm of purely spiritual essences did not stop with the first batch of angelic creatures a number of whom promptly rebelled against Him. Mjomba suggested that the work of creation in that realm likely was continuing - just like the work of creating humans only begun with the coming into being of Adam and Eve.

Mjomba believed that humans had a somewhat primitive concept of these "angelic" beings. He in fact thought that it amounted to a denial of the fact that the Prime Mover, Himself being the personification of splendor and wisdom, was capable of designing and bringing into existence creatures whose elegance and charm was beyond the appreciation of humans whether in this life or the next.

As it was, Mjomba wrote, humans appeared patently incapable of cherishing and appreciating the beauty that was immanent in themselves; because, if they had been, their preoccupation of choice would be meditation for the purpose of glorifying the Prime Mover for being such a brilliant designer. They would for one have less time for mischief (which arose from being idle) and ultimately little or no interest in material things and self-indulgence.

Since humans were not driven by pure instinct like the lower life forms, there would be a general tendency to neglect things like feeding, sleep, etc. Purely human relationships, including marriage, would also suffer. Mjomba surmised that this sort of altruism, were it to prevail among humans, would hasten their anticipated reunion with their Lord and Maker in eternity.

The biblical injunction that one must needs lose one's life - or essentially die, not just metaphorically but truly, even though in a spiritual rather than physical sense - in order to preserve it would not be such a preposterous idea anymore in these circumstances, and every human who could stir would be looking for opportunities to do precisely that in that "Utopia"!

Rephrasing what the Scriptures said in that regard somewhat, Mjomba wrote that the seed - another word for life in its germinal form - was sown from the moment a human was conceived in the Prime Mover's mind in eternity to the moment in time when a human was conceived in the womb. Before it could germinate and bear fruit due at the point it was set to pass on to the after-life (actually the real life for humans), it had to die and not just allegorically but actually if imperceptibly in the physical sense.

For the seed that did not die or at least germinate in the period between one's conception and one's passage to the "after-life" so-called, the possibility of inheriting the eternal kingdom receded accordingly. A seed in this category was one that had essentially landed - not by accident but through its own intransigence - on rocky ground.

For the seed that did die during that stage, it entered a new phase right there and then.

Representing a completely different kind of existence, that phase started as the seed first germinated, then solidified as a prelude to bearing its fruit. It culminated in the seed's transition to the equivalent of a fruitful vine around the time the Sower returned to reap his fruit. And the act of reaping presaged yet another phase. That phase was of course analogous to physical death, and actually marked the seeds' inclusion in the granary holding the rest of the farmer's priceless harvest.

Mjomba wrote that there was, perhaps, something to the idea, mirrored in the cultural beliefs of peoples in the Eastern Hemisphere, that a transmigration of souls occurred. Because, typically, a granary would be stocked with seeds that were ready to be sown in fields in a move that would in our case begin the cycle all over again! The problem with that, though, would be that there would be no rest for the individual souls involved, and would go counter to the original idea that the seeds represented souls which, with the Prime Mover's grace, would already have bagged their victory over sin and intransigence at that juncture, and would be well on their way to eternal rest without any opportunity to revisit Mother Earth as members of a different species!

The parable of the farmer who went out to sow seed hinged entirely on the premise that humans were spiritual creatures first and foremost, and rational *animals* only in a secondary sense, according to Mjomba. He went on to suggest that it was precisely because humans were first and foremost spiritual in nature rather than flesh or solid matter that their actions, the accompanying motivations included, were not really concealable. Even when their actions were done out of sight or in the dark, they appeared to be hidden only on the surface! The scheming that went on behind closed doors or in darkness - or even inside the heads of humans - might as well be done in day light in full view. The resulting shame - or exultation in the case of laudable deeds - might be physically felt, Mjomba wrote; but its real impact was spiritual.

The Paramount Prime Mover...

In the after-life, the hypocrisy and the evil plots hatched behind closed doors would not only be exposed to all and sundry, but would come back to haunt those guilty of the hypocrisy when it was too late for them to do anything to rehabilitate themselves in the society of humans.

But lest one be tempted to underrate the Prime Mover in any way, wrote Mjomba, the fact of the matter was that the Prime Mover was also another one - to put it mildly. Mjomba suggested that He was the only being to whom the word "invincible" applied without qualification. This was because, no matter how depraved or downright stupid humans became, almost by design they always ended up according Him recognition and rendering Him homage even though it was frequently in disguised and sometimes contradictory expressions and epithets - Good Luck,

Hard Luck, Chance, Blessings, Horoscope, the Stars, Mystery, *Élan Vital*, Evolution, *El Niño*, Life, Nature, Unknown God, etc. The nice part of it all was that this recognition of the Prime Mover's almighty power did not appear to be dependent on the disposition of humans but was accorded involuntarily.

Mjomba argued that shouts of joy, screams of pleasure, and anguished cries and other similar expressions to which humans gave vent were all instances of explicit acknowledgement of the Prime Mover's presence and power. Any yearning, or longing for anything whatsoever, was as much an act of faith in the Prime Mover as the solemn recital of the renowned "*Credo*". The same went for smiles, grins and laughter so long as these were not contrived or fake. That was one reason, Mjomba argued, why humans alone could laugh, smile or cry! These emotions sprung from the core of the human being, and it was there that the Prime Mover maintained his dwelling.

Acknowledgement by humans of the Prime Mover's omnipotence was implicit in the guilty consciences they found they apparently could not stifle each time they did something they knew was wrong. But tacit recognition for the Prime Mover's power and authority also came clocked in the instantaneous swearing and in the other acts of desperation that humans resorted to as they kept discovering that they could not explain their so-called good or bad fortunes!

Sometimes this acknowledgement was cloaked in the vain attempts to escape the responsibility for their actions by giving in to impulses to end their own lives and often the lives of others as well when, after squandering valuable time and resources, they discovered that they were on the brink. Mjomba explained that the real problem was not that they found themselves on the brink, but that they were reluctant to come even, admit wrong doing and follow that up with a display of remorse that was commensurate with the hurt caused by their actions, things that required a certain amount of humility. But, while they knew very well that they had violated cardinal rules which had adversely affected their spiritual well-being, they were too ashamed to own up, come clean and start all over again.

Mjomba wrote that recognition of the power and might of the Creator by humans came in many forms and shapes precisely because it was inevitable, whether humans liked to admit it or not. It was, he explained, inevitable because the constitution of humans allowed them to choose between following their reason or doing what went against reason. Thus, even though "free" creatures, to the extent that they were creatures, they were not free from the *obligation* of doing what was right, and there was a price to be paid for being in what was in effect a rebellion against their own nature. By extension it was, of necessity, also a rebellion against the One who originally designed and accorded not just to the human nature, but to the nature of everything in creation (or that had come to be) an existence and, along with that existence, a purpose that was in line with the divine scheme!

According to Mjomba, admission that the Prime Mover's rule over creation was paramount was likewise implicit in the constant yearning for fulfilment and in the ceaseless search for purpose in life even by those who refused to openly confess that He was the supreme Lord of all. And this admission was also manifest in, of all things, the contrived modesty of sinners! This was because modesty that was insincere evidenced an absence of godliness and what he termed a haunting emptiness!

Humans acknowledged the omnipotence of the Prime Mover in the very act of sinning, Mjomba wrote. Without Him, not only would the occasions for acts of sin not have arisen, but the acts of sins themselves, consisting in the distortion of the original goal and purpose of creation, would themselves not have been possible. And above all, without freedom of the will which He had included in His design of human nature, sin would have been impossible. Sin as a notion boiled down to an attempt to pull off a coup d'état with the intention of expropriating assets to which only the Prime Mover as prime cause of everything that existed had a rightful claim, and/or denying Him full credit for copy rights held in regard to things He designed and brought into existence out of nothing.

Acknowledgement by humans of the might and power of the Prime Mover was unavoidable and was, indeed, manifest in the very act of sinning. Sinning or betrayal, Mjomba wrote, could be reduced to the statement "I am a mere human; but, guess what, I also want to be a Prime Mover - or at least to pretend that I am one! At the very least, however, I am not about to use my talents in the real Prime Mover's service. I would even rather bury them, if I may say so!"

The dependence of humans on the Prime Mover was especially evident in the commission of sins of self-indulgence. Self-indulgence was entirely dependent, he argued, on the fact that the God-given nature of humans was human; that if that had not been the case, things like concupiscence - or even lust - not only would not have had any meaning, but would not even have constituted occasions of sin.

According to Mjomba, lusting after someone else's spouse was possible only because the individual who was the object of the lust had been constructed in the particular manner in which he or she had been constructed; but, more importantly, that individual was human and the lusting individual happened to possess a complimentary human nature. If that were not the case, humans would in fact not even be in a position to derive the temporal or passing pleasures that they now derived from self-indulgence.

If the nature of one of the parties had not been human, humans would almost certainly not be in a position to feel any attraction to each other the way they now did, and perhaps even not at all. Instead of feeling attracted to each other, humans quite possibly would be repelled by each other. According to

Mjomba's thesis, lust and things like that were possible only because humans could identify with each other as creatures that enjoyed the same human nature. But that was not all. The material things to which they now found themselves attracted and, in some cases, enslaved would probably be quite unattractive and possibly even repellent.

Humans, Mjomba asserted, were dependent on the Prime Mover to that extraordinary extent. But the tragedy, he went on, was that when humans indulged themselves, they did it at precisely the time they would have been much better preoccupied giving glory and praise to the Prime Mover for the very same reasons they now turned their backs on Him. And so, in one stroke so to speak, these humans were squandering what really was an immense opportunity for giving back to the Prime Mover something in return for bringing them into existence through self-denial. Instead, they were chafing for battle with each other over the Prime Mover's blessings to humankind - which sins of concupiscence, lust and greed amounted to.

By emptying themselves through self-abnegation, abstinence, fasting and things like that, humans gave themselves a chance to lust after and eventually enjoy, not pleasures that were short-lived because they were engendered by aspects of creation that were changing and were therefore not permanent or long lasting, but the One and the Only Unchanging Being and Author of Life, and Creator of the World and everything that was in it.

Sin thus included an explicit, albeit grudging, acknowledgement not just of the Prime Mover's existence but of what he was capable of accomplishing as well, namely bringing humans (and other creatures) into existence out of nothing.

Now, humans were, according to Mjomba, free to exercise their freedom of speech and to say anything that came to mind. But they made complete idiots of themselves when, acknowledging that they were not there at a given point in time and had been gratuitously brought into existence by someone who had to be immeasurably bigger than themselves, turned around on impulse and casually - and in the same breath - rejected the existence of the Prime Mover! They did that in the exact same casual way they "forgot" to treat other humans the way they themselves wanted to be treated, but started howling foul as soon as the roles were reversed! They were free to try and ignore the obvious - but only for so long. When humans acted like that, they were not just in denial - they lied and were dishonest!

The purpose of discussing that subject, Mjomba wrote, was to show that when humans offended the Prime Mover, they knew exactly what they were doing, even if they chose, after the fact, to play sissy by claiming that the devil made them do it, by pleading ignorance or coming up with some other excuses in an attempt to escape accountability for their actions.

Mjomba believed that if humans were serious and really wanted to, they would see the power and might of the Prime Mover revealed wherever they would care to look in a literal sense. The stinging pain from a small bruise on the sheen would speak volumes about the Prime Mover for His brilliance and foresight in designing humans who might otherwise overlook serious injuries sustained by them until too late. The almost instantaneous clotting of blood stemming any further hemorrhage would not fail to remind them of the Prime Mover's ingenuity and foresight, and would be further evidence of the fact that He remained in total control, the intransigence of humans notwithstanding.

According to Mjomba, the rebellion of Lucifer and his lackeys exemplified this aspect of sin clearly. Prior to his sin, the devil, more than any other created being, was fascinated and dazzled by the majesty and boundless power of the Prime Mover, before jealousy and lust for power got the better of him, and he decided that he was going to try and usurp that grandeur and authority and set himself up as an alternative god. Even after Satan and the spirits he had successfully drawn into his plot were cast into hell, it was the same magnificence and power of the Prime Mover that they continued to battle, while Michael, the Archangel, and the other hallowed spirits were doing the opposite.

Mjomba contended that the rebellion of Lucifer and his minions, whose specialty was sowing the seeds of death through spreading lies about the Truth and trickery, would lose its sting and not constitute a revolt if it did not include an acknowledgement that the Prime Mover remained the one and the only "prime mover" and in charge of things, the rebellion notwithstanding. This was a paradox of sorts, Mjomba wrote, adding that it was precisely because the renegade spirits had never expressed regret for their failed attempt to try and unseat the Prime Mover that they continued to stand condemned. Pure spirits who knew at the very outset that any coup attempt or declaration of war on their part was irrevocable, they had apparently worked themselves into an awkward spot from which they could not retreat.

The brazen intransigence of Beelzebub made him dangerous enough that the Deliverer Himself saw the need to personally draw the attention of humans to the perils he continued to pose to creatures with a capacity to choose between good and evil. The fact that He did so suggested that Beelzebub was very richly endowed at creation. And now, like a disgraced prince charming/chairman of the joint chiefs of staff whose position previously made him privy to the most sensitive information, the Evil One, aided by the fact that he was invisible to the human eye and jealous and resentful to the hilt, literally had nothing on his hands apart from roaming the corners of the earth in search of human prey.

Talking about Beelzebub and about intransigence, you would think that the devil would be the last person to proclaim the greatness of the Prime Mover, Mjomba wrote. Satan occasionally found himself cornered in a way that left him no option but to proclaim loudly and clearly the greatness of the Creator, and it went without saying that he found all such occasions humiliating in the extreme, according to Mjomba. Some of the devil's most embarrassing moments, Mjomba went on, were recorded in graphic detail in the New Testament, and showed Beelzebub belatedly announcing the arrival on Earth of the Deliverer as he himself took to his heels!

That led Mjomba to the conclusion that all transgressors in the moral arena knew they were transgressing, even though they often tried very hard to make their less than sterling lives appear normal. There really was such a thing as a conscience, Mjomba wrote, adding that it apparently remained active regardless of efforts of transgressors to stifle it.

And so, while some "silly" humans, who even knew their dates of birth, had the audacity to question the existence of a Creator, Beelzebub and his lackeys in the Underworld had never done that. Silly, Mjomba explained, because, dream creatures endowed with spiritual gifts, they preferred to imagine that their place was in the animal world rather than in the blessed realm of spiritual beings. They equated themselves with creatures that were not only incapable of thinking aright, but that could not "think" at all because they did not possess the wherewithal for that sort of thing, namely souls!

And thank God it was only humans amongst creatures that roamed the earth that possessed souls and could think, Mjomba observed. Even though they belonged to the same human race, Mjomba could not recall a time in history when they were not at war with each other over nothing. Mjomba imagined, with good reason no doubt, that if the divine plan had called for other 'earthlings' that could also 'think' to share Planet Earth with humans, the warring would not only be constant, but the ongoing slaughter, as the two groups of earthlings battled for control of the earth's scarce resources, would make the wars amongst humans like mini-storms in tea cups!

Mjomba wrote that regardless of how "scholars" and others described the phenomenon of conception - regardless of whether they attributed it to "genetic mutation" or to natural or artificial "insemination", a spiritual essence came into being at the time a human was conceived in the woman's womb. The spirit or "soul" certainly did not create itself; and, of course, it could not just spout out of "matter" - whether living matter or dead matter, including what is called "semen" - because that could not happen in accordance with the well-worn maxim *nemo dat quod non habet*!

And, anyway, whoever said that the Prime Mover - because He was a prime mover - could not use His creatures to prepare conditions that facilitated "implantation" inside a woman's womb of a brand new "human soul" at the right moment in time, if doing so was going to result in a unique "human" creature. Yes, a human creature - Mjomba wrote - in which a physical part (body) and a spiritual part (soul) would be fused together in such a way that the end, "Man", was subject to natural law and supernatural law at one and the same time!

Mjomba went on that those silly people, by denying the existence of a Prime Mover, also automatically denied the existence of pure spirits since a pure spirit (or any "creature" for that matter) could not simply materialize out of nothing with no other Entity intervening to facilitate its "spiritual conception", an Entity that itself had to be uncaused or what Thomas Aquinas referred to as "First Uncaused Cause", or *Primum Movens* (Unmoved Mover) as Aristotle aptly put it. But, again, assuming that pure spirits existed, since they could not possibly create themselves or will themselves into being (in accordance with the maxim *nemo dat quod non habet*), the case for a Prime Mover "willing" them into existence was all too evident.

And they were silly because, in denying the existence of a *Primus Movens*, they also implicitly denied that they themselves existed! And, of course, that effectively removed them *and* their arguments from the picture at least in so far as Mjomba was concerned.

The seminarian did not fail to point out that, if one accepted that humans lived on after death - just as the so-called "animists" claimed - the case for a Prime Mover willing them into existence and sustaining them in their after-life also became self-evident.

That was why, in addition to Anubis, the Egyptian "God of the Dead", Nephthys, the Egyptian "Goddess of the Dead", and their other "gods", Egyptians (representing Africa), also believed in the existence of "the Hidden One", or so-called "primordial creation-deity", Mjomba argued. He wrote that the closest equivalent among the gods of Greeks and Romans (representing Europeans for whom "animism" is still taboo to this day), was Zeus or Jupiter (the Greco-Roman "Captain of Gods") and perhaps Apollo, the Greek "God of Sun", and Cupid or Eros, the Greco-Roman "God of Love" - mythological deities whose power did not include the "power to create entities out of nothing".

It was all "silly" because individuals who had a *perishable body* and an *immortal soul*, but preferred to act as if the situation was otherwise, were in denial. And, even though they were free to do as they wished (which was fine and well with Mjomba), being in denial was fine and well only for so long. Those who were now "in denial" would in time discover that the *animists* - the "stupid Africans" - were correct after all! Those individuals would also discover that after they "kicked the bucket", they didn't vaporize (as they might have wished). Mjomba wrote that mounds of earth meant to keep buried human remains respectfully out of sight did not hinder spirits of humans who had passed on from "matching on", as Louis Armstrong put.

The silliest part was the fact that many, who did not now exist, would at first be all agog on finding themselves sharing the same habitat with other animal species here on earth (including mammals that couldn't smile, laugh, or communicate - or think - in the same way as they themselves did) only to turn around and start pretending that they were exactly like those other life forms which, perhaps, did indeed owe their existence to something as impersonal as evolution!

And if the Prime Mover was an essential party to procreation where humans were concerned, did it mean that the act of procreation was sacred? Mjomba's response was in the affirmative, and not so much because the Prime Mover was directly involved as because the act of procreation, just like any other human activity - tilling the fields, planting, harvesting, eating and resting, interacting with fellow humans and saying one's prayers, etc. - took place in the presence of the Prime Mover.

According to Mjomba, He (the Prime Mover) watched over His creatures in the literal sense and sustained them from the moment they came into existence and continued throughout eternity. He did not stop at being a "prime mover" or "creator". He even made it His job to welcome humans into eternity after their sojourn on earth.

Following in the example of Adam and Eve who by and large had every intention of doing everything they did, in the wake of the Prime Mover's promise of a deliverer, to His greater glory and honor, throughout the ages, humans have implicitly dedicated their lives to the service of the Prime Mover after recognizing that positive human activity was sacrosanct. Accordingly, the ancient Egyptians paid homage to Ptah (the creator), Set (the god of evil), Osiris (lord of the dead), Meskhenet (goddess of childbirth), Re (the sun god), Heh and Hauhet (deities of infinity and eternity), Thoth (the god of wisdom), and even Ammit (devourer of the wicked), amongst others.

It was in a similar vein that the Greeks and Romans paid homage to Jupiter (the king of gods from whose name, a combination of *Zeus* and *Pater*, we got the words *Deus* or God and *Pater* or Father; Apollo (that supposedly handsome and beardless god of the sun, light, knowledge, poetry, music and oracles, art, archery, plague, healing and disease, etc.); Venus (the goddess of love); Volcanus (the god of the "raging" fire); Minerva (the goddess of wisdom, the arts, and commerce); and others. According to Mjomba's thesis, the same applied to the Chinese, the Indians, and the world's other ancient civilizations.

Mjomba wrote that humans in the twentieth century gave expression to homage, perhaps unwittingly, in pop songs, rapping, sitcoms, and other "Hollywood acts", when they were not doing gigs in prayer palaces and paying lip service to worship of the divinity from pulpits and now increasingly in telecasts. All of which, according to Mjomba, said something about the extent to which humans had strayed from reality.

Returning to the subject of conscience, Mjomba asserted that it did not matter how emphatically or for how long those who transgressed tried to disavow the reality. It did not matter how crafty or how powerful the transgressors were. It did not matter how loudly and for how long the benefits from the sinful practice were trumpeted; or how successful humans were in perpetuating the deception. It did not matter how socially acceptable, how popular and fashionable; or how widespread the sinful practice was. It did not matter what the pay back in material benefits or convenience the sinful practice engendered; or even the security, economic or otherwise, which the sinful practice guaranteed.

And it did not matter what the cumulative benefits from the sinful practice were in the short term or the long term. And it did not matter how pleasurable and satisfying, how exciting or addictive, the sinful practice was. It did not even matter if Church figures turned up and endorsed or even blessed the sinful practice. Transgressors, whatever their station in life, could never totally suppress their consciences, Mjomba wrote.

Later, as he defended his thesis, Mjomba would remark that the human conscience was not something apart from the soul. It was the soul, created in the image of the Prime Mover, and it was revolted by any and all irreverent tendencies that crossed the individual's mind. Those who transgressed and tried to pretend otherwise were in effect trying to promote the lie; and, as with all lies, "you could lie all the time but not to everybody" just as "you could lie to everybody but not all the time" Mjomba wrote.

The extent of lying sometimes amounted to an invitation to the archenemy to take over full control of their person. But humans could, even then, never douse the spark of light within that attested to the enabling presence of the Prime Mover in human souls.

According to Mjomba, whenever one's conscience beckoned, it was in fact the Prime Mover Himself who was calling out and saying to the transgressor in unmistakable terms: "Foul, you. And, listen up, creature - that is another one too many!"

According to Mjomba, the harping by humans concerning their God-given right to choose, when taken in conjunction with the fact that their consciences were never silent every time they transgressed, ironically made it more difficult for them to turn around and say they were not culpable for sins committed.

Mjomba's little "scheme"...

Mjomba made some of his most controversial statements as he was responding to questioning during his oral defense of the controversial thesis. He suggested, for instance, that engaging in sinful practices for monetary gain was, at least in some if not all cases, like making a "secret" pact with, of all people, the archenemy; and he added that the time inevitably came when the turncoat, going back on his word as he was wont to do, broadcast the terms of that pact to all and sundry to demonstrate his skills in cheating, or more precisely hoodwinking, "the simpletons and the unwary" to use the devil's his own words.

371

He surprised the professors and his fellow students with some of his assertions. He claimed, for instance, that he was a great deal better off than the prince of darkness, even though he was not as talented or as blessed at creation as the spirit. Mjomba thought he could even say "infinitely" - assuming, of course, that he himself didn't end up flopping the CTET. Mjomba announced to laughter that, apart from the fact that Lucifer (it had never surprised Mjomba that the devil operated under many pseudonyms - Satan, Beelzebub, Mephistopheles, Lucifer, etc. - for obvious reasons) could lie from both sides of his mouth or so they said, there was absolutely nothing about the Evil One which gave him, Mjomba, any reason to feel envious.

Satan, according to Mjomba, had been disgraced and had been banished from the sight of the Perfect One eternally, losing everything he had ever had in the process - with the exception of his ability to make trouble, that is. But he himself, with the modest gifts he had received from the Prime Mover, still stood a good chance of breezing past the embittered Lucifer and sneaking into heaven and happiness that had no end!

But Mjomba did concede that Satan, had he not made the one - and likely the only - mistake he ever made of thinking that be was so talented and comfortable that he could tell the Prime Mover to take a hike, would have been the envy of every creature that ever existed. Mjomba commented that it was the same pitfall into which Adam and Eve and other humans had fallen - a mistake that was far worse than seizing a machete and trying to chop off the hand that fed you, or using a saw to bring down the branch on which one sat.

Sin, because it assumed that high ideals which were in fact achievable might not be after all and went on to give precedence to that which was temporal or ephemeral over that which was eternal automatically implied an inferiority complex on the part of the sinner, the devil not excepted.

Mjomba, accordingly, argued that Mephistopheles, by far the most egregious sinner, had to be the one who suffered most from having an inferiority complex. And that, Mjomba wrote, made him decidedly the least enviable creature ever. Even though he railed against the Evil One like everyone else did, it was apparent from the start that Mjomba had a very special interest in - of all things - the devil! It was an interest the seminarian did not make any real effort to conceal.

Satan's Manifesto...

The fact was that, in selecting the topic for his theological thesis, Mjomba had been influenced by one thing above all, namely the role that was traditionally played by the so-called Devil's Advocate in the canonization process in Rome. Mjomba reasoned that if it was fine for a cardinal - a Prince of the Church - to step in the shoes of Diabolos and not merely play-act, but represent the Prince of Darkness in a matter of such gravity as the canonization of a saint, there couldn't be anything wrong with a seminarian heading off into the library and bringing himself up to date on everything that had been written about Beelzebub, and then stepping into the shoes of the accursed one and using him to do what he hated to do, and that is work for the salvation of souls instead of their damnation! Actually, Mjomba's plan was to have the devil reveal his dirty secrets in what would be the equivalent of Satan's "Manifesto" or "State of the World Address"!

In Mjomba's mind, his scheme, if it were to succeed, would amount to a real coup against Diabolos and his Underworld. He imagined that it would be like getting the most determined and vicious anti-Catholic that ever lived to suddenly come out swinging in defense of the Church he or she had spent a whole lifetime trying to demolish.

Mjomba knew that if anyone, especially a member of the seminary's faculty, were to get wind of his little scheme, he would probably be roundly denounced as a reckless person who wasn't heeding the wise admonition that good folks stayed clear of Satan and his tricks for their own safety. And for all he knew, it could lead to his instant dismissal from the seminary! Mjomba had accordingly decided to just go ahead and prove to the world that there was nothing wrong with trying to exploit the devil and, above all, using the Evil One to enlighten the world on matters relating to the study of *Theos* or the divinity.

It would not only revolutionize theology; but by getting the devil to broadcast his secrets, humans who might otherwise fall for his tricks and end up serving him would be alerted to the fact that they were very dirty tricks indeed, and would not fall for the devil's wiles - at least not as easily. And, if successful, his scheme likely would cause pandemonium in the Underworld, and with a bit of luck might actually drive some of the demons - especially the little (Mjomba imagined also "frail") demons - to despair and cause them to abandon their ruinous missions targeting the poor forsaken descendants of Adam and Eve!

Mjomba had proceeded to research his subject, taking note of what everybody from Thomas Aquinas to the children of Fatima wrote or said about Beelzebub. Mjomba was obviously surprised to discover that the devil was actually a very knowledgeable figure, and that his strength lay therein. An apostate archangel, who was expelled from the presence of the Prime Mover in the wake of his rebellion with the combined force of St. Michael the Archangel (whose name denotes "Like God"), St. Gabriel (whose name means "God is mighty"), and St. Raphael (whose name means "God Heals"), the former "Light Bearer" (as his name "Lucifer" signified), and now also "Demon-in-Chief", was no dummy.

Quoting St. John of the Cross, Mjomba argued that Diabolos knew that he could accomplish far more through a little harm done to souls that were advanced in holiness than through great damage to the rank and file of sinful and sinning humans; and the devil's strategy of passing himself off as non-existent to profligate and dumb humans while at the same time subjecting the advanced souls to the most terrible temptations involving false piety and humility, presumption, and subtle temptations to abandon mental prayer was an admirable and a winning strategy that was executed by the former Archangel of Light with precision and an eye to results. The "Prince of Wickedness" was determined to use his commanding grasp of matters pertaining to the spiritual realm to try and throw humans, with their inclination to sin, under the bus (as they say). Mjomba wrote that Diabolos was extremely well versed in Philosophy and Theology, and he could apparently convince you that a sin, which might be related to presumptuousness, false humility, or even downright hypocrisy wasn't a sin after all!

It was not long before Mjomba started dreaming about the possibility of showing that the Catholic Church was a very special target of the devil and his minions. If he could prove that this was indeed the case, and that the devil didn't really take much notice of the other churches and even less the non-Christian religions, Mjomba would have demonstrated beyond any doubt for anyone who had eyes to see and ears to hear that the Catholic Church was the one true holy Church. And so Mjomba had gone for it. That was how Mjomba found himself using Satan in his thesis as his mouthpiece when he needed to expound on Church doctrine particularly the teachings that were very controversial.

Mjomba did not have any qualms whatsoever about having the Prince of Darkness take the position that Catholicism was the true religion and all others false. To garner credibility for the phantasies they churned out, Hollywood consistently did it; and Mjomba himself thought that if his character (the Prince of Darkness) was going to be credible, he had very little choice but to portray him as a 'fallen' Catholic. Indeed, for someone like Lucifer who (prior to being disgraced) had filled the role of Master of Ceremonies, as the highest choirs of Seraphim, Cherubim, and the Thrones ministered to the Prime Mover, Mjomba was tempted on a number of occasions to portray his character as a fallen "Prince of the Church" or a defrocked priest - or ex-seminarian (like his namesake Judas Iscariot). But Mjomba also took comfort from the fact that the now quite famous (infamous to a dwindling minority) "Canadian Scrolls" contained incontrovertible evidence that the Catholic Church alone (and none other) could claim to be the true Church.

The "Eleventh" Commandment...

It was always apparent that Mjomba was careful not to underestimate any one gender in matters of the soul. And he said as much in his face-to-face exchanges with the panel during the oral defense of his thesis on Original Virtue. What, after all, was the gender of the devil, he asked rhetorically. Was Diabolos male or female?

Mjomba did not fail to point out that, increasingly, preachers were suggesting in their sermons that it was possible for humans to "have sex" with the devil, with many (of the preachers) making a special point of warning their flocks from time to time about the inherent dangers of exposing themselves to that kind of temptation. That also chimed in with the traditional position that humans should be wary of engaging in any sort of dialogue with the Evil One, presumably because that would expose them to seduction by the Tempter *or* Temptress if they did so!

Mjomba conceded that the notion of beatific vision and a love relationship between two members of the Church Triumphant that *excluded* other members were incompatible; and that marriages did not occur in heaven for that reason. The most important reason for marrying, according to Mjomba, was so that the earthly "couple" could help each other and their issue attain self-actualization. According to him, there was no practical problem in choosing a partner on earth from fellow humans who were seeking self-actualization.

Because souls in heaven had already attained self-actualization in their union with the Prime Mover, and also enjoyed different levels of self-actualization in the Church Triumphant, there would have been a practical problem in choosing a 'partner'. But a bigger problem, according to Mjomba, was the fact that when humans chose spouses back on earth, they did so out of self-interest. The so-called "exchange of vows" during nuptials was simply an affirmation by the parties that they now belonged to each other and to no one else! Now, that was really the antithesis of selfless love.

Of course there was such a thing as the "Sacrament of Matrimony" (CCC 1601). But, buried inside the covers of the voluminous Catechism of the Catholic Church that only a scant few if any Catholics - and even less non-Catholics - ever opened, the fact that marriage was sacred remained for most a distant fantasy. Why otherwise were there no movies and tv shows showcasing that divine gift. Instead the movies and tv shows showcased escapist love stories that had the exact opposite of what you would term "moral underpinnings".

According to Mjomba, earthly marriages were therefore not love relationship in any sense at all - they were pacts in which the parties promised to avail each other for mutual exploitation. That was why as soon as the marriage unions encountered problems that called for mutual understanding and personal sacrifice, the parties to those 'contracts' as a rule called everything off without any regard for the effect of their action on the wellbeing of their offspring, and went their ways.

But Mjomba also argued that the fact that no marriages occurred in the afterlife did not in itself rule out the possibility that gender as an idea applied to pure spirits as well. For one, the idea of unions or liaisons was not restricted to life on earth. It was certainly not at all unusual to talk about the sacred union between spiritual entities on a spiritual plane.

Perhaps one could also make a case for a spiritual union (or a liaison) being licit and holy, and for proscribed unions or liaisons between two or more spirits.

Humans were, of course, spiritual beings first and foremost, and that was why one could even talk of licit and illicit unions (or licit and illicit liaisons) between members of the human race. That being the case, the idea of licit and illicit unions or liaisons in the afterlife did not at all appear to be all that far-fetched as an idea. There was clearly logic behind it, and it seemed to flow naturally from the idea of marriage between two human beings, which in turn appeared to be linked to the mystery of the Blessed Trinity.

Illicit unions or liaisons between two or more spirits that were united in common cause against all that was good or sacred? That sounded like a very good description of the unholy trinity between Diabolos who was the author of death, Diabolos' minions consisting of disgraced members of the choirs of angels, and the "poor banished children of Eve" who were determined to squander their second chance! And that description certainly did one thing: it made a very compelling case for the hypothesis that gender - or what approximated to it - formed an important attribute of pure spirits just as it did in the case of humans.

It was, according to Mjomba, one of the legacies of original sin (which was an alternative description for "the state of losing "original virtue"") that terms such as "union" and "love" now invariably aroused feelings of shame and even disgust in humans. This was especially true among those humans who were supposed to be knowledgeable in matters of the spirit - preachers.

But, assuming that "original virtue" - which humans had admittedly lost - was still a valid concept, perhaps, liaisons, both sacred (when they occurred between individuals here on earth who were in a state of grace or between members of the Church Triumphant) and perverted (when they occurred between sinners or when they involved the inhabitants of hell) did indeed reflect gender attributes regardless of the locale in which they occurred!

This in turn pointed to the real possibility that the devil had gender attributes that, in the case of a pure spirit, probably meant that it was both a he as well as a she! Which, in its turn, would seem to confirm that it was indeed possible for a human to fall for the temptation to have sex with Diabolos! Mjomba confessed that it was a possibility that was utterly boggling to the human mind - certainly to his mind!

But it was a possibility that was also very "puzzling", according to Mjomba. For if some humans could successfully "sleep" with the devil in an illicit union, that would constitute a very grave sin - the kind that would undoubtedly have merited it a place on the list of proscribed activities on the "tablets" Moses had been carrying after his historic encounter with the Prime Mover on that mountain in the wilderness. Mjomba thus had his doubts regarding the feasibility of sexual activity between humans and Satan as suggested by the preachers.

But his doubts also invariably raised the question of the responsibility of those who used the pulpit to spread such "false" alarm. Preachers doing so in those circumstances were, in Mjomba's view, not just indulging in something that could just be passed off as mischief. Their action amounted to an attempt to re-visit the Ten Commandments and substitute what the Prime Mover had inscribed on the "tablets" and in the consciences of men and women with something they had concocted using their own fertile imagination.

The effects of sin...

Elaborating on the subject of sin, Mjomba wrote that whereas one could make a distinction between the purely physical acts (which were of themselves neither good nor bad) and the intentions of the actors (which made all the acts sinful or meritorious) when talking about humans, the same was not possible when talking about pure spirits. Mjomba supposed that pure spirits were incapable of committing venial sins; and he also supposed that, while any transgression by a pure spirit inevitably translated into a mortal sin, it also invariably was in the nature of an unforgivable sin.

Mjomba speculated that, until the first man and the first woman lost their innocence through the act of eating of the forbidden fruit from the Tree of Knowledge of Good and Evil, they were repelled by any form of temptation to disobey the Prime Mover almost as a matter of course. He wrote that, while their friendship with their Maker was intact, even the most minor violation of the sacred trust that was vested in them by virtue of being creatures that were fashioned in His image and also the very first humans to roam the earth loomed as something that was loathsome in the extreme. Consequently, it mattered very little what the nature of the Man's first act of disobedience was according to the seminarian.

The act of disobedience of Adam constituted a very grave "original" sin that had the effect of cutting off Man's friendship with his Maker! In a sense, that original sin was a lot worse than the mortal sins that humans now committed almost at a whim, and that included the derelict acts of betrayal of Judas Iscariot, the apostle Peter and the murderous adventures of Paul of Tarsus.

But, according to Mjomba, the ability of pure spirits to see the full consequences of their actions at the very outset, or what he called "real time", ruled out the possibility of transgressions that could be designated as minor or venial sins, or transgressions that were serious or mortal but pardonable in their case. Mjomba supposed that humans were also quite capable of committing transgressions whose very nature precluded forgiveness, and feared that they too committed them.

After all, if humans were capable of landing themselves in a frame of mind that left no room for regretting acts that were out of bounds, and if they were also capable of willfully mounting a rebellion against their Prime Mover while in that frame of mind, it would, Mjomba contended, be tantamount to suggesting that humans were only nominally free creatures if they could not be bad boys or bad girls in that respect and also actually roast in hell as a consequence of their willful actions!

And there was, of course, also the inevitable question of discrimination, if pure spirits that committed transgressions of the same gravity were treated differently from their human counterparts by the Final Arbiter. Consequently, if humans were denied the chance of reaping what they were sowing, they would be in a position to claim that there was something wrong with a process that discriminated against them for no reason!

According to Mjomba, the fact that humans could end up in hell made an argument of sorts in favor of the Sacrament of Confession. Because it would not have made sense to have humans, who were free and capable of transgressing, not also be capable of receiving forgiveness for their transgressions - provided they were sincerely repentant and prepared to make restitution as necessary.

Mjomba wrote that anyone who "accepted" the bible as an authoritative source of revealed truth, but was not prepared to accept that the Sacrament of Penance was divinely instituted had a real problem on his or her hands. He/she had to be prepared to explain away (among others) the words of the Deliverer to the apostles to the effect that if they decided not to forgive but to retain sins, they would be retained!

But that notwithstanding, Mjomba would have found it hard to conceive of the Sacrament of Baptism, signifying the reconciliation of humanity with the Maker, in the absence of the Sacrament of Penance which took cognizance of the propensity of humans to sin (because of the legacy of original sin) on the one hand and the fact that, even though humans were "weak" in the flesh, their spirit was quite capable of "willing" to break out of the cycle of sin.

Then, claiming that he was making a point everyone else appeared reluctant to make, Mjomba wrote that the real probability that there were humans in hell militated against the proposition that it was *a sola fide* (by faith alone) that humans attained salvation. Mjomba went on that, if one accepted that *faith* was *a gift* (of the Prime Mover) that humans were free to accept or reject, accepting the mere possibility that humans could end up in hell made the first proposition (justification by faith alone) untenable. One had to conclude that it could not be by *faith* alone that humans became saved because that undermined the fact that humans were *free* to begin with. But their freedom was not just in relation to the gift of faith (which they could choose to accept or reject), but in relation to a host of other things -

both good and bad - that they could choose to do or not to do.

The freedom to accept or reject divine gifts (of which *faith* was just one) was something that was already extraneous to *faith*; and, as was obvious from the situation of the first Man and the first Woman before their fall from grace, making a choice as to whether to eat or not to eat of the forbidden fruit (a choice that was unrelated to *faith*) determined if they were on the path to perdition or not. If they had continued to steal fruits from the Tree of the Knowledge of Good and Evil *after* the promise of a deliverer, they would definitely have made themselves ineligible for a heavenly reward, and would have ended up with Diabolos in a "hell" of their own choosing. Their faith in the Prime Mover's promise - that a Deliverer would come along and reconcile them (humans) with Himself - became an *additional* requirement, and did not absolve them of the need to strive to stay clear of the Tree of the Knowledge of Good and Evil and the fruits that dangled from it at all times while they waited for the Deliverer.

The attempt to absolve humans who belong to later generations from responsibility for their actions thus also militated against the fact that Adam and Eve and their issue were all equal in the eyes of the Prime Mover, and subject to the same requirements for gaining eternal life. But more importantly, since the gift of faith could not possibly be foisted upon humans by the Prime Mover (regardless of whether they were willing to accept it or unwilling to do so), *choice* in its regard by individuals automatically became critical, which in turn proved that humans were *capable* of making critical choices both before *and* after faith came into play.

And, while there was absolutely no evidence to suggest that those other critical choices (before *and* after faith came into play) had been determined (by the Prime Mover and/or by the Deliverer, or by the Holy Ghost that united them in eternal love) at any time as being irrelevant to the salvation of humans, the exact opposite was true. That is not to say that humans, in making *any* choice that was critical to their eternal salvation, could do so *without* the help of grace that was merited by the Deliverer through His passion and death on the cross! By no means - but that was a completely *different question* altogether.

To be credible, those pressing the point that it was only by faith *alone* (that individuals were saved) had to prove a number of things among them the following: that Adam and Eve had a different nature from that of their posterity (which, if proved, would raise even more intractable questions regarding redemption); that the Prime Mover expected more of Adam and Eve - even after the fall - than He now expected from their descendants; that the descendants of Adam and Eve were incapable of making critical choices (in spite of being endowed with gifts that were specifically designed to make them capable of making such choices); that the Prime Mover made a mistake and created humans who were supposed to be accountable for their actions, but who were now (supposedly) incapable of taking responsibility for actions directly stemming from the choices they made; that the Prime Mover was in the business of "foisting" His gifts, including the gift of faith, on willing and unwilling humans; that the gift of faith actually absolved believers from keeping the ten commandments, and that it also made the Deliverer's admonition to humans to take up their crosses and follow Him redundant.

They also had to clarify what they meant by "faith". Was it merely faith in the power of the Deliverer to forgive sins? Or was it also faith in the fact that the Deliverer came, died for humans and, after He was raised up and given power over heaven and earth, and left a specified group of individuals whom He had individually asked to leave all behind and follow Him (His apostles) a special commission to go to the ends of the world and spread the message of the Crucified Deliverer, and to forgive sins in His name? They moreover had to also explain how an individual could be saved by "faith alone" in the Deliverer if that individual in the same breath refused to recognize those whom the Deliverer had called to succeed the apostles as His instruments of divine grace and to press on with the commission that had the full backing of the Holy Spirit.

The Deliverer's Mother, born without the stain of original sin, much like Adam and Eve, didn't become the "Queen of Heaven" by dint of "grace alone". Growing up in this cruel world of ours and subjected to temptations like all other humans, she refused, albeit with the help of the grace that her Son (the "Second Adam") would merit through His death on the gibbet, to cave like the first Adam and his wife Eve had done. She earned her queenship by enduring the temptations and untold trials she faced while on earth, like witnessing the crucifixion and death of the Son of Man as He paid the price for the sins of the "poor forsaken children of Adam and Eve" at the hands of the very people He had come to save! That was the antithesis of being "saved by grace alone"!

And the Deliverer Himself (who was like us in everything except sin) certainly didn't claim His victory by anything close to "grace alone"! He did it by strenuously doing the will of His Father in heaven. And grace alone is certainly not going to save any "poor forsaken child of Adam and Eve" who might be looking for some easy way out, especially after the Savior of Mankind challenged all His would-be disciples not just to keep His commandments (if they loved Him) but to take up their crosses and to follow Him!

But, also guess what, if it had been in the divine plan that the "poor forsaken children of Adam and Eve" would be saved by "grace alone", the Son of Man would Himself have said it very loudly and clearly. But He did say this: "Wonder not at this: for the hour cometh wherein all that are in the graves shall hear the voice of the Son of God. And they that have done good things shall come forth unto the resurrection of life: but they that have done evil, unto the resurrection of judgment." The Council of Trent thus rightly declared: "If any one saith, that man is truly absolved from his sins and justified, because that he assuredly believed himself absolved and justified; or, that no one is truly justified but he who believes himself justified; and that, by this faith alone, absolution and justification are effected; let him be anathema."

According to Mjomba's thesis, in addition to the foregoing, it was imperative for proponents of the "thesis" of *justificatio sola fide* to both provide an authoritative and incontrovertible source for *their* peculiar interpretation of the gospels, and to show that they themselves had standing in this matter and consequently *could* speak on behalf of the body of believers as successors to the apostles (or for the Mystical Body of Christ) or because of some special commission they might have received from the Deliverer. But it was even then clearly moot to ask whether the Deliverer, who had paid such a high price for the redemption of humans and then taken the unusual step of handpicking His apostles before laying His hands on them so they could receive the Holy Ghost, and sending them off to continue his work, could possibly give a commission of that nature to any other party (or parties), particularly a party (or parties) that was likely to contradict the teaching of His *Sancta Ecclesia* (or "Holy Church") however "deficient" it might appear in anyone's eyes.

Talking about the commission, the Deliverer's instructions to His twelve apostles (when He sent them out to go preach to the lost sheep of the house of Israel) were quite clear, specific and indeed explicit. As they went forth out of the house or city that did not welcome them or hear their words, they were to shake off the dust from their feet. (Matthew 10:14; Mark 6:1; and Luke 9:5) But then He had added ominously, saying: "Amen I say to you, it shall be more tolerable for the land of Sodom and Gomorrha in the day of judgment, than for that city…". Mjomba wrote in his thesis that it was hard to ignore the similarities between "the separated brethren" so-called and what the Deliverer referred to as "the lost sheep of the house of Israel".

Mjomba went on that the claim by proponents of that doctrine of *Sola Fide* that the Prime Mover actually *foisted* the gift of faith upon some humans (His chosen) and in the process predestined them for heaven, regardless of whether the lives they led were worthy of creatures that were made in the image of the Prime Mover or not - created more problems for them than it solved. Or could it be that the Prime Mover *foisted* the gift of faith on *all* humans, but only the chosen or predestined ended up in heaven? Any of those options - in which the gift of faith *worked* for some humans and *did not work* for others - automatically laid the blame for *forfeiting salvation* on the "saving" *gift* itself. One ended up implicitly blaming the Prime Mover for offering a gift that was only efficacious for some and not for others

But where was the evidence that the Prime Mover did any such thing any way, Mjomba asked? He supposed that the idea that some humans were predestined for salvation while other humans were not clearly sought to minimize the personal responsibility of individual humans in the spiritual arena, a very serious thing to try to do in an arena in which the Prime Mover has been very careful to make His expectations very clear. The angels fell from grace because they disobeyed, as did Adam and Eve. To try and exempt later generations of humans from that divine law was a very serious thing indeed, and those who went along with any "doctrine" that was in conflict with that law were evidently in denial and were trying to escape the reality that all humans faced.

According to Mjomba, the doctrine of a *sola fide* was fallacious because it also militated against the infinite goodness of the Prime Mover who would certainly not have brought humans into being, endowed them with a free will with which they could accept or reject His divine gifts, and then turned around and refused to keep his covenant with those who diligently chose to do His will on the grounds that He had not predestined *them* for heaven, and who decided that some who did not diligently choose to do His bidding, because *they* were predestined for good things, could enter heaven. Mjomba contended that suggesting that predestination was orthodox automatically called into question the Prime Mover's infinite goodness as well as His infinite mercy.

On the contrary, Mjomba argued, humans, created in the image of the Prime Mover and with spiritual faculties of reason and free will in addition to sense faculties, had to stir to cooperate not just with the gift of faith, but with the other graces that were available to all humans through the Mystical Body of the Deliverer - graces the apostles became capable of dispensing once the Deliverer laid His hands on them as He prepared to send them out into the world with a commission to be "fishers of men", and which the apostles' successors, who comprised the Church's hierarchy, continued to dispense.

Mjomba added that humans, inclined to sin, were clearly incapable of good works on their own without the help of grace. Now, as creatures who understood their limitations (and all humans who accepted to be like little children did), all they needed do was ask - ask that, despite their weakness and propensity to evil, with the help of the grace that was merited for them by the Deliverer and Son of Man, they eschew deeds that were degenerate, amoral and diabolic, and (like the fruitful vine) produce works that were worthy of creatures made in the Prime Mover's image.

The fact that humans who *asked* would *receive*, and the fact that *knocking* on the door of divine mercy would always *cause it to be opened* were, according to Mjomba's thesis, perhaps the best repudiation yet for the doctrine of Predestination. Unless the Deliverer was lying, if any one (including humans who were presumed to be 'predestined for hell') asked, the vaunted predestination (a doctrine that certainly did not originate with the Deliverer) automatically went out the window.

Mjomba pointed out in passing that while these were things his seminary professors wanted to hear, they certainly were not things that proponents of the doctrine of *Salvation by Faith Alone,* or the related doctrine of *Predestination,* would want to hear. They disliked the routine and tradition, yet the Deliverer had specifically left instructions to the effect that His followers continue to "break bread" in His memory, and things like that. That was in addition to establishing a Church to *continue* His work of redemption. Mjomba wrote that they wouldn't be true to themselves if they came upon his thesis and didn't think it was inspired by the devil or something.

Mjomba asserted that his objective in making the comparisons was to point out that what he believed was a distinct possibility, namely that there were humans in hell contrary to what some believed. During the oral defense of the thesis, Mjomba would ruffle quite a few feathers with a reference to what he called the big question. This was whether or not the Church's hierarchy discriminated against those who, while perhaps not members of the visible Church, were members of the invisible Church! The same question, put differently, was whether the Church's hierarchy unduly favored members of the visible Church over other members of the Mystical Body of Christ!

Mjomba suggested that the Church's hierarchical structure made for a Church organization that was inward looking rather than outward looking, something which inevitably led to bias of one form or another. And, what with the external trappings of power enjoyed by the Church's clergy and the carefully nurtured corporate image of what, indeed, had once upon a time been a citadel of power in the world, the Church looked more like a laid-back world government or a Church Triumphant fan club than an organization of humans who were seeking to be delivered from the pranks of Satan and human frailty.

And, instead of being all over the airwaves in this age of mass communications and reaching out to the millions out there who were hungry for word about the Deliverer (following in the example of the Deliverer Himself who crisscrossed Galilee and Judea drawing crowds who could never have enough of him), the Church's hierarchy incredibly remained aloof. The only people who ventured out there in the fields that were ripe for the harvesting were the Mill Hill Fathers (Saint Joseph's Society for Foreign Missions), the White Fathers and Sisters (Society of the Missionaries of Africa), Mother Theresa's Missionaries of Charity, the Basilian Fathers (the Congregation of St. Basil), the Maryknollers, and the Franciscans according to Mjomba, who believed that the detached attitude of members of the hierarchy arose from the erroneous belief that they had a monopoly over truth!

Even though going on the air carried with it certain risks of its own, including the risk of sensationalizing the patently serious business of saving souls, there was no excuse for not exploiting the media - as others, who really didn't have very much to offer, did. While noting that there were very real risks of converting sermons and Church services, including the Holy Mass, into empty shows and entertainment for television audiences, Mjomba wrote that the time had definitely come for seminaries to prepare seminarians to remain calm and recollected as they faced cameras, and to resist the temptation of just going on the air for the sake of basking in the lime lights.

Having panels of eminent theologians critique and dissect the theses submitted by seminarians at the conclusion of their years of study in major seminaries seemed like a good way to start. And, even better, the authors could be asked to defend their theses on "catechetical TV networks" which the Church could specially commission for that purpose.

But even as he was floating those ideas in the course of his own oral defense of the contents of his paper on Original Virtue, Mjomba noted that, regardless of their merits, any such ideas would almost certainly be viewed by the neo-conservatives who dominated the Curia in Rome as a threat to their positions and particularly their influence on the development and direction of catechetical instruction. Permitting any discussion or debate in that vein would be depicted as a reckless challenge of papal authority, and would consequently be banned, according to Mjomba's assessment.

Later, alone with fellow students with none of the professors around, Mjomba spoke more bluntly saying that clergy were holed up in mostly empty churches as if still awaiting the advent of the Comforter. He claimed that they were, at best, helping those who were already in line awaiting the bride. That they were preoccupied with that group of people who already had candles, but seemed unconcerned about the importance of keeping the candles lit - which, in Mjomba's opinion, was hardly fair to those who were not even aware that the "Wedding of the Millennium" (as Mjomba called it) was on, let alone having a candle to keep alight.

This, according to Mjomba, was a decidedly a raw deal for the many out there whose hunger for the message of salvation was such that it would be unconscionable for them not to accept to feed on crumbs offered them by other do-gooders who did not have anything better to offer.

Mjomba thought it went without saying that the Church's hierarchy, at least judging from the attitudes of some senior prelates, was that you were deemed to be lost and irredeemable if you were ostensibly living in sin or not yet a member of the "flock". And if you were paid a visit by a Church official, the chances were that the visit would be for the purpose of serving you papers of excommunication rather than for the purpose of attempting to reconcile you to the Church - which was the same as saying that the discrimination against those who were regarded as unsaved was total!

In contrast, the twelve apostles, far from being "holed up in mostly empty churches", were all over the place planting the faith in all corners of the globe despite having had the benefit of only three years in seminary. The difference might be that their "seminary" had the Son of Man Himself as Rector, and also that they had learnt to allow the Spirit to lead them where on their own they would not have gone. And, predictably, with the odd exception here and there, they went on to pay with their lives for their labors as fishers of men.

Simon Peter, after witnessing to the faith in Jerusalem where he was twice arraigned along with John, set off on his missionary journeys which took him to Lydda, Joppa and thereon Caesarea, becoming instrumental in the decision to evangelize the Gentiles. And before long, he was in Corinth and Antioch in Greece en route whence Peter got an opportunity to debate the notorious Simon Magus. Also along the way he found time to ordain Zacchaeus as the first bishop of Caesarea and Maro as the first bishop in present day Lebanon. Peter founded the Church in Antioch and Rome with Paul. But before moving shop to "Babylon" as Rome was referred to metaphorically, Peter spent seven years as the Church of Antioch's first Patriarch.

The Apostle Andrew, who died a martyr in the city of Patræ in Greece, preached the Gospel in Scythia in present day Iran, and along the Black Sea and the Dnieper river as far as Kiev; and traveled from there to Novgorod in the heart of Russia. En route he founded the See of Byzantium (present day Istanbul), installing Stachys as bishop there. Hippolytus of Rome wrote that Andrew also preached in Thrace, which is bounded by the Balkan Mountains to the north, the Aegean Sea to the south and the Black Sea to the east.

The Apostle James, who had the same father (Zebedee) as John the evangelist and was the first one of the twelve apostles to lay down his life for his faith (put to the sword by Marcus Julius Agrippa better known as Herod Agrippa I), trekked from Jerusalem all the way to Spain, spreading the Gospel of the crucified Deliverer.

The Apostle John, younger brother to James, was one of the "pillars" of the Church in Jerusalem. But he ended up in exile on the Island of Patmos in the Aegean Sea.

According to legend, the missionary journeys of the Apostle Bartholomew saw him trek to Ethiopia in North Africa, Mesopotamia, Parthia and Lycaonia, all the way to the City of Kalyan in India, and then back to Armenia (in present-day Turkey) where he was skinned alive and then beheaded for winning converts to the Lord Jesus.

The Apostle Philip was sent with his sister Mariamne and the Apostle Bartholomew to preach the Gospel in Greece, Phrygia, and Syria. And then there is the story of the Ethiopian eunuch, the treasurer of Candace, Queen of the Ethiopians, who was sitting in his chariot reading the Book of Isaiah as Philip chanced by, and who begged to be baptized by the evangelist on learning that the passage in Isaiah that he was reading had found fulfilment in the Nazarene.

The Apostle Thomas (also known as Didymus and Thomas the Doubter) travelled outside the Roman Empire to preach the Gospel, trekking as far as Tamilakam (an area covering present-day Tamil Nadu, Puducherry, Lakshadweep and the southern parts of Andhra Pradesh, Karnataka and Kerala in India). According to tradition, Thomas reached Muziris, (modern-day North Paravur and Kodungalloor in the state of Kerala, India) in AD 52. According to one legend, the Apostle Thomas met the biblical Magi as he made his way to India.

The Apostle Matthew (also known as the Levi or Tax Collector) concentrated on preaching to the Jewish community in Judea before heading off abroad to other countries. His tomb is in the crypt of Salerno Cathedral in Italy.

According to tradition, the Apostle Jude (also known as Judas Thaddaeus) preached the Gospel in Judea, Samaria, Idumaea, Syria, Mesopotamia and Libya. Apostles Jude and Bartholomew are traditionally believed to have been the first to bring Christianity to Armenia. Tradition has it that the Apostle Jude suffered martyrdom around 65 AD in Beirut, in the Roman province of Syria, together with the Apostle Simon the Zealot.

Simon the Zealot (also known as Simon journeyed all the way to Egypt on his evangelizing mission. According to the "the Golden Legend", Simon joined Jude in Persia and Armenia or Beirut, Lebanon, where both were martyred in 65 AD, with the latter undergoing crucifixion for his role as the Patriarch of Jerusalem.

According to one tradition, Matthias, who succeeded the betrayer Judas, planted the faith in and around Cappadocia and on the coasts of the